DEADLY

LIES

A gripping detective mystery full of twists and turns

CHRIS COLLETT

Revised edition 2017 by Joffe Books, London.

First published by Piatkus in 2004 as "A Worm in the Bud."

www.joffebooks.com

ISBN-13: 978-1-912106-50-9

For Richard

Author's Note

This is the first mystery featuring Tom Mariner. It is set in the early 2000s, when the internet was in its infancy, mobile phones had yet to evolve into smart phones, and people still read print newspapers.

CHAPTER 1

Mariner glanced at his watch again. Only ten to eight, yet it felt as if he'd been here for hours. Getting here first had been his way of keeping control, but now, as his stomach knotted with anxious speculation, he wished he hadn't been so keen.

He'd managed to secure the only vacant seat in the crowded bar: a stool positioned directly under an air-conditioning vent that blew a steady stream of cold air down inside the unbuttoned collar of his shirt. Twenty-four hours ago this idea had seemed a good one, a simple solution to a growing problem, but now the doubts were creeping in faster than the chill descending his spine. Had he been a smoker he'd have hacked his way through half a packet of Silk Cut by now.

The only reason he'd bought last night's *Echo* was to check that his advert had been correctly placed in the 'Accommodation to Let' section. It had. *Double room with en-suite facilities. No pets, non-smoker preferred.* Placing that ad had been a big step, and not one he was completely sure he'd wanted to take, but mortgage rates were climbing steadily, and it was the only foreseeable way of sharing his house without necessarily having to share his life. Having placed the ad, he'd stayed in all evening absently leafing through the rest of the paper while he waited for the phone to ring. That's when the 'Solos' page had caught his eye. Mariner had yet to see the appeal of internet dating. But lulled into a state of misplaced confidence by three pints of Brewmaker's Traditional (one of his stronger concoctions), and charmed by the old-fashioned simplicity of the small ad, he had picked up the phone. Impulsiveness wasn't normally one of his traits, and now, as his apprehension gathered momentum, he remembered why.

Noting the assortment of ill-matched couples around him, Mariner sensed that his venture wasn't unique. The comfortably anonymous mix of blond wood, brushed steel and pale blue leather upholstery made the bar of the Chamberlain Hotel perfect for any assignation — business, pleasure or both — and he had to fight a sudden hysterical urge to get out his warrant card and watch the place empty.

'Derek?'

Mariner's stomach lurched. The girl who approached him was sleek and attractive with thick, chestnut hair and eyes the colour of dark chocolate.

Recovering, Mariner shook his head and watched hope fade from her face. For a minute there, she must have thought her luck had changed. He was tall, reasonable-looking (so he'd been told) and — thanks to Greta's past influence over his wardrobe — he was pretty sharply dressed tonight. Derek, her as yet unknown client, would almost certainly turn out to be a middle-aged, fat and balding suit, like the majority of the girl's customers. Mariner had no doubts that she was a tom.

With a brief smile that left her eyes untouched, she tottered away on ludicrously high heels to take a seat on one of the squashy sofas, crossing her long, tanned legs. For a moment Mariner half wished he was Derek. Being

Derek would have been so much simpler. And his intention wasn't so very different. Same planned outcome, just glossed over with the flimsy veneer of social respectability. Suddenly the knot felt ready to explode and he had to make a dash for the gents.

Emerging minutes later, Mariner scanned the room, not allowing his eyes to rest on anyone who might conceivably be looking out for him. The brunette was on her feet again, engaged in animated discussion with a man. Not Derek, Mariner decided. This man was a rough diamond, unshaven with collar-length dark hair, in jeans and a well-worn leather jacket, the Harley Davidson logo stretched across his broad back. The body language was pure agitation: shoulders bunched, semaphore arms. Now he had his wallet out flashing money, cajoling. Her pimp, or just an over-attached regular? Whoever he was, he was giving her a hard time about something. At one point he grabbed the girl's arm but she wriggled free. Then, before Mariner's eyes, her resistance seemed to crumble and with a last cursory glance around the room for Derek, she slung her bag over her shoulder and reluctantly followed the Harley man towards the sliding glass doors.

The whole exchange made Mariner uneasy, putting up just the excuse he needed. Feeling only a minor twinge of guilt for his own date, he tailed the couple out of the hotel and into the orange sodium-glare of Broad Street, to where an eight-year-old Porsche with a dented boot squatted on double yellow lines, its hazard lights flashing. Concerned for the woman's safety, Mariner watched the couple get into the car . . . but Harley man was visibly calmer now and, as they drove off, the woman seemed more irritated with him than anything else. Mariner perceiving trouble where there was none. *You got the wrong idea, mister.* Occupational hazard.

* * *

Left alone on the pavement, Mariner stared through the window to the hotel bar, where the 'attractive blonde, seeking male 35-45 for discreet fun' was even now anticipating his arrival, and knew he wasn't going back in there. He'd phone her tomorrow and apologise, maybe. Turning away, Mariner threaded a path through the snarled traffic to the opposite side of the road and into a dark and rowdy Australian bar. Over a pint of foul-tasting non-alcoholic beer he watched the closing minutes of what most of the city's male population were glued to this evening: the live cup tie between Blues and Wolves. But after an uninspiring and goal-less second half, followed by the usual inane discussion from the pundits, Mariner retraced his steps to the Chamberlain's underground car park.

With nothing to distract him on the drive home, Mariner reflected on the evening's non-event, knowing deep down that it had never been a viable option, however desperate the circumstances. Was he desperate? It was nearly a year now since Greta had left. For a while Mariner had really believed that they had something. But that was before Greta turned forty and mutated into his mother, running his life for him and imposing unreasonable expectations until finally trying to force a commitment he couldn't make. That she'd abandoned him after that was no big surprise. The mystery was that she'd taken his confidence with her. Not his social confidence — his small talk had always been pathetic — but his confidence in bed, something he'd never had trouble with before.

That last time, when he'd been unexpectedly invited to spend the night with a young WPC, he'd resorted to distraction tactics. As intimacy progressed, he'd tried mentally rehearsing the names of the actors who had played the Dirty Dozen and the Magnificent Seven respectively. It had worked like a dream until he had inadvertently spoken Steve McQueen's name out loud.

'What?' She'd halted him mid-thrust, the expression on her face enough to precipitate his collapse, leaving them both agonisingly frustrated and Mariner with a big enough question mark over his head to discourage her from ever seeing him again. That had been nearly six months ago and Mariner hadn't had the guts to pursue anything or anyone since.

Tonight's quick fix was the intended solution, but if he couldn't keep it up with the assistance of Hollywood's finest, how would humiliating himself with a total stranger help matters?

'Delta one to all units.' The car's radio, tuned to the NPU wavelength, cut through his maudlin train of thought. 'Request for urgent assistance at 34 Clarendon Avenue, Harborne; informant an unidentified female.' It was just a few streets away, on this same patch.

Under normal circumstances Mariner would have ignored the call. It was one for uniformed patrol and, in any case, he'd been off-duty for hours. But he was in no hurry to go home and, judging from the lack of any other audible response, there was no one else nearby. Resources tonight would be concentrated around St Andrews, keeping the rival fans apart and diverting any trouble. Like the comforting glow of a distant refuge, Mariner felt himself drawn towards the secure predictability of work. He'd take a small detour to check whether the incident was already attended. If it was, he would simply drive on by. Making a second circuit of Five Ways traffic island, Mariner peeled off in the direction of Harborne.

Almost immediately the nervous energy of Birmingham nightlife melted away into silent darkness, taking with it Mariner's own anxieties. Typical of Birmingham's mongrel suburbs, Harborne had its rough patches but was inhabited in pockets by university professors and consultants from the Queen Elizabeth Hospital, their relative affluence reflected in the sprawling detached houses that were set in immaculately tended gardens.

Clarendon Avenue was easy enough to find, but locating the house itself was a different matter. Here, the properties were modest and compact, but set back from the road, hiding behind hedges and wrapped in swathes of ivy and wisteria, making individual identification in the dark almost impossible. There was no outward indication of any disturbance or any sign of a police presence at any of them.

Picking out a number at last, Mariner counted along, hugging the kerb as he went. Thirty, thirty-two, thirty-four . . . that was it, a mock-Georgian detached, ablaze with lights and standing out like a bloody carnival float. Then Mariner noticed the eight-year-old Porsche with a dented boot parked on the drive, and a sudden draught stirred the hairs on the back of his neck.

Mariner got out of the car and walked up the gravel driveway, past the Porsche and stepped into a narrow porch. From inside the house he could hear the babble of a TV, mainly because the front door swung slightly ajar. It was not a good sign. His warrant card at the ready, Mariner advanced cautiously along a bare, parquet-floored hallway, alert to any possibility. 'Police!' he warned, easing open the nearest internal door, already visualising the brunette cowering in a corner, her face bruised and bloodied. But in the event there was no blood, only a sterile and unnatural calm.

CHAPTER 2

The man lay sprawled on the sofa, his arms widely splayed.
Even from a distance, Mariner could see that his eyes were
glazed, his complexion waxy. The right sleeve of his
leather jacket was pulled up to above the elbow and a
hypodermic syringe dangled grotesquely from his inner
arm, its needle still tugging at the vein. A message beside
him, scrawled in block capitals on a curled scrap of paper,
was short and to the point: 'NO MORE.' Had he rolled
him over, Mariner would have seen Harley Davidson
advertised across the man's back.

There was no sign of the brunette but the TV
chattered on, with a youthful Carol Vorderman providing
an obscene accompaniment. Struck by the strangeness of it
all, Mariner moved quickly across the room, his footsteps
crunching on debris underfoot. Checking for signs of life
at each of the pulse points, twenty years of experience
already told him that he was too late, while his mind
struggled to reconcile the fact that only a couple of hours
earlier he'd seen this man so very much alive.

'Anyone home?' Though loud, the voice was too
guarded to be a threat, and even in those three words

Mariner thought he recognised a familiar intonation. 'In here,' he called back.

A uniform appeared, confirming his hunch. PC Tony Knox, formerly of the Merseyside Police, was about Mariner's age but had moved with the times, his number two buzz-cut obscuring the onset of baldness and combining with his sinewy build to make look him every bit the hard man he was reputed to be.

'Sir . . . ?' The question hung in the air unanswered as Knox took in the scene. 'Shit. Is he dead?' As Knox squatted down to verify it, Mariner watched him try to make sense of things. Finally his brow creased to a frown. 'What are you doing here?' he demanded at last, subtlety never one of his strengths. The exact reason for the transfer from Liverpool had never been made explicit, but rumour had it that it wasn't entirely Knox's decision. In this case, however, the question was justified. A DI wouldn't normally be first on the scene of a bog-standard disturbance.

Mariner hoped it wouldn't complicate things. 'I was in the area and heard the call,' he said. 'When I got here I recognised the car on the drive.'

'You know him?'

'Not exactly.' Mariner briefly recounted what he'd witnessed earlier that evening. If Knox wondered what a senior officer was doing hanging around the bar of the Chamberlain Hotel on his night off done up like a dog's dinner he was, for once, astute enough not to ask.

'It's ironic,' added Mariner. 'The way this guy was behaving made me afraid for the woman's safety. But then, that was more than an hour ago.' And, as they both knew, practically anything could have happened in the interim.

As he inhaled Mariner caught a whiff of something, a sort of unwashed smell. At first he assumed it was the dead man, but studying Knox more closely he noticed suddenly the grimy rim around the collar of his white shirt and the thin sheen of stubble coating his chin. Thanks to tonight's match they'd be short of police around the city, which probably accounted for why Knox was solo, but even so. 'How long have you been on duty?' Mariner asked him.

'Since two,' Knox shifted uncomfortably. 'The wife has locked me out so I had to kip in the car last night. I'll get a shower at the end of the shift.'

'Good idea,' said Mariner with feeling, making an effort at shallow breathing and shaking off any speculation about why Knox might have been barred from his own home.

Taking the hint, Knox got up and moved away. 'I'll check over the rest of the house.'

'It'll be a start. Our friend here drove off with the brunette, and it was a woman who made the emergency call, so there's a strong possibility that it's the same one. She looked more like a tom than a user to me, but this guy was waving his money around, so it's possible that she supplied and serviced him. Let's make sure that she isn't still hanging around somewhere, then get Scenes of Crime out of bed.'

Whatever the circumstances might imply, this was a sudden unexplained death and in the absence of any reliable witnesses they would have to remain open minded for now. It didn't look much like many other crime scenes Mariner had attended — unless the reckless dispersal of potato snacks had suddenly become a felony — but until they found conclusive evidence of suicide nothing was certain, and they would treat the scene accordingly.

'You'll need these,' said Knox. Throwing Mariner a small polythene packet, he went off to search the rest of the house, speaking into his lapel radio as he went. Mariner opened the packet and squeezed his hands into the tight latex gloves, grateful, as always, that he was only a policeman and not a vet.

Knox reappeared. 'We're on our own,' he confirmed, tactfully keeping his distance. 'No sign of life. And SOCO are on their way.'

'Good.' Taking care not to disturb the syringe, Mariner slid his hand into the inside breast pocket of the dead man's jacket to retrieve the soft leather wallet he'd seen earlier. It contained a hundred and thirty in notes, along with a variety of standard credit and loyalty cards, plus a larger, laminated press card, conveniently displaying a photograph of the deceased. He'd been right. This wasn't Derek. But it seemed he'd been way off the mark about everything else. 'Edward Barham,' he read out loud, for Knox's benefit. 'And this is his place, according to the address.' He made a swift mental calculation. 'Age thirty-nine, and a paid-up member of the National Union of Journalists.'

'A hack,' said Knox. He walked the length of the room and stopped in front of a fitted cupboard, on top of which, high up and almost beyond Mariner's line of vision, was a row of plaques and trophies. 'He was a good one too, if this lot's anything to go by,' he craned his neck to read the engraving: 'Midlands Reporter of the Year three years running.'

'But modest enough about his achievements to stick them way up there, almost out of sight,' observed Mariner. 'Christ, and is that what I think it is?' Staring out from the corner of the ceiling, was the beady eye of a miniature, remote controlled video camera.

'Journalist, junkie and security nut,' announced Knox.

'This is a prime area for burglaries, it would have been a reasonable precaution.' But even as Mariner spoke he was conscious, studying it for the first time, that the design of this room represented security taken to its extreme. The substantial TV and DVD housing was bolted to the polished wood floor, while the state-of-the-art sound system, CDs and rows of books were all present, but locked away behind elaborately reinforced glass inside the same floor-to-ceiling cupboards that ran the entire length of one wall. Apart from those items, the four-seater sofa was the only other piece of furniture in what was a cavern of a room. Everything was obsessively, uncompromisingly minimalist.

Truth be told, it was Mariner's kind of place, but the overall impression was stark and empty, with none of the usual clutter accumulated in most homes. No pictures, photographs, pot-plants or the army of candles that these days seemed to be practically mandatory. The only aberration was a pile of dog-eared catalogues that stood in a jumbled stack by the door, topped by two weighty hardback books.

And then there were the funny little symbols. Black-and-white laminated line drawings were posted here and there, on the side of the TV, the back of the door, beneath the window sill. Knox was studying one at close quarters. 'What do you suppose they are? Something to do with the occult?'

Mariner was dubious. The images were simple and childlike — although there was little other indication that children lived here — but they did have a kind of alien quality.

Knox had already made up his mind. 'I bet this guy had one of those weird compulsive disorders,' he said. In many ways it made sense. Suicide could be just a short step away from mental disturbance, but it was still a big assumption.

'On the other hand, he could have just been security conscious and tidy,' countered Mariner, Knox's tendency towards the forgone conclusion starting to rankle. 'And be grateful. Whatever the purpose of that camera, if what happened here has been filmed it's going to save us a hell of a lot of trouble.' Mariner turned his attention back to the wallet, which also contained a couple of personal business cards and a folded page recently torn from a newspaper. Flattened out, Mariner recognised it as the same column for personal services as he'd used, well-thumbed and with several of the numbers emphatically ringed in black ink. He wondered if one of them was the brunette's.

Something stale invaded Mariner's nostrils again. Knox was back peering over his shoulder. 'See,' he concluded, uncompromisingly. 'What kind of sad git gets his sex life out of the paper?'

'We don't know that he did!' Mariner rounded on him, feeling his colour rise. 'There could be any number of explanations for this. He was a journalist, remember?' He knew he'd jumped in too soon and too defensively, conscious of the arrangement he himself had made only the night before. Okay, so he hadn't followed it through, but he'd made it all the same.

'No, well, perhaps you're right, boss.' Knox's expression was inscrutable, but Mariner could almost hear him adding two and two to make five. It was no more than Mariner would have expected. Blessed with the Scouse gift of the gab, Knox would never find himself in that sorry position, but chances were that had something to do with why Mrs Knox had thrown him out.

'I'm just saying we shouldn't be making any assumptions at this stage,' Mariner said, regaining his composure. He was tempted to say more, but let it go. Instead he turned his attention back to the cutting. 'These numbers will need to be cross-checked with the calls made on Barham's phone.'

'I'll have a vowel, please Carol,' piped up one of the contestants on the TV.

'Not what I'd choose as the background for my final, dramatic gesture to the world,' Knox said, momentarily distracted by the screen. 'Shall I turn it off?' But neither of them was inclined to, not while it provided a diversion from the bleak silence of death.

'Let's get searching.' Mariner said. 'We need to turn up a relative or two.' Yellow potato rings cracked beneath his feet as he stood up. 'What is all this crap?'

'Hula Hoops,' Knox obliged, nodding towards a wrapper beside the sofa. 'But only one packet — not much of a party.'

A loud knock echoed down the hall. Great, nosy neighbours, that was all they needed. Where were they a couple of hours ago? But it wasn't neighbours. It was Stuart Croghan, the police surgeon, carelessly dressed and bleary-eyed, making Mariner wonder enviously whose bed he'd just left. Why was it that when your own love life was on the skids, everyone else seemed to have it on tap? Close behind Croghan, the SOCO team had arrived, too. This was fast turning into rent-a-wake.

'Stuart,' Mariner nodded a greeting.

'Tom. What have we got?'

'Edward Barham. Pretty much as we found him, except that I've relieved him of his wallet.'

Croghan's gaze took in the suicide note. 'No more what?' he wondered aloud.

'Monkeys, bouncing on the bed?' suggested Knox. He caught Mariner's glare and left the room before the DI could interject. 'Next of kin, sir. I'll get on to it.'

Mariner had nothing to gain by hovering over Croghan either. So, leaving the surgeon pulling on overalls, he followed Knox up the stairs.

'Where the hell did you learn something like that?' he asked.

'My granddaughter.'

Knox spoke so quietly, Mariner thought he must have misheard. He hoped that the thud of his jaw hitting the ground wasn't audible. 'Granddaughter?'

'That's right.' Knox turned to face him, his eyes challenging Mariner to make something of it.

'I never had you down as a granddad,' Mariner said, truthfully.

'Neither did I,' Knox replied evenly. 'But some things are out of our hands, aren't they, sir?' And with a minimal lift of his eyebrows, he turned and continued up to the landing. Subject closed.

Of the four first-floor rooms, the most promising appeared to be a small back bedroom that had been converted into a home office complete with computer and printer. In stark contrast to the lower floor, this room was by far the untidiest and therefore was probably the one that mattered most. Papers were piled haphazardly over every horizontal surface and drawers were pulled open to varying degrees, revealing their contents.

'Almost as if he was looking for something, too,' remarked Mariner.

'An anti-virus programme if he had any sense. Look at that.' Mariner tracked Knox's gaze to the computer screen. The machine had been left running, and, as Knox nudged the mouse, the screen-saver cleared to reveal a scene of technological devastation. Trailing across the screen in ragged rows, Mariner could still make out the ruins of a meticulously crafted Excel document, now a tangle of symbols and characters, devoid of all meaning.

Although he could type on them, Mariner's interest in computers pretty well ended there. This was the first time he'd witnessed a virus in action but even he understood the implications. 'This document . . . can you recover it?' he asked.

From the expression on his face, Mariner guessed that Knox shared his level of IT expertise: basic at best. 'It might be possible to save anything that isn't already corrupted,' he said.

'Get on with it, then,' said Mariner. 'It might be important.' Like holding the key to why Edward Barham had just killed himself.

Knox sat down on the swivel chair and the first thing he did was to clear a space to the left of the keyboard and move the mouse and mouse-mat over to it. He noticed

Mariner watching him. 'I'm left-handed,' he said, defensively.

'Okay,' said Mariner uncertainly. Meanwhile, he rifled through the rest of the desk, looking for any personal papers that might help them to build a picture of Edward Barham's life in the days leading up to its close. The journalist, it appeared, was nothing if not methodical, and it wasn't long before Mariner found some useful material contained in a single suspension file squeezed between dozens of others in the bottom drawer and labelled, 'Finance: Current.' In it were bank statements, credit-card bills and invoices, some going back as far as a year. Making further inroads into Knox's supply of evidence bags, Mariner tipped in the entire contents. They could sort it out back at the station. None of the other files of correspondence, newspaper cuttings and assorted instruction manuals, looked as immediately relevant. They could be checked later if necessary.

Closing the drawer Mariner straightened, and as he did so, noticed a Filofax that had fallen on the floor, down the side of the filing cabinet. He picked it up and placed it beside Knox.

'While you're at it, here's your chance to multitask,' Mariner added. 'Have a flick through that for any likely names and addresses.' And leaving Knox to his endeavours, he went to look over the rest of the house, glad to escape the stuffy office and to breathe some sweeter smelling air.

Unsurprisingly the remaining four rooms lacked the hi-tech input and were furnished more in keeping with the age and style of the house. Old-fashioned Mariner would have called them, though the lingering smell of paint hinted at recent decoration. Only one, the master bedroom, was obviously inhabited, although a single bed in the spare room was also made up. Mariner opened drawers and cupboards. No trace of any female apparel — ruling out the brunette as a wife or live-in partner — but several wardrobes, including those in the spare room, were full of men's clothes and shoes. There were a couple of suits and some formal shirts but mainly it was casual wear: Next, Gap, off-the-peg stuff. Reasonable quality, but like the leather jacket, most of it well worn. Mariner sensed Barham wasn't a man who had lived extravagantly. There was a slight fluctuation in size, though, making Mariner wonder if Edward Barham had been battling with his weight. In any event there seemed far more clothing here than one man could reasonably wear. Again, up here the strange symbols were posted in places, including the bathroom, an otherwise pretty standard affair, which gave little away until Mariner came to the medicine cabinet. Prying open the flimsy lock he found inside, among the standard remedies, six vacuum-packed plastic syringes.

As if on cue, Stuart Croghan's voice echoed up the stairs. 'I've finished the preliminaries, Tom. All right with you if we get him taken away?'

Mariner took the stairs down two at a time. 'First impressions?' he asked, knowing that it was completely unreasonable to expect anything concrete at this stage.

'Only what you've already worked out.' Croghan was replacing instruments in his kit bag while the scene photographer flashed some last minute shots from varying angles. 'The body temperature would suggest that it occurred not long ago, maybe not more than an hour or two; no sign of rigor yet. The post-mortem will establish what he injected, but I'm sure we're all thinking the same thing. Enough of the stuff would have done the business within a matter of minutes. Strange that there's no preparation equipment,' Croghan observed. 'Unless he bought it pre-packed. The ultimate in convenience shopping, eh?'

It was something that had puzzled Mariner at first, but was in keeping with the general orderliness of the place and with his idea of the brunette's role in the proceedings. Alternatively, Knox could be right about a compulsive disorder. 'Could it have been an accident, a miscalculation?' he asked Croghan.

'It's possible, of course. There's nothing on the face of it to show that he was a habitual user, so it could have been an experiment gone horribly wrong. Apart from the fatal puncture mark there don't seem to be any others, and the point of insertion makes it look like an amateurish job,' he pointed to Barham's pale and lifeless arm. 'See where the skin is torn?'

Mariner thought back to the computer mouse. 'He bungled it?'

'Could be. But if it was an accident I'd say it was bloody bad luck. And you do have the note.' Safely protected within an evidence bag, the note would, along with the syringe, be sent to the forensic science service laboratory over at Bordesley Green. 'Besides, if you were about to relax and enjoy yourself over a quiet fix, wouldn't you at least take your coat off first?'

Croghan was right. The scene had a definite air of urgency. And Mariner recalled Barham's agitation in the hotel bar. But something didn't sit right. He kept his thoughts to himself for now. He was doubtless seeking complexity where there was none — one of his more annoying habits, as he'd frequently been told. Talking to those around Edward Barham to establish his state of mind would soon settle the matter and Knox had at last found a promising name and address.

Mariner and Knox waited around until the SOCOs had finished, but after that there was nothing more to do except secure the scene. On the TV, the *Countdown* audience went wild.

'Turn that off, will you?' said Mariner. Knox did so, and immediately a different noise became apparent.

Mariner listened hard. 'What's that?'

'What? I can't hear—'

'Sshhh!!' Barely discernible in the background was a faint, high-pitched keening sound. Mariner tracked it out of the room to a small, low door under the stairs, fastened on a snib-lock. He opened it and rubbed noses with what felt like a battering ram.

CHAPTER 3

Anna Barham stretched lazily in her king-sized bed. Although the hollow remained where Jonathan's head had been on the pillow, the other side was cooling fast and in the darkness she could just distinguish his shadowy figure as he hastily pulled on his clothes. Fully dressed, he leaned over and kissed her on the forehead, his goatee lightly scratching her skin. Anna wished he'd shave it off. Goatees had gone out of fashion long ago but apparently his wife liked it, so it had to stay. She feigned sleep, knowing that he preferred to think she didn't hear him go. Moments later she heard the front door close as her digital clock clicked over to 12:13 a.m. Hmm, earlier than usual. Niggling doubts resurfaced as Anna wondered if her suspicions that Jonathan was cooling towards her were more than just unfounded paranoia. The uneasiness had started soon after Melanie Pick joined the firm, her induction programme seeming to demand rather a lot of Jonathan's time. But that was ridiculous. She and Jonathan had a great thing going.

Not that a part-time relationship with a happily married man was every woman's dream, but at this time in her life it suited Anna's requirements perfectly. With one disastrous, blink-and-you'll-miss-it marriage behind her, the last thing she wanted was any kind of commitment. She and Jonathan had fun together, they had fantastic sex, but Jonathan's family kept him right where Anna wanted him: at arm's length. He didn't want to move in with her and permanently impinge on her space. He wouldn't start wanting babies with her, because he already had three of his own. And children were definitely not on Anna's wish list. Okay, there were downsides too: the occasional lonely night she had to endure when Jonathan was unable to get away, and the odd troubling pang she felt when she thought about his other life (occurring more frequently lately than she cared to acknowledge), but all things considered, it was a small price to pay for her to remain exactly the way she liked and needed to be: in control.

She dozed and awoke again — almost immediately after Jonathan had left, it seemed — to a lightening sky and the humming undercurrent of the city stirring into life. Sliding into her blue silk kimono, Jonathan's gift from his last visit to Tokyo, Anna opened the blinds and relished her view, as she'd done on every single morning of her three-year occupancy. As part of the city's prestigious canal-side development, the outlook from her apartment was like a picture postcard: freshly painted black-and-white bridges arching over the canal that snaked darkly towards the shops and restaurants of Brindley Place. All this set against the backdrop of the showpiece Symphony Hall, with its pale blocks and tinted glass — today rendered clear and sharp by a burst of February sunshine.

Anna took a long shower, choosing gel, shampoo, exfoliating cream and moisturising body lotion from rows of accumulated preparations. Applying her make-up, she noticed that her hair would need trimming in a couple of weeks, which meant ringing the studio today if she was to stand any chance of getting Nicky. She was down to the last dregs of her Chanel too, so it was as well that she'd be passing through duty-free next weekend on her way back from Milan.

In all, her whole morning routine took a leisurely hour, ending, as always with a circuit of the flat as she straightened the cushions, swept up a few imaginary crumbs and replaced three CDs in their boxes, slotting them back into the neat rank. Finally, she parcelled up last night's empty takeaway cartons to take down to the bin and wiped over the already spotless kitchen counters one last time. Walking out of the door, she took a last look around, getting a thrill, as always, from the knowledge that when she came back in again this evening, everything would be exactly as she had left it.

As much as anything else, Anna had chosen her flat for its proximity, via a network of side streets, to the office where she worked. But all this week she'd been inconvenienced by road closures along her usual route while cables were being laid. To follow the suggested diversions would mean lengthy detours into heavy rush-hour traffic, so she'd developed a simple strategy. Ignoring the no-entry notices, she consigned herself to the 'emergency access' category for three quarters of a mile, before swinging into the corporate car park only minutes after leaving home. Lowering the window of her fiery red company Mazda3, she tucked her pass card into the machine before drawing to a halt in her reserved parking space. Getting out of the car, she smoothed the skirt of her dove grey Donna Karan suit, grabbed her briefcase and laptop from the passenger seat and setting the remote electronic alarm, strode towards the modern office block that was home to Priory International Management Consultants.

Flexi-time ensured that Anna was early enough to have pre-empted the arrival of most of her colleagues but not Becky, her brilliantly efficient PA, who emerged from behind her work station to pick up Anna's stride like a well-trained relay racer.

'Hi, Anna,' she said as they walked. 'The first draft of the contract for Milan is ready on your desk for you to approve and I've confirmed your flights for next weekend. Mr Waterhouse has booked a table for eight thirty this evening at da Paglia.'

'Perfect.' Anna nodded approval. Helping Jonathan to wine and dine prospective clients was becoming an increasingly important feature of her job, and Robinson's Logistics PLC, their guests tonight, were potentially among the biggest they were ever likely to get. Even better, Robinson's had been Anna's find. She'd been the first to pick up the rumours of their sliding profit margins and a timely phone call had generated just the response she'd hoped. The following day, her call had been returned and, so far, the chance of a deal was looking promising. All Anna had to do now was to make sure that she was the face of Priory Management most visible to Robinson's chief executive. If she could front the securing of the contract with them, it would earn her a barrow-load of brownie points with Jonathan — something she suspected she was in need of right now.

'These are your phone messages.' In place of a baton, Becky passed across a sheaf of papers. 'And,' she added casually as Anna rested her hand on the door handle, 'there are two policemen waiting for you in there.' So they'd got her.

Taking a deep breath, Anna pushed open the door that bore her nameplate in shiny brass. The room seemed darker than usual, the view over Birmingham's city centre obscured by the tall man who stood with his back to her looking out of the window.

The other man, a uniformed policeman, had been sitting in the visitor's chair but now clambered awkwardly to his feet, weighed down by all the occupational hardware. It was he who spoke first. 'Anna Barham?' he asked, waving identification in her face and not waiting for her reply. 'I'm Police Constable Knox and this is Detective Inspector Mariner.'

The tall man turned to face her holding out his warrant card which, this time, she got the chance to see. Thomas Mariner, Detective Inspector, she read. The mugshot adequately portrayed the pale features and the glacier-blue eyes, but not the hideously bruised and swollen nose he bore in reality. Anna had to stop herself from staring.

Talking herself out of difficult situations was one of Anna's specialities, but in the half-minute or so she'd had, she'd already decided to come clean. They must at least have her license-plate number and had probably filmed her in the act of defying the diversions with CCTV, although she was staggered that such a petty traffic offence should provoke a personal house call from two police officers, one of them a detective. 'I'm really sorry,' she began, apologetic, but coolly professional just the same. 'I know I shouldn't keep ignoring the signs, but I forget and before I know it, I'm just way past—'

PC Knox looked blankly at her. 'Sorry?'

Anna helped him out. 'The diversion signs. I should follow them, I know.'

'This isn't about driving.' PC Knox was suddenly floundering.

Anna glanced up at Mariner's battered face. 'Well, I don't remember assaulting a police officer . . .' she said, instantly regretting her flippancy.

'It's nothing you've done, Miss Barham,' Knox persevered, with a touch of irritation in his voice.

'You may want to sit down,' Mariner intervened, his voice thick and adenoidal, so that Anna had to fight a bizarre urge to pinch her nose and respond in the same way. He gestured towards her chair, and more from surprise than anything else, she did as she was told.

'Your brother, Edward, was found dead in his home, late last night.'

Wow, this guy knew how to make an impact. He may as well have punched her in the stomach, and for several seconds her vision distorted and the room seemed to sway. 'No!' Anna blurted out uncontrollably. 'No, he can't be.' A sudden vision flashed through her mind of the occasion all those years ago when she'd got home late from a party to find Eddie himself waiting for her. *'Ann-ann, there's been a terrible accident—'* Now they were telling her that Eddie was dead too? It was impossible.

'I'm sorry,' said Mariner.

'When? How?' She was so sure that this couldn't be right.

The constable had taken out a small, black notebook. 'We were called to a house late last night, 34 Clarendon Avenue,' he said. It was Eddie's address all right.

'As yet we're not looking for anyone else in connection with his death,' Mariner added.

It was common enough police-speak and it took Anna only a few seconds to catch on to what he meant. 'You think Eddie killed himself?'

'It appears so. He left a note.'

'Where? Can I see it?'

He turned to Constable Knox, who was ineffectually digging around in his pockets. Eventually he produced a folded, crumpled photocopied sheet, which he passed to Anna. 'Does it look like his writing?' he asked.

Staring at the print, Anna gave the slightest shrug of her shoulders. There was little that was distinctive about the scrawled block capitals.

'Your brother seems to have died from a drug overdose,' Mariner went on.

Now Anna knew for certain that they'd got it wrong. 'That's nonsense,' she told them. 'Eddie didn't do drugs.'

'When did you last see him?'

'I'm not sure exactly,' Anna hedged.

'Days ago? Weeks?' Mariner probed.

'Weeks, I suppose.' Suddenly Anna knew what he was getting at and resented the assumption. Her eyes flashed angrily. 'But I know he wouldn't have killed himself. It's absurd.'

'It would help us if you could make a formal identification, Miss Barham. Do you feel up to it?'

Anna looked from one to the other of them. 'I will,' she said, eventually, 'but I really think you've got this horribly wrong.' She glanced up at the outer office. 'I'll have to arrange for my PA to cancel my diary appointments. Could you just wait for a moment?'

'Of course.'

Anna went out to where Becky sat at her desk, printing off documents. 'Becky, incredible as it sounds, these policemen think my brother has killed himself. They want me to go with them and identify a body.' Telling it how it was helped Anna to keep a grip on herself and ride out her friend's shocked reaction. Then she returned to the office to pick up her bag, feeling the first chill of apprehension as she allowed herself to consider the seriousness of what she'd been asked to do. 'Right,' she said. 'Let's get this over with.'

* * *

Apart from the ominous creaking and whirring of the lift mechanism, the trio descended to the ground floor in silence while Mariner gave Anna Barham time and space to absorb what she'd been told. For once Knox was exercising some discretion, too. Thanks to Mariner, he did at least present as a respectable officer of the law this morning. After they had finished at the station last night, Mariner had given Knox the spare front-door key to his house and ordered him to go and get a shower and borrow a clean uniform from somewhere, before returning. 'I'm not breaking the news to the relatives accompanied by a tramp.'

Mariner had worked this routine a hundred times before and was prepared as ever for shock and anger, even denial. Suicide in particular threw up all kinds of powerful and unwanted emotions. But this one was especially interesting. He couldn't work out whether Anna Barham really didn't believe them, or simply didn't want to. Or did the lady just protest too much? Mariner hadn't, of course, overlooked the possibility that Anna Barham herself could be involved. A woman had made the emergency call, and if not the brunette, why not her, making her reaction part of an elaborate attempt to cover up for her brother? But somehow he didn't think so. What would be the point? And her initial surprise had seemed genuine enough.

Then there was that newspaper cutting, the list of small ads for personal escort services, leading them in one swift move back to the brunette. Mariner hadn't changed his view of her and Knox hadn't appeared to disagree. It was becoming increasingly commonplace for some of the higher-class call girls to supply, and if that was the case it would explain why everything had been left so neat and tidy. A pro would have cleaned up before she left. It could easily have been the way Eddie Barham had planned things, a discreet and distinctly impersonal service. But even that explanation left one significant outstanding loose end. He was waiting for Anna Barham to come to that.

Hers was an unusual reaction; indignant and affronted, as if they were wasting her time. And she was taking the whole identification procedure surprisingly in her stride, leaving Mariner considering the dubious possibility that she'd done it before. But he knew better than to make any judgments at this stage, because death is much the same as life. Everybody handles it in his or her own unique way. Shock can do funny things to people. And right now, as Knox manoeuvred them out into the soupy mid-morning traffic of the Hagley Road, Mariner was content to bide his time. They'd know for sure soon enough.

CHAPTER 4

The city mortuary on Newton Street was housed in an anonymous-looking square Georgian edifice labelled, innocuously enough, 'Coroner's Office' by the standard brass plaque. The sign that had always afforded Mariner a darker satisfaction was the red-topped 'T' at the entrance to the street, so fittingly declaring the byway a 'dead end.' Within the bowels of the building, in a tastefully and sensitively furnished suite of rooms, Anna Barham did reluctantly provide them with a positive identification of her brother.

Afterwards, Mariner carried two beakers of grey scalding tea from the vending machine to where she sat in what was generally referred to as the recovery lounge. It was a misnomer in most cases, though occasionally relatives managed to regain their outward composure, as Anna Barham seemed to have done. Now faced with the truth, she was clearly shocked, as Mariner would have expected, but still far from being distressed. Instead she appeared more puzzled and detached, as if presented with a conundrum.

'Are you all right?' Mariner asked anyway.

'Yes.' With a brief nod of thanks, she awkwardly relieved him of one of the flimsy, polystyrene cups. 'Just can't believe it.' Mariner took a seat opposite, and her tawny-brown eyes looked directly into his, steady and unblinking. No avoidance, but no trace of any tears either. She read his thoughts. 'You must think I'm hard.'

It wasn't an apology and Mariner only shrugged. 'Everyone reacts differently in these situations,' he said. 'You'll probably cry your eyes out when you get home.'

Anna Barham smiled weakly. Christ, it was a stunning smile. 'That's tactful of you,' she said. 'But I don't think so. Eddie and I weren't what you'd call close. It isn't weeks but more like months since I last saw him, even though we live only a few miles apart. I left home to get married when I was quite young.' There was diffidence to her admission and from the bare fingers of her left hand Mariner guessed that the marriage hadn't lasted.

That aside, none of this was beyond the scope of his comprehension. The week-old answerphone message from his mother tweaked at his conscience, but he pushed the thought away again. He braced himself. 'Miss Barham, coincidentally I saw your brother earlier yesterday evening in the bar of the Chamberlain Hotel. He was with a woman, about five ten, with long, reddish hair and brown eyes. Do you have any idea who she might be?' He'd keep his own opinions about the brunette to himself for now.

She thought for a moment. 'No, I'm sorry. As I said, I'm a bit out of touch.'

He couldn't resist. 'Yet you seem very sure that Eddie hadn't taken up a new recreational pursuit.'

She flushed with annoyance. 'I do know Eddie. We may not have seen each other often, but I know he wouldn't have done that. He didn't smoke, he hardly ever drank—'

'People change. Sometimes pretty dramatically.'

'Not Eddie. He wasn't a user,' she insisted.

'He doesn't have to have been. It looks as if it was his first time.'

'No!' Again the anger flared.

When the silence stretched to breaking point and she still made no reference to the other item outstanding, Mariner said quietly, 'There was another man in the house.'

His words had a more dramatic effect than anything he'd said so far and she jumped violently, almost spilling the tea. 'Jamie! God, of course! I'd completely—' Forgotten? Now that *was* unbelievable. 'But I don't understand — he shouldn't have been there. Is he all right?' She finally got round to asking.

'Oh, *he's* fine.' Involuntarily, Mariner touched his swollen nose and elicited a smirk of understanding from her. 'Although that skull of his should be classed as an offensive weapon,' Mariner said. 'He is—?'

'My younger brother.' It was confirmation of what they'd already guessed from the physical resemblance to the dead man. He was struck by her likeness to her brothers, too. Though smaller and more fragile, she had the same fair hair, tinged with red and cut boyishly short so that it curled into the nape of her neck. Her eyes glinted dark and dangerous. They were like peas in a pod, the Barhams. 'Where is he?' she asked.

'At the station. We're waiting for him to come down so that we can talk to him.'

'Come down?' She was momentarily confused, but as realisation dawned, she broke into a humourless laugh. 'Oh great, now you're going to try and tell me that Jamie's on drugs, too.'

'Miss Barham, Eddie was found with a hypodermic needle sticking out of his arm. There's not much doubt about the way he died. And we found more syringes in the bathroom—'

'Yes, probably left over from a time when Jamie used to have seizures,' she said matter-of-factly. 'Afterwards, he needed an injection of Valium to help him calm down and sleep it off.'

'And head-butting people is a normal part of his behaviour, is it?' Mariner persisted. 'We found him hiding in a cupboard under the stairs and when we let him out, he went crazy.' Her reluctance to face facts was understandable and nothing he hadn't had to deal with before. 'Look,' he went on, patiently, trying to help her out. 'You don't have to pretend to me, I've had years of experience of users.'

'And what's your experience of autism, Inspector?'

'Autism?' It came at him from out of left field.

'Jamie isn't on drugs, he's autistic. He freaked out because he was frightened. He didn't know you. It's that simple. If he was shut in a cupboard, he would have been terrified. He was always afraid of the dark.' Her voice carried a triumphant ring.

It took Mariner a few seconds to fully digest what she'd said, but gradually it began to add up. The kid's raw terror, his apparent total lack of understanding of anything they'd said to him, the peculiar mannerisms. 'Autistic,' he said at last. 'That's why we couldn't find any tracks.'

'I'm sorry to disappoint you, Inspector, but Jamie won't be "coming down" from anywhere. That's the way he is, all the time.'

'We're going to need to talk to him,' Mariner reiterated, eventually.

'You can talk away,' she said, with obvious amusement. 'Jamie will completely ignore you. His understanding of spoken language is virtually non-existent, and the only things he says are words and phrases that he's learned, mainly from the TV. He just echoes what he hears.'

'Echoes?' It was out before he could stop himself. Mariner groaned inwardly. This was worse than he'd thought. The video camera had been wiped, so finding Jamie Barham had been the next best thing. They were banking on him as a key witness. Mariner had felt confident that however high he might have been, he would be able to demystify at least some of the events of the previous evening. 'Maybe if *you* talked to Jamie?' he suggested, hopefully.

'Me?' Another wry laugh. 'You must be joking. Eddie's the one you need.'

'We will have to interview Jamie, and the sooner the better. It would help if you could be there. And then you can take him home.'

'Home?'

'He's not under arrest. We're only holding him for his own safety until after questioning. He's free to go at any time.'

'But not with me!' And for the first time she seemed truly appalled. 'I'm flying to Milan in a few days. I can't look after him.'

'So is there someone else we can contact?'

'I don't know. He goes into respite care at the weekends but the rest of the time—' Her shoulders sagged as suddenly the fight went out of her and finally the tears looked as if they might come. 'With Eddie gone there's nobody. God, what a mess.'

'What about your parents?'

'My parents are dead.'

So she might have been through this before. Shit. Nice work, Mariner.

* * *

From the mortuary, it was a twenty-minute drive to Operational Command Unit two, Granville Lane police station, where Jamie Barham was being held. The station was Monday-morning busy, nonetheless allowing the desk sergeant the opportunity to call out cheerily as they passed. 'That bloke you brought in last night has been creating havoc in the cells.'

'Doing what?'

'Trying to crack his head open on the walls, mainly. Andy Draper's moved him up here for his own safety.' Draper, the station's on-call police surgeon would have been called in to check Jamie over.

'Where is he?' asked Mariner.

'Observation Room Four. We're keeping an eye on him. No traces of drug use either; just your average nutcase.'

'Cheers.' Mariner flashed Anna an apologetic smile. So far, locking up Jamie Barham had been nothing more than a misunderstanding and he'd been hoping they could keep it that way. 'Through here.' Moving swiftly on, Mariner led the way through a maze of brightly lit corridors until they reached a door, which he pushed open, standing back to allow her in.

The room itself was empty but a window ran almost the entire width of one wall and on the other side of it was Jamie Barham. Mariner immediately sensed Anna's unease. Wearing only underpants and a single sock, Jamie paced restlessly around the perimeter of the room, stopping now and then at some random spot to spread the fingers of both his hands on the wall, laying his cheek in between, as if listening for something on the other side. His matted and spiky hair gave him a wild, agitated appearance that was compounded by the deep graze on his forehead, which had streaked blood down one side of his face and onto his pale wiry body. Here and there, terracotta-coloured prints adorned the stark white walls of the room — decorative stencilling gone grotesquely wrong. But even in that condition Jamie Barham was strikingly handsome, with the sort of intense good looks that stared insolently from monochrome aftershave ads.

'So if he's autistic,' Knox broke the silence. 'Does that mean he's really a genius? Like Rain Man?'

Anna scoffed. 'You can forget the toothpick trick. Jamie's no mathematical genius. He's what they poetically call "low functioning." On top of the autism, he has learning disabilities too. Unless Eddie's worked miracles, he can't even dress himself without considerable help.'

Knox nodded towards a pile of linen in the corner. 'We gave him those, but he wouldn't put them on.'

'Where are his clothes?'

'They had blood on them, they're being analysed.' Mariner told her.

She hesitated. 'Eddie's blood?'

'Some of it was mine, but apart from that we don't know yet.'

'So what happens now?'

'We would like to talk to Jamie. It's just an informal chat, but he has the right to legal representation—'

They seemed to be doing a good job of keeping her amused. This time she laughed out loud. 'I hardly think that will be necessary. What you'll need is some kind of incentive just to get him to sit down and take notice of you.'

'Like what?'

'I've no idea. I don't know what he's into now. It always used to be Monster Munch: pickled onion flavour.'

'Hula Hoops,' said Knox.

'What?'

'At the flat,' the constable reminded him. 'There were Hula Hoops all over the floor, remember? Perhaps his taste has improved.'

'That sounds the right kind of thing,' Anna agreed.

'I'll see if they've got some in the canteen,' Knox left them alone.

'Can I get him dressed first?' asked Anna.

'Of course.' Mariner stood and watched from behind the two-way mirror as Anna Barham entered the room with her brother. The intercom was switched off, so the scene ran before him like a silent movie being played in slow motion and was one of the most bizarre encounters between human siblings that Mariner had ever witnessed.

CHAPTER 5

Closing the door behind her, Anna's lips moved in a soundless greeting. Jamie ceased pacing momentarily and turned towards her with a wary sideways look. Anna walked slowly to the other side of the room to retrieve the clothes. Picking out a T-shirt, she held it out towards her brother and began to gradually advance towards him, her lips moving all the while, in what Mariner imagined was some kind of soothing encouragement. Jamie visibly tensed, bringing his hands up parallel with his ears and flapping his fingers in agitation. Anna stopped momentarily and waited. Eventually he brought his hands down again to pluck at his crotch like a nervous toddler. Anna resumed her approach and as soon as she was near enough, slipped the T-shirt over his head, guiding his arms up into the sleeves in one swift, fluid action. She repeated the whole process with the other items of clothing; trousers, shirt, socks and shoes, the second shoe going on just as Knox returned from his quest.

'Look at that,' breathed Mariner. 'It's like dressing a kid.' As he spoke Anna turned to the mirror, giving the thumbs-up signal for them to join her.

Mariner and Knox came into the interview room, Mariner with some caution, the memory of his last face-to-face encounter with Jamie Barham still fresh in his mind. His fears were unfounded — Jamie had other more pressing concerns. With the speed and accuracy of an Exocet, he homed in on the crisp packet, hovering over Knox while he and Mariner seated themselves at the table.

Mariner slipped a tape into the recording machine. 'Even though this isn't a formal interview, it might be helpful,' he explained to Anna. For the benefit of the tape he set the scene — date, time, persons present — before turning back to her across the table. 'Off we go.'

'Okay. As I told you, he won't understand much of what you say to him,' she said. 'You'll need to keep your language very simple. Short questions, using just the key words. And say his name first each time to get his attention.' Taking the Hula Hoops packet from Knox, she held it up, deliberately scrunching the wrapper, dangling the proverbial carrot.

Jamie made a grab for it but missed. 'Loops. Want a loops!' he said.

'Jamie, sit down,' Anna patted the fourth chair beside her and Jamie obediently sat without taking his eyes off the crisps.

'Good,' said Anna. 'Good sitting.' She rewarded him with a single Hula Hoop which Jamie held up to the light turning it round in his fingers, before putting it in his mouth then holding out his hand immediately for another. With years of experience, Mariner considered himself to be up to the mark with most interviewing techniques but this one was something else. Anna gave him the nod.

'Jamie,' he began. Jamie glanced briefly in his direction as if newly aware that there was someone else present. 'What happened last night, at your house?'

No response. Jamie's attention had reverted to the Hula Hoops. Seizing Anna's free hand, he pushed it towards the packet. Anna pulled away. 'Not yet, Jamie,' she said, then *sotto voce* to Mariner, 'Try "at home."'

Mariner cleared his throat. 'Jamie, what happened last night at home?'

This time the response was instant. 'Home! Home now!' Jamie shouted and jumped up grabbing Anna's arm, dragging her off the chair and towards the door.

Anna wrenched herself free. 'No, Jamie, not now. Look, Hula Hoops,' she held up the packet and regaining his attention led him back to the table.

'Loops,' Jamie echoed, reaching out for another.

As he sat down Anna gave him another of the snacks. 'Yes. Jamie sit down, that's good sitting,' she looked over at Mariner. 'Try something different,' she suggested.

'Jamie, what happened to Eddie?' Mariner said.

'. . . Eddie,' the word echoed back at him.

'That's right,' said Mariner, encouraged. 'What happened, Jamie? What happened to Eddie last night, what did he do?'

'Eddie,' Jamie repeated once more and then, as if in sudden realisation, he leapt up tipping back the chair with a crash and began to restlessly pace the room.

'You've said too much,' said Anna. 'It's confusing him.' Jamie came to a halt, resting his face against the wall, murmuring to himself.

'What's he saying?' asked Knox. They listened.

'Sounds like "Sally-Ann,"' said Mariner. For a split second, Jamie glared at him, angrily.

'No Sally-Ann! No Sally-Ann!' he shouted.

'Sally-Ann who? Who's she?'

Anna pulled a face. 'I don't know.'

They listened again as Jamie's chanting grew in intensity. Then suddenly, without warning, Jamie began banging his forehead against the wall, in time with the chanting, over and over and with increasing force. Anna and Knox, who were nearest, jumped up and managed between them to drag him away, Knox firmly gripping Jamie by the shoulders to restrain him.

'Jamie, stop!' said Anna. 'It's all right, there's no Sally-Ann. Stop!' Slowly Jamie ceased struggling against Knox and calmed down.

Anna turned to Mariner. 'I told you, it's a waste of time. He doesn't understand abstracts. He's only interested in here and now. Concrete things. Things that are important to him, like Hula Hoops.'

'How about if we took him back to the house?' Mariner asked.

Anna sighed, wearily. 'I suppose it might be worth a try.'

'Get a car organised, will you, Tony?'

* * *

In the light of day, 34 Clarendon Avenue looked like any other house in the street, with nothing except the narrow strip of crime-scene tape to mark it out as different. And even that didn't look entirely out of place alongside what resembled a small building site in the garden next-door, half of it covered by a brand-new expanse of block paving.

On the approach to the house, Jamie had become manifestly more unsettled, flicking his fingers by his ears, his eyes panning anxiously from one side to another. Once Knox had pulled into the drive, the two officers stood back while Anna attempted to coax her brother out of the car.

But before they'd even unlocked the front door, with a sudden shout of 'No black mouth!' Jamie took off running down the street.

Knox was off like a shot, too, but it was Mariner who got there first, catching up with Jamie, grabbing him and propelling him, struggling, back to the car. 'What does he mean, "black mouth?"' Mariner asked Anna, trying not to let his breathlessness show.

'I don't know. I'm as much in the dark—' she stopped. 'Wait. You said he was shut in the cupboard? Maybe he thinks we're going to shut him in the "black mouth" of the cupboard again. We've brought him back here too soon. This is too frightening for him.'

'Terrific.' So it was going to be like that. Another avenue barred, though not entirely. As they prepared to leave, the front door of the adjacent house opened and a woman emerged, carrying a small fluffy canine. She stepped delicately around the piles of sand and bricks.

Seeing an opportunity, Mariner jumped back out of the car and, introducing himself, thrust his ID towards the woman, over the low hedge. She squinted at it, before looking over Mariner's shoulder towards the unmarked police car. 'Have you got Jamie in there? I thought I heard him.'

'And you are . . . ?'

'Moira Warren.' She shook her head sadly. 'I can't believe that such a dreadful thing has happened to poor Eddie. He was wonderful with Jamie.'

News travelled fast, but only apparently one way. Mariner had already been told that so far the house-to-house had turned up no worthwhile information. Nobody had seen or heard anything the previous night. It hadn't helped that there had been some kind of social gathering down the street early on, which meant that cars had been coming and going for most of the evening. Anything happening at number thirty-four would have just blended into the activity.

'And you didn't notice anything out of the ordinary yesterday?' he asked the old lady.

'No. I've had the workmen here all over the weekend, working on the drive. This job should have been finished in three days, but you know what it's like. They start something and then there's a problem. Five days it's been going on and it's still—'

'Did you know Eddie and Jamie Barham well?' Mariner cut in.

'Not really, no. We only moved in two years ago, this February gone, and we hardly ever saw them. I know the last people used to help out with Jamie, sitting with him sometimes. I did try once, but—'

'But?'

Her tone became defensive. Conscience kicking in. 'It was difficult, officer. Jamie's a grown man. He's strong and I'm not getting any younger. My husband said I shouldn't do it. I already told all this to the young policeman who came to see me.'

'So you haven't helped out recently?'

'No. But I don't think Eddie needed anyone lately because of the girl.'

'What girl?'

'I thought she must be Eddie's girlfriend. I never actually asked. You don't like to be nosy, do you?' That took a stretch of the imagination. 'We were just pleased to see that Eddie had a young lady. He must have missed out on so much because of, well, you know.' With a glance in Jamie's direction she lowered her voice, though not quite enough to prevent it carrying as far as the car. 'To be honest I'm not surprised it all got too much for him,' she intimated. 'There's a sister, you know. Haven't seen hide nor hair of her since we've been here but she's out there somewhere. You'd have thought that she might have—'

'This girl. Was her name Sally, or Sally-Ann?' Mariner interrupted again.

'It might have been, we were never actually introduced.'

'What did she look like?'

'She was a pretty girl, tall, with lovely long dark hair. But a bit . . . you know.'

'What?'

'Well, sort of cheap-looking. You know what these young girls can be like these days. Tiny little skirts that leave nothing to the imagination.' Eddie and the brunette were sounding like more than just a one-off. And were she and Sally-Ann the same person?

'Did you see this girl around last night?' Mariner asked.

'No.' The micro-hound had begun to wriggle and whine in her arms. 'I'll have to go now, Oscar needs to do his business. But if I can be of any more help, officer—'

After what he'd just heard, Mariner doubted that she could, but he nodded his thanks anyway. He went back to the car, mulling over the new information. 'Could this Sally have been Eddie's girlfriend?' he asked Anna.

'I didn't even know that Eddie had a girlfriend,' she replied, testily. 'As you heard, I've never been near the place.'

'Well, whoever she is, we need to find her.'

'So what now?'

'We'll take you home.'

'No!'

Mariner was unprepared for the force of her response, but then, if he imagined a home as perfectly turned out as Anna herself, and the potential effect on it her brother might have, he could understand the reaction.

'Jamie goes to a day centre on the other side of Harborne,' she was saying. 'I think I can direct you to it. If we take him there first, it will give me time to arrange things.'

They drove in near silence as she issued hesitant instructions to Knox, which left Mariner wondering how sure she was about where they were going. 'Eddie worked for the *Echo*, didn't he?' he said, firming up facts as they drove.

'Yes.'

'Doing what exactly?'

She seemed relieved to be able for once to answer him. 'He was a reporter,' she said. 'It meant he could work flexible hours and be around for Jamie.'

'Do you know what sort of stuff he covered?'

She was out of her depth again. 'All sorts, from what I remember,' she said, vaguely. 'You'd need to talk to the paper.'

It was on the list.

Judging from Jamie's reaction as they drew up outside a low, modern building, Anna's memory of where he spent his days was accurate. He bounded in like an eager puppy, visibly relaxed and clearly at home. Knox waited in the car.

'Greenwood Day Centre' read the logo emblazoned on the chest of the middle-aged woman who emerged from an office to greet them in the foyer. 'Joyce Clark. I'm the centre manager. Can I help you?'

Mariner produced his warrant card yet again, which Joyce accepted as though visits from the police were an everyday occurrence. 'We were wondering where Jamie had got to,' she said. 'Eddie's usually good at letting us know if he's going to be late. Has he been running away again?' So perhaps they were.

'It's more serious than that,' Mariner said, in an attempt to prepare her. 'I'm afraid Eddie Barham is dead.'

Joyce just gaped at them. 'When? How?' she ventured when she finally found her voice.

'Late last night,' said Mariner.

'Oh my goodness, poor Eddie, poor Jamie. What on earth will happen to him? Where will he go?'

Taking her cue, Anna put out a hand. 'Hi, I'm Anna, Jamie's sister,' she said.

'Oh.' Joyce seemed startled. 'I had no idea . . .' That he had a sister? As the women shook hands, Mariner completed Joyce's statement in his head. A pattern was beginning to develop.

'I'm so sorry.' Joyce was flustered now. 'This is such a shock.' She turned to Mariner. 'You don't know—?'

'It's early days,' he said. 'But anything you can tell us might be helpful. For instance, when did you last see Eddie?'

41

'Well, as far as I remember, he came to collect Jamie from the centre on Friday afternoon as normal. Most of our clients travel on the centre transport, but for the last few weeks Eddie has been bringing Jamie in and fetching him himself.'

'Why was that?'

'I'm not really sure of the precise reason. I presumed that it fitted in more conveniently with Eddie's working pattern. If he wasn't home at the right time to receive Jamie—'

'But I thought Jamie was going to Moorcroft for the weekends to give Eddie some respite?' said Anna. 'That's where he should have been.'

Joyce looked embarrassed. 'Not any more. Eddie withdrew Jamie from the Moorcroft about two months ago.'

'Oh.' Anna reddened. So she really was that out of touch. 'Why?' she asked.

'It was the medication, I think.'

'Medication?'

'They wanted to put Jamie on something to help his sleeping, but Eddie wasn't keen. The next thing we knew, Jamie was back home at the weekends.'

'How did Eddie seem on Friday?' Mariner asked.

'Oh, I didn't speak to him myself. I only saw him briefly from a distance. You'd need to talk to Jamie's key worker, Francine, although I'm afraid she's tied up with supervising lunch at the moment. The last time I spoke to Eddie personally would have been a couple of weeks ago. We had been having some issues with Jamie's behaviour, so he came in to discuss them.'

'What sort of issues?' Anna asked, warily.

As they talked, people wandered past them in the corridor and realising they were being overheard, Joyce ushered them towards her office. 'It might be better to continue in here, where it's a bit more private,' she said. 'And if you can wait a moment, I'll just go and settle Jamie with his group.' She walked over to Jamie. 'Lunch, Jamie,' she said, gently touching his arm. And without a murmur, Jamie turned and followed her down the corridor. Mariner went with Anna into the cluttered office where Joyce returned to join them a few minutes later.

'You were going to tell us about Jamie's behaviour,' Anna prompted, before Mariner could say anything.

Joyce began cautiously. 'Well, in recent months, it's as if Jamie has suddenly developed some kind of sexual awareness,' she told them. 'Eddie had started having problems with Jamie exposing himself, masturbating publicly, that kind of thing. Only a week ago he walked up to a woman in the swimming baths and made a grab for her breasts. Eddie thought she was going to bring indecent assault charges.'

'It must have been worrying for Eddie,' said Mariner, seeing the alarm on Anna's face and wanting to steer the conversation back round to Eddie.

'It was,' Joyce said. 'We were all concerned. It's not an uncommon situation with the young adults we work with here, a child's mind inside an adult body and all that, but it doesn't make it any easier. To put it in simple terms: while it might be reasonable to ignore a three-year-old playing with his private parts in public, at twenty-nine it's a different matter entirely. It's vital for Jamie to learn about what is unacceptable social behaviour, so we discussed some strategies for managing it. Eddie took it very seriously. He even went as far as installing a video camera at home so that we could monitor progress.' The camera. That knocked Knox's theory on the head.

'Jamie's other obsessions were worsening too,' Joyce continued. 'For some time now he's had a fixation with mobile phones. He recognises all the brand names and for months he made Eddie drive past the same billboard on the way to the centre because it displayed an advert for Vodafone. When they changed the poster, Jamie got very distressed.'

'He was like that with pylons and radio transmission masts when he was little,' Anna remembered. 'Insisted on dad driving past them every time we went out. He could spot them from miles away.'

'Will Jamie be staying with you now?' Joyce asked.

Anna's eyes widened. 'I'm not sure. It's difficult,' she stalled. 'I feel as if I hardly know him.'

And after what we've just heard . . . thought Mariner.

'Oh, I'm sure it won't take long for you to get to know each other again,' Joyce was cheerfully encouraging. 'As I said, he likes to go swimming, and Eddie used to take him to McDonald's a lot. He loves his Big Macs.'

But this was evidently not what Anna wanted to hear. 'It's not really as simple as that,' she persisted. 'I have commitments. Do you know if there's anywhere that Jamie could stay, temporarily, while I get things sorted out?'

Joyce looked doubtful. 'Nowhere that could be accessed immediately. Residential places are like gold dust. There just aren't enough of them in the city. Other parents at our support group might be able to give you some ideas, though. You could try coming to their meeting on a Thursday evening. I know respite care is a regular discussion topic.'

'I'll think about that,' said Anna, though it didn't look to Mariner as if it would occupy her thoughts for long.

'One more thing,' he said. 'We tried to question Jamie about what happened last night, but we couldn't get much out of him.'

Joyce nodded knowingly. 'It would be difficult. Jamie has very little understanding of spoken language.'

'Is there anyone here who could talk to him? Try to find out if he does know anything?'

'Francine would be the best person, she knows him better than anyone. But to be honest, all you're likely to get is the odd word. It may not mean much.'

'Well, if she could give it a try and let me know the outcome.' Mariner gave Joyce his card. 'Someone Jamie did mention is Sally, or it could be Sally-Ann. Have you any idea who she might be? Eddie's girlfriend perhaps?'

Joyce looked blank. 'I wasn't aware that Eddie had a girlfriend. With Jamie to take care of, I'd be surprised if he had the time.'

Back at the car they roused Knox from a snooze.

'Where can we drop you?' Mariner asked.

Anna was decisive. 'Back at the office; life has to go on.'

In those five short words Mariner could hear the desperate desire for the world to revert back to what it had been before they'd come along and so shockingly disrupted it — a need to step out of this surreal sequence of events and return to normality. It was a common enough feeling for anyone following traumatic events, and one with which he was all too familiar.

CHAPTER 6

'Hungry, boss?' Knox asked hopefully. They were watching Anna Barham walk back into the Priory Management building, where a security guard let her in with a smile. Food wasn't at that moment featuring anywhere in Mariner's thoughts but now that Knox raised the subject, he realised it was the middle of the afternoon and he'd eaten nothing all day. No wonder he felt light headed. Knox could be forgiven for feeling the same.

'So what's it to be?' Knox put the car into gear. 'Drive thru McDonald's?'

But Mariner shook his head. 'Something infinitely better.' He directed Knox back into the city centre, casting his eyes about as he had been all morning in the vain hope that a statuesque girl with long chestnut hair might suddenly emerge from around a street corner.

On the Ladypool Road, Knox waited in the car while Mariner went into Nazeem's and picked up six assorted samosas and a couple of bottles of Evian. They parked up in a side street of Edwardian villas to eat.

Knox peered suspiciously into the brown paper bag. 'This isn't food,' he grumbled.

'Get it down you. It's good stuff,' said Mariner.

'So what do you think?' Knox asked, through a mouthful of spicy vegetables, but he wasn't talking about the samosa.

'I think we can't do much until we've had the post-mortem findings,' Mariner replied. 'Best case scenario is that they'll prove conclusively that Eddie Barham killed himself by injecting an obscene amount of heroin. He was under stress so he took the easy way out. Case closed.'

'It'll take more than a coroner's verdict to convince Anna Barham.'

Knox was right. From where they sat, the reason for Eddie Barham's death looked obvious, so how was it that Anna Barham was still so convinced that her brother, from whom she was effectively estranged, hadn't taken his own life?

'The one person who should be able to clear this up is the brunette,' said Mariner, in between swigs of water. 'Who might, or might not, be called Sally-Ann.'

'If we can find her,' said Knox. 'She's hardly likely to just walk up and present herself, is she?'

'Well, Eddie had been trawling the small ads so maybe that's where we'll find her too. We can start by going through his phone records, too,' he said. 'See if any of the numbers match up.'

'And I could try ringing round the agencies themselves,' Knox added. 'We've got a description and a name, so with any luck the two belong to the same person. Somebody must know her.'

'And I want to talk to Eddie's workmates.' said Mariner. 'Even if they can't help identify the woman, it'll help to know what Eddie's been up to during the last few weeks. See if there's anything else that might have pushed him over the edge.' Although he was beginning to think that they already had all the motive they needed. Jamie Barham alone was probably more than enough. Not having siblings himself, Mariner found it impossible to

47

imagine a situation in which he could be wholly responsible for another adult, let alone one who had apparently turned into an obsessive willy-waver. Eddie Barham was sounding like a saint. But even saints had their limits.

'Sounds all right to me,' Knox agreed.

As a straightforward suicide, since he'd made his statement about the discovery, Mariner should really have handed Eddie Barham over to uniform, in this instance Knox, to complete the formalities. But in the early hours of this morning they had agreed between them that having been at the scene, Mariner would be present to break the bad news to Anna Barham. Now he could reasonably bow out and leave the rest to the junior officer. Mariner though, for reasons that he couldn't quite pinpoint, wasn't ready to let go yet and Knox was apparently happy to keep him involved. 'Aren't we always being told what good practice it is for CID and uniform to work in collaboration?' he said now, with more than a hint of cynicism.

'Absolutely,' said Mariner.

'But that's the last time you get the dinner,' said Knox, screwing the empty brown paper bag into a ball in disgust. 'That tasted like shite.'

* * *

Boasting the biggest circulation in the West Midlands, the *Birmingham Echo* was the *Birmingham Post*'s tarty younger sister, a tabloid that thrived on melodrama, running regular banner headlines and editorials decrying the police, amid dramatically soaring crime statistics — statistics that were always, naturally, isolated from context and hugely exaggerated. But sensation sells, and had earned the *Echo* an impressive-looking imitation of New York's cone-topped Chrysler Building, deep in the heart of Birmingham's business quarter. This was the district that tried hard to ape its more sophisticated European equivalents and had, to a limited degree, succeeded. One of its triumphs was the complete lack of parking space, so it was fortunate for Mariner that today he had a chauffeur to take him there. 'See you back at the ranch, boss,' said Knox as he dropped him off.

Inside a vast open-plan atrium, Mariner flashed his ID at one of a whole bank of receptionists who hardly gave it a glance. One day he'd stick a picture of Mickey Mouse over his photograph and see if that provoked any kind of reaction. 'I'd like to talk to Ken Moloney,' he said. Thanks to the extensive blood clots that had taken up residence in his nasal passages, Mariner made it sound like 'baloney,' which, by pure coincidence, also summed up his opinion of the newspaper.

Mariner was directed to a glass-sided lift, which would transport him up to the eighteenth floor, a ride that afforded him a panoramic view over Birmingham's sprawling urban skyline and gave him a sudden yearning for the more poetic craggy towers of the Rhinogs in North Wales. For most of the time, Mariner was a man at ease with the city, along with all its noise, dirt and blissful anonymity. But now and again he felt the need to get away. He had some leave due. Maybe when this was cleared up he'd take a few days in Snowdonia.

Alerted to Mariner's arrival, editor-in-chief Ken Moloney greeted him at the door to his office, which, unlike the rest of the building, Mariner noted, was not a smoke-free zone. Moloney stood swathed in a bluish haze like a science fiction time lord, if at close range a pretty raddled one, a half-smoked Marlboro clamped between his knuckles. The effects of this forty-a-day habit, along with a lifetime of burning the midnight oil to meet spiralling deadlines, were imprinted in Moloney's coarse complexion. Add to that the folds of several chins and lank, thinning hair, and Moloney hardly presented an attractive role model for his profession.

Mariner declined offers of tea, coffee or mineral water. Some kind of breathing apparatus would have been of benefit given his constricted airways, but that wasn't, it seemed, an option.

'What can I do you for?' Moloney asked drolly, when they had settled either side of an enormous mahogany desk that was as battered and scarred as Moloney himself, much of its surface covered with paper.

'I'd like to talk to you about Eddie Barham.' Mariner said.

Sizing up Mariner's damaged nose, Moloney broke into a broad nicotine-stained grin. 'Oh yes. What's he done now?'

'He was found dead at his home last night,' said Mariner. 'He appears to have committed suicide.'

That took the wind out of Moloney's sails. In fact, judging from the effect on his face, it had scuttled the whole boat. 'God Almighty,' he wheezed, taking a long drag on his cigarette. 'Are you sure?'

Mariner nodded. 'That's certainly how it looks.'

'God,' Moloney repeated. 'I knew things had taken a turn for Ed, but I didn't know it had got that bad.'

'You must have known him pretty well, then.'

'We weren't what you'd call bosom-buddies, but he'd been around the block a few times, you know? He must be, *have* been, one of our longest serving reporters. A lot of kids see us as just a stepping-stone to the nationals, but Eddie started as a cub years ago and stuck with us. Poor bastard.'

'What do you mean, "things had taken a turn?"' Mariner probed.

'A few years back, Eddie was right there at the top,' Moloney explained. 'You could send him anywhere, anytime and you'd be sure to get cracking copy from him. His talent was for the slow-burn investigative stuff. You could always rely on something good from him.'

'Always?'

'Eddie had a strong sense of social justice. Once he got hold of something he wouldn't let it go. He could be very persuasive and was very good at getting people to talk to him. People seemed to trust him, you know? And he was patient. He'd just bide his time and eventually get out of them what he wanted.'

Praise indeed, and no doubt justifiable. Mariner thought back to the scene in the Chamberlain Hotel, when the brunette had capitulated. 'So if he was so good at his job, what went wrong? Drugs?' he hazarded.

But Moloney seemed genuinely appalled at the suggestion. 'No. Eddie wouldn't be the sort to do drugs. He was a very down-to-earth guy,' he sounded absolutely certain. 'Nothing went wrong as such. He just chose to take a step down. He took a demotion, a couple of years ago, back onto the local desk, writing fillers for the main pages.'

'Things were getting too much for him?'

'In a way, but not at work. He had a forced change of circumstances. He lost both his parents very suddenly some time back, and there's this brother, he's mentally handicapped or something—'

Mariner touched his nose. 'Jamie. We've met.'

Moloney smirked. 'Gotcha. Yeah, well, he's been here once or twice. Bloody liability. Anyway, he needs a lot of looking after, someone there all the time. He goes to some day-care place and in the early days, Eddie had some arrangement with the neighbours, too, but suddenly all that changed. He struggled on for as long as he could, but eventually he asked for a move to nine till five. I tried to negotiate something, but whatever Eddie takes on he throws himself into, one hundred percent. It was like that with the boy. For the big stories, we need someone who can go where the action is any hour of the day or night, and Eddie said he wasn't prepared to do that anymore.'

'So it was his decision?'

'He knew the score.'

'And did he seem unhappy about it?'

51

'He was more philosophical. I think he felt that there wasn't a choice. There is a sister around somewhere, but there didn't seem to be any question that Eddie would take on the kid brother. Sure, he must have found the change frustrating, but he was never the sort of guy to whinge on about things. Ironically, although he was working regular hours then, we saw less and less of him. He did his job then went home. Either way, he still made his deadlines, so it didn't bother me. He never stopped being reliable. The original Steady Eddie.'

'And would you have known if things were getting too much for him?'

It took Moloney several seconds to meet Mariner's eye. 'The man was a pro. He wouldn't have found it acceptable to have his home life interfere with his work.'

Mariner let him off the hook. 'Who were Eddie's close friends?'

'I'm not sure that he had any what you'd call close friends. Eddie got along okay with most people, but he was a bit of a loner. Not much choice I suppose, given his domestic set-up.'

'Did he have a girlfriend?' Mariner asked.

Moloney shook his head. 'I never got the impression that there was anyone, but I suppose there could have been.'

'Do you know a girl called Sally, possibly Sally-Ann?'

'No, can't say I do.'

'When was the last time anyone here would have seen Eddie?' asked Mariner.

'Friday, he was in for work, as usual, as far as I know. He'd have been working with Darren Smith, one of our photographers. They'd got to be quite a team. They worked together on a regular basis.'

'I'll need to speak to Darren. And I'll want to look at Eddie's workspace and see what's on his computer.'

'Sure.'

The interview had run its course. 'Well, thanks for your time, Mr Moloney,' Mariner said.

'No problem. Anything we can do to help.'

Mariner stood up and even though it was only a few paces, Moloney walked him to the door. Something was still bothering him. 'We can run this as a story?' he asked at last. So that was it.

'It's news, isn't it?' said Mariner, drily.

'So what can we print?'

'Let's go for novelty. How about the facts?'

The sarcasm slid off him. 'Which are?'

'That Eddie Barham was discovered dead at his home late last night. Police are not currently looking for anyone else in connection with his death, but would like to speak to a woman who may have been at the scene, and who made the emergency call.'

Moloney nodded, sadly. 'Eddie was a good bloke,' he said. 'A lot of people round here will miss him. And I think we'll all feel bad that we didn't see this coming.'

He sounded entirely sincere. Who'd have thought? A journalist with a heart.

On the wall by the door to Moloney's office Mariner's attention was caught by one of several framed front pages: 'LOCAL HOMELESS CHARITY EXPOSED,' the byline was Edward Barham's. Mariner scanned the page. 'This was one of his.'

'Yeah. Caused quite a stir at the time. Eddie won a couple of awards for it, too. I think his only regret was that Frank Crosby didn't get put inside. Still, the publicity didn't do the bastard much good.'

Frank Crosby. Although Mariner had never personally had dealings with the man, Crosby's was a name you heard bandied around the station canteen with frightening regularity, in connection with just about any illegal activity. Drugs, gambling, prostitution — Crosby was up to his ears in it. That was an interesting link.

Darren, Eddie Barham's erstwhile co-worker, it transpired, had called in sick, so interviewing him would have to keep until another day. If indeed that proved to be necessary. For Mariner, a picture was emerging of a man under pressure, and he still hoped that the path report would remove any remaining traces of doubt.

CHAPTER 7

Returning to the office, Anna couldn't help but remark on the contrast with her entrance earlier this morning, when the world had been a different place and she'd been in command of her life. Now, in a matter of hours, she felt as though chaos theory was being tested out at her expense. She tried not to dwell on it. If she was going to keep on top of things, she needed to focus on her job again.

Becky came in, full of concern. 'It's true? Anna, I'm so sorry. Are you okay?'

Anna smiled bravely. 'I'm fine. It's a shock, of course, but we weren't exactly close.'

'Do you want us to re-schedule tonight?' Becky asked.

Anna didn't know what she was talking about. 'Tonight?'

'Robinson's at da Paglia,' Becky reminded her.

'Oh, shit.' With all that had happened, the dinner engagement had flown completely out of her mind.

'If you're not feeling up to it, I'm sure Jonathan will understand.'

Anna didn't share her friend's optimism. The meeting with Robinson's had been set up weeks ago and to cancel it now would be a PR disaster, both for Priory and for her personally. 'It's not that. Remember my younger brother, Jamie?'

'Yes, of course.'

'Well, with Eddie gone, I'm left with him.'

'Oh God. What will you do?'

'Try to find someone else to look after him, I suppose.' She'd have to. There was no alternative. Anna thought suddenly of Becky's partner. 'Mark's a GP. Would he know anyone who could help?'

'He might. I can ask him.'

'Tell him I'm desperate.'

'I'll see what I can do.'

Becky had been gone less than a minute when a second knock preceded Jonathan, as suave as ever in a navy blue Paul Smith suit, his well-chosen tie providing a tasteful splash of colour. He closed the door behind him. 'I heard the news, Anna. I'm so very sorry.' For a moment he looked as if he might hug her, but then, remembering that they were in full view of the outer office, he settled for taking Anna's hand in both of his. It was one of those few occasions when it wasn't enough. Anna wanted to sink into his arms and be held, close and tight. 'You'll need a few days off,' he said. 'Take as much time as you like.'

'No, it's okay, I'll be all right.'

Jonathan allowed a respectable pause. 'What about Robinson's, tonight?'

'It shouldn't be a problem,' Anna said, with far more conviction than she felt.

'Are you sure? I mean, obviously we can't call it off at this late stage, but if you don't feel up to it, I'm sure I could ask Melanie to stand in for you.'

'No. I'll be fine. Really.' The offer of Melanie as substitute had come a little too quickly for Anna's taste. Fine or not, she was damn sure she wasn't going to let that little cow muscle in on her deal. She was already beginning to play a more prominent role around here than Anna was happy with.

'Good,' Jonathan smiled. 'I told Gillian it would be a *very* late night.'

Anna liked the sound of that. Now it was imperative that she find somewhere for Jamie. Alone once more, she turned her attention to her in-tray, firing off rapid responses to memos and emails where she could, filing those that required more attention. After a whole morning out, there was a lot to catch up on if she was to be ready for Milan by next weekend. So much so, that when Becky put her head around the door to say she was going, Anna didn't notice how empty the outer office had become. The phone rang and kept ringing, and glancing up irritably from her PC monitor, Anna suddenly realised it was dusk and everyone else had gone.

She picked up the handset. 'Hello?'

'Hi, this is Francine,' said a cheerful voice.

'Francine?' Anna didn't know a Francine.

'I'm Jamie's key worker at the centre,' the voice explained. 'I was wondering when you were coming to collect him. All the other clients have gone home—'

Jamie! Shit! 'I'll be there as soon as I can,' she said, already on her feet and stuffing papers into her briefcase.

When she got to the centre it was practically deserted, apart from the omnipresent cleaning staff. Jamie sat alone in the foyer, head bent, gently rocking.

'Hi, Jamie.'

He didn't even look up. He wasn't punishing her for being late. He just wasn't interested.

A young dark-skinned woman emerged from the office. 'Hi, I'm Francine, you must be Anna?'

'Yes. Look, I'm really sorry, I completely lost track of the time.'

'That's okay,' Francine smiled generously. 'I had some paperwork to do and Jamie didn't seem to mind.' She hesitated. 'I'm so sorry about Eddie. I couldn't believe it when Joyce told us. It must be hard for you.'

'It's bad timing,' Anna agreed. She still had this evening's little problem to solve. Taking advantage of Francine's sympathetic smile, Anna tried a long shot. 'Actually, all this couldn't have come at a worse time for me. Do you know if there's anywhere that would be able to just look after Jamie for tonight?' But predictably, Francine didn't.

* * *

In the early evening gloom, Tom Mariner sat at his desk in a similarly deserted office. His nose throbbed painfully despite assurances that it wasn't broken, and every time he exhaled, he emitted a low whistling sound. A bag of frozen peas sent up by some joker in the canteen was generating a slow-spreading puddle on one corner of the desk, like the dull ache that was inching its way around his skull. He'd been through the files of a number of local known prostitutes over and over now, hoping he'd missed her the last time and willing those brown eyes to gaze out at him. Once, he even thought he saw her, but he was kidding himself. Either she was new or she was careful, or she wasn't what he thought.

Knox had finished for the night, stating his intentions to go and try to and patch things up with 'the wife,' but sounding more as if he was trying to convince himself than anything. Mariner's plans for this evening, which had at one time included the digitally restored version of Hitchcock's *Rear Window* playing at the MAC, had been comprehensively sabotaged: he was loath to squander the cinematographer's talents on his intermittently blurring vision. The rain that had in the last hour begun beating relentlessly on the windows precluded a walk, even for him. So, other options closed, courtesy of Jamie Barham, Mariner was left flicking through the information gathered by the canvass of Eddie Barham's neighbours.

Apart from what he'd already learned from Moira Warren, it didn't amount to a fat lot, even though Eddie Barham had lived in Clarendon Avenue all his life. Neighbours hardly seemed to know him and certainly nobody had heard or seen anything the previous night or, at any rate, was admitting to it. Glimpses of Eddie or Jamie over the whole weekend were sparse. No one seemed prepared to get involved. The John Donne line kept coming back to him. 'No man is an island, entire of itself.' Maybe not in the seventeenth century, when Donne had first made the observation, but these days, despite mobile phones and email, not to mention social media, the gulfs between people seemed to be widening all the time. More people than ever were choosing to live alone, and cars, personal computers and home entertainment systems all made it increasingly possible to exist without the need for social interaction of any kind. And there, at the extreme end of the scale was Jamie Barham, for whom even the simplest human exchange was meaningless. Even Mariner had read about the growing so-called autism epidemic: evolution's ironic kick in the teeth for the golden age of communication.

But perhaps in the end, the lack of background intel wouldn't matter. Reviewing what had been gathered so far, Mariner was already getting a sense of a man potentially near enough to the edge to take his own life. In practical terms, Eddie Barham couldn't have had an easy time of it. Living with Jamie must have been a challenge, to put it mildly. Add to that the stifling of any career ambitions Eddie might have had, and an explosive cocktail was beginning to develop. But was it enough to make him throw in the towel without even going to their sister for help?

Eddie's computers had been brought in to the IT department to see what could be salvaged, but the lads in that section were stretched and Mariner had been warned that it would be a couple of days, at least, before they could come up with any kind of result. The only other items to plough through were contained in the pile of zip-lock wallets of paperwork harvested from Eddie Barham's house. Mariner began with the least interesting first: the bank statements. There was a year's worth folded into each other. Spreading them out over his desk he started with the oldest, scanning the columns of figures in search of any anomalies. No competition for Grace Kelly, but they did turn out to be more interesting than expected.

The first obvious fact was that from last summer, Eddie Barham had been sailing close to the wind with his finances to the extent that, over time, significant debts were beginning to accumulate. By the end of every month Eddie was in the red, with a growing overdraft. A closer look at his expenditure revealed that a large portion of his monthly salary was paid out to an organisation called 'Bright Care.'

Mariner had seen that name before and, hunting through the other wallets, he found that the amounts corresponded with invoices issued from 'Moorcroft,' the respite care home that Joyce Clarke had mentioned. The puzzle was that those payments only began to appear on the current account statements back in June, while Mariner was under the impression that Jamie had been attending Moorcroft for some years.

The answer to that query lay deeper in the wallet, where Mariner came across a now-redundant building society account book. The account dated back going on for twenty years, when it had been opened with a substantial sum and some irregular deposits. From ten years ago, there were monthly standing orders to 'Bright Care' along with the occasional additional payment. But though these outgoings were regular, from what Mariner could see there had been no cash paid into the account during this time, and by June of last year the account had dwindled to nothing. CLOSED was stamped in forbidding letters over the remaining empty pages.

The timing of that closure corresponded with the sudden appearance of the debits to 'Bright Care' on Eddie's current account statements, which solved one mystery — payment switched to another account. The debits were then recorded until, in line with what Joyce had told them, suddenly ceasing two months previously, when Jamie must have left Moorcroft. The absence of payments in January and February alone left Eddie's bank account looking healthier. Mariner couldn't help wondering to what extent these numbers had given impetus to Eddie Barham's death. Medication may have been one of the reasons Jamie left the respite provision as Joyce Clarke had told them, but it looked to Mariner as if the monetary constraints were greater. Like any other human, Eddie would have needed some relief from the demands of caring for Jamie, but he simply couldn't afford it. Nor could he put in the overtime to make more cash because there was no one to look after Jamie. Catch twenty-two. This was building up to look like a solid case, and Anna Barham's doubts about suicide receded a step further.

After a while, the figures on the paper began to jump around before Mariner's eyes and his throbbing head felt ready to burst. Aside from the injury, he'd also barely slept in forty-eight hours. It was time to go. But as he started to gather up the statements, something else sprang out at him. At the end of December, Eddie's bank account had taken a sudden, unprecedented upward turn, thanks to a single deposit made by standing order from another unknown account. When Mariner checked, the same sum appeared again on the same day in January. On the day of his death, on Sunday, Eddie Barham had been a comparatively wealthy man as each of those payments was for five thousand pounds. Suddenly it turned everything he'd been thinking on its head, but right now Mariner hadn't the stamina or the inclination to figure out the full implications. The crux of it all would be the post-mortem report, which Mariner felt confident would be categorical enough to allow them to tie this thing up and move on, but so far this evening the telephone had remained mute.

Leaving a note instructing Knox to follow up the source accounts for those standing order deposits, which Mariner felt sure would turn out to be cosmetic, he retrieved his jacket from the hook on the back of the door, and switched off the lights as he left.

CHAPTER 8

There was one more job to do before he went home. The bar of the Chamberlain was quieter than it had been on Sunday night, so she would have stood out as much as he did, drawing half-concealed stares from around the room. But one look around told Mariner that the brunette wasn't working here tonight, unless she'd been in earlier and he'd missed her. The same barman was restocking the bottles of garish alcopops. In the absence of a photofit Mariner gave him as close a verbal description as he could muster, but it was to no avail. If the girl was regular here she'd struck a deal with the barman to keep *shtum*.

Eschewing the inflated prices of the Chamberlain, Mariner deferred having a drink himself until he was closer to home, and even then he wasn't sure. Being the centre of attention was becoming wearisome. But some ten minutes later he pulled into the car park of the Boatman. His vehicle brought the total number to five, mainly because most of the Boatman's regulars were beyond the age when it was safe for them to drive. Lacking the dubious attractions of piped disco music, fruit machines or wide-screen satellite TV, the pub was on borrowed time, ripe to be snapped up by one of the larger brewery chains and turned into one of the 'fun pubs' that in Mariner's experience, were too much of an assault on the senses to be anything like fun. An old man's pub Greta had dubbed it, and not as a compliment.

Locking his car, Mariner decided to risk a pint, in the hope that the few customers knew him well enough by now to leave him alone. He'd be the first to admit that he wasn't an attractive sight, but if anyone else asked where he'd been 'sticking that,' he didn't quite trust himself not to give them one to match.

The only sounds to greet his ears in the Boatman were comforting, including the clatter of dominoes that underpinned the gentle banter from four elderly gents playing fives-and-threes up one end of the lounge bar. This was occasionally bolstered by the ebb and flow of the murmured conversation of a younger couple on one of the side benches. Irish landlady Beryl was on her own, gliding gracefully under the weight of her extravagantly bouffant hair, which, like the pub, belonged in a different era. Seeing Mariner and without prompting, she slid a straight pint glass under the Marston's Pedigree tap. 'You've been in the wars then,' she commented blandly, as Mariner approached the bar, her gaze lingering just a little too long.

'Walked into a door,' said Mariner, stealing the line he'd been given in countless domestics over the years. He wasn't sure whether Beryl caught the irony, but she certainly took the hint, allowing Mariner to retreat to a corner table to enjoy his beer without further interrogation.

'I'll leave the car,' he told Beryl, twenty minutes later, replacing his second empty glass on the bar.

'Right you are, darlin'.'

It was something Mariner did regularly, making the hundred or so yards back to his house on foot. The pub car park was as secure as anywhere, overlooked as it was by the small, local Kings Mead police station. The rain had stopped and though it was mild for February, a fresh breeze blew as Mariner wound his way along the sixties-built cul-de-sac that was to the one side of the pub, and into the small service road that few people even knew existed. Ominously, a silver Ford Focus was parked just down from his house, and walking up the path of the narrow, three-storey, Victorian red-brick cottage, Mariner noticed the blue-tinged flickering of a TV in the darkened window of his living room. He opened the front door and flicked on the light.

'Fancy a spring roll, boss?' asked Knox, brightly. He'd made himself at home, slouching on the sofa with his feet up on the coffee table amid a litter of greasy takeaway cartons, from which emanated the pervasive smell of egg fried rice. On screen, the subjects in a reality TV show were arguing loudly.

Mariner felt his anxiety level crank up a notch. 'I take it the peace negotiations didn't go as planned,' he said, closing the door.

Knox killed the sound on the TV. 'Not exactly, although she did chuck me down some clothes, so at least I'll be clean. All right if I kip here tonight, sir.' Mariner couldn't work out if it was a question or a statement.

'I suppose so,' he said, doubting the decision already, though at least there was a room ready and waiting — the one on the second floor that he'd advertised for rent. 'As long as you remember that we're off-duty,' Mariner reminded him. 'You don't have to call me sir here.' Interestingly Knox had never bothered with the formality at the station, so it was puzzling that he should start now.

'Right.' Knox held up a glass of brown liquid. 'And I helped myself. I hope you don't mind.'

'No,' Mariner said, dubiously. 'What do you think?'

'It's all right,' Knox was unenthusiastic. 'Though I'm more of a lager man myself.'

Mariner was disappointed. He'd thought it was a good brew. To check it out for himself, he went and fetched a bottle.

'You've got a nice place here,' said Knox, when Mariner returned, 'very neat and cosy.'

'Yes, well, I have my last girlfriend to thank for that,' said Mariner. 'She took an immediate dislike to the place and refused to set foot in it until it was what she called "liveable."' Mariner could still remember the buzz he'd got from seeing the For Sale sign on the property, the day he'd come across it. Right from when they'd first met, Greta had been nagging him to make the move from renting to owning a house that they could share, but unfortunately this wasn't the sort of place she had in mind. Her dream was of a brand-new build on a regimented estate of clones, not an ancient, run-down cottage in the middle of no man's land. The writing was on the wall even then.

Having been owned for years by an elderly bachelor (Mariner liked the symmetry there), the property had been virtually derelict, something Greta seemed to interpret as a deliberately constructed obstacle to their cohabitation. Nevertheless, under her close scrutiny, Mariner had, in the space of a few short months, sanded the wooden floors, slapped a coat of emulsion on the walls and had central heating connected to the wood-burning stove. Despite her initial reservations, Greta had helped out with the furnishings. Not that there was much for her to do. The original builder, clearly unfamiliar with the advantages of a spirit level, had compensated by covering every irregular nook and cranny with doors. The result was hoarders' heaven, the small, compact rooms resembling the cabins of a boat. Every square inch of space was utilised, with numerous tiny cupboards and hideaways, many ornately inlaid with varnished walnut and oak.

'It looks liveable to me,' said Knox. 'So where is she?'

'It didn't work out,' said Mariner, making the understatement of the century.

Displaying unprecedented tact, Knox didn't pursue it.

'So if she didn't even like the place, what was the big attraction?'

'I'll show you.' Mariner got up and walked out of the snug living room and into the galley-like kitchen. Opening the kitchen door, a dank smell greeted their nostrils and as their eyes adjusted to the darkness, it was just possible to make out the oily black ribbon of the Worcester canal, the trees on the opposite bank a wall of spiky silhouettes against the indigo sky.

'I wanted to be by the water,' said Mariner. 'That was the attraction.'

'Must be something to do with being a mariner,' said Knox. 'It's the nearest you'll get to the sea around here.'

Mariner chuckled. 'Do you know, I'd never even thought of it like that.'

Just outside the door, under the kitchen window, in the small garden that separated the cottage from the canal's towpath, was a stone bench, sheltered by the overhanging eave. Mariner sat down on it and Knox joined him.

'There's canals everywhere round here,' said Knox. 'I've noticed that. But I didn't know about this one.'

'It's part of the Worcester and Birmingham,' said Mariner. 'What with the Birmingham-Fazeley and the Grand Union, we've got over a hundred miles of man-made waterways in and around the city,' Mariner said. 'More canals than Venice, so they say, though hardly with the same romantic appeal. Not easy to picture a gondolier punting his way down past the Tyseley incinerator waxing lyrical about love and romance. It's getting better though.' In recent years Mariner had walked for miles along the towpaths, watching whole sections transformed from decaying industrial wastelands to gleaming fashionable walkways with shops and restaurants to accommodate the growing tourist industry. Here though was far enough out of the city to have escaped the cycle of urban renewal, and

Mariner liked his shabby, unpretentious section of the waterway.

'Not so much traffic here as in Venice either,' surmised Knox.

'There would have been once,' Mariner said. 'A hundred years ago, even at this time of night, this stretch would have been as busy as the M42,' he said. 'Constant flow of barges. Sometimes you can almost hear the boatmen shouting at each other—' He broke off. Knox would think he was suffering from concussion.

But the constable was just soaking it all in, and hardly seemed to notice. 'I like it,' was his final verdict. 'It's got style.'

'Well, that's not what Greta thought. She spent most of her time complaining about the damp and the huge spiders. I didn't dare tell her about the rat.'

'You're a lucky bastard,' Knox said, after some consideration. 'You've got it made; good job, a great house and you're still single. Birds must be throwing themselves at you.'

Mariner had a sudden mental image of sparrows and pigeons hurling themselves at his windows. 'Oh, all the time,' he said. But his sarcasm drifted off into the darkness.

'To the single life,' said Knox, raising his glass.

His heart not really in it, Mariner joined in the toast. 'So, are you going to tell me why your missus threw you out?'

'It's complicated,' said Knox, vaguely, which Mariner decoded into 'mind your own business.' He let it go.

Instead, it made sense to bring Knox up to date with what he'd learned at the *Birmingham Echo*, and the payments he'd found on Eddie Barham's bank statements.

'What do you think they're for?' Knox asked.

'I don't know. They could be anything: fees for a story—'

'Or his sister could have been subbing him.'

'Hm, I'm not sure that's very likely. But whatever it is, we're going to have to ask a few more questions. And check out more paperwork.'

'I can't wait.' Swallowing the dregs of his beer, Knox got to his feet. 'But first I've got some kip to catch up on,' he held up the empty glass. 'And this stuff may not taste much, but it's knocked me out.'

'Mission accomplished,' said Mariner.

After Knox had gone Mariner sat on his own a while longer, breathing in the cool air as best he could through his blocked nose, and listening to the low, distant rumble of the city, punctuated incongruously by the occasional croon of nocturnal wood pigeons. His phone ringing jolted him back to the here and now, and he scrambled inside to get it. Knox had disappeared upstairs, but, Mariner noticed with some appreciation, had cleared up the debris from the living room before he went. Maybe this arrangement wouldn't be so bad. He picked up the phone.

'Tom? It's Stuart Croghan.' He was working late. It was nearly eleven. 'I've just finished writing up the case notes on Edward Barham,' he said. 'I thought you might like a preview of the main findings.'

'Technically it's PC Knox's case,' Mariner reminded him, without real conviction, thinking at the same time that Knox was only a few metres away. 'You should talk to him first.'

'Like I said,' Croghan repeated cheerfully. 'I thought you might like the main findings on Edward Barham. We've turned up some interesting stuff.'

Upstairs, everything had gone quiet and Mariner caved in immediately, feeling only slightly guilty about his failure to summon Knox to the phone. 'Let's have it then,' he said, grabbing the nearest piece of paper, which happened to be a grease-stained napkin from the Rising Sun takeaway.

CHAPTER 9

Taking Jamie into her flat for the first time was like guiding a blind man. Anna could sense his fear, but at least he wasn't actively resisting. Switching on all the lights, she hung back to allow Jamie to set his own tempo. Gradually, reassured that it was safe, he began to pace, touching the walls and surfaces, checking them over. A Jo Malone candleholder smashed loudly to the ground, but Jamie ignored it. Anna followed him at a distance, when he moved a photograph she moved it back again. Jamie slapped his hand to his mouth and bit down hard, Anna returned the photograph to where he had placed it.

Eventually, having completed his tactile exploration of the room Jamie gravitated to the TV, which he switched on without hesitation and using the unfamiliar remote control almost instinctively, channel-hopped until he found something he liked, loud and brash with canned laughter. Then choosing a corner of the room he lay down on his back on the polished wood floor, his knees raised and both hands in front of his face, peering through his fingers at the light cast on the ceiling by the standard lamp.

Anna stood watching for a moment, waiting for him to get up again but he didn't. She suddenly recalled his favourite 'spot' at home behind the sofa, where the sun shone in through the window to highlight the top of the radiator in a series of lines and curves that had kept him transfixed for hours on end. Right now Anna couldn't see what had attracted him to this particular place in her flat but in time she might. Meanwhile Jamie seemed contented enough and she had things to do. In less than an hour she had to be at da Paglia, looking her most alluring. And before she could even think about that, she had to enlist some help.

Despite Joyce's well-intentioned encouragement, Anna had already made up her mind that her priority was to find residential accommodation for Jamie as soon as possible, preferably tonight. She was not about to be sucked into playing a more active role in his life than she needed to. It wasn't as if it would make the slightest difference to Jamie anyway, as long as he had his Hula Hoops and a TV he'd be happy enough.

Picking up the phone, she tried the number for Moorcroft without giving her name, but it was as Joyce had predicted, they were full. A swift search online turned up the next number she needed, and after being re-routed three times by recorded messages, she was finally greeted by a human voice. 'Hello, is that the Social Services department? I'm looking for somewhere for my brother to stay. He's autistic.'

But several minutes of questioning established that the voice at the other end was unable to assist. Unless Anna was homeless herself it was assumed that she would be responsible for Jamie. She was not considered to be an emergency. Long-term they may be able to help her to find residential care, and could even furnish her with a list of establishments that was only slightly out of date, but could offer nothing at seven fifteen on a Monday evening: 'so sorry.'

That was a blow. Time for 'Auntie Anna,' the one-time babysitting queen, to call in a few favours. But Nigel and Sue were going out themselves tonight, to the gym Nigel cheerfully told her, having recently taken on this *wonderful* new au pair.

'Have a great time,' Anna said, distractedly, her mind already exploring the next possibility. She had obliged her old school pal Kate on odd occasions, well once at least, and an exhausting experience it had been taking care of the two little dears. Now would be a good time for Kate to reciprocate. Her kids must be old enough to look after themselves by now.

Anna punched in the numbers. 'Hello, Kate? It's Anna. I'm fine, how are you? Look, I need a favour. My younger brother is staying with me at the moment but I've got a really important business dinner tonight. Is there any chance you could sit for me?'

Kate was clearly confused by the request, having forgotten about Jamie.

'He's twenty-nine,' Anna reminded her. 'But he's—' But by now Kate's memory was restored and in the same instant she also suddenly remembered a prior, but unspecified, engagement that she couldn't possibly rearrange. Anna brought the conversation to a polite close between gritted teeth and tried Becky's number.

'I'm sorry,' declared the irritatingly cheery automated message reply. 'There is no one here to take your call . . .' Anna slammed down the phone in frustration. She searched through her address book. She flicked through it again. One last hope. She pushed buttons and thankfully a real voice answered.

'Hello? Auntie Helen, it's Anna, your goddaughter.' Auntie Helen sounded surprised to hear from Anna. 'Yes, I know, it's been a while,' Anna conceded, but ignoring the pangs of guilt, she came straight to the point. 'Actually, Auntie, I'm in a bit of a fix and wondered if you could help. I need someone to take care of Jamie for me—'

It was to no avail. Learning that Auntie Helen had only left hospital the previous day following an angina attack made Anna feel worse than ever. 'Oh, I'm sorry to hear that,' she said. 'No, of course not. Never mind. You just concentrate on getting yourself well again. I'll be in touch soon. Bye.' She hung up. 'Shit.'

And now it was twenty to eight. If she was to stand any chance of getting to the restaurant on time she needed to get ready right away. By five past eight she had showered and dressed in a smart two-piece; not too casual, not too formal. She'd also reached a decision, and walked purposefully into the lounge where Jamie sat in a corner of the room flicking through an Ikea catalogue he'd found. In an hour he'd hardly moved.

'Right, Jamie,' Anna announced to no one, in an attempt to strengthen her own resolve. 'You're going to have to stay here on your own.'

Before leaving, Anna made a quick tour of the flat, unplugging any unnecessary appliances to minimise the risk of fire or electrocution. In the kitchen she stowed away the food processor and removing all the sharp implements from the drawer, tucked them into a high cupboard out of sight. Throughout, Jamie stayed where he was, on the same spot on the floor. It would be fine.

Anna walked down the hall. 'See you later, Jamie. Be good.' And she closed the front door on him, listening for the Yale to click. On her way out she would just alert Ted, the doorman, to the fact that Jamie was in her flat, then if there was a fire . . . a fire. Her train of thought suddenly began moving along an unwelcome track. What would happen if there really was a fire? Ted wouldn't go up three flights to get Jamie out. And if the fire started on her floor . . . ? *Don't be ridiculous*, she told herself. There had never been a fire. Why should there be one tonight of all nights?

Then, as she was getting into her car Anna remembered her bedroom window, the one with a broken lock that she'd yet to report. Had she closed it? She couldn't remember. Straining her eyes in the darkness, she turned and looked up at the building, searching for her own flat and at the same time thinking about Jamie's penchant for climbing. Then she saw it. Open. Abandoning her car, Anna ran back into the building and up the stairs. She fumbled at the lock to her front door. 'Jamie!' she yelled, bursting back into the flat. Jamie looked up disinterestedly from where he lay on his stomach, turning the pages of this week's *Grazia* magazine, in exactly the same spot as she'd left him. Anna's heart pounded and her knees went weak. She felt faint. Oh God, she couldn't do this. How could she possibly concentrate on a business meeting, knowing that Jamie was here alone? It wasn't even as if she could phone to check up on him. But she had to get to that meeting.

'If you can't stay here, Jamie,' she said out loud. 'You'll have to come with me.'

But time was running out. Jonathan would be at the restaurant now, the Robinson's reps due to arrive at any minute. Taking Jamie's arm Anna encouraged him to his feet. 'Oh God, look at you.' The ill-fitting police-issue clothes smelled of the day centre and he badly needed a shave. On the plus side, designer stubble was practically a requirement where they were going. But the clothes . . . then Anna remembered Jonathan's emergency overnight bag. Not much in it, but there were the basics: a Ralph Lauren shirt and dark chinos.

Still clinging to the magazine, Jamie stood impassively and allowed Anna to dress him. Jonathan was bigger than him though and the clothes swamped him, the main problem being the trousers, which were several inches too big in the waist. From Anna's own wardrobe she unearthed a broad, black leather belt to tighten them up but the length left them baggy at the ankles, Charlie Chaplin style. He didn't look great, but it would have to do. Then she washed Jamie's face and combed his hair, before foolishly attempting to relieve him of the catalogue.

Jamie held on tight. Anna tried again, eliciting a sustained moaning until finally, she wrested the catalogue from him with a jolt, leaving him jumping on the spot, flapping his hands and wailing loudly.

That was when Anna reached the crushing realisation that whatever Jamie might be wearing, she was never going to be able to pass him off as a fellow executive. She'd been mad to think that she could do it. Practically throwing the catalogue back at him, she sank down onto the sofa, raking her hands through her hair in frustration. Finally she made herself pick up the phone. Luckily, Jonathan had his mobile switched on.

'It's me,' Anna said, in a small voice.

'Hold on.' There was a pause and some scuffling, during which Anna heard Jonathan making excuses before moving to somewhere more private. 'Where are you?' he said at last. 'What's happened?'

'Nothing — at least, nothing more. I couldn't get anyone to have Jamie.'

Another pause while Jonathan took this in. 'Well, can't you just leave him in your flat? He's a grown-up, isn't he?'

Immediately Anna could hear the contest between lover and manager playing itself out. 'In years, I know, but . . .' She looked over at Jamie who was already tugging at his trousers, fidgeting with the unfamiliar belt. 'It's complicated.'

'Jesus, Anna. What am I supposed to say to our guests? They're here. We're waiting to order.'

'You'll just have to tell them I've been taken ill or something.'

'Leaving me to do all the work. Thanks. I really wish you'd thought of this earlier.' Short contest, settled already, and suddenly Anna felt angry. Whatever happened to sympathy?

'Well, I didn't know it was going to be such a problem, did I?' she snapped. 'Where do you think I'd rather be? Do you think I planned for my brother to kill himself?' That last was a cheap shot, but it had the desired effect.

Jonathan was grudgingly contrite. 'Okay. I'm sorry. Look I'd better get back.'

'Good luck.'

'Thanks.'

'You'll be—' But he'd cut her off.

By now, Jamie had discovered a programme he liked on the TV, and Anna had little choice but to sit miserably beside him in her Karen Millen suit and ridiculous strappy sandals, drinking her way through a bottle of red wine. She had a sudden horrible premonition that this was what her future life would be like, and she'd be consigned forever to drinking cheap wine and watching sickeningly smug TV presenters striving to turn Mr or Mrs Boring from East Sussex into millionaires. It had been a long day and she was almost asleep when, much later, the phone rang.

'Hi.' It was Jonathan. Anna looked at her watch. It was ten thirty.

'Why are you calling?' she slurred, unsteadily. There was a din in the background. He was driving.

'Mrs Robinson needed her beauty sleep,' said Jonathan. 'And boy, does she need her beauty sleep.'

'It's over?'

'It's over, and it was bloody hard work, but I think they're hooked.'

'That's great. Well done you,' said Anna, trying to muster some enthusiasm.

'So, what I thought was, I'm just around the corner, I could come and celebrate my triumph with you. I can be with you in less than five minutes.'

A mild pain was beginning to throb just behind Anna's eyes and she thought longingly of her comfortable bed and the prospect of a long, deep sleep. 'It's a nice idea, Jon, but actually I'm whacked.'

'Oh come on, Anna. I'm sure you can find some energy from somewhere.' His voice went low and sexy. 'I'm practically bursting out of my boxers here.'

Anna looked across at Jamie, still wide eyed and engrossed in a TV show. 'I'm sorry, Jonathan, I can't. I'm not on my own, remember?'

A sigh. 'Does that matter?' Her lack of response was his answer. 'I see.' His plans thwarted, Jonathan's voice hardened. 'Look, you're due some holiday, Anna. Why don't you take a few days off? Get things sorted out?' It was more of an instruction than a suggestion.

'But Milan's coming up,' Anna reminded him. 'There's preparation I need to do.'

'Well, it's not essential that *you* go, is it?'

'What's that supposed to mean?'

Jonathan relented a little. 'Look, see how things go over the next couple of days, eh? I'll give you a call.' With that he broke the connection, and in that same instant Anna felt her flimsy bond with the outside world being severed, too.

Using one of Jonathan's emergency toothbrushes, she helped Jamie to clean his teeth before settling him down in her guest room. 'Good night, Jamie.' Turning off the light, she went through to her own room, but climbing into bed saw that Jamie had followed her back and was hovering in the doorway.

'No, Jamie,' she said. 'Not in here.' She took him back to his room. 'This is your room. Jamie sleeps here.' They repeated the same routine four more times before Anna had to give up and sit on Jamie's bed beside him until, at twenty-nine minutes past three in the morning (not that she was counting), Jamie finally fell asleep and she could go to bed, too.

CHAPTER 10

It felt like only moments after closing her eyes that a crash startled Anna awake, and she looked up to see Jamie flash by her bedroom door. Naked? Naked. In the bedroom his underwear lay on the floor in a soggy heap and there was a funny unidentifiable smell. He'd wet the bed. Ripping off the sheets, Anna bundled them into a heap and took them into the kitchen, stuffing them furiously into the washing machine.

The TV blared out from the living room but Anna tracked Jamie to the bathroom where he was busily working his way along her row of toiletries, sniffing at each container of moisturiser, shampoo and exfoliator, before pouring its contents into a congealed sticky mess on the floor.

'Jamie!' Anna struggled to hold back her anger. Jamie ignored her and kept on emptying. Her fury ruptured its banks. 'Stop!' she yelled. Jamie stopped what he was doing then calmly walked over to her, taking her hand and pressing it to his rough chin.

Anna sighed. 'I know. You need a shave.' After making a bad job of it with her Ladyshave, she turned on the shower and tried to persuade Jamie under the jet of water. He wouldn't go near it, so she ran a bath and Jamie climbed in happily, so happily that twenty minutes later when the water was tepid, he didn't want to get out. They were going to be late for the day centre at this rate. In desperation Anna grabbed the TV remote control and, dangling it in front of him as bait, pulled out the plug. It gurgled loudly and Jamie leapt out of the bath, snatching the remote and running through to the lounge, still dripping wet. Anna gathered up what remained wearable of his sorry collection of clothes, resolving to fetch him some clean ones from the house as soon as possible, just enough to last until she could find somewhere permanent for him to stay.

She hooked the T-shirt over his head. 'Come on, you help. I'm not going to do it for you.' But Jamie had other ideas and Anna found herself manipulating him into every garment while he sat with his eyes glued to the TV screen.

By the time they were hurrying out through the door, Anna was exhausted. She'd managed somehow to throw on jeans and a sweater after a quick shower but make-up was a complete non-starter. They both looked as if they'd spent the night on the streets, leaving Anna to pray that they wouldn't meet anyone she knew.

The day centre was buzzing with activity when they got there and Francine greeted them cheerily. 'I like the kit,' she said. 'How's he been?'

'A nightmare.' Anna had already decided to play it straight. 'I never realised what a powerful weapon passive resistance could be.'

Francine chuckled. 'You need to be firm with him.'

'But he just looks at me as if I'm mad.'

'Probably because he doesn't understand what you want him to do,' Francine said. 'Jamie's much better at picking up visual clues than auditory ones, so we use a lot of pictures to help him. Eddie had photographs showing things like getting dressed, eating, going out, so that Jamie could see what's about to happen and what he's meant to do. If he knows what's going on, he's much more likely to co-operate.'

By way of a demonstration Francine took Jamie by the hand and led him over to a wall that was covered in strips of photographs. 'This is his timetable,' she told Anna, then, turning back to Jamie, 'Jamie, look.' Familiar with the routine, Jamie followed where she pointing.

'Work first, then drink.' As she spoke, Francine moved her finger to a photograph or line drawing that illustrated each activity while Jamie watched her out of the corner of his eye. She went back to the first. 'Work now. Jamie, sit down.'

Without hesitation Jamie went to sit at one of the tables set up with light packing work for which the clients at the centre were paid a token wage.

Anna couldn't help but be impressed. If they achieved that kind of result, pictures might be good, even in the short-term. 'I'll see you this afternoon,' she said to Francine. 'I'll try not to be late.'

* * *

Waiting for Jamie to drop off to sleep last night had given Anna an opportunity to start planning a strategy, and her first stop this morning was the surgery of the man who had been their family doctor for years. Eddie had stuck with him because it was easier to continue with someone who knew Jamie well, and it was equally important to Jamie to visit someone he trusted. Doctor Owen Payne, whose name had provoked a lifetime of hilarious quips, had always been more like a family friend than a GP as Anna was growing up, and she was hoping that today he would be able to offer some advice. Although Anna had long since transferred to a more local practice, walking into Dr Payne's waiting room was an oddly familiar experience. During her childhood years, she'd spent countless mornings here helping to keep Jamie occupied and out of trouble while awaiting consultations.

Today Anna queued at reception with the intention of merely making an appointment, but while she was standing in line, Dr Payne emerged from his consulting room and, seeing her, did a double take. 'Anna?'

Anna returned the smile, 'Hello, Dr Payne.' She was amazed that he'd recognised her so quickly. It must have been a good fifteen years since they'd last met. Although the Celtic, dark good looks were fading to grey and the raw Scots brogue had softened to a southerner's lilt, he remained as engaging as ever.

'Are you here to see me?'

'It's Eddie.'

'Eddie?'

'He's— he—' suddenly her predicament was impossible to describe, but seeing her distress, Dr Payne stepped out and put an arm around her. It felt like coming home. Even after all this time, he was more comforting than Anna could have imagined, the nearest she could get to sharing the awful news with Mum or Dad.

'Come with me.' Looking over Anna's shoulder, the doctor squared things with his receptionist. 'Give us a few minutes, would you?' Always accommodating, nothing had ever been too much trouble for Dr Payne. When Jamie was first diagnosed, he'd been a constant visitor to the Barham household at all hours of the day and night, and again at the onset of the epilepsy, becoming virtually an honorary member of the family. Anna could recall her Mum joking on more than one occasion that Dr Payne should have his own front-door key. That was back in the days when doctors made twenty-four-hour house calls themselves, without relying on night-time deputising services.

On top of that, Dr Payne had been a brilliant support to Anna and Eddie too, at a time when they had needed someone to listen but Mum and Dad were too busy with

Jamie. As a consequence Anna had developed quite a teenage crush on Dr Payne and she was slightly disconcerted to find as she walked through to his office supported by his guiding arm that those feelings hadn't entirely dissipated.

In his consulting room, he sat her down. 'Now tell me what's happened.' When she finally managed to articulate the sequence of events as they'd been told to her, his reaction was exactly as Anna would have expected, mirroring her own horror and disbelief.

'I'm so very sorry Anna,' he said. 'How can your family have suffered such terrible tragedy again?'

'It's becoming a habit,' Anna agreed, darkly.

Standing abruptly Dr Payne paced the room, coming to rest with his back to Anna and palms pressed down on the windowsill. 'Anna I have a confession to make.'

'Confession?'

He turned to face her. 'Eddie's been to see me several times during the last few weeks. Jamie was going through a difficult patch.'

'It's what he's good at,' Anna said. 'The day centre staff have already been candid about what's been going on.'

'So you know that the respite placement at Moorcroft had broken down?'

Anna nodded. The knowledge had done nothing to assuage her mounting guilt.

'It was a blow,' Dr Payne went on. 'But unfortunately, all I did was to try and solve the problems with Jamie. I had no idea that Eddie was in such a state himself.'

'You couldn't have known,' Anna assured him. 'Eddie was an expert at hiding his feelings.'

'But I should have guessed. He took his care of Jamie so seriously.'

And you didn't? Anna studied Dr Payne's face for any implied meaning, but saw none. She was being oversensitive.

'I should have seen that he needed help too, but instead I focused all my energies on Jamie,' he paused. 'How's Jamie doing?'

'He seems fine. It's almost as if he hasn't noticed that Eddie's gone.'

'And there are no ill effects from his ordeal that night? Is there anything to indicate that he's distressed by what happened?'

Anna thought back to the police interview. 'No, although someone called Sally-Ann seems to be on his mind. You don't know her, do you? One of Eddie's friends perhaps?'

Dr Payne shook his head. 'Not someone I know, I'm afraid, but then I wasn't party to Eddie's social life. Look, it might be an idea if I checked Jamie over at some point. Is he staying with you?'

'At present, yes he is. But that's what I wanted to talk to you about. I'm finding it really hard—' Anna floundered. She didn't want this to sound whingeing, but she needn't have worried, as the doctor was immediately sympathetic.

'Of course. Although he'd withdrawn Jamie from Moorcroft, I know Eddie hadn't ruled out the idea of finding alternative care for Jamie. In fact, despite your parents' views, he'd expressed an interest in something far more comprehensive. We talked at length about what the options might be. I took that as being a wise long-term precaution, but now I wonder if his motive was different altogether.' Like planning his way out.

Anna paused. 'Well, the thing is, I was hoping you could help me in the same way.'

Dr Payne was already with her. 'I'd be happy to. I compiled a list of possible facilities for Eddie to try. I'm sure I must still have a copy somewhere. Bear with me one moment.' Getting up, he went out of the room, returning moments later with a handwritten list on a sheet of headed A4 paper. 'I'm afraid it doesn't look much, mainly because provision for adults with special needs is pretty scarce. It's a case of phoning up each setting and arranging a visit. As I advised Eddie: have a good look, be thorough and don't be afraid to ask questions — these places vary enormously in what they offer for the price. And there may be some hard choices to make, particularly around things like the use of medication.' He frowned. 'The other thing you must be prepared for is that none of these places are cheap.' So there was the rub. Despite the encouragement, was that final comment subtly designed to discourage her?

Whether or not that was the case, as Anna left the surgery, those were the words that resounded in her head. She felt ruthless looking into this so soon, but the next logical step was to establish where she stood financially. From Dr Payne's practice, Anna drove to the small block of offices on Harborne High Street that accommodated the Barham family solicitors. It seemed unlikely that Eddie would have made any kind of will. After all, he wasn't yet forty . . .

'But actually he had.' Paul Jenner was someone else who had, for years, lurked on the margins of Anna's life. That he was a junior partner in the firm was a misnomer as he must be fast approaching retirement and had been the one to assist Eddie and Anna through the legal minefield that had followed the death of their parents. As Anna had told him the news, he'd blanched and called to request tea from his secretary — as much for himself as for Anna — before moving on to business.

'Fortunately Edward's forethought will make things much simpler. You'd be amazed at the mess that can be left behind in some instances,' he said. 'But prudence would seem to be a strong quality in your family. Edward came in to see me a few weeks ago to talk through the arrangements. Then he came in to sign the finished document a week or so later.' Jenner looked uncomfortable. 'I'm sure he even said: *in case anything should happen*, which, naturally I took to be a superstitious reference to your parents' accident. But now of course — if what the police say is correct — it shines a new light . . . I'm so sorry.' He drew to a faltering close leaving Anna to consider further proof, were it still needed, of the way in which Eddie's mind was working. Anna had been so sure that the police were wrong, but little by little, her certainty was being undermined.

Moving to the back of his small, conventionally furnished office, Paul Jenner flipped through the top drawer of a filing cabinet before removing from it a slim folder, which he brought over to the desk. Taking out two documents, both of which bore Eddie's signature, he passed one to Anna.

'Here we are. As I said, he seemed in a hurry, so he asked me to act as sole executor.' Jenner shifted uneasily. 'I expect he didn't want to trouble you. And it's all very straightforward. Edward's entire estate has been left to James.' Suddenly he was finding it hard to meet Anna's eye.

Then it dawned on her. He thought she'd come to claim her share of Eddie's legacy for herself. 'That's good,' she said, to allay his anxiety. 'A huge relief.' But her words seemed to have little impact.

'As you already know, the house was left to James as part of your parents' bequest, not to be sold until professional care for him becomes essential.' Providing Jamie with lifelong security and at the same time making explicit her parents' desire that Jamie should, until it was no longer viable, be cared for in the family home. 'I seem to remember that Edward and you were compensated by the will accordingly.'

'We were,' Anna agreed. The sum of money allowed her to put a deposit on her first flat. Eddie, she recalled had been rather more impulsive. That was when he'd developed his taste for Porsches, albeit second-hand ones. The house was something she'd have to consider.

With a bit of lateral thinking, she was sure it didn't have to be the millstone it had become for Eddie.

'The most effective way of administering the residue of Edward's estate will be through a trust fund, naming yourself as the sole trustee.' At last he met her eye. 'Edward didn't mention any of this to you?'

'No.'

'Well, as I said, it seemed to have been quite a sudden decision. Perhaps he was planning to discuss it with you.' And perhaps not. Why make excuses for the fact that she and Eddie had hardly spoken to each other for years? 'For the moment,' Jenner concluded. 'It will make James quite a wealthy young man—'

'Wealthy enough to be able to afford some kind of long-term residential care,' murmured Anna. She was thinking aloud, but now that it was said, Jenner's uneasiness compounded before her very eyes. 'I'm not sure if that's what your parents had in mind when—'

'My parents are dead, Mr Jenner,' Anna quietly reminded him.

'Yes, of course.' Now she'd really embarrassed him. He covered his confusion with the professional matter in hand. 'Once probate has been granted, it will take me a week or so to draw up the papers. After that I'll need to ask you to come in and sign them.'

Anna nodded to indicate that she'd understood, feeling better than she had done since the news of Eddie's death. It was what she needed to hear: that she would not have to bear the financial burden of residential care for Jamie entirely on her own, which, in turn, meant that she could find him somewhere good and find it soon. The house was a complication, but not one that couldn't be overcome. Her relief was palpable. 'Thank you,' she said, and began gathering together her things.

'Your brother did leave one other specific item with me,' Jenner added, almost as an afterthought. He disappeared into a walk-in cupboard, emerging moments later carrying, somewhat bizarrely, an old shoebox tied with string. 'I'll leave it with you for a few minutes.' He walked out before Anna could demur.

As the door closed behind him, Anna slipped off the string and inside the box found a bundle of letters held together by an elastic band. Big deal, she thought. They looked old, but as Anna riffled through them, she saw that some had numbers scrawled on them in what looked like Eddie's handwriting. She freed one of the letters from the pile and scanned it. It was addressed not to Eddie, but to her father. At first she couldn't see any relevance, but by the second paragraph, she was hooked.

'. . . our daughter Ellen was born at full term,' it read. 'Delivery was normal and she weighed 5lbs 4oz. She was a happy, healthy baby, a joy to everyone, until at around eighteen months, she suddenly began to scream.'

An unexpected pain speared Anna as a vivid memory of one of Jamie's first 'screaming days' came rushing back to her. A hot summer day, they had gone to visit Auntie Meg and Uncle Keith down in Gloucestershire. Jamie, who would have been about two at the time, had started crying as soon as they got there, but for no identifiable reason. The crying had quickly escalated into screaming — in terror or pain, it was impossible to tell, but every time Mum tried to comfort him, he pushed her away, recoiling from her touch and screaming even louder. More plainly than ever, Anna could picture her mother's face, stricken with the knowledge that she couldn't even soothe her own child. The incident had shocked Anna because it was the first time she'd seen her mother cry. It wasn't to be the last. And even then, at the age of seven, Anna knew that the other adults were looking on and making their own judgments. What she hadn't understood, couldn't have understood, was that their lives would never be the same again.

The neat copperplate handwriting blurred in front of her eyes. Blinking back tears, Anna glanced over one or two more of the letters. Not all were as fluently written and there were subtle differences to each: a child who was eerily passive and undemanding, another whose obsession with light switches had become intolerable. But from every page came the painful desperation of parents living with a child beyond comprehension. Anna couldn't imagine why on earth Eddie had kept the letters, unless it was to punish her.

Paul Jenner cleared his throat, making Anna start. She hadn't noticed him come back into the room. 'It seemed important to Eddie that you got those,' he said. 'Perhaps they're of particular sentimental value?'

Mm. Or perhaps in the last few weeks of his life, Eddie had been going slowly insane. Suddenly Anna was overwhelmed by an urge to be outside. Making an effort to pull herself together, she handed the shoebox back to the solicitor. 'It's all right, you can keep these, for now.' And with a brief thank you and goodbye, she hurried from the building.

Out in the air again, part of her was relieved, knowing now that Jamie was financially sound, and that she could safely turn her mind to some serious research. But her relief was tempered by everything else that was falling into place. Eddie had been making arrangements. He had been planning. Doing all things you would expect of a man who was about to take his own life. It was not an easy thought.

Anna was still brooding on it when she met Becky for their regular lunch date at Chez Jules.

'How are you doing?' Becky asked.

'Not wonderful,' Anna had to concede. 'When the police told me Eddie's death looked like suicide I wouldn't believe them, but now it seems obvious. The things he'd done, preparations he'd made. It's all beginning to fit.'

'That's awful.'

'Not least because it leaves me with the knowledge that I could have done something about it. I keep asking myself, how could Eddie have been so desperate and I didn't even know? I'm his sister for God's sake. Why didn't he talk to me?'

'You weren't close,' said Becky. 'You said it yourself. How could you have known? What you need is some retail therapy to cheer you up. There's a mid-season sale at Selfridges. Come on, let's go.'

They settled the bill and left the restaurant, but for once, even shopping couldn't shake Anna from the sudden depression that had descended on her. Her attention snagged on a newsstand headline: *City journalist found dead*. Eddie, she thought, numbly. And suddenly, trying to find a sweater in exactly the right shade of blue seemed a totally pointless exercise. 'Actually, I think I'll give it a miss,' she told Becky. 'I'm not very good company today.'

Becky didn't put up a fight. 'What have you got planned for this afternoon?' she asked.

'I need to get some of Jamie's things.'

'How's that going? I heard about what happened last night.'

'Oh, did you? Yes, I suppose it's all round the office by now —unreliable Anna. It pretty well sums up the way life is going. I'm hoping that there might be things back at Eddie's house that will keep Jamie occupied so that I can start trying to get back to normal. I'll go straight there now I think.'

Becky shuddered. 'Rather you than me,' she saw Anna's look. 'Sorry, but you know what I mean.'

'It's only a house,' said Anna. But driving out to Harborne, she knew precisely what Becky meant, and her apprehension began to grow.

CHAPTER 11

Even under normal circumstances Anna didn't look back on 34 Clarendon Avenue with any great fondness. It wasn't that her childhood had been unhappy, it had just never been quite right, and she'd hardly returned here since her parents died. Contrary to their wishes, she and Eddie would both have preferred to sell the oversized house along with all its memories, but at the time their reasoning had seemed sound: that whatever other dramatic changes there might be in Jamie's life after they were gone, here, at least, there would be continuity.

On the approach to the house, the police squad car at the kerb-side heightened her anxiety, and she was mystified to see another car parked on the drive behind Eddie's, until she recognised it as the one belonging to the detective, Mariner. Its presence slightly tempered her fears. Having never knowingly entered a building where someone had died, let alone committed suicide, her usual confidence seemed to have deserted her.

Inside the squad car a young uniformed officer sat eating his sandwiches. What could be more normal than that? Walking up the drive Anna took a deep, calming breath. All she needed were a few of Jamie's clothes, his toothbrush and shaving kit. A quick in and out was all it would take. Beyond the strip of crime-scene tape, the front door was open, leaving her free to enter, so why wasn't she pleased? Anna ducked under the tape and went in. Inside, the place had an illusory look to it where surfaces had been painted with grey metallic fingerprint dust. Following the sound of movement, she pushed open the lounge door.

'I wouldn't mind a place like this—' PC Knox was saying.

'It's one of the few perks of losing your parents prematurely,' Anna interrupted, and both men reeled around to face her.

'How did you get in here?' Mariner's frown mirrored his accusatory tone.

'Through the door, the same as you,' Anna defended herself. 'It was open.'

'It shouldn't have been.' He glared at Knox.

'I just need to get some of Jamie's things,' Anna said.

Mariner's expression softened. 'How is the Hula Hoop kid?'

'His clothes are beginning to smell. He could use some more.'

For a moment their eyes locked. She should do it now, but admitting she was wrong had never come easily. Oh well, here goes. 'You were right,' she said, eventually. 'About the way Eddie died. It's all beginning to fit. He had begun making plans for Jamie. His GP knew it, and he'd even made a will. Hindsight is a wonderful thing and I'm sorry I doubted what you said. At the time it seemed impossible, but I suppose that's what everyone says. I still find it hard to believe that Eddie didn't stick around long enough to see Jamie settled, but it shows how desperate—' She tailed off, all at once seeing that both men were staring at her. Something was off kilter. 'What?' she said. 'Why are you here?'

Knox gave Mariner a 'go on, tell her' sort of look and the tall man sighed. 'Eddie didn't stick around to see Jamie settled because he didn't take his own life,' Mariner said. '*You* were right. It wasn't suicide. I was going to contact you to let you know.'

'What?' Anna struggled to take in what he was saying.

'We've had the post-mortem report. Eddie was murdered. But someone went to great lengths to make it look like suicide.'

For the second time in two days, Mariner watched Anna Barham absorb what to many would be devastating news, with impressive self-control. He'd been pretty shocked himself, when Stuart Croghan had broken it to him late last night. Everything they'd turned up so far pointed to Eddie Barham as a man at the end of his tether taking up his final option, but now that theory had been completely overturned.

'How can you be so sure?' Anna Barham asked, repeating word-for-word Mariner's own question to Croghan.

'Eddie's killer made one or two mistakes,' he said. 'Either hadn't thought things through, or was in a hurry — probably the latter.' Suddenly he saw how wobbly she looked. 'Why don't we—?' Mariner gestured towards the sofa and she sat at one end, while Mariner took up the opposite corner, a pair of bookends propping up an empty space. 'We were right about the drugs, of course,' he went on, gently. 'Eddie definitely died from a massive overdose of diamorphine — heroin to you and me — but he didn't administer it himself. Eddie was right-handed, wasn't he?' Mariner had known that from Knox's remark about the computer mouse.

'Yes.'

'But he'd injected into his right arm. Not the most natural thing for a right hander to do.'

'Somebody did it for him,' she said, dazed.

'That's the implication. And Eddie wasn't exactly co-operative about it. There's indication that he was being forcefully restrained at the time he died.' Extensive bruising to the wrists and upper arms, Stuart Croghan had said, consistent with being held down. Along with some old cuts and bruises whose provenance was unclear. 'We've run some basic forensic tests on the syringe, too. Significantly, there were no fingerprints on it, not even Eddie's. Meaning that whoever injected him either wore gloves or deliberately wiped it clean afterwards. It's not something suicides generally do.'

'You'd know more about that than me.'

'The other curious thing is that the heroin used was of a particularly pure grade, although we're not sure how important that is at this stage. And the preliminary analysis of the blood that was on Jamie's shirt shows that although it's consistent with the timing, the blood isn't his or Eddie's. Some of it's mine — big surprise — but there was someone else in the flat, too. We have to conclude that it was Eddie's killer. Or one of them.'

'Is that why Jamie was in the cupboard?'

'It's possible Eddie put him there for his own protection. But it's more likely that Jamie was shut in there out of the way while Eddie was dealt with. It was an effective strategy. Jamie could tell us nothing about what happened, even if he was able to.' Only this morning, Francine the care worker at Jamie's day centre had rung to confirm it. Using a photograph of Eddie she'd tried to elicit something, anything, from Jamie, but without success.

Anna frowned. 'But what about the note?' she asked, suddenly. 'You found a note.'

'Mm.' Mariner felt the blush rising from his neck. It had been so obvious in retrospect. 'Half a note, actually. There was a post-script,' he said. 'We found it stuffed in the hedge outside. Fitted together again with the so-called "suicide note," it would have read: "NO MORE MILK UNTIL THURSDAY THANKS, NO. 34."'

'Oh.'

It was one of the things that had jarred with Mariner; that a man who made a living from words would make his last message to the world so brief. 'Eddie must have left it on the doorstep that evening,' he said. 'It was a gift to whoever killed him. It may even have influenced the way they set things up.'

Anna shivered as Mariner watched her efforts to digest what he had just told her. 'It's funny,' she said, eventually. 'I thought it would make me feel better to know that Eddie hadn't taken his own life, but it doesn't.' Her eyes glazed over as she momentarily drifted off into her own thoughts, and Mariner could only guess at the images crowding her head. It was the stuff of nightmares. He began to wonder if he'd given her too much information too soon, but in a matter of minutes she seemed to come round again.

'So what happens now?' she asked, at last.

'At the moment it'll help if we can keep all this to ourselves,' Mariner said. 'If Eddie's killer is still around, it suits us that he or she should think that we're still treating the death as suicide. It's good that you're here, though. You may be able to help. Tell us if you see anything else unusual, anything about the place that strikes you as odd.' He wasn't holding out much hope, especially in such austere surroundings, but it was always worth a shot.

'I wouldn't know,' she confessed, looking absently around her, at a home she must have once known intimately. 'I've only been here once since my parents died. And that time Eddie succeeded in making me feel so guilty that I just walked out again.'

'Guilty?' It seemed an odd choice of word.

'Well, look at it,' she raised her arms. 'This room is like a monastic cell.'

Mariner nodded, grimly. 'And we thought it was all fashionably minimalist.'

'Fashion doesn't come into it. There are only so many times an insurance firm will pay out for "damage caused by autistic sibling." Add into that Eddie's own little fetish for order. We used to joke that he was on the spectrum too.'

'Sorry?' She'd lost him.

'The autism spectrum,' she elaborated. 'These days it's pretty well accepted that autism is a continuum, with "normal" at one end and severe at the other. If you take it to the extreme, we're all on it somewhere, with our own little routines and obsessions,' she smiled suddenly. 'I'm sure you must have some autistic traits.'

From the corner of his eye, Mariner saw Knox suppress a grin. Okay, so he kept his desk tidy. What was wrong with that? 'I can live without Hula Hoops, if that's what you mean,' Mariner defended himself uneasily.

'Either way, it all screamed "sacrifice!" at me,' Anna said. 'Which is exactly what Eddie wanted.'

'Why?' Mariner sensed a sudden reluctance. Maybe she didn't expect him to understand. Maybe he wouldn't. But he wanted to know.

'Because after our parents died, Eddie was prepared to take Jamie on, and I wasn't,' she explained with great patience. 'It upset a lot of people. After all, I'm the woman, so in theory, the nurturer. The fact that I had a husband and a home to run, as well as a successful career didn't count for anything.'

There was an awkward silence, which Mariner wasn't sure how to fill.

'Families, eh?' Knox chipped in, and the word hung in the air for several seconds, where Mariner was content to leave it, for now. After all, what did he know about families? 'You wouldn't know if Eddie had any enemies, then?' he asked, moving on.

With the change of subject Anna perceptibly relaxed. 'I've already told you. I have very little idea of what was going on in his life. But it's hard to imagine that he would have. Eddie was such an easy-going guy. Except where I was concerned, of course.' She shot Mariner a wry look. 'Does that confession make me a suspect?'

He managed a smile. 'I don't think so. Although it would help, for the record, if you could tell me where you were between the hours of nine and midnight on Sunday night.'

'That's easy. I was at home with my boyfriend. He's "happily married," so we don't go out much.' Something nipped at Mariner's gut, but he couldn't quite identify it as disapproval or disappointment.

'Will he back that up?' he asked.

'As long as you don't ask him to broadcast it on the six o'clock news, it shouldn't be a problem. What do you think happened?'

'That's what we're here to try and find out. It's not looking like a robbery. Nothing valuable seems to have been taken and Eddie's wallet, when we found it, was still stuffed with cash. And there's no sign of a forced entry. If Eddie went out leaving Jamie at home, would he have left the door on the latch?'

'He might have.' She was unsure.

'If not, we have to conclude that it was someone who knew Eddie and wanted something from him.'

'Eddie had made a will. He told the solicitor it was in case anything happened to him.'

Mariner nodded. 'If he was feeling under threat from someone, he might have started to make those kinds of preparations. And it might explain why he'd begun collecting Jamie from the day centre himself, too. He could have believed that someone would try to get at him through Jamie.'

'But who? And why?'

Mariner was beginning to formulate some ideas about that, but he wasn't ready to share them yet. 'It was someone who was well organised. They had a purpose and they came prepared. They apparently weren't keen to broadcast that they were here, either. There were men working on the driveway next door all weekend, so they had to wait until a Sunday night after dark, when everyone had gone home. And what we haven't got yet is any kind of motive.' Though if pressed Mariner would have laid bets on a connection with those large payments of money into Eddie Barham's bank account.

Knox had been researching those, but so far his investigations had drawn an intriguing blank. The account wasn't from a UK bank and so far they hadn't even managed to identify its country of origin, let alone any other details. Mariner didn't imagine Anna Barham having access to an offshore bank, but the question had to be asked. So he asked it. 'Did Eddie ever talk to you about money?'

'No. It wasn't something we ever discussed.'

'So you haven't lent him any recently?'

'I'd be the last person Eddie would come to for money,' she said. 'And anyway, he wouldn't need to. He wasn't rolling in it, but he was solvent. His solicitor told me that Eddie left a substantial sum.'

Mariner decided to spare her the details for now. 'He did,' he agreed. 'We're currently trying to identify the source of two large payments into Eddie's bank account in December and January.'

'How large?'

'Ten thousand pounds each. They were paid by standing order. Any idea about where they may have come from?'

Her response was in the negative, as he'd expected, and as she seemed unfazed by the line of questioning Mariner was inclined to believe her.

'We really could do with finding Sally-Ann,' he said. 'If that's her name.'

'You really think a woman might have done it?'

'I saw Eddie with a woman earlier on Sunday evening, they drove off together. It may have been the same woman who later made the call to the emergency services. She has disappeared and so apparently has Sally-Ann. It's quite a coincidence. Whether or not she's implicated, she was one of the last people to see Eddie alive.' Mariner braced himself for what could potentially be a sensitive area. 'In Eddie's wallet we found a page torn out of the local newspaper. It was the list of ads for personal services, escort agencies, that kind of thing.' Mariner hesitated. 'It was well used. I'm pretty sure the woman I saw him with was in that line of work.'

'What are you getting at?' she demanded.

'Do you know if Eddie was ever in the habit of using the services of prostitutes?'

'Absolutely not!'

'It could have been connected with something he was working on, of course, but we have to check out all the possibilities,' Mariner said, to cool things down again. 'We're trying to recover what remained of Eddie's computer files, too.'

'You think it could have happened because of something he was writing?' It was perhaps easier to bear than the alternative.

Mariner shrugged. 'Or something he'd written in the past. People bear grudges.' Men like Frank Crosby did it big time.

Knox's mobile trilled. 'I'll take it outside, boss,' he said fumbling for it. In his haste to leave the room, he tripped over the two large volumes propping open the door, sending one of them sliding across the floor. Mariner got up to retrieve it, inspecting the spine as he did so. It was a dated edition of *Gray's Anatomy*.

'Was Eddie's reading always so light, or was he thinking of going into medicine?' he asked Anna Barham, turning over the book in his hand.

As Anna took the weighty tome from him, a trace of recognition registered. 'It's one of Dad's old medical books,' she said. 'I didn't know Eddie had kept them.'

'Your father was a doctor?'

With a brief smile, Anna shook her head. 'A frustrated doctor maybe. He taught chemistry and biology at St Mark's Comp. But he had his own little research projects on the go all the time, too.'

'His autistic trait?'

'Something like that.'

'What was he researching?'

'What else? Bloody autism. The bane of our lives.'

'Trying to do what? Find the cure?'

'Cause or cure, he thought the one would lead to the other. But above all he wanted to prove to my mother that Jamie's condition wasn't her fault.'

'Was that necessary?'

'Oh yes. At the time when my parents were first told about Jamie's condition, some of the thinking was that autism happened as a result of the mother's failure to bond with her child. They called them "refrigerator mothers."'

'That sounds like a lorry load of antiquated Freudian crap.'

'It does now, but at the time little else was known. So, not only did my mother have this miserable, screaming, uncommunicative child, but she had to live with the experts telling her that *oh, and by the way, it's your fault that he's like that*. Never mind that she's already got two happy, healthy children.'

'And your father didn't believe it?'

'Dad never took anything at face value. He was a scientist so the psychological stuff didn't cut it for him. Then when people began to realise that there could be other, more tangible explanations for autism it was all the encouragement he needed. Now, of course, it's pretty much accepted that there are a whole range of biological and genetic factors at play.' She could tell that Mariner was impressed.

'You know a lot about this, don't you?' he observed.

Despite herself, Anna laughed. 'Something must have sunk in from the endless discussions we were dragged into over the dinner table. Dad was obsessed. It was his little one-man campaign. Looking back, I think it was his way of dealing with Jamie. Our lives were like a rollercoaster, each time some new theory or therapy or medication came out, there was hope or there was guilt. We were a pretty dysfunctional family. Dad shut away in his study for hours on end, Jamie taking all Mum's time and energy—'

'And not much time for you and Eddie.'

'It's probably why we hated each other so much.'

'Hate's a strong word.'

'Maybe, but whatever it was, we took out our anger on each other.'

'Did any of your father's work get published?'

Another sardonic smile. 'No.' Then a pause as something stirred in her memory. 'Although they did print some letter he wrote to an autism journal, expounding one of his theories. I was living away from home by then, so Mum sent me a copy. She was so proud of him. She claimed it had created quite a stir. But I was sick to the back teeth with autism. I'd left home to get away from it, so I didn't even bother reading it. It went straight in the bin. It's one of those stupid things I regretted, because only a few weeks later Mum and Dad were dead.'

'What happened to them?'

'Their car skidded off an icy road and went into the canal. They were both killed outright. Dad learned to drive quite late in life and he was never a very confident driver. It was a shock, of course, but we could understand how it might have happened.'

'I'm sorry,' Mariner said.

Anna shrugged, 'It was a long time ago.'

'How long?' asked Mariner.

'Fifteen years or so. It was a great year. Within months, my marriage hit the rocks and my parents were killed. Still, at least Mum and Dad weren't around to say *told you so*.' By Mariner's calculation that would make it two years after the building society account was opened.

Knox reappeared in the doorway, distracting them both from further morbid thoughts.

'I've been called back to the shop, boss. They're short of bodies. And that photographer at the paper has surfaced so I said that you'd be down there,' he said. 'I've arranged for you to look at the office, too.'

'Right.' Mariner turned to Anna. 'We'll leave you to it then. SOCO have done a pretty rigorous job, so forensically you can't do any harm. PC Hunter outside will lock up when you go.'

She nodded assent. 'Of course. It's probably a stupid question, but I have to ask. How likely is it that you'll find out who did this?' she asked.

'It's too early to tell,' said Mariner. 'But I suppose this is where I say, "If we get any leads, I'll call you."' He drew back his mouth in a terrible Humphrey Bogart impression that at least made her smile. 'And in case you think of anything else that might be important.' He handed her his card, complete with his office and mobile numbers.

CHAPTER 12

Hearing the front door close behind the two policemen, leaving her alone in the house, Anna tried hard not to feel spooked. It wasn't just the recent events that haunted her, but more than thirty years' worth of history. She climbed the stairs slowly, unwillingly. After their parents died, Eddie had moved into the master bedroom and both that and Jamie's room had since been decorated, but her own room was almost exactly as she'd left it, two months before her twentieth birthday. She fingered the lock that she herself had inexpertly fitted in an attempt to safeguard some privacy from her marauding younger brother. A consequence of too many days of coming home from school to find that he had pulled records off the shelves, destroyed her school project or ripped her precious pop posters from the walls. Mum and Dad had refused to secure Jamie's room, insisting, reasonably enough it seemed now, that he wasn't an animal to be caged. So she'd fitted a lock on hers instead, and retreated to her own safe haven at every opportunity.

Dad's sanctuary had always been his study, the room that now housed Eddie's computer. It was where their father had laboured night after night, the angle-poise lamp highlighting his thinning hair as he frowned with concentration over his work, barely even noticing when, in rare moments of consideration, Anna had set a mug of tea or coffee down in front of him. *Families*, Knox had said. Anna couldn't remember them ever having been much of a family. Mariner's lack of response was significant, she thought, virtual proof that a perfect wife and two beautiful children awaited him at home.

Jamie's bedroom was largely untouched by the police investigation. Under the bed she found a holdall, and, opening drawers, packed into it a selection of underwear, shirts, jeans and sweaters. Not too many. She wasn't expecting to host Jamie for that long.

The phone rang, splitting the air and making her jump. For a moment she just stood, frozen to the spot, reluctant to answer it, before chiding herself. *It's just the phone, for God's sake.* She picked up the computer-room extension. 'Hello?'

A male voice responded. 'Eddie, it's Andrew Todd. We need to talk.' The man's voice was tense, urgent.

'Mr Todd, this is Anna Barham, I'm Eddie's sister,' she took a deep breath. 'I'm afraid my brother is dead. He—' A click and the line went dead too. Anna was left suspended in mid-air. 'Mr Todd? Hello?'

She tapped down on the cradle, punched in 1471 and was rewarded with the standard recorded message telling her that the number had been withheld. No surprises there. But Mr Todd, whoever he was, obviously hadn't seen the local papers.

Downstairs in the lounge, Anna sorted through the extensive DVD collection. She uncovered an entire collection devoted to vintage *Countdown* . . . which didn't surprise her in the slightest. If Carol wasn't in it, then Jamie wasn't interested. In the kitchen there was little. She threw away the remains of a carton of milk and half a stale loaf, but took with her the multi-pack of Hula Hoops that was in the pantry. Something she was learning: you could never have enough Hula Hoops.

On her way out, Anna realised she'd forgotten Jamie's shaver. She retraced her steps to the bathroom, where she found toothbrushes, but the only razors were disposable ones. Had Eddie wet-shaved Jamie every day? Jamie would never have managed it himself without cutting his face to shreds. It was yet another measure of Eddie's devotion to his younger brother. She picked up a few, along with a can of shaving gel. In the bathroom cabinet, its child safety-lock forced open, doubtless by the police, were more deodorants and hair gel, and beside them, a bottle of aftershave. On impulse, Anna uncapped the lid and briefly held it to her nose. The effect was disturbing in its familiarity, as though Eddie was suddenly standing beside her in the room. Tears welled up in her eyes and she wiped them away irritably.

'Shit!' she spoke aloud. 'Why did this have to happen, Eddie? What had you got into?' Through blurred vision she gathered up the rest of the things she needed and feeling suddenly, overwhelmingly claustrophobic, headed for the door.

* * *

With the revelation of Eddie Barham's murder came a shift in the dynamics of the enquiry. This was now a criminal investigation, giving Mariner no option but to take over as senior investigating officer. There were plenty of detective constables at his disposal, but he was inclined to reciprocate Knox's generosity and keep him involved as much as he could. Knox had been in at the very beginning of the case and, other duties permitting, would want to see it through. So far they'd worked well together. Like Mariner, Knox was a pragmatist who had no interest in station politics, but simply wanted to get the job done. Right now though, he was hostage to the flu virus that was sweeping Granville Lane and had been called back to base. He dropped Mariner off at the *Echo* offices on the way.

This afternoon Mariner was directed to the basement canteen where he was told photographer Darren Smith was finishing off a late afternoon lunchbreak. The cafeteria was a subterranean vision in chrome and melamine, loud with clattering cutlery, with a generously subsidised menu; a brave but unsuccessful endeavour to keep employees out of the surrounding bars.

Illness hadn't apparently suppressed Darren's appetite. Mariner, who hadn't eaten since a snatched slice of toast this morning, had to make an effort not to salivate as the younger man, who looked about fifteen by Mariner's reckoning, tucked into a particularly juicy looking medium-rare steak. The lad looked as if he could do with the nutrients. His close-cropped hair and sallow complexion gave him the appearance of a death camp survivor, although the scales would have probably shown a healthy reading, thanks to the extensive metalwork threaded through ears, nose and eyebrows. He made Mariner feel middle-aged and past it.

News that Eddie's death was not after all self-inflicted had by now permeated and though less demonstrative, Darren appeared as distressed as his chief had been. 'I've been Eddie's partner for the last three years on and off,' he told Mariner, in his lyrical Black-Country accent, and dispelling the age myth at once. 'I can't believe it. He was a straight-up bloke. Why would anyone want to do that to him? You don't know . . . ?'

Mariner shook his head in response.

'God. And I was only with him Friday.'

'He didn't talk to you about his plans for the weekend? Whether he was meeting anyone?' Mariner asked.

'No, he never talked much about what he did after hours.'

'It would help now if you could tell me a bit about Eddie,' said Mariner. 'What was he like?'

Darren shrugged. 'There's not much to tell. Eddie was all right.'

This might be an exercise in getting blood from a stone. 'And the two of you got on okay?'

Darren's alibi was solid, he'd been drinking in a pub in Cradley Heath with his mates all of Sunday evening, but it was still worth asking. 'Yeah,' he said. 'Eddie was really good to me when I first started. We worked well together.'

'Was there was anything about his behaviour during the last few weeks or days that seemed odd or out of character?'

Darren shipped his knife and fork with a clatter. 'No. I mean, I keep going over it, trying to think. But Eddie was never a conventional sort of bloke.'

And you would know? Mariner eyed the rows of assorted rings that adorned Darren's ears, and the studs in his left nostril. Unconsciously his finger and thumb strayed up to the two puncture holes remaining from his own modest youthful rebellion. The extent of Darren's pierced bits was extravagant by comparison, but then maybe with a name like Darren Smith, you had to find other outlets for self-expression.

'What did the two of you get up to then?' Mariner prompted in an effort to get him talking.

'Oh, we covered local stories, the really exciting stuff,' Darren said, meaning exactly the opposite. 'You know, "Edna the dinner lady retires after thirty years," "Terry the fireman cycles up Everest for charity."' He feigned a yawn.

'Must have been quite a change from what Eddie had been used to,' observed Mariner.

'You can say that again.'

'Did Eddie seem to mind?'

'I don't think so, not really. One of the things he taught me was: no matter how small it is, a story always has potential. You never know when the small tug on the line might turn out to be a big fish. Eddie took all our assignments seriously. He was old-school. And in any case, he usually had his own agenda to keep him going.'

Mariner's interest stirred. 'What do you mean?'

'Eddie always had his own little private investigations on the go. Force of habit, I guess, but he was always on the lookout for the big story.'

'What sort of big story?' asked Mariner.

Darren smiled, shaking his head. 'I never knew exactly what. He just liked to chuck out these hints from time to time; that he was working on something more important than the crap we got landed with.'

'Like what?'

'He never told me. Things. Sometimes he used to just disappear without telling me where he was going. He used to say he had leads to follow up.'

'And you didn't mind that?'

'We weren't joined at the hip. I'm a picture man. If there wasn't anything to photograph, there wasn't much point in me going, was there?'

'And when he did his disappearing act, there were no hints about where he was going?'

'No, although he told me once he had a big drugs story. He said it was the drug story to beat all drug stories. Made out like it was really something.'

'When was this?'

'Oh, I don't know, few months ago. It never came to anything,' Darren added, dismissively.

'Was that drugs, as in narcotics?' Mariner persisted. He'd already noticed the redness around Darren's nostrils, but maybe it was a cold that had kept the lad away from work.

Darren snorted. 'I didn't get the impression he was on about Sanatogen.'

'What else did he say about this story?'

'Nothing that I can remember. That was pretty well it — oh, and it was personal.'

Again Mariner's antennae twitched. 'As in personal services? You know, like the columns of ads in the paper? Or could he have meant personal as in revenge, some kind of vendetta?' He caught the whiff of a distant motive, but Darren didn't seem inclined to help him out.

'I don't know.' His brow creased to a frown. 'It could have been either or neither, I suppose. To be honest, half the time I used to think he was just winding me up. Letting me know that he hadn't lost his touch, that he still could be one of the major players if he wanted.'

'Eddie was involved in a big prostitution case a few years ago. He ever say anything about that to you?'

'No. When we first got together I asked him about it, but he didn't say much.'

'Did he ever talk to you about a man called Frank Crosby?'

'I've heard of him.' Darren's eyes widened. 'Do you think——?'

Mariner cut that one off at the pass. 'Eddie ever get involved in any rough stuff? Anything that was likely to get him into trouble physically?'

'No. He didn't take chances, if that's what you mean. But he did get mugged the other week,' said Darren, absently, giving Mariner the growing impression that he wasn't actually all that bright.

'When?'

Again a pause while Darren thought it over. 'It must have been about three weeks ago.'

'What happened?'

'Eddie turned up for work with a black eye, cut lip, all that.' Darren glanced up at Mariner's own battle scars. 'He said he'd been mugged the night before.'

Mariner sensed Darren's discomfort. 'Did you believe him?'

'When I asked if he'd reported it to you lot, he said he wasn't going to bother. In fact, he got really annoyed, told me to stop banging on about it because it was his business.'

Mariner's thoughts came back to the brunette. 'What about women?' he asked.

'Oh girls liked Eddie. They all fell for his charm. Not that he seemed to notice.'

'So there wasn't anyone special.'

'Not that I knew about. He's got this brother—'

Mariner raised a hand. 'I know all about Jamie.'

'Well, you'll know that he came first, then.' Darren picked up his knife and fork in a less than subtle hint.

Mariner was content enough to take it. He'd probably got as much as he was going to squeeze out of Darren. 'Thanks, Darren. You've been very helpful. I'm going to have a look round Eddie's office now. Will you be around if there's anything I need to check with you?'

'Sure, I'll be back at the office, reviewing photos from the latest thrilling shoot.'

'Great. And if you should think of anything else—' Mariner finished the sentence by sliding his card across the table. Darren picked it up and studied it for a moment before tucking it into his shirt pocket and returning his attentions to what must now be a considerably less appetising stone-cold steak and chips.

Ken Moloney himself had taken time out to escort Mariner to Eddie Barham's workspace. Mariner took the opportunity to quiz him again as they travelled up in the lift. 'Eddie's piece on Frank Crosby must have been a pretty big story.' Mariner had been considering those payments. 'Would anyone else have been interested in it?'

'Like who?'

'Was it the kind of thing Eddie could have syndicated to the nationals?'

'I wouldn't have thought so. It was a local story, pretty shocking at the time, but every city has a similar tale to tell. It wouldn't have been anything that unusual.'

Besides, thought Mariner, it was old news. So why would anyone have been interested in it as recently as three months ago?

'Though as a matter of fact, he did come back to me on that with a proposal for a follow up story,' Moloney added.

'When was that?'

'Maybe six months ago.'

'And?'

'I nixed it. Not enough substance to it, and anyway, the world isn't ready for another exposé yet.' Mariner wondered if Eddie Barham would have agreed with that.

They had come to the corner of an expansive open-plan office. Islands of desks were randomly scattered, many topped with flat-screen monitors, and the room hummed to the tune of phones and photocopiers. That none of the handful of staff present gave them a second glance, told Mariner that Moloney's approach was hands-on. They were used to the chief wandering in.

Eddie Barham had created himself a small zone of tranquillity in one corner by blocking off a section with tall filing cabinets.

'Eddie liked his own space,' confirmed Moloney.

'Sensible man,' said Mariner.

It was an orderly workspace, everything neat and tidy — the way it might have been left by a man who knew he may not be returning. Moloney called over someone called Phil who logged Mariner into Eddie's computer, then they both left him to it. But Mariner already had a feeling that he wouldn't find much here. The virus on Eddie's home computer was a clear sign that anything important had been stored there, which is why he, or someone else, had taken steps to eliminate it. The only documents they'd so far managed to salvage from it were a few fairly low-key stories and the remains of a database, the meaning of which they had yet to fathom. Eddie's work computer was networked, meaning that practically anyone could gain access to his files. If he really was onto something big, it was unlikely that he'd leave key information here.

Eddie Barham's particular little obsession appeared to be databases, which he kept for everything. His file management system was a detective's dream: methodical and transparent, electronic documents arranged as neatly as the hard copies. The first thing Mariner did was a search for Sally-Ann and all other possible permutations of the name, but unsurprisingly, it yielded a nil return.

Eddie's diary and work-log in the weeks prior to his death revealed nothing that particularly stood out either. Specific assignments were coded and most of the items on the work-log tallied with his computer files, the stories he'd been working on. True to Darren's word, it was pretty mundane stuff and nothing to get Mariner's pulse racing or to justify any five thousand pound pay-outs. There were one or two blank spaces on the schedule, but cross-referencing with Eddie's diary explained some of these as meetings at Greenwood, and on one occasion at Moorcroft, along with what looked like routine medical appointments for Jamie. For now, Mariner noted the few slots that were unaccounted for, like half a morning on 14 November with only a telephone number occupying the space.

Out of curiosity, Mariner picked up the receiver by Eddie's desk and tapped in the number. As he did so, he heard a distinct click echo somewhere down the line. Ken Moloney keeping track of the calls made by his staff? It seemed a bit excessive. The ring tone sounded.

'Charles Hanover and Associates,' said an efficient PA, announcing one of the largest law firms in the city.

Mariner identified himself. 'I'm trying to trace the last known movements of an Edward Barham,' he said. 'And on the morning of 14 November I see that he had an appointment with someone at your firm. I wonder if you could check that for me.'

'One moment please.'

She returned quickly. 'That's right, sir. The appointment was with Mr Lloyd.'

'Could I speak to Mr Lloyd?'

'I'm afraid he's away on holiday at present. He won't be back until the twenty-first.' Almost a week away.

'Is there any indication of what this meeting was about?' Mariner asked.

'I'm sorry, I can't access Mr Lloyd's files, they're confidential. We'd have to wait until he returns.'

As an afterthought Mariner asked, 'Does Mr Lloyd have any kind of specialism?'

'He's one of our best compensation lawyers,' she said, with such pride that Mariner wondered if Lloyd's PA perhaps had the tiniest crush on her boss.

With luck, Darren would be able to shed some light on that.

The remainder of the system revealed Eddie Barham as a journalist of eclectic interests. Other computer files were given over to the copy for old news stories and reference material, some of it dating back years and covering a huge range of topics. Even during the last few months he'd been researching variously the National Front, GM foods and something called Foetal Valproate Syndrome. Mariner didn't even pause to speculate on what that might be. It sounded vaguely medical but a check on the date revealed that it had come to Eddie's attention only after the appointment with Lloyd, so was unlikely to be related. It was impossible to pick out any single project that may have contributed to his death, unless size was the criterion.

By far the largest folder was one dedicated to Frank Crosby. According to the machine the file had last been modified four years ago, but that wouldn't have prevented Eddie Barham from using it for reference or from putting fresh material on his home computer. Out of curiosity, Mariner glanced through some of the notes, which began with records of interviews with street kids. The little Mariner saw made uncomfortable reading.

'How's it going?' Darren's sudden appearance startled Mariner into minimising the file, but not before noting the occurrence of DI Doug Lowry's name, which he made a mental note of. 'Fine,' he said. 'Though there are a couple of things you can help me with.'

'Sure.' Darren pulled up a chair.

'There are some gaps in Eddie's diary, I noticed. Would these be the sort of occasions where Eddie was pursuing his own lines?'

'They might be.' Darren dug into a khaki rucksack, one of the army surplus store's best, and produced a dog-eared diary. 'What have you got?'

Mariner flicked back through Eddie's notebook. '12 January, p.m.,' he said

Darren looked it up. 'That afternoon we had a union meeting.'

'And 14 November. This appointment. He's got a telephone number that belongs to a compensation lawyer. Any idea what that would have been about?'

Darren thought for a couple of minutes, swiping idly through the diary. He stopped at one particular page. 'The only story I can think of was this couple we went to see who were suing the health authority. They'd already got four kids and they weren't supposed to have any more, the woman had been sterilised, but then she got pregnant again. '

'Do you remember the name of this couple?'

Darren thought for a minute. 'Powell, I think. Yeah, I'm sure of it, Mr and Mrs Powell.'

'Thanks.' Mariner checked and sure enough the name and number of Mr and Mrs Stephen Powell were recorded on one of Eddie's databases. When Darren had gone, Mariner called them up but the line was engaged. The STD code was for an area Mariner would pass through on his way home. Perhaps he'd stop by and talk to them instead.

Finally he rang Knox to see if there had been any progress on tracing those bank accounts.

'Sweet FA,' was the concise response. 'We've narrowed down the location though. It's a bank in Guernsey, we're trying to identify which one. We'll probably need an access warrant to get anywhere near.'

'Well, see that it's—'

'I already have, boss.'

CHAPTER 13

Back home Anna made coffee and took out the list of residential accommodation that Dr Payne had given her. At first glance there seemed to be half a dozen possibilities, all within a radius of about twenty miles. She chose the most attractive sounding one, middle-distance, and picked up the phone.

A woman answered her call almost immediately. 'Hello, the Limes.'

It was a jolly voice, and Anna tried to reciprocate. 'Hello, I'm looking for residential care for my brother,' she began.

'I see. Is he an older gentleman?' asked the woman.

The question threw Anna. 'No, he's twenty-nine, but he's—'

'I'm sorry,' the woman cut in. 'This is a retirement home.' Brilliant. She terminated the call. The next was more promising. It was, as Anna established straight away, a home for adults with learning disabilities of all ages, but there was a hitch.

'We don't have any vacancies at present,' a woman with an equally cheery voice told her. But there was hope.

'We operate a waiting list and you're welcome to come and have a look. How about next Monday? Around two o'clock?' It was a start.

'I'll do that. Thank you.' Leaving her name, Anna replaced the phone, punching the air with a triumphant, 'Yes!' Once she was there she might be able to persuade them to take Jamie anyway, especially as she could pay. She could be very persuasive.

At the thought of Jamie being taken care of by someone else again, her depression lifted, slightly. Their relationship could be restored to a safe distance and her life returned to normal. Anna felt a sudden ache for Jonathan, the touch of him, the smell of him. She was learning something from Jamie. Celibacy didn't suit her.

To avoid being late in fetching Jamie from the centre she'd set her alarm, but halfway there, realised she hadn't done any shopping. They'd have to do it on the way home, she decided, dismissing nagging memories of Jamie as a boy, throwing himself on shop floors and screaming if he couldn't have or do what he wanted.

Fortunately Francine had given her an envelope of photographs, duplicates of the ones Eddie had been using at home, so that consistency could be maintained between home and the day centre. As Francine had suggested, she prepared the ground first. 'Going shopping,' she said, thrusting a snapshot of Sainsbury's in front of Jamie. 'We'll get you some Hula Hoops,' even though her cupboard at home was bursting with them. It was unashamed bribery.

Jamie didn't care. 'Loops,' he echoed, contentedly.

To begin with, the expedition went reasonably smoothly, if painfully slowly, and Jamie for his part appeared to enjoy it. Being one of the busiest times of the week, the store was crowded. But after an initial wariness, Jamie developed a profound interest in the dates and serial numbers written on packets and tins, in fact, so much so, that he wanted to stand and examine each item he picked up for several minutes.

Anna reminded herself to be patient, especially when Jamie selected things that caught his attention, sniffing, shaking and squeezing them, before absently dropping them on the floor. Anna simply replaced them. No problem. They spent a good five minutes at the display of 'pay as you go' mobile phones while Jamie recited the brand names one after the other, touching the appropriate box as he spoke, until Anna could move him on. They were awarded some funny looks; that was all.

Along the way Anna grabbed what she needed as quickly as she could. Decisions that in other circumstances she would have taken some time over, were made in an instant. For once she didn't care whether the chicken was free-range or battery farmed, the coffee decaffeinated or packed with stimulants, she just hurled it in the trolley and kept on moving, dragging Jamie along behind her. They'd made it to the last aisle, frozen vegetables, the end in sight, when Anna spotted a new and exotic stir-fry mix. Jonathan was passionate about Thai food — well, that and other things — and right now she could do with topping up the brownie points. She stopped to study it for a few minutes. It was expensive. Should she get it?

A child's shrill voice pierced her consciousness. 'Mummy, what's the man doing?' and something made her look up. For a few seconds she couldn't see Jamie and began to panic that he had run off. Then she caught sight of his rear end, he was leaning so far into one of the vast chest freezers that he was almost in it.

'Jamie, what are you—?' Anna walked over to see what was so compelling and froze with horror. With consummate skill, Jamie was systematically prising the lids from the cartons of chocolate ice cream, before plunging his hands into the soft, icy mass and scooping out handfuls to shovel into his mouth.

'Jamie!' Anna dragged him out of the freezer. He had chocolate ice cream up to his elbows and his face was Coco the clown on a very bad day.

'Ice 'ream,' he said, beaming at Anna, as a blob of melted chocolate dripped off his chin and onto his sweater.

'I'll give you bloody ice cream!' hissed Anna. 'You can't just eat it. We have to pay for it!' Holding him back, at arm's length, she ran a quick visual inventory. Shit. He'd despoiled at least five cartons that Anna could see. Fortunately there was now no one else nearby, and for several seconds Anna was tempted to replace the lids on the tubs and bury them. But her conscience got the better of her, so abandoning the rest of the shopping she stacked the cartons one on top of the other and headed for the checkout, propelling Jamie along ahead of her.

'Somebody couldn't wait then,' commented the checkout girl helpfully, giving Anna a wary look. 'Did you want school computer vouchers with these?'

Anna gave her an icy glare, fumbling for cash with one hand while using the other to fend off Jamie's sticky hands. Ignoring the fascinated stares of other shoppers, she re-stacked the ice cream and marched out of the supermarket.

In the car park she strapped Jamie into the car before gingerly loading the rapidly thawing ice cream into her boot, noting the interesting stains that were being added to the upholstery. Jamie, sensing the atmosphere perhaps, was uncharacteristically quiet and subdued.

* * *

Rarely had Anna been so relieved to retreat to the safety of her own home. Hurrying inside, she began stuffing what she could of the ice cream into the freezer. The buzz of the intercom startled her, and Anna half expected to find the supermarket manager at her door with a policeman, accusing them of product abuse. But it wasn't.

It was Jonathan, smiling and stomach-churningly handsome. Glancing at Anna's chocolate-covered hands he grinned, lasciviously. 'This looks like fun. Can anyone join in?'

'Don't,' said Anna. 'I'm not in the mood.' When she told him what had happened, the story only seemed to amuse Jonathan even further and eventually Anna was able to see the funny side too.

'Except that I had to leave a trolley full of shopping at the supermarket.' She smiled sweetly. 'Would you do me a favour and just sit with him for half an hour, while I go and get it? It won't take long.'

'What, now?'

'I'll make it worth your while.' Anna ran a hand down his shirt front and lower. Then she grabbed her keys and hurried out of the door before he had the chance to object. The full trolley was still where Anna had left it, and by now the queues had diminished, so she was back well within the half hour.

As she unpacked in the kitchen, Jonathan crept up behind her and slipped his hands around her waist and up over her breasts. 'Now Dicky Stiff wants his reward,' he said, pressing himself against her.

Through in the lounge Anna could just see the top of Jamie's head as he sat, intent on the TV screen. 'I'm not sure about this,' she said, uncertainly.

'Come on,' Jonathan was persuasive. 'He's not a baby. You don't have to watch over him all the time, do you? We can go to your bedroom. He needn't know what we're up to.' He turned her towards him and his lips touched hers.

Anna moved her head away. 'I need a glass of wine first.'

The shopping stowed, Jonathan poured her a glass of Merlot and brought it to where she sat near to Jamie. Leaning over the back of the sofa, Jonathan began to massage her shoulders. It felt wonderful. Then he leaned down and murmured in her ear: 'Why don't we continue this in the bedroom?' And taking her hand, he practically dragged her along the hall.

Closing the door behind them, Jonathan's arms went around her, his mouth on hers, hungrily seeking her out. Anna could feel his excitement, but for some reason, she was unable to reciprocate. Instead she felt somehow uncomfortable, as though she was setting some kind of double standard. She worried that Jamie might walk in on them. What would he make of it?

Jonathan hardly seemed to notice. 'God, I've been dying for this,' he breathed, but Anna pushed him away and broke free. 'What?'

Anna didn't really know what, and stood for a moment, helplessly, looking at him. 'It's very quiet in there,' she blurted out.

'What do you expect? He's watching telly.'

'If he is still watching. When he gets bored he gets up to all sorts. I think I'll just go and check, I won't be a minute.'

'Okay,' Jonathan was humouring her.

Creeping back along the hallway, Anna peered into the lounge. Jamie was exactly where they'd left him, three feet from the TV, his eyes fixed on the screen. 'He's fine,' she told Jonathan on her return.

'Of course he is.'

So why couldn't she relax? Jonathan reached for her, trying a different, gentler tack. Slowly unbuttoning her shirt, he slipped it down from her shoulders. There was a crash from the lounge.

'What was that?' Anna pulled the blouse back on.

With Jonathan's frustrated groan ringing in her ears, Anna went back out to the lounge. Jamie had pulled the pile of magazines onto the floor and was sprawled out and happily occupied flicking through their pages. She perched on the edge of the sofa watching him for a moment, not wanting to return to the bedroom, but not really knowing why. She glanced up to see Jonathan come in, buttoning his shirt.

'What are you doing?' she asked.

His eyes gleamed with barely repressed anger. 'What does it look like? I'm obviously wasting my time here.'

'I'm sorry. I just can't relax. He could walk in on us at any time. Look, I know it's difficult, but you don't have to go. Couldn't we just watch TV, talk for a while?'

Jonathan stopped dressing and stared at her. 'Have you any idea how hard it was for me to get away tonight? You honestly believe that I'd want to spend all night in front of the TV? And while we're at it, if I wanted to childmind, I could do that at home, with my own kids.'

'He's not a—' Anna began, but was halted by the image that for months had lain dormant on the edge of her consciousness, of Jonathan's wife, Gillian, at home managing the constant demands of three small children, while her husband was out indulging his own selfish pleasures, egged on by Anna. Her desire to argue evaporated. As Jonathan pulled on his jacket, Anna trailed behind him to the door, stepping over Jamie, who remained blissfully oblivious.

As an afterthought Jonathan turned back to Anna. 'There was something else,' he told her. 'The panic is off about Milan.'

'Oh. Have they cancelled?' asked Anna, stupidly.

'No, I'm sending Melanie in your place.'

'What do you mean? There's no need. I'll have something fixed up for Jamie by then!'

But Jonathan was adamant. 'I can't rely on you at present, Anna. When things have settled down, I'll give you a call.'

Anna made a flash decision. 'No, please don't bother.'

'All right, if that's the way you want it,' Jonathan regarded her evenly for a moment.

'It is.'

'I'll see you at the office then, when you're ready to come back. Goodbye, Anna.'

Anna closed the door on him and leaned her forehead against it. 'Thank you so much for your support,' she murmured.

As she walked back into the living room, Jamie jumped up and took her hand, pulling her towards the kitchen. 'Want a drink,' he said.

'Don't you ever say please?' Anna snapped back at him, the hurt, frustration and confusion of the evening spilling over.

'Please,' Jamie echoed, cheerfully. Despite herself, Anna smiled and complied. The packet of photographs Francine had given her was on the kitchen table. If they were to be of any proper use, she'd need to sort through them and see what there was. She tipped out the contents and shuffled through the pile: Jamie at the day centre, Jamie in the garden. Jamie with a woman Anna had never seen before. She stared at the picture. She was a pretty woman, with long chestnut hair and dark eyes. Anna remembered Mariner's description of the woman he saw with Eddie. Was this Sally-Ann? On impulse, Anna showed it to Jamie. 'Jamie look,' she said. 'Sally? Sally-Ann?'

But Jamie frowned as he reached out to touch it. 'Kay,' he said. 'Kay no cry.'

'She's not crying Jamie,' Anna said. 'She's happy, she's smiling.'

'Kay,' Jamie insisted. 'Kay no cry.'

CHAPTER 14

Mr and Mrs Stephen Powell lived on the Bournville Village Trust, the model estate created by George Cadbury in 1885 to accommodate the employees of his newly built chocolate factory. Of varying shapes and sizes to meet the needs of workers at different levels of income, the houses carried a distinctive collective style of orange brick and Georgian-style or leaded windows. Along with the narrow winding streets fronted by tidy, pocket-handkerchief gardens, the impression was of a child's toy village, perfect in every detail. As Mariner climbed out of his car the image was completed by the sound of the distant melodic chimes of the Carillion as it struck the quarter hour.

The Powells' home was semi-detached and set back behind an expansive green, where in the gathering dusk the 'No ball games' sign was being used as a goal post by a group of noisy young boys. Mariner wasn't really sure what he was looking for or whether the Powells' story was likely to be of any importance, but he was curious about why Eddie Barham would have contacted a top-notch compensation lawyer, and this had seemed the only remotely viable possibility.

Steve Powell answered the door and immediately Mariner was aware of the family Darren had described — a horde of boisterous children rushing past their dad and up the stairs, shouting and yelling.

'Detective Inspector Mariner,' Mariner raised his voice above the racket and held out his warrant card. 'This is nothing to be alarmed about Mr Powell, just a routine enquiry. Would it be convenient to talk to you for a few minutes?'

'Sure, if you can stand the chaos, come in.' Closing the door, Powell led him through to the quiet oasis of a lounge where a young woman sat bottle feeding a tiny infant. 'This is my wife, Ceryn, and our daughter Isobel.'

Sitting down as invited, Mariner found himself mesmerised by the scene: the baby's delicate hands clasping the bottle, huge dark eyes wide and unblinking, gazing up at her mother as she suckled. With some effort he turned his attention back to Steve Powell and briefly explained the purpose of his visit. When he got to the part about following up Eddie Barham's death, both Ceryn and Stephen were shocked, but then with five young and demanding children in the house (Mariner could hear the continued thudding of feet running around upstairs), the opportunities for keeping up with local news events must be limited.

'That's terrible. He was such a nice man,' Ceryn said.

'We contacted him back in September of last year,' Stephen Powell told Mariner. 'At the time, Ceryn was about seven-and-a-half months into the pregnancy. We were tearing our hair out. We didn't know how on earth we were going to cope with another child. I work up at Longbridge, where the threat of redundancy never seems far away. We sought legal advice on taking action against the health authority and a friend suggested that the publicity would bring some additional pressure to bear. That was why we phoned the newspaper.'

'And Eddie Barham came to talk to you.'

'He brought a photographer too,' said Powell. 'But after some discussion we decided that it would be more effective to run the piece after the baby was born, when we were due to start proceedings. So we waited, and then Isobel came along and we changed our minds.'

'About the publicity?'

'About suing. We dropped the action. We rang the paper to tell Eddie.'

'When was this?'

'The beginning of December, shortly after Isobel was born.' It would have been only weeks after Eddie's meeting with Lloyd.

'And what was his reaction?'

'He was surprised. He said he thought we had a very strong case, and obviously he recognised it as a good story. But we'd already made up our minds that we couldn't go through with it. Touch wood, we're not badly off and we had a beautiful, healthy baby. We felt that to try to blame someone for Isobel's birth would be an act of betrayal. I mean, look at her,' Steve Powell relieved his wife of the now replete infant, who blinked uncertainly towards Mariner. 'How could anyone not want one of these?'

Mariner did look, and for some inexplicable reason, he found a lump rising in his throat.

'Have you got children, Inspector?' Ceryn Powell asked, but fortunately Mariner was saved from making a reply by a thud and a loud wail from upstairs. Never a comfortable question, right now Mariner would have been hard-pressed to answer truthfully. Ceryn hurried from the room to attend the incident and as Steve Powell was engaged with his youngest child, Mariner saw himself out.

Driving away from the house, Mariner couldn't help imagining what it might have been like to hold that tiny infant in his arms, while Steve Powell's words rang inside his head: *How could anyone not want one of these?* How indeed? Mariner needed a drink. Along with the seven-and-a-half thousand dwellings on the Bournville Estate were the churches, schools and shops required to serve the residents' needs. Unfortunately though, thanks to the Cadburys' Quaker roots, the one glaring deficiency was a decent pub, indeed any kind of pub, so Mariner was forced to return to the Boatman.

Over his pint of Boddington's, he considered where this case was going. The Powell family appeared now to be a complete red herring. No money had apparently changed hands, and in any case, the Powells would have been paid for their story, not the other way round. And Mariner couldn't quite imagine them keeping their funds stashed away in some offshore account.

All they were left with then was a partial database lifted from Eddie Barham's corrupted hard drive, and a fragile link with Frank Crosby. Not much to offer at the inquest. He could do with showing that database to Anna Barham. It was possible that she might have an inkling of what it was all about, though somehow he doubted it, given the tenuous nature of her relationship with her brother. They should go back to the original clues, too, namely the page of small ads. So far those had yielded nothing, but Mariner couldn't shift the feeling that there might be something there.

After a couple of pints he wandered home. Despite the Focus parked outside, the house was unexpectedly dark and quiet, meaning that Knox was either on a night out, or had turned in early. Switching on the living room light, the mystery was solved by a pair of pink patent leather trainers neatly aligned with Tony Knox's size eleven Doc Martens. This hadn't been part of the deal, and Mariner's immediate thought was that he wished he'd discussed the point. Too much to hope for that it could be Mrs Knox, come round for a reconciliation.

Again Mariner pondered on the stupidity of Knox's behaviour. 'You've got it made,' he'd told Mariner, failing to realise that actually he was the one with all the advantages of a loving wife and family. A grandkid.

Something that Mariner had started wondering lately if he would ever achieve.

Until Greta had come along he'd been content to be alone. It had always been his natural state. Most of his relationships tended towards the purely functional and he'd only ever really cultivated friendships because somehow it seemed to be an expectation: of his mother, his teachers or his girlfriends. Left to his own devices he'd always preferred to be entirely self-reliant. Now though, he'd reached that age where some kind of settled family life had begun to look vaguely appealing. The irony of the situation wasn't lost on him. Just at the time when he felt ready for a long-term relationship, the possibility had begun to recede rapidly into the distance. The reasons for this he tried not to dwell on too much, but someone, it seemed, was determined that he would.

He'd only been in bed ten minutes when he suddenly became aware of low, rhythmic groans emanating from the room above his. They got louder. If this was a reconciliation, then it was a pretty comprehensive one. He tried to ignore the noises and go to sleep, but he was startled and ashamed by how much the undulating, animal-like sounds aroused him. And when, eventually, they built to a screaming crescendo, his own climax followed soon afterwards, leaving him feeling self-disgusted, like some dirty little voyeur, rubbing salt into an increasingly festering wound.

* * *

For Anna Barham, the days that followed were marked out by the rituals of sudden death. The nature of Eddie's demise necessitated an inquest, which, in the event, was blissfully short. Mariner had already talked her through the process and it went pretty well as he'd predicted. Once the pathologist had presented his findings — cause of death a lethal injection of pure-grade diamorphine — the request for an adjournment was duly granted for fourteen days pending police enquiries. Meanwhile, permission was given to release Eddie's body to be laid to rest, allowing Anna to make the final arrangements.

The Friday of his funeral was bitterly cold, with a biting wind and a blanket of thick grey cloud that pressed claustrophobically down over Lodge Hill Crematorium. It seemed not so very long ago that Anna and Eddie had come to this very place, on a crisp, sunny afternoon, to say the last goodbye to their parents. For that brief window in time, united in grief, they had almost been like a normal brother and sister, although even then, Anna seemed to remember, they'd found time to argue about Jamie.

Like then, today was a day of ghosts and strangers, and Anna found herself surrounded by a group of unknowns, who paradoxically all seemed to know her. It was like being on the wrong side of a two-way mirror and one of the rare circumstances when she wished she wasn't on her own. Despite what had happened last night, it would have been comforting to have Jonathan beside her to soak up some of the attention from all those sympathetic eyes. Even DI Mariner would have been a welcome presence. He'd rushed off after the inquest and she hadn't yet had the opportunity to pass on the photograph she'd found. She would have quite liked just to talk to him, but she wasn't sure why, unless it was simply that right now they shared a common cause.

Auntie Helen managed to come along; looking ill and making Anna feel guilty about that phone call. There were some remaining distant relatives Anna barely recognised, who presumably had seen the newspaper story, along with a clutch of younger people who Anna took to be Eddie's former work colleagues. Glancing behind her once again, Anna was relieved to eventually catch sight of Becky and Mark slipping into the back of the chapel of rest at the last minute and acknowledged with a smile Becky's reassuring wave.

She'd kept the ceremony brief and simple, the eulogy read by the same minister who had officiated at her parents' cremation. Anna had furnished him with what few details she could about Eddie, but had no desire to stand up herself and spout hypocritically. Honesty, she felt, was the least she could give him in death. Eddie's dedication to caring for Jamie formed the main theme and Anna was glad. It was only during the last few days that she had got a real measure of that devotion. Afterwards, Anna led the mourners back out into the foyer past the floral tributes.

As Becky and Mark caught her up, Becky gave her a much-needed hug. 'How are you doing?'

'I'm coping,' Anna took Mark's outstretched hand.

'I'm really sorry, Anna,' he said.

'Yes.'

'I've brought you this.' Reaching into his pocket, Mark took out a slip of paper. 'Becky said you were looking for a place for Jamie? This one is new, and it's a bit out of town, but it's got an excellent reputation.'

Anna took the paper from him. She didn't recognise the address from Dr Payne's list, so it presented another option. 'Thanks, Mark.'

'We've got to go,' Becky was apologetic. 'Jonathan has allowed me two hours exactly.'

'That's very generous of him,' Anna struggled to keep the sarcasm from her voice.

'I didn't know if he might have come himself,' Becky went on. 'Moral support and all that.'

'No,' said Anna, unable to keep the bitterness from her voice. 'Far too public.' Becky gave her an odd look, but Anna left it at that. Her friend would find out soon enough, and now was hardly the time.

'Will you be all right?' Becky asked.

'I'll be fine.'

'Well, keep in touch,' Mark said. 'And if there's anything else we can do—'

How about babysitting my twenty-nine-year-old brother once a week? Anna was tempted to say, but she just smiled thanks and retained the thought.

As Becky and Mark moved away, a youth, tall and loose-limbed with a shaven head and facial features dotted with hoops and studs, broke away from the group and loped across to Anna. 'Darren,' he said, simply. 'I worked with Eddie at the paper.'

'Thank you for coming, Darren,' Anna said automatically, noting that Eddie's co-workers looked considerably more interesting than her own.

'No problem. Eddie was a good guy, I'm really going to miss him.'

'We all will,' said Anna, with feeling. There seemed little more to add until she suddenly recognised an opportunity. 'Darren, you may be able to help me,' she said. 'You may know that Eddie and I weren't particularly close, and I've never met his girlfriend. Is she here today?'

But Darren just looked confused. 'I told that copper; I didn't know Eddie had a girlfriend. He never talked about one.'

Rifling quickly through her bag, Anna took out the photo of Jamie and the unknown woman. 'I thought this must be her. Do you know who this might be?'

Darren pulled a face. 'I've never seen her before. I'd remember a face like that, I'm sure of it. Pretty girl.'

'Oh, well, thanks anyway.'

'Sure, and hey, I'm really sorry.' He dipped his head before moving back to the group.

'Thanks,' said Anna.

Darren's place was immediately taken by an older woman, her greying hair set off by an elegant claret-coloured tailored suit. She smiled warmly. 'Hello, Anna. I'm so sorry about Eddie.' She accepted Anna's blank expression with a smile. 'You won't remember me. I'm Liz Trueman,' she obliged. 'Richard and I were friends of your parents. It was a long time ago, I know, but you visited us once or twice when you were all children.'

'Oh, yes, of course.' Thankfully her words began to strike a familiar note with Anna. Mum and Dad had got to know the Truemans along with several other families when Jamie was young. The Truemans had subsequently moved to a bigger house in Sutton Coldfield, to the north of the city, that Anna vaguely remembered visiting. Michael had the autistic diagnosis, like Jamie, but any similarity ended there. Michael had seemed to make so much more progress and had lots of language, although he didn't always know how to use it properly. Anna's overriding memory of Michael was having him follow her around their garden all day because he'd taken a liking to her then waist-length hair. 'How is Michael?' she asked now, out of politeness more than anything.

Another smile. 'He's doing really well. Especially since he's been on his new medication. He was on the same one for years, but it started to have a very odd effect on him. It was very worrying. But what he's taking now is brand new and so much better. He's got his own flat now, with a lot of support from his dad and me of course, but he holds down a part-time job, so he helps to pay for that himself.'

'That's great,' said Anna, struck by the huge contrast. Hard to imagine Jamie living in his own place, however much support he was given.

'He's still Michael though,' Liz added, tempering her enthusiasm as if she too had recognised the discrepancy. 'And that will never change.' She put a hand on Anna's arm. 'I do know how hard it can be. And if you and Jamie ever want a day out sometime, change of scenery, you know where we are.'

'Thank you.' It wasn't until later that Anna wondered how it was that Liz had even known about Eddie's death. To the best of her knowledge they hadn't been in touch for years. But then, they did get newspapers in Sutton.

Before Anna had time to work it out, she was confronted with yet another sympathetic smile, but this time from Dr Payne. Anna relaxed, pleased to see a familiar face.

'How are you bearing up?' he asked.

'I'm managing,' Anna said.

'Good. And what about Jamie?'

'He seems to be okay. Life just goes on for him, doesn't it?'

'I suppose so. You haven't noticed any ill effects?' he asked. 'Nothing bothering him?'

'Nothing obvious, no. Give him a packet of Hula Hoops and he's as happy as a sand-boy.'

'Good, and the staff at the day centre haven't reported anything? He's still at Greenwood, isn't he?'

'Yes, he seems to really like it there. I don't know how I'd manage without it.'

'Well, if there is anything I can do, you know where I am.'

'Yes, thank you.'

The undertaker was hovering tactfully nearby. 'When you're ready, Miss Barham,' he intervened.

'I must let you go. Your car is waiting.' Dr Payne grasped her hand and squeezed it hard. 'I really am so sorry, Anna.' As always, he was taking it so personally.

And when Anna looked back from the car window, it was Dr Payne who caught her eye again, deep in conversation with one of the many people at the funeral she didn't know.

CHAPTER 15

Anna was so relieved to get the funeral over with, that collecting Jamie was almost a pleasure. 'I'm worn out, Jamie,' she told him, getting into the car. 'Let's go to McDonald's.'

'McDonald's. Big Mac. Big Mac,' Jamie grinned. At this time on a Friday afternoon, the car park at the fast-food restaurant was almost full. Anna squeezed the car into a far corner and they walked across the car park, Jamie trailing his customary five yards behind. A party of about twenty effervescent children was advancing from the opposite direction.

'Come on, Jamie, keep up,' Anna urged. Although they pre-empted the children, they still had to join a long queue, but for once Jamie stayed calm. Tucking a hand into the crook of Anna's arm, he waited patiently, with a half-smile on his face. It was good to see him happy and Anna could understand why Eddie had been a regular customer here. Her focus shifted from Jamie's face to beyond the window, where she noticed a man sitting in a silver-grey Mercedes, parked in the spaces reserved for customers to 'eat out.' She noticed him mainly due to an odd sensation that she'd seen him before. But she couldn't think where . . . The queue shuffled forward.

'Can I help you?' asked the acne-studded teenager behind the counter, revealing a set of metal-plated teeth, and by the time he was limply encouraging them to 'Have a nice day,' the identity of the man still eluded Anna and the car had gone. She'd probably been mistaken anyway; chronic fatigue could play tricks like that.

* * *

Back home, Anna was uncorking a much-needed bottle of Pinot Noir when the phone rang. It was DI Mariner. His voice was a welcome sound, but since they'd returned from McDonald's Jamie had been prowling restlessly, making talking difficult. Cordless phone in hand, Anna was following him from room to room, trying hard to concentrate on the conversation.

'I'm sorry I couldn't make it today,' Mariner was saying. 'Something came up.'

'A policeman's lot, eh?' quipped Anna, finding herself strangely comforted by his voice. 'I'd half expected to see you lurking in the background, waiting for the murderer to give himself away.' That glass of wine she'd drunk was going straight to her head.

'Another media myth,' Mariner assured her. 'How did it go?'

'It was a good turn-out. At least fifty people I'd never seen before.'

'Well, it's over now. You can move on.'

Said with such quiet authority, even the cliché was a consolation. But Mariner hadn't called just to ask about the funeral. 'There's something I need you to see,' he said. 'We've come up with the remains of some documents on Eddie's computer. Most of them look like the drafts of some minor stories he was working on, but there is one thing that we're not sure about. It may be significant, so

I'd like you to see it as soon as possible. Would you be able to call in at the station sometime tomorrow?'

'Yes, that should be all right.' Anna thought of the photograph. 'Actually, I've turned up something that might interest you, too.' A sudden impulse overcame her. 'You could always come here,' she said. She hadn't intended to be so blatant, but the wine she'd drunk was taking effect, and the truth of it was, she was desperate for some normal adult company, even a policeman's.

Perhaps she'd overdone it, though. There was silence at the other end of the phone; the sound of a man weighing up his chances, or working out how to politely refuse? 'Okay, that would be helpful,' Mariner said at last, coolly professional. 'The sooner we can do this the better. I could finish up here and then call round.' He was going to play. 'What time would suit you?'

'Any time you like.' Anna watched Jamie as he carefully selected his place and lay down on the floor. 'We're not going anywhere.' Replacing the receiver, Anna had a sudden inexplicable urge to tidy the house, before changing into jeans and a loose shirt, in a colour that she knew suited her. It was more comfortable. She was checking her hair in the mirror when the intercom crackled noisily and she buzzed down to let Mariner in.

The detective looked as if he'd had a hard day at the office, but then maybe he had. His grey suit was creased, his tie was loosened at the collar and there was the dark shadow of a beard around his jaw line. He wasn't going to win any 'best dressed man' awards tonight, but to Anna he looked pretty good. Now that the bruising around his nose was subsiding a bit, he wasn't a bad-looking bloke underneath. Reining in her wayward thoughts, she took Mariner into the lounge, where his arrival was completely ignored until he fished in his jacket pocket and brought out a bright red foil packet.

'Loops!' Jamie jumped up and made a grab for it.

'Jamie, say please,' Anna prompted automatically. Jamie muttered something unintelligible in response, simultaneously snatching the pack from Mariner's hand.

'You don't have to bribe him to like you,' she said.

'Who said it was bribery?'

Anna saw Mariner's gaze take in the bottle on the kitchen counter, a third already gone. 'It's been a long day,' she said, only partly in self-justification. 'Would you like a glass?'

Mariner glanced at his watch and a million questions ran through Anna's head, all of them far too personal to voice. At last he nodded. 'That would be great, thanks.'

They retreated to the kitchen, mainly to escape from Carol Vorderman, and while Anna poured the wine, Mariner took off his jacket and slung it over the back of a chair. Anna, pulled up a chair to sit opposite him. 'Right,' she said, impishly, encouraged by the wine she'd already consumed. 'I'll show you mine, if you show me yours.'

Mariner smiled. 'I'm afraid you might find mine a bit of a disappointment,' he said, holding her gaze. Was he flirting with her? Momentarily, perhaps, but that was all. Almost immediately he was back to business as he reached into the inside pocket of his jacket and took out a single sheet of folded paper. 'The most interesting thing we found on Eddie's home computer was a powerful virus. Someone made a deliberate attempt to destroy all his files.'

'His—?' Anna couldn't bring herself to say the word 'killer.'

'Possibly, or it may have been Eddie himself, if he knew he was under threat. Whoever it was did an effective job. The only thing of any interest we managed to rescue was this.' He was right. It wasn't much. The A4 sheet that he spread out on the table was a database of some kind, rows and columns divided by gridlines. The left-hand column contained only letters, and the row next to it numbers, but beyond that, halfway across the page, the data began to be replaced by rows and rows of meaningless hieroglyphics, where the virus had begun to corrupt this document too. Anna had witnessed a similar effect when a bug had entered the system at work.

'As you can see,' Mariner said. 'We're not left with much, even on this. But this is our starting point.' He traced a long, pale finger down the left-hand side of the page. His nails were clean and neatly trimmed, Anna noticed. No ring, but that could be a matter of personal choice. He didn't seem like a man who'd go in for any kind of jewellery. She dragged her thoughts back to the task. The column of figures Mariner was showing her appeared to be initial letters, paired with dates. 'Any of them mean anything to you?' he asked.

Anna studied them dutifully, but none of them did, and he didn't seem particularly surprised. 'At the moment we're thinking that they probably relate to the escort agency ads. We've checked these initials against the names Eddie had highlighted in that personal services column and one of them did match up, although as we don't have the date go with it, it's too early to say whether that's just coincidence. They could be the names of the girls working out of those particular agencies. Or it could be that these are places Eddie's already checked up on, and those highlighted in the newspaper are the ones he had yet to add to the list. Without knowing what the other details mean, we can't be sure.'

'But why would he do that?' Anna wanted to know, not entirely comfortable with this line of enquiry, though at least Mariner seemed to have moved away from questioning Eddie's personal life.

He shook his head. 'We're not sure, yet. When I spoke to Ken Moloney, Eddie's boss, he told me that Eddie had done a story on prostitution some time back. He won some awards for it.'

'Yes, it was a sore point. I didn't go to the presentation ceremony.'

'Well, according to Moloney, it was a mission neatly accomplished, except that one of the key players, Frank Crosby, got away with it. We're considering the possibility that Eddie had developed a renewed interest, possibly tied in with drugs this time, too. Drugs and prostitution are not exactly mutually exclusive these days and Darren, who he worked with, gave the impression that Eddie had been working on something of that kind on his own initiative. He did it all the time apparently, going off on his own for hours on end.'

'It sounds like his style. I met Darren today at the funeral.'

'Did he tell you that Eddie had been mugged?'

'No. Do you think that was to do with what he was working on, too?'

'There are some pretty hard guys tied up in that kind of racket and if Eddie had been ruffling the wrong feathers . . .' he left her to draw her own conclusions.

'I asked Darren about possible girlfriends, too. But he's saying the same as everyone else. As far as he knew, Eddie didn't have one.'

'And nobody we've talked to yet has heard of Sally-Ann either. Apparently she's disappeared off the face of the earth. Unless, of course, she never existed in the first place.'

'I don't know,' said Anna. 'I was beginning to think it could just be a name Jamie's picked up from the telly, but then I came across this.' Reaching for the photograph she slid it across the table to him. 'Francine gave it to me. Eddie was using photographs to communicate with Jamie, people and places he might know, to help him to prepare for change. This was among them. I've never seen her before and neither had Darren.'

'I have,' Mariner looked up at her, eyes gleaming. 'This is the woman Eddie was with on the night he died. The brunette. That's brilliant! You've found us a connection!'

Anna flushed with unexpected pleasure. She'd always been a sucker for praise. For one bizarre instant she thought he might be going to kiss her, but he was studying the picture again. 'Yes, it's her all right. And if her name happens to be Sally-Ann, we've hit the jackpot.'

Anna shook her head. 'I don't think so. Watch.' Taking the picture from him, she got up from the table and took the photograph through to where Jamie sat on the floor in front of the TV. 'Jamie, look.' She held out the picture again, for Jamie to see.

He glanced momentarily at it. 'Kay, Kay no cry,' he said before turning his attention back to the screen.

Anna came back to the kitchen. 'Meet Kay,' she said.

'Christ, how many mystery women can a man have?' Mariner wondered aloud, visibly disappointed. 'I'll need to take that to make a copy,' he went on. 'We can show it around, see if anyone else recognises her. Somebody made that emergency call, and presumably it wasn't the invisible woman.'

His sarcasm was drowned out by a clatter from the living room. Mariner and Anna rushed in to find Jamie on the rampage, running the length of the sofa, pulling things from the shelves as he went. His TV programme had ended.

'Jamie, get down! Down! Now!' Anna commanded.

'Jesus.' Mariner looked on with disbelief as Jamie jumped down from the sofa and ran off down the hall, sweeping his arm along a radiator shelf and knocking its contents to the floor.

With a weary sigh of resignation, Anna knelt and began to retrieve them. 'He does this,' she explained. 'One minute he's perfectly settled, the next this sudden burst of intense energy.'

Mariner bent down to help. 'You could do with some space. You haven't got a garden here?'

'Oh there's a garden all right. The only problem is, it's on the roof, with very little to separate it from a two-hundred-foot drop. Jamie wouldn't last five minutes.'

Mariner glanced back at his watch again, and Anna waited for the inevitable 'actually-I-must-be-going' routine, that any of Jamie's more extreme behaviour was guaranteed to prompt in people.

Instead Mariner said, 'Why don't you come and keep me company? I was on my way to the Wall.'

'The Wall?'

'The indoor climbing centre. You could get in as my guests and Jamie can climb as much as he likes there. He'd have to wear a harness of course, and a helmet, but if you think he can handle that we'll give it a go.'

'Game on,' said Anna and somehow she meant more than the climbing.

CHAPTER 16

'Are you sure this is no trouble?'

'None at all. It'll ensure that I actually go. I've had about as much use out of the membership as your average person gets from the gym. Somehow there's always something more important to do.'

'Well, I appreciate it. I had no idea what a comprehensive service the police offered these days,' said Anna.

'Hadn't you heard? It's all about keeping Joe Public happy. Even the felons get a customer satisfaction questionnaire.' Mariner was watching in the rear-view mirror as she strapped Jamie into the back seat of the car beside her. Deep down, he knew that he was pushing the boundaries of professional conduct with this, although if it came to it, he could fully justify his actions. Jamie Barham provided the link with his brother's killer. All Mariner was trying to do was build enough of a relationship with him to get at the truth. Anna Barham's presence was just a necessary but pleasant by-product. Wasn't it? He felt sure Tony Knox would have approved.

The Wall was actually more like a vast cavern lined with layers of towering moulded and riveted panels, lending it the surreal appearance of an old set from *Dr Who*. Once a disused firearms factory, abundant EU regeneration grants had helped to reinvent it as a comprehensive climbing centre with a thriving clientele. Despite being a long-standing member, Mariner continued to be treated with the customary cool suspicion afforded police officers in most social situations. It did mean, however, that there was no argument about Jamie and Anna gaining entry.

Mariner had brought a bag in with him and once inside, left Anna and Jamie to go and get changed. Returning minutes later, wearing khakis and a T-shirt, he felt more relaxed, and sensed Anna Barham looking at him differently too. Jamie had at first seemed overawed by the new surroundings, but as they walked round to the climbing area, he suddenly came to life and was at the nearest wall in a couple of bounds, forcing Mariner and Anna to physically restrain him.

'Wait, Jamie,' Mariner said, firmly. 'Helmet and harness first, then climbing.' Jamie complied, but getting his harness on and ensuring its safety was like trying to keep hold of a wriggling eel. Mariner was worn out before they'd started. The beginner's climbs provided fixed ropes, making the walls simple and safe for anyone to try. But it soon became obvious that for Jamie these were an unnecessary precaution. Quick and unerring, he reached the top of the first wall in a matter of minutes. A small audience gathered to watch as Mariner gradually introduced Jamie to increasingly complex climbs. He had, it seemed, an insatiable appetite, but after an hour Mariner called a halt.

'It's taken me years to achieve this level,' Mariner told Anna. 'I refuse to be completely humiliated by a novice. Let's get a drink. Jamie drink?'

'Drink,' echoed Jamie happily.

'I thought he didn't have any special talents,' Mariner said, bringing over two bottles of beer and orange juice to where Anna sat watching Jamie as he prowled.

'So did I,' said Anna.

'He's a natural. Most of us have to give it some thought. You sure he hasn't climbed before?'

'Apart from at every opportunity around the house? How would I know? One of the things I've learned in the last week is how little I've ever really known about him or Eddie, or for that matter, my parents. And now they're all gone and it's too late.'

'Does that bother you?'

'Well, I never thought I'd hear myself say this, but yes, in a way it does. It's weird, knowing that there's only Jamie and me left. No one else to answer to.'

'Sounds all right to me,' Mariner said, without thinking.

'Oh, yes? Nobody keeping tabs on you?' she asked, cheekily.

'My gaffer mainly,' smiled Mariner, trying to keep it professional.

But she wasn't satisfied with that. 'What about family, brothers and sisters, Mum and Dad?'

'There's just me. I see my mother from time to time. I never knew my dad.'

'Oh, I'm sorry.' She'd misunderstood, as people often did.

'No, I mean, as far as I know he's still out there somewhere. I've just never met him. Don't know who he is.'

'Oh.' Naturally she didn't know what else to say. It was a situation people generally seemed to have difficulty in grasping, which is why Mariner on the whole kept it to himself. In fact, he didn't have a clue why he should be talking about it now. Apart from Greta, he hadn't told anyone in years. But perhaps he felt that Anna deserved something back from him. Through her brother's murder he was uncovering more and more of the intimate details of her life, it only seemed fair to reciprocate on some level. 'My mother's never told me,' he said, in response to her unasked question. 'She doesn't think it matters.'

She'd also made it clear that his father didn't want to know. She'd been fobbing him off, of course. This was back when the consensus was still that children ought not to be troubled with the complexities of adult lives. To his mother's credit, Mariner couldn't ever remember being lied to, she just kept the details vague: his dad was an important and very busy man, so he couldn't live with them in the same way that other dads did. In other words, he was already married. By the time Mariner entered his teens, fantasies about his father's identity ranged from astronauts to movie actors to sports stars, depending on his mood. By the time he was old enough for his questioning to be more probing and direct, his mother had conveniently developed migraines and any talk of his father was guaranteed to induce an attack, long before any answers were forthcoming. Repeatedly he was dismissed with a vague promise that one day, 'when the time was right,' he would know. The few friends he had were those who took him for what he was, and when he began, in his mid-teens, to attract girlfriends, his predicament afforded him an aura of mystery that he used shamelessly to his advantage.

'And what do you think?' Anna Barham jolted him back to the present.

'I think there are times in my life when it's been more important than anything else in the world, and other times, like now,' Mariner shrugged, 'when it seems pretty much irrelevant.'

'It must have been hard, growing up though,' she said. It was a simple observation, no more.

'Difficult for my mother at times,' Mariner agreed, deliberately deflecting any imminent concern she might feel for him. 'She got to be very dependent.'

'On you?'

'I was all she had. She gave up a lot to raise me.' Mainly her itinerant lifestyle. Marching for world peace wasn't so easy with a toddler in tow, so the sisterhood had come to her. 'It got a bit intense sometimes.'

Anna was pensive. 'I'd always thought I had a raw deal, not getting enough attention. I'd never considered the possibility that too much could be worse. What did you do?'

'I stuck it for as long as I could. Then I ran off to join the police force.'

'Very romantic.'

'Yeah, well, this was during the great twentieth-century circus shortage.'

'And you lived happily ever after.'

She was right. He'd made it sound glib. But then, he'd missed out a couple of chapters in the middle. There seemed little point in telling her about the filthy squalor he'd moved into, the near starvation or the months of depression that had followed. It was a bad time in his life, when the boundaries had become blurred and chaotic — dismal days and black, lonely nights when, unable to sleep, he had sought out the open spaces and prowled the dark chasms of the canals that on occasions had looked so very inviting. For a while he teetered on the edge of a slippery slope, until a young detective constable had thrown him a lifeline. Even now, years later, he never failed to appreciate the comfort of clean sheets and clothes and an orderly, disciplined environment.

'Not so straightforward for you then, either,' Anna remarked, bridging the silence that followed.

'It hardly equates with having a disabled sibling,' Mariner said. He looked around him. 'Where is Jamie?'

Jamie, who only minutes ago had been hovering near an adjacent fruit machine, was now nowhere to be seen.

'Oh God,' said Anna. 'He does this all the time.'

A loud 'Hey!' pointed them in the right direction, as they saw a young man snatch back the phone that Jamie had helped himself to from a table. He relinquished it, but only under protest, leaving Anna to make profuse apologies. She and Mariner were still laughing about it going out to the car park. She had a terrific laugh. A little later, Mariner dropped them outside the apartment block.

'Thanks for that,' Anna said. 'Jamie loved it.'

Him and me both, thought Mariner. 'No problem,' he said, lightly.

'So did I,' she added, unexpectedly. 'I mean it's great to have some normal adult company again. And who knows, Jamie might even sleep tonight.'

'Let's hope so.'

She'd sat in the front passenger seat for the return journey and was smiling up at him, a warm, encouraging smile. Mariner breathed deeply, getting the merest hint of her perfume, sweet and heady. All he'd have to do was lean a little closer—

'Consernut please, Carol,' piped up Jamie from the back seat. They laughed again, and the moment, if that's what it was, had passed.

* * *

Mariner thought his timing for getting home would be about right, but his heart sank when, on the approach, he saw that the ground-floor lights were still on. To compound his irritation, he'd decided tonight to drive right up to the service road, to find it blocked not only by Knox's car, but also a scarlet Fiat Panda.

Inside, a touchingly domestic scene greeted him. Knox and his female friend were watching TV together. Or at least they might have been, if the blonde hadn't been draped across Knox's lap treating him to some alternative entertainment. As Mariner walked in they leapt like a pair of teenagers caught in the act, though in fairness, one of them at least appeared to accurately fit the age profile.

'Hi, boss,' Knox said, running a nervous hand over his cropped scalp. 'Erm, this is Jenny.'

'Hello, Jenny,' said Mariner, politely.

Petite and stunningly attractive, Jenny stepped forward and offered Mariner a hand, the same one that only moments before had been groping around inside Tony Knox's police-issue shirt. 'Hi. Tom, isn't it?' she said turning on a beaming white smile that looked used to getting its own way. 'Nice to meet you.'

Mariner nodded but declined the hand.

'I love your house,' she went on, effusively, as if seeking to justify her presence.

'Thanks.' Mariner was non-committal.

In recognition of the sudden awkwardness, she cast a meaningful glance at Knox and nodded towards the stairs. 'I'll go on up then.'

'Sure,' said Knox. 'I'll be there soon.' The two men stood and watched her go. 'Hope you don't mind, boss,' Knox said, sheepishly, when her small, shapely bottom had disappeared from sight.

Mariner gave an indifferent shrug that belied a powerful and irrational urge to punch Knox's lights out. Instead he said, 'How did you two meet?'

Knox squirmed like a guilty schoolboy. 'She's a second-year medical student at the uni. I responded to a burglary at the hall of residence a couple of weeks back.' He left Mariner to fill in the rest.

'I take it she's the complication.'

'You could say that, yes.'

What the fuck are you playing at? Mariner wanted to ask. *You've got a wife, a family, and a grandchild for Christ's sake. How can you throw it all away for a five-minute fling with kid who's probably just turned on by the uniform?* But he didn't say anything. Mariner couldn't begin to understand what Knox's motives might be. And perhaps underneath it all he was just jealous, plain and simple.

'Well, cheers, anyway,' said Knox, clumsily.

Mariner just nodded.

'I'll say goodnight then.' There seemed little else to add.

Tonight, Mariner noted, lying awake below them, their lovemaking lasted a mere seventeen minutes. Short by most standards, but still enough to be a painful reminder of what he was missing.

In a moment of half dream, half rampant fantasy, he imagined asking out Anna Barham, taking her out for dinner or to see a film, and back home afterwards. And then what? Dazzle her with his non-existent conversational skills? Mariner had never had any problem attracting women, but until Greta came along his relationships had rarely strayed beyond the superficial. 'There's less to you than meets the eye,' one former girlfriend had unkindly commented. A psychologist would have had a field day — an only child, bled dry by his mother. What else could you expect?

Over the years he'd come to rely heavily on sex, but now he couldn't even manage that. Drastic action was called for. Ignoring his problem in the hope that it would go away hadn't worked. And he hadn't had the guts to go through with the one-night-stand remedy. What any sensible man would probably do was see the doctor, but he just couldn't face it. Somewhere at the back of his mind was a nagging worry. Didn't a man reach his sexual peak at nineteen or something ridiculous? He was more than twice that age now. What if it didn't get better and he was over the hill?

An ecstatic cry erupted from the room above his, and Mariner shoved his head under the pillow and tried to block it out.

CHAPTER 17

The following cold and blustery morning Mariner was scheduled to appear at the Queen Elizabeth law courts in the city centre to give evidence in a fraud investigation he'd been involved in sixteen months previously. Small and unassuming, Faisal Ibrahim had single-handedly relieved the insurance firm for which he worked of forty thousand pounds over a six-year period. His ingenuity was spectacular. If it weren't for the fact that he'd broken the law, Mariner would have had a sneaking admiration for him. Mariner's contribution to the prosecution case was over by mid-morning and as he was in the vicinity, he took the opportunity to drop in on DI Doug Lowry on the Vice Squad, based at police headquarters at Lloyd House.

It was not a comfortable experience. Amid the overflowing in-trays, out-trays, stacks of files and empty coffee mugs, the only feature absent from Lowry's office was seagulls circling overhead. Mariner found the mess almost unbearable.

'Sit yourself down then,' Lowry insisted cheerfully, leaving Mariner wondering if he was expected to perch on top of the filing cabinet. Instead, he shifted a pile of dubiously stained paperwork from a moulded plastic chair. Lowry's office was windowless, airless and overheated, and already the big man was sweating profusely. Mariner hoped this wouldn't take long. 'You knew Eddie Barham, didn't you?' he kicked off.

'That journalist you lot thought had topped himself? Yes, I did.'

Mariner let the implied criticism go. 'What did you think of him?'

'That he wouldn't be the sort to kill himself, for a start,' said Lowry, smugly.

Mariner refused to rise to the bait. 'What sort was he then?' He pressed on.

'To be honest, I quite liked the guy,' Lowry admitted. He made it sound like a major confession, and understandably felt the need to qualify his remark. 'He was down-to-earth and pretty straight as reporters go. Had an unusual propensity for wanting to get at the truth.'

Mariner tugged at his collar. If he'd been in a cartoon, a jet of steam would have escaped. 'When was the last time you heard from him?'

Lowry shook his head. 'Not for a long time. But I worked pretty closely with him on a story a few years back.'

'Frank Crosby?'

'That's right.'

'Tell me about that.'

'You must know most of it,' he said. 'About four or five years ago. Eddie Barham was researching a story for the *Echo* about kids who were sleeping rough on the streets in Birmingham. It was going to be one of those social conscience pieces, you know. Shocking that this could be happening on our doorstep. He got to know one or two kids who used the drop-in centre on Alcester Street, the one run by the Streetwise charity.'

Mariner nodded, he'd driven past the place frequently. 'They do some good work, I heard.'

Lowry snorted, 'Most of the time, yeah. Anyway, Eddie Barham got to know this one kid in particular, built up a friendship with her. She was bright, articulate, but had a bad start. Stepfather had knocked her about, so she'd run away. She'd ended up sleeping rough and God knows what else.' Lowry told the story as if it was a normal everyday occurrence, which in his line of work, it probably was. *There but for the grace of God*, thought Mariner, grimly.

'Anyway, one evening this kid had arranged to meet Eddie for an interview, but she didn't show. Next time he saw her, the explanation was that the guy running the drop-in had offered her some alternative work, and as it was well paid, she'd gone for that instead. Barham managed to wheedle out of her that this "work" was of the largely horizontal variety, in a seedy hotel with a fifty-year-old Dutch businessman who was visiting our fair city. When pushed, she admitted that it was common practice. Other kids, girls and boys, from the drop-in were regularly "employed" in exactly the same way. Some of them considerably younger than her.' Lowry paused to allow that to sink in.

'Underage?'

'As young as eleven and twelve.'

'Jesus Christ.'

'No, Paul Spink — one of the workers on the project. Seemed he had a direct link with Frank Crosby and was lining his pockets nicely by procuring youngsters for Frank's customers. If the kids turned him down, they were no longer welcome at the drop-in. And most of them weren't in much of a position to refuse.'

'How do you mean?'

'Rumour had it that Frank supplied them, too. If they didn't co-operate, it was cold turkey time, whether they liked it or not.'

'Shit.' Blackmail was never more cruel or effective.

'Over a three-month period Eddie Barham documented all this, with the help of the girl. Then he did the sensible thing and brought it to us,' Lowry went on, 'on the understanding that he got the rights to the story and a couple of good quotes from yours truly. I was impressed. He'd been bloody thorough — had photographs, dates and places. He as good as handed us Frank Crosby and a couple of prominent local councillors on a plate. The rest is history. The news story exposed the drop-in for what it was, the guy working there was successfully prosecuted and his little racket was stopped.' So Eddie Barham wouldn't exactly be flavour of the month.

'What about Crosby?'

'He was the weak spot. Although Eddie Barham wrote a damning indictment of his involvement, Crosby's no mug. He must have known that it was only a question of time and he'd been very good at covering his tracks. We couldn't get anything in the way of hard evidence to charge him on. Apart from a bit of adverse speculative publicity, he got away scot-free. Barham was pretty pissed off about that, as you'd expect.'

'Did anybody else go down for it?'

'A couple of councillors lost their jobs over it, but Spink, the guy working the shelter, was the real scapegoat. He was the only one to get time. About eight years if I remember rightly, for procuring minors.'

'Is he still inside?'

'No idea. He had no previous, so it's possible he could be out on parole by now.'

And maybe thirsting for revenge, thought Mariner. 'What happened to the girl?'

'Vanished. Before she was due to testify, in fact. Not that we were dependent on her. She and Barham had already given us enough. It wouldn't surprise me if Eddie Barham helped her to get away. Protecting his source. I think he felt sorry for her.'

'And Barham hasn't been back to you since?'

'No.'

'Am I right in thinking that Frank Crosby deals in more upmarket stuff, too? Escort agencies, that kind of thing?'

'Frank Crosby deals in any shit that's going. He owns a lot of properties across the city, rents out to all kinds of undesirables.'

'Would he have anything to do with the kind of agencies that might supply their clients with optional extras — chemical optional extras, if you take my meaning.'

'He's probably one of the market leaders, why?'

'Looking at what he left behind, Eddie Barham seems to have developed a recent interest in that area, too.'

'Really?' Mariner waited patiently while cogs turned in Lowry's head. 'You think he was planning to have another pop at Crosby?'

'What do you think?'

'I think Eddie Barham wasn't the sort of bloke to let someone like Frank Crosby get away with it.'

Precisely what Mariner was thinking. 'And if Frank Crosby got wind of it, he's unlikely to sit back and wait for Eddie Barham to come to him,' he completed the equation for both of them. 'One more thing,' he took out the photo of Kay. 'Do you know this girl?' Lowry shook his head.

'Could she have been Eddie Barham's source?'

'I don't know. I never met her. Like I said, Eddie was protective.'

'Do you remember her name? Could it have been Kay?'

Lowry shook his head. 'Eddie gave the girl an assumed name, but I don't think that was it.'

'Have you ever heard of a Sally-Ann?'

Lowry hadn't. But then, who had?

'There's something else,' said Mariner. 'Eddie Barham came into some money a couple of months before he died,' Mariner said. 'It was paid in from an obscure offshore account which we've yet to trace. Does Frank Crosby have any connection with organised crime?'

Lowry was doubtful. 'I wouldn't have thought Frankie moved in such sophisticated circles, but on the other hand—'

'Yes?'

'I wouldn't rule it out either.'

It was what he'd wanted to hear, and Mariner emerged from Lloyd House into blissfully cool, fresh air and an unexpected burst of spring sunshine with adrenaline pumping through his veins again. It felt like progress.

* * *

Back at Granville Lane, Tony Knox was less optimistic. Before Mariner had even had the chance to take off his coat, he appeared in the doorway.

'I must have phoned every bloody massage parlour in the city,' he complained. 'It's a wild fucking goose chase. Nobody's heard of Sally-Ann anyone.'

'That's because we might be looking for Kay instead.'

'What?'

Mariner showed him the photograph and told him about Jamie's reaction. 'You may need to start again.'

'Oh thanks, boss. I had nothing else planned for the next three years.'

'What about those bank accounts?' Mariner asked.

'We've identified the bank. The Charlemagne Investment Trust.'

'Never heard of it.'

'Could be because it's based in Belize. I've faxed through the access warrant and they're "following their security procedures," whatever that means. They're going to get back to us with the account holder.'

'When?'

'I'm not holding my breath,' said Knox. 'Any chance of letting me in on where all this is going, boss?'

'In the right direction,' said Mariner.

'What are we trying to find?'

'The same two things that Eddie Barham was in pursuit of before he died.'

'Money,' said Knox.

'What else?'

'I don't know. You tell me.'

'Frank Crosby.' Knox was as blank as a new cheque. Mariner persevered. 'A little while back, Eddie went to his boss with a new proposal that would happily combine both of those interests; a follow up to the exposé he'd written. You remember I told you about the original case? Well, our Eddie wasn't happy with the way that it ended, and I think he wanted to have another pop at Crosby. He knew, probably through his earlier research, that among other things, Frank Crosby deals in high-class call girls who also illegally supply drugs.'

'So?'

'How about: Eddie decides to find one that he likes — a brunette, say, Sally-Ann maybe, or Kay, who's also run by Crosby. He cultivates a relationship, invites her to his place, then asks the girl to supply the additional extra, too. He captures it all on film. He gets a great story and also the potential to get Crosby put away for running a highly illegal operation.'

'So why didn't it happen?'

'Eddie's boss wouldn't buy it. According to him, Frank Crosby is old news. And why would *Echo* readers be interested in the sordid lives of toms? It lacks the sympathetic "this could be your daughter" element of the earlier piece. But Eddie could have decided to go ahead with it anyway. The only thing he wouldn't get out of it would be the money, unless—'

'He got it by extortion,' said Knox.

'Right.' Mariner felt a surge of elation. If Knox could so easily reach the same conclusion he had, then it must be beginning to make sense.

'Christ. He really did have a death wish if he was trying to blackmail Frank Crosby.'

'Eddie was desperate for the money. Without it he couldn't afford respite for Jamie. This way he could kill two birds with one stone.'

'What do you think went wrong?'

'Crosby found out what was going on and saw his own chance to get Eddie Barham off his back once and for all. He played along with it, let Sally-Ann, or Kay, go with Barham, but then he sent over a couple of minders. They sorted Eddie Barham for good, got rid of any evidence, and rigged it to look like suicide. Sally-Ann disappears. QED. I just hope to God that we don't have another body show up. What do you think?'

'Sounds feasible.' Though Knox didn't sound entirely convinced.

'All we need is some firm proof.'

Knox shot him a look. 'Oh, that all?'

'And first I'd like to find out whether Crosby had an accomplice, someone else with an equally powerful motive.'

'Like who?'

'I was wondering what became of Paul Spink.'

It didn't take long to locate Spink on the PNC. After an initial stint in Winson Green, his 'exemplary behaviour' had earned him a transfer to Hewel Grange category 5 open prison that sits between Birmingham and Bromsgrove.

Mariner put through a call. 'Have you still got a Paul Spink in residence?'

The person at the other end went away, returning a few moments later. 'Not anymore.'

This was looking promising. 'He's out?'

A pause. 'In a manner of speaking. Spink hanged himself in his cell last March.'

'Shit.' Mariner passed on the news to Knox.

He was philosophical. 'Okay, so the joint revenge theory's down, but that still leaves Crosby trying to guard himself against another onslaught from Eddie Barham. And that must be solid enough.'

Mariner agreed. 'We need to go back to the small ads. The brunette holds the key. Let's concentrate our efforts on her.' In between uniformed duties Knox had done a sterling job in phoning round the agencies, but so far had achieved nothing. It was time to try a more direct approach.

* * *

The house looked like any other large rambling Victorian detached along Birmingham's outer circle route. Set into the thick beech hedges that topped the boundary walls was a discreet sign, announcing it as 'The Beeches.' Anna pulled onto the small tarmac driveway and sat for a moment, critically inspecting the exterior of what could potentially become Jamie's new home. From the outside, the building could have been anything, from a refuge to a dentist's surgery. Everything looked well cared for, paintwork was in good condition and the hedges were neatly trimmed. A promising start, and Anna approached the main door high on anticipation. This marked the first step towards reclaiming her life. It was going to be so much better for her and for Jamie.

Going to the main entrance, she pressed the security buzzer next to the door, which crackled into life with a muffled: 'Hello?'

'Anna Barham,' said Anna. 'I have an appointment to look round.'

'One moment.' But it was several minutes before the huge panelled door swung open and Anna was greeted face to face by a smiling middle-aged woman in M & S spring range skirt and sweater, who introduced herself as Linda Kerr, the manager of 'The Beeches.' 'Please do come in.'

Anna stepped into a wide, ornately tiled vestibule and into a very specific atmosphere. The combined smell of cleaning fluids and cooking food was heavily reminiscent of the nursing home in which Anna's grandmother had spent her final years, and the first impression was everything she'd hoped it wouldn't be. And when, thirty minutes later, she emerged from the same door, her enthusiasm had been all but extinguished.

The contrast between the homely exterior of the building and the functional, institutional interior was stark. An occasional picture on the wall and a pile of dog-eared magazines on one of the tables in the communal lounge was the extent of the finer touches. Elsewhere, walls were grubby with finger marks, the carpet stained in places and there were few comforts.

'As you can see,' Linda said, encouragingly. 'There's a lovely outlook from the back of the house.' A large lawn surrounded by shrubs and dotted with benches. 'The residents spend a lot of time out there in the summer months,' Linda was saying. A sudden graphic image appeared in Anna's mind's eye of Jamie, sitting alone on one of the benches gently rocking, as dusk fell around him. She felt a sharp inexplicable pain in her chest.

Upstairs, the small, cubicle bedrooms were simply furnished. A single bed, wardrobe and nightstand in each, some adorned with soft toys and posters of sports or pop stars, while others, by far the majority, were bare and impersonal, like cells. Anna thought of how confining Jamie would find it.

'Do all the . . . er, residents have autism?' Anna asked.

'Oh no. Most of our younger clients have learning disabilities of some kind, but we also have one or two older EMI residents.'

Anna tried vainly to work out what EMI meant, but couldn't get beyond the record label. Later she discovered that it referred to Elderly Mentally Infirm. Hardly Jamie's peer group.

'Normally we try to group according to age and ability,' Linda was saying, 'but with staff shortages, we sometimes have to be a little more . . . flexible.' Her honesty couldn't be faulted.

The tour over, Linda took Anna back to the reception area and the office, so that she could 'take some details.' This appeared to involve completing a long and detailed questionnaire on every aspect of Jamie's life so far. And Anna stumbled on the second question, Jamie's date of birth. She knew it was March, and she knew he was twenty-nine, but was it 15th or 17th? Unable to bring herself to admit her ignorance, she took a guess. If it was wrong, she'd have to change it later and tell them she'd made a mistake.

The written application complete, Anna stood to go, but Linda hadn't finished. There were, she said, some 'more sensitive' issues to discuss. 'Does Jamie have any . . . er, challenging behaviours?' she asked, her attempt at sounding casual not quite succeeding.

Now we're getting to it, Anna thought, *not unless you count public masturbation.* She played ignorant. 'Such as?'

'Violent outbursts?' Linda suggested. 'Smearing?'

For a moment Anna really didn't know what she meant, Jamie wasn't exactly up to spreading malicious gossip about anyone. 'Smearing?' she repeated.

'Faeces,' said Linda calmly.

'No!' Anna was horrified, Linda clearly relieved.

'And how is his sleeping?' she asked, moving quickly on.

'He doesn't,' said Anna, candidly. Even after the climbing Jamie had only lasted four hours the previous night.

'And does he take any medication for that?' asked Linda.

'No.'

'Is it something you have considered?'

'No.' Was it Anna's imagination or did Linda suddenly appear less welcoming?

'And where does Jamie live at present?'

'He's staying with me, but it's really not convenient. If he was to come here, how soon could he move in?'

'Well, as I said on the phone, we do have a waiting list, but clients do "move on," especially the elderly ones, if you know what I mean. We could probably take your brother in about two months.' Two months? That was eight weeks.

'No sooner than that?' Anna asked, in desperation, seeing her life slipping from her grasp again. 'I can pay—'

'It's not a question of money. I'm afraid we just don't have the space,' Linda reiterated. 'But I can contact you as soon as we do. And we'll send someone out to see Jamie, too. We'd like to meet him first.' To check on the challenging behaviour, no doubt. And with a neatly manicured handshake, that was that.

Back in her car, Anna sat for a moment and attempted to visualise Jamie living at The Beeches. But however hard she tried, the image wouldn't present. Instead, unaccountably her eyes filled up and the pain in her chest returned. She couldn't look after Jamie, but nor could she consign him to that kind of place. It had to be somewhere sunny and caring, not a place where there might be staff shortages and imposed 'flexibility.' If she couldn't care for him, she wanted a place where people would understand Jamie's needs and take the time to communicate with him, using his photographs if necessary. She felt suddenly angry to have been put in this impossible position, angry with Eddie and the person or people who killed him. She would look back at Dr Payne's list and the name given to her by Mark. There had to be other, better places and she'd visit them all if necessary. After all, she had at least eight weeks to make up her mind.

CHAPTER 18

There were hundreds of escort agencies and massage parlours in the city and Knox couldn't be expected to handle them all. Questioning of this kind could potentially take weeks, so division of labour had to be fair, without concession to rank. The plan was to start close to Eddie Barham's home and work their way out. By the following afternoon, Mariner was on his third house call, this time seeking Heaven's Gate, although, on the face of it, the main drag through Selly Oak hardly seemed a promising location for the portal to the land of milk and honey.

Once a thriving shopping centre and community strung out along the main arterial road south out of Birmingham towards Bristol, Selly Oak was now mostly neglected, economically shored up by the term-time influx of university students. Boarded up shop fronts, shaggy with torn and blackened fly-sheets, were interspersed with an assortment of fast-food outlets and laundromats, like the last decaying teeth in an old man's mouth. Parking up on a side street, Mariner zigzagged his way through clusters of the nation's most privileged youth dawdling their way to afternoon lectures.

The Heaven's Gate Agency was accessed through a door to the side of one of the suburb's increasing number of Balti houses, where the smell of garlic and coriander hung richly in the air, even at this early hour.

At the top of the perilously narrow staircase, an effort had been made on a small budget to create a welcoming reception area with a faded sofa and a low wood-effect coffee table bearing heavily leafed *Motor* and *Amateur Photographer* magazines, along with the mandatory portfolios of beauties. Further portraits of attractive young women gazed seductively down from the walls, a number of them exotic looking, possibly eastern European.

St Peter's female counterpart was speaking into the phone on the other side of a cheap melamine desk, and was a projection of the pictured models across twenty years. Comfortably into middle age, the auburn hair was from a bottle and the glowing complexion thickly crafted from the latest in the Avon range. She apparently and quite understandably assumed that Mariner was there for an appointment and with a demure smile, gestured him towards the sofa. Thankfully it was clean enough to sit down on.

'I'll book you in with Sonia at ten thirty then?' she said into the receiver, her voice bright and business-like. 'Your usual rendezvous?' she asked. 'Right you are, duck, Sonia will be there. Thank you.' Cradling the phone, she turned a beaming smile on Mariner. 'One of our regular clients,' she confided, stressing the word 'regular.' As Mariner got up and approached the desk, she offered him a hand crowded by heavy, jewel-encrusted rings and topped off by lethal looking scarlet talons.

'Maureen,' she purred. 'Your hostess at Heaven's Gate. You're new to our agency, aren't you?' At close range the perfume was overpowering. Mariner made an attempt at shy and, taking this as encouragement, Maureen looked around at the portraits, 'Do you see anyone you like? We can accommodate all desires.' She gave him another smile.

Mariner smiled back and with impeccable timing, opened out his warrant card for her to see. 'You should be able to accommodate me then, Maureen.'

The effect was instantaneous, as the charm evaporated into the ether. 'The first thing I'll tell you is that I run a legitimate, respectable business,' she retorted. She switched her attention to rearranging the papers on her desk, though there was nothing Mariner had seen that she needed to hide. 'What do you want?'

Mariner took out the accumulated documentation, beginning with the photograph of Eddie Barham. 'I want to know if this man has ever been here.'

A definite, but almost imperceptible flicker of recognition passed over her face and was gone again. 'I couldn't say, I have to protect my clients' confidentiality, you know—'

'He was a client then.'

She reddened. 'Not exactly—'

But Mariner wasn't interested in 'not exactly.' 'Listen, Maureen,' he cut in. 'Eddie Barham, that's his name in case it had slipped your memory, couldn't give a toss about confidentiality any more. He was found dead in his own home, just over a week ago.' Maureen paled a little under the layer of foundation. 'He died from a drug overdose. Any of your girls provide "optional extras?"'

'No!' she was affronted.

'Are you sure about that? Is that what they'd say if we talked to them? Of course we'd need ID before we could interview them: passports, work permits and all that.'

Maureen capitulated. 'All right, he did come here, but it's not what you're thinking. I couldn't help him.'

'Oh? I thought you catered for "all desires."'

'It wasn't that. He wanted a girl to go to his place. We don't do that. It's too much of a risk.'

'Anonymous bars and hotel rooms are safer, eh?'

'As a matter of fact, they are and you know it.'

'So you didn't help him at all? I'd like to remind you that this is a murder enquiry. We might have to delve a little deeper into your working practices.'

'All right, he did look through the book. Poor bugger seemed as if he'd really built himself up to it and when I turned him down, he didn't know what to do. I persuaded him to have another look in the book and then he saw a girl he liked.'

'Who? Was it Sally-Ann? Or Kay?'

Maureen looked blank. 'Neither. It was Kerry.'

Kerry? Kay? Too close to be coincidental, surely. Mariner felt the satisfying sizzle of a connection being made. 'This her?' he produced the second photograph.

'Yes.'

'Show me.' He waited while Maureen leafed through the book until she came to the picture. It was the same girl all right, the chocolate brown eyes staring out at him. 'And did you fix up an appointment with Kerry for Eddie Barham?'

'I couldn't, she doesn't work for me anymore. She stopped working here weeks ago.'

'So why is her photograph still in your book?'

Maureen actually had the grace to blush under the thick make-up. 'I must have forgotten to take it out.' Nothing to do with the fact that the girl was a stunner.

'What happened to her?'

'She just left. Decided to go independent. Good luck to her, that's what I say.'

'Did you tell Eddie Barham who she was?'

'Not to begin with. I tried to offer him an alternative, but he wasn't interested. He'd made up his mind.'

'Did you tell him where he could find Kerry? Or is that bad for business?'

'I told him all I knew. It was no skin off my nose, was it? I gave him one of these.' Pulling open a desk drawer, she rifled through it, eventually coming up with a business card that she handed to Mariner. 'She left me a handful of them, but I don't know if the number still stands.' The card was cheaply and inexpertly printed:

Kerry, for all your personal needs. At a glance the number, a mobile, gave no clue about location, but hopefully it could be traced.

'She was hoping I might put some punters her way,' Maureen said. 'But she knows I don't operate like that. They either work for me or they don't. I like to take care of my girls.'

Along with a substantial portion of their earnings, too, thought Mariner. 'And you didn't recommend anyone else to Eddie Barham? How about a Sally-Ann?'

Maureen frowned. 'I don't know any Sally-Ann.'

On balance, Mariner thought she was probably telling the truth. 'Is there anything else you can tell me about Kerry?'

'Not much more than you can see there. She's pretty, like I said, and classy. Got a nice voice and knows how to make the best of herself. To be honest, I was sorry to lose her, she was popular with the punters, especially round here. I get the occasional university professor, you know. But she thought she could do better on her own.'

Mariner had a sudden thought. 'Who was setting her up? Did Kerry have someone backing her?'

'I don't know, but she knew Frank Crosby, so she said. Poor cow seemed to think it was something to be proud of.'

Mariner's stomach flipped. 'Did you tell Eddie Barham that?'

'I don't think so. Why would I?'

But maybe she hadn't needed to because Eddie already knew. 'Any idea where Kerry was planning to go?' he asked.

'No.'

'Do you have an address for her?'

'No.'

'Do you know if Eddie Barham tried to contact her?'

'How the hell would I know that?'

'But you're certain it was an appointment he wanted and not just information.'

'What do you mean?'

'Eddie Barham was a journalist. I think he might have been following up a story.'

Mariner could tell from her face that it was news to her. He stood up to go, he'd got what he came for. 'If Kerry gets in touch again, call me straight away.' He gave her his card, but he wasn't convinced that he'd get a result that way.

Fired with enthusiasm, Mariner tried Kerry's number as soon as he got back to the car, but all he got was: *The number you have dialled has not been recognised; please hang up and try again.* Somehow he wasn't surprised.

* * *

Anna was pleased when Becky had rung her to say that there was a lunchtime leaving celebration for Gareth from Human Resources. It would be an opportunity for her to spend some time in the normal world again and remind people that she was still around.

But after only ten minutes in the noisy city centre bar, she realised what a mistake it was to have come. Eddie's murder seemed to have created a wall around her and beyond offering their condolences people didn't know what to say. In addition, six days' absence had cast her so far adrift from the rest of her colleagues that her knowledge of office gossip was wildly out of date, putting her at a significant conversational disadvantage.

Taking Becky on one side yet again, to fill her in on the who, the what and the wherefore of yet another anecdote, Anna realised that even her friend was beginning to find her tiresome. What's more, the gripes and grumbles about the meagre bonuses and narrow range of available company cars seemed banal and juvenile. Anna felt like a grown-up being forced to spend an afternoon at a child's birthday party.

In an attempt to involve herself in the chat, she tried recounting some of Jamie's escapades, but got only polite but uncomprehending smiles in return. They're humouring me, she thought. She was sure the supermarket story would go down well, but it fell flatter than the Norfolk fens, and afterwards she felt wretched for having used Jamie as some kind of cheap entertainment. She wondered how he was doing. He'd looked a bit pale when she'd dropped him off at the day centre this morning and it had crossed her mind that he might be sickening for something. Perhaps he was beginning to pine for Eddie after all.

A roar of raucous laughter broke out, signalling the punchline to yet another story Anna had completely missed, and suddenly she couldn't stand it anymore. Making her excuses about 'things to sort out,' she wished Gareth good luck and walked out of the bar.

To kill some time before collecting Jamie, she wandered around some of the city centre shops, drawn unexpectedly towards the menswear departments, imagining how Jamie would look in some of the gear. She bought him a couple of new shirts and a pair of up-to-the-minute cargo pants and took some pleasure from planning what he'd wear. Even so, she managed to be early at the day centre, and was rewarded by Jamie coming over to her, taking her hand and putting it to his face. 'Ann-ann.'

Anna found herself unexpectedly moved by the gesture. It was the first time in years that Jamie had fully acknowledged her, even if his version of her name did make her sound like a giant panda.

'How's he been?' she asked Francine, for once genuinely wanting to know how Jamie had spent his day. He looked okay now, his colour was better, and Francine was reassuring. 'He's been fine,' she said. 'Didn't eat much lunch, but then, it was spaghetti Bolognese, so what's new?

Are you staying for the parents and carers support group tonight?'

The innocent enquiry threw Anna onto the back foot. 'I don't know,' she blustered. In truth, the prospect terrified her.

'I thought that perhaps it was why you were here early,' continued Francine cheerfully. 'Jamie loves the activity club they run alongside it. And it might help him to get rid of some of his excess energy.'

It was a dilemma. Worrying about Jamie was one thing, getting involved in his life was something else.

'I'm sure Eddie was involved in arranging the speakers tonight, too,' Francine chattered on, persuasively. 'One of the topics up for discussion is sleep issues. Mightn't that be relevant?'

It was enough to entice Anna in. A couple of hours of her time seemed a minor commitment, and Francine was right, she might learn something useful. With Jamie in tow, she followed Francine's directions back to a large recreation room, which already echoed to the sound of loud pop music. Various activities had been set up and a number of other adults, some with visible disabilities, but others like Jamie whose needs were less clear, were already engaged with volunteer helpers. Jamie hovered initially on the periphery, hands flapping, but pausing now and then to watch the others, until a young student, evidently an old friend, encouraged him to get involved in a basketball shoot.

Anna watched with fascination as Jamie went to join in, responding with a smile to some gentle teasing from the other adults. This was his social life. She'd never for one moment imagined he could have one. After a few minutes, she pried herself away to follow the flow of people to another communal room, where chairs had been set out in rows. Wanting to remain inconspicuous, Anna took a seat towards the back. Gradually the room filled with other people, mainly women, mainly middle aged or beyond, who quickly huddled into small knots to talk. Eavesdropping shamelessly, Anna caught snippets of strangely reassuring conversation.

'How's she doing this week?'

The woman addressed held up crossed fingers. 'Only up three times last night, so we were really pleased.'

'—then he just knocked his dinner all over the floor. It was so embarrassing.'

Feeling that she was blending into the background nicely, Anna began to relax, but the anonymity didn't last for long.

Like many there, the woman who approached her was of her parents' generation, attractive without make-up and casually dressed in jeans and T-shirt. 'It's Anna, isn't it?' she said.

'Yes.' Anna was wary.

'I thought I saw you with Jamie. I'm Gail. Our daughter Susannah is here at the centre, she's autistic too. In fact, we used to know your parents quite well. We were all terribly shocked to hear about Eddie. I'm so sorry.'

'Thanks.'

'How's Jamie coping?' Gail asked. 'He must miss Eddie dreadfully. Eddie was so good with him.'

'He seems to be okay.'

Gail smiled, encouragingly, 'Well, it's great that you're taking him on.'

'There wasn't much choice really,' Anna reminded her.

'No,' said Gail. 'There isn't for any of us.'

There was a beat of self-conscious silence before Anna felt compelled to set the record straight. 'Actually, Jamie will only be staying with me as a short-term measure,' she said. 'I've already been to look at a residential home and it seemed very nice.'

'Oh, I see.'

Did Anna sense a cooling towards her, or was it paranoia striking again? 'It's called The Beeches,' she elaborated. 'Do you know it?'

Gail looked uncomfortable. 'No. We've never considered anything like that. I couldn't think of having anyone else care for Suzie. We haven't left her with anyone else in nineteen years.'

Anna was appalled. 'What do you do if you want to go out?' she asked.

'We don't,' was the simple reply. 'We haven't been out together since she was born.'

Anna didn't know what to say. It seemed like a life-sentence that Gail was proud of and suddenly Anna wondered how her parents had coped.

'It's good to see you here anyway, Anna,' Gail was saying. 'I hope you enjoy the evening.'

'Yes. Thank you.'

Shortly after that, the meeting was called to order, but to Anna's great embarrassment, the first item on the agenda was the news of Eddie's death, followed by her introduction to the group as Jamie's new carer, making her feel more fraudulent than ever.

The session then began encounter-group style with a general sharing of problems, especially relating to sleep. Anna listened to people describing many of the difficulties she'd already experienced with Jamie, though often far more extreme, leaving Anna marvelling at the resilience of the human spirit. One couple admitted to never having had an unbroken night since their twenty-seven-year-old, doubly incontinent son had been born.

Although it made caring for Jamie sound like a picnic, there was a ring of familiarity to it all, and Anna began to find some small comfort in the knowledge that she was not alone. In fact, she realised, with a jolt, that somehow she felt less of an outsider here than she had done in the pub earlier in the day.

The first guest speaker of the evening was an alternative therapist, who recommended the use of aromatherapy and massage in encouraging good sleeping habits. Her philosophy sounded wonderful, although the large woman sitting next to Anna remained healthily sceptical, 'My Andrew would love it,' she murmured, to no one in particular, her voice laced with sarcasm. 'Considering he can't stay still for two minutes and he hates being touched, it would be perfect.'

The alternative therapist was followed by a clinical psychologist, who advocated the use of behavioural techniques for the management of routines. The principles seemed to be well founded in theory, and successful — if individual intervention could be given for twenty-four hours a day.

Professor Ivan Fellowes, the final speaker, was tall and authoritative, and was introduced to the group as a visiting consultant from the Queen Elizabeth Medical Centre and specialist in the treatment of sleeping disorders, particularly for people with autism.

Not surprisingly, his was the more conventional medical approach, advocating the use, in certain circumstances, of drugs. He explained that while in the early days treatment had been confined to some fairly crude anti-depressants, in recent years much more refined versions of the treatments had been developed. He reeled off a list of names that could have been varieties of potato for all the meaning they had for Anna.

His presentation was altogether much more professional, with accompanying slides, copious handouts and an almost scripted commentary, beginning with a detailed look at different areas of the brain and the impact that certain substances might have. He talked at length about a group of recently developed drugs, known as PSTIs, that worked, he said, mainly on the serotonin system, helping to regulate sleep, aggression and anxiety levels.

But as the professor went on to describe in great detail the various neuro-chemical processes that could be influenced by the use of pharmacological treatments, Anna could see him being far more at home addressing other medical experts, and noticed faces beginning to glaze over. Almost a week of disturbed sleep was taking its toll on her, too, and her powers of concentration were suffering. Interest was briefly revived as Professor Fellowes described some highly successful trials of recently developed medications, which made them sound like wonder drugs, until he followed that with a damning indictment of the potential and actual side effects. Anna drifted away again, her parents' opposition to medication for Jamie apparently vindicated. They had travelled this route years ago, with endless visits to Dr Payne and even an assessment with an expert in London, before rejecting the idea of medication outright.

When the lecture ended, Anna found herself standing in the queue for coffee beside Professor Fellowes and felt obliged to offer some comment. 'It was a very interesting talk,' she said, neutrally.

The professor smiled an acknowledgement. 'But was it useful?' he wanted to know.

'Not really in a practical sense, drug therapy isn't an option for my brother, Jamie. He was removed from a respite placement for that reason.'

But having been present when Anna was introduced, the professor looked surprised, 'It was Eddie who invited me to come and speak tonight,' he said. 'He seemed keen to learn more about what the possibilities for Jamie might be.'

'Did he?' Now it was Anna's turn to be surprised.

'Oh yes, he was very interested in the effects of particular medications. We had several telephone conversations about it. I'm only sorry that, in the event, we were unable to meet.'

So what had changed Eddie's mind? Afterwards, when the main body of the meeting was over and people were beginning to disperse, Anna went with all the other carers to collect their charges from the recreation room. On the way, she went to thank Gail for an interesting evening. What followed seemed to come from nowhere. Gail's husband wandered over while they were talking. 'We ought to be getting back, love,' he said to his wife, smiling at Anna.

'Yes, of course. Well, it's nice to meet you Anna,' Gail said, rather formally. 'And if there's anything we can do . . .' The now habitual offer tailed off, but Anna was nonetheless grateful for it.

But as Gail moved away, her husband lingered a moment and suddenly and unexpectedly, his expression hardened. 'I hope you're not going to start stirring things up, like your brother did,' he hissed at Anna, under his breath. 'There's no point in dragging up the past. We all have to move on.' And with that he walked away, leaving Anna flabbergasted.

Francine, standing a few feet away, had witnessed the exchange.

'What was that all about?' Anna asked her, baffled.

'Oh, don't worry about Jim,' Francine was dismissive. 'It doesn't take much to get him going. He gets a bit intense. It was just that your brother had a journalist's instinct. He asked a lot of questions. It didn't always go down well.'

But the incident left Anna feeling unsettled and angry.

CHAPTER 19

It had been another long evening. After time spent pursuing mobile phone companies only to establish that Kerry's number was untraceable, Mariner had whiled away a couple of hours attending to overdue paperwork, before reluctantly deciding that it was time to go home. On his way out, he almost fell over a box of assorted hardware in the corridor. 'What's all this?' he asked the duty sergeant.

'The surveillance techs have been spring cleaning,' said the sergeant. 'That's all the obsolete stuff waiting for disposal.'

Something lying on the top of the pile caught Mariner's eye. He knew who could use one of those, and what's more, it would give him the perfect excuse to take a detour on his way home.

'So it's all being thrown away?' he checked again.

'Waiting for the bin men, so to speak,' the sergeant confirmed. 'Help yourself.'

Mariner did, and sorting through the rest of the box he came up with the unit's other component part, batteries even included. He ran a quick check to make sure that it still functioned. It did. That would do nicely.

Turning into the residents' parking bay outside Anna Barham's flat, however, he was disappointed to note that her car wasn't there. He had the choice of waiting it out or going home. A brief flashback of Jenny's orgasmic cries came into his head, and he settled for the former, flicking on the radio to keep him occupied.

Erectile dysfunction, or impotence, can affect any man at any age for a variety of reasons, a health expert was saying. *And in tonight's programme we'll be exploring how this and other common problems. . .* God, but life was full of cruel coincidences. Mariner reached out again to switch it off. His love life might not be at its best right now, but impotent? No way, Jose. His finger hovered for a moment over the on/off button. On the other hand, he had precious little else to do right now. Leaving it on, he slid down in the seat, closed his eyes and pretended not to listen.

Dazzling headlights sweeping over him roused Mariner from a graphic description of the premature ejaculation avoidance technique. Anna and Jamie Barham were home. He jumped up, and in his haste to silence the radio, banged his knee hard on the dashboard. Shit! He turned the radio off, refusing to allow his mind to speculate on where Anna and Jamie might have been until this hour, but was reassured that at least that they were alone. Mariner waited while Anna parked up, then picking up the tracking device from the seat beside him, climbed out of his car.

He hadn't expected to be welcomed with open arms, but, as he limped over, carrying in his hand the small black box sprouting wires, he saw how tired she looked and noted, with some disappointment, her apparent indifference towards him. He pressed on regardless, holding up the equipment for her to view. 'Hi. I saw this, and thought of you,' he said.

'Thanks,' she said, forcing some kind of enthusiasm towards the so-far unidentified object. 'What is it?'

'It's a Kestrel Short Range,' said Mariner, helpfully.

'Oh,' she said. 'Do you want to come in, then?' It was a reluctant, ungracious invitation, but she'd made it, so Mariner accepted. If the tracker was to be of any value, she needed to know how it worked.

'I'd almost given up on you,' he said, conversationally, as they travelled up in the lift. 'Been somewhere nice?'

'A lecture about PSTIs,' Anna said, provocatively.

'Pesticides? That must have been fascinating.'

That raised a smile at least. 'Not pesticides, P . . . S . . . T . . . Jamie!!' Her shout came from nowhere. As the lift doors opened onto the third floor, Jamie bolted out ahead of them, not in the direction of the flat but towards a gaping doorway at the end of the landing. Running after him, Mariner grabbed Jamie's sleeve and hauled him back just in time, slamming the door shut before he could escape.

'God, why are people so thoughtless!' Anna said, white-faced. 'That's the door leading up to the roof garden. It's meant to be kept locked.'

'Do you have a residents' group?'

'I've already told them—'

'Perhaps I should have a word.'

Her resigned sigh said, 'Suit yourself.' Safely inside her flat, Anna settled Jamie in front of a DVD, while Mariner made himself comfortable at her kitchen table. When she joined him, he attempted to demonstrate the finer features of the tracking device. 'It's easy to use,' he explained. 'You just attach this clip to his clothing somewhere, and the receiver will tell you where he is in relation to you. Just set the central arrow in the appropriate direction and Jamie's position will be shown on the screen.' The LCD display he showed her looked like a miniature radar. 'It's only a basic model,' he admitted. 'But it will give you an idea of direction and distance for up to a mile, so if you use it straight away, it should be effective.'

'Thanks,' Anna said. It was grudging, but there nonetheless, and he hadn't done this for gratitude, had he?

'So, tell me about these pesticides,' he said.

'PSTIs: Potent Serotonin Transporter Inhibitors,' she recited, struggling to remember the terminology. 'They're the types of medication used to help with sleeping.'

'Oh. And are they any good?' Mariner asked, out of politeness, after all, he'd started this.

'It was complicated,' Anna said. 'Too much for my limited brain capacity. But Eddie had arranged the talk, so they said, and I felt obliged to display some interest.'

'You sound surprised.'

She frowned. 'I am. It's not something I would have expected Eddie to think about. You heard what Joyce, the centre manager said. He'd taken Jamie out of his respite care placement precisely because he didn't want Jamie put on medication.'

'And because he couldn't afford it,' Mariner reminded her.

'Yeah, whatever. But after what I heard tonight? Frankly it's enough to put anyone off.'

'Even if it means a good night's sleep?' Mariner had already noticed the dark circles under her eyes. 'Perhaps Eddie was having second thoughts.'

'He wouldn't have. Mum and Dad were always completely opposed to medication for Jamie, too. He wouldn't have gone against their wishes.'

'But that was then, this is now. Things move on, don't they?'

'Not that much. Some of the side effects described tonight were horrendous.' She shuddered.

'Perhaps you need to weigh those against the benefits,' said Mariner.

She shot him a look, but then probably the last thing she needed was someone else offering unwanted advice. 'So how's your investigation going?' She asked, blatantly turning the tables.

Now it was Mariner's turn to shrug. 'Slowly,' he said. 'There are a couple of things we're following up.'

177

'Escort agencies?' She wasn't comfortable with that line of thinking, but Mariner could only be honest with her.

'Eddie had definitely been making enquiries in that area,' he said. 'We're on the trail of the woman I saw Eddie with, the one in your photograph, too. But I think her name is Kerry, not Kay. We haven't exactly found her yet, but we do know who linked her up with Eddie.'

'So, tell me the worst.' She was daring him to.

'It seems she is some kind of call girl,' Mariner said, with reticence. 'Eddie was very specific about wanting a girl who would come to his place. And she fits the description his neighbour gave us of his "girlfriend."'

'Oh.'

'She could easily relate to a story he was working on,' Mariner said, quickly.

'But you don't really think so.' She was beginning to read him like a book. Mariner didn't like that much.

'It just seems odd that no one at the paper knew anything about it.'

'Darren knew about it though, didn't he? He said he thought that Eddie was working on some story on his own initiative. Maybe Eddie had found something really big and didn't want someone else getting to it first.'

Mariner was loath to disillusion her. He could understand her unwillingness to believe that her brother would pay for the services of a prostitute. Fortunately, Jamie chose that moment to wander into the kitchen, saving him the trouble. Ignoring Mariner, he tugged at Anna's arm.

'What is it, Jamie? What do you want?' she asked. She took out a bundle of pictures and spread them out on the table. 'What?'

Jamie scanned them until he found the picture he was looking for, picked it up and gave it to Anna.

'Good. Jamie wants Hula Hoops? Say, Loops, please.'

'Loops,' said Jamie.

'Please,' Anna prompted, waiting patiently.

'—please.'

'Good. Good talking, Jamie.' She went to the cupboard and got out a packet, opened it and gave it to him. With a brief transient smile, Jamie took them and retreated back to the lounge.

Mariner had watched the whole exchange with interest. 'So that's what all those pictures are about,' he said, thinking back to the line drawings in Eddie's house.

'They help Jamie to make sense of what goes on around him. He finds pictures easier to understand than words. It's why he had the picture of the girl. Kay, Kerry or whatever.' Meaning that the girl had been a feature of their lives. Suddenly Mariner saw her understand that fact, and she didn't like it a bit.

As a distraction, Mariner picked up one of the longer strips. 'So what's this? A whole sentence?'

Anna shook her head. 'That's Jamie's timetable. It helps him to predict what's going to happen next during each day. He finds it hard to handle change, so the pictures act as a kind of early warning system to let him know what's coming up.'

Mariner studied the pictures. 'Okay, the breakfast cereal, the car and the day centre I understand, but I don't remember it snowing today.'

'It's not snow, it's a snowflake.'

'Of course.' Clear as mud.

'A snowflake stands for "something unexpected,"' Anna explained. 'Eddie and Francine were trying to get Jamie used to the idea that sometimes there are events you can't predict, that you have to be prepared for the unknown. That's what the snowflake means. Something unknown is going to happen. I wasn't sure what we were going to do this evening; hence the snowflake.'

'Clever stuff,' said Mariner. 'You two are beginning to behave like the odd couple.'

'Yes, well, as long as he doesn't get too comfortable,' retorted Anna immediately. 'I've started looking into long-term residential care for him.'

'Oh.'

'Unfortunately I'm coming up against the same thing as Eddie. They want to use medication if necessary.'

'So why bother. He seems pretty settled here. I'd have thought—'

'My God, don't you start!' she cut in, accusingly.

'Start what?'

'Trying to make me feel guilty.'

Although it was obvious that she didn't need his help. 'I wasn't—' he began.

But she wasn't listening. 'And if one more person tells me how "wonderful" Eddie was with Jamie, I'll strangle them with my bare hands. There, I'm confessing to that one in advance.'

'I'll make a note of it,' Mariner said, evenly, holding her gaze.

She maintained eye contact, but he could see the inner struggle going on, as she fought to keep a lid on her emotions. 'I just want to get on with my life,' she said, her voice breaking ever so slightly. 'Is that so unreasonable?'

'Of course not,' said Mariner.

'You have no idea what it's like. Only two weeks ago I had a job, friends, a social life. I did all the things that normal, independent adults do. I got up, went to work, stayed late if I wanted to, went to the pub afterwards if I wanted to, ate what I liked, saw who I liked. As a matter of fact, I wouldn't blame Eddie for seeing a prostitute,' she went on. 'There's bugger all opportunity for any other kind of love life with Jamie around. He's been with me less than a fortnight and I've become a social pariah.' In a visible effort to hold it all together, she pushed back her chair and strode the length of the kitchen to bang down her mug in the sink. When she spoke again her voice was a whisper. 'I can't go back to that. I know I should, but I can't.'

Mariner watched a single tear escape in a wet trail down her cheek, before she turned away from him, pretending to be fascinated by the view from the window that she saw so many times each day. But he could see from the movement of her shoulders that the battle had been lost. Mariner felt he ought to do something, but he wasn't sure what. He'd never been much good at this stuff. Prepared for rejection, he went over to her and rested his hands lightly on her shoulders. 'I'm sorry,' he said. 'I really didn't mean to—'

But the rest was left unsaid as she turned and clutched at him, all the pent-up stress and emotion of the past few days pouring out in great wrenching sobs, her head pushing into his chest, while Mariner put his arms around her, holding her close. Sod professionalism.

After a while her crying subsided and she stepped back from him, rubbing angrily at her eyes. 'Oh God, I'm so sorry, that was stupid.'

Mariner could think of several words to describe her behaviour, but stupid wasn't one of them. 'It's been a tough time,' he said, inadequately.

She managed a short, staccato laugh. 'You're the master of the understatement, aren't you?' She took a gulp of air. 'The irony is,' she went on, 'that this is the last thing in the world Mum and Dad would have wanted. They knew first-hand what hard work Jamie can be. They never intended for either Eddie or me to have to take care of him. Look out for him, yes, of course, but not wash him, dress him, feed him, clean his teeth, day in day out. They didn't expect that of us. It's always people on the outside who make the judgments.'

'I wasn't judging you,' said Mariner truthfully.

'Oh, it's not your fault—' she tailed off, exhausted and spent. 'Sorry, I've made your shirt wet.' She patted the damp patch and Mariner thought her touch would burn a hole in his chest.

'That's all right,' he said. 'I've got another one at home.' He stepped away so that she wouldn't notice the effect she was having on him.

'Not in that colour, I hope. No offence.'

Mariner took the weak attempt at humour as a good sign. 'None taken,' he said. 'Do you keep any brandy?' She told him where and Mariner found it and poured her a generous measure.

'I was wrong about what I said before,' she said, taking it from him and leaning back against the kitchen units.

'What?' Mariner sat down again, finding that he couldn't quite trust his knees to support him.

'About Eddie being a martyr. It wasn't his problem it's mine. I was the one who felt guilty, about leaving him to cope with Jamie. At first I could use my marriage as an excuse. By the time it was over I'd convinced myself that Eddie didn't need my help, he had it taped. He and Jamie were a team.' She fixed her gaze on the brandy as she swirled it around the glass. 'When Jamie was born Eddie was old enough not to mind,' she said. 'He was the grown-up, responsible one who helped out whenever he could. Jamie responded to that. He'd do things for Eddie that he wouldn't do for anyone else. I suppose in a funny sort of way I was jealous of their special relationship. I'd always resented Jamie like hell, because until he came along and wrecked everything, I was Daddy's sweet little girl. That's why I was determined that it wasn't going to happen all over again. Perhaps I still am. I'm the selfish one. I've had enough of autism and what it does to you. I just want a normal life.'

'Nobody can blame you for that.'

She looked up at him, her eyes shining. 'No. But it doesn't stop me from blaming myself.'

CHAPTER 20

To his considerable relief, Knox and Jenny had already retired when Mariner got home. So, safely alone, Mariner got out the dictionary and looked up PSTIs in the abbreviations section. It wasn't listed. He tried the word potent: 'cogent and strong' it said, so little to be learned there. Then, almost unconsciously, his eye slid down the page to 'impotent.' It didn't make for comforting reading. *Powerless; helpless, decrepit; wholly lacking in sexual power, unable to copulate or reach orgasm.* Hm. Not all bad then. He didn't have any problem with reaching orgasm, just as long as no one else was involved. With the right woman, at the right time it would be resolved. It was just a question of finding the right woman. He refused to allow himself to speculate on whether he already had. God, he'd badly wanted to kiss Anna Barham tonight and that was a new and worrying experience. Never before had he been tempted to overstep that particular professional line. And there had been no shortage of opportunity. Right from his first week in the job on his first solo call-out when he'd been asked to attend a domestic, the door had been answered by a young woman in a negligee so sheer it needn't have been there.

Only when she insisted on encouraging his attentions had he realised it was a set-up. It was his initiation into the squad, which no one would let him forget for months. Since then, unlike Tony Knox, he'd kept everything well under control, until now. This deprivation was beginning to impact on everything.

Crawling up to bed, Mariner passed the small hours in a restless sleep and by the time the birds began singing, he'd resolved to at least phone the doctor. He wouldn't be offered an appointment for weeks anyway, so he'd have time to prepare.

'If you can you pop down to surgery in about twenty minutes, Mr Mariner, we've just had a cancellation.' The receptionist's response the following morning wasn't the one that she'd given during his nocturnal rehearsal, and he almost bottled out. But surely it couldn't be that big a deal. In his head it had all gone pretty smoothly. A brief chat with the Asian guy he'd seen last time—

But things weren't going Mariner's way. Dr Suliman was on holiday, and in his place was a young female locum, fresh out of sixth form, judging from her youthful appearance, and a fully paid-up member of the Spanish Inquisition to boot. 'How can I help?' she asked.

Her innocent gaze fixed earnestly on him, and all of Mariner's careful, mentally prepared descriptions of the problem deserted him. 'I can't keep it up,' he blurted out, with rather less eloquence than he'd intended.

'Is the problem erection, ejaculation, or both?' she asked, as if she was offering him a choice of pizza toppings.

'Erection,' Mariner said, shrivelling inside.

'Since when?' She turned to his records on the computer screen.

'About a year.'

She looked up. 'You've waited a long time before seeking help.'

'I thought it would get better.'

184

'Mm.' Despite her youth, she'd evidently heard that one before. 'Take off your jacket and roll up your sleeve, would you?'

It seemed a novel approach, but Mariner did as he was told.

'How old are you, Mr Mariner?' she asked, slapping a strip of inner tube around his exposed bicep and pumping it up until all circulation to his lower arm had been staunched.

'Forty-three.' Compressed air escaped with a hiss.

'I see. That's fine.' He took that as a comment on his blood pressure and not his age. 'Any other health problems?'

'Not that I'm aware of.'

'You're not on any medication?'

'No.'

'How's your peeing?'

Mariner looked blank.

'Bladder control okay, steady stream and all that?' the doctor prompted.

'It's fine,' said Mariner, not knowing what else to say.

'And is your difficulty in achieving an erection, or maintaining it?'

'Maintaining it.'

'Okay then, let's have a look.' A look? 'Take off your things and get up on the couch please.' Mariner wanted to ask if this was strictly necessary, but presumably she wasn't just doing this for fun. Presumably. Feeling vulnerable, with only his shirttails to protect his dignity, Mariner hoisted himself onto the couch, praying that he wasn't about to be caught in a lie. He needn't have worried. Her cool, latex-sheathed fingers had an intimidating effect.

'Well, physically everything seems in order,' she assured him. 'We'll need a urine sample to rule out diabetes, but that's unlikely if you're getting no other symptoms. You can get dressed.'

But after he'd pulled on his clothes there were further questions. They started innocuously enough. What was his occupation? Was it often stressful? Had he felt particularly stressed during the last year or so? No more than usual. That seemed to disappoint her, so she tried a different, more intimate tack. Did he masturbate successfully? Well, yes. Was there a pattern to when he lost his erection, was it always at the same point during intercourse? Yes, just prior to consummation, he just — collapsed.

Ah. Was he in a stable relationship? No, his last one finished just over a year ago.

'Tell me about that,' she said.

Despite reservations about the relevance of this line of questioning, Mariner found himself pouring out the whole sorry tale about Greta. It had started off so well until she moved in with him and started holding him to account for every minute of his day. Even just thinking about it made him feel physically sick, as the memory of that final evening replayed itself in his mind.

'Dinner won't be long,' Greta had chirped from the kitchen the second he'd walked in the door. He groaned inwardly. After a harrowing day spent interviewing an eighty-two-year-old woman who'd been brutally beaten in her own home, he needed space to recover himself. To this end he'd retreated to the bathroom, but he hadn't yet got around to fitting a lock and Greta had pursued him there, wrapping her arms around him as he leaned over the washbasin.

'Who's a clever boy, then?' she smiled enigmatically back at him from the mirror, a hand straying down over his groin.

Mariner wished she wouldn't talk in riddles all the time. 'What?' he asked irritably.

'You're going to be a daddy.'

Mariner had almost passed out. Horror was not the desired response, he could tell immediately from Greta's face, but he couldn't help it, he was horrified.

'I thought we wanted a family,' she wailed, her misery quickly equal to his. And maybe he did, somewhere in the safe and distant future, in an abstract kind of way, but not now. Occasionally since then he'd wondered if he could have compromised. But he couldn't, not over something so big. And the experience had shaken him, because up until that point he'd always considered his mother and himself to be the wronged parties, when they'd been abandoned by his own father. But now, for the first time he could see it from the opposite perspective. Had his mother sprung the same unwelcome surprise on his dad?

Greta was distraught, and later that night Mariner had tried to make it up to her but had failed dismally, as he had done ever since.

'So it's since then that this problem has developed?' asked the doctor, bringing Mariner back to the present.

'Yes.'

'And did your girlfriend go ahead with the pregnancy?'

'I assume so, yes. Not long after that we went our separate ways.' Even though he'd tried contacting her to offer financial support, Greta had completely stonewalled him. It wasn't enough, she'd said. She didn't want his money. She wanted a husband and father for her child. After a while he'd just given up.

'Well,' said the doctor after a considered pause. 'I think this is all in your mind. You're feeling guilty.'

'Guilty about what?' Mariner was indignant. He wasn't the one who'd walked out.

'Well, you must surely have thought from time to time that you might be a father, that there could be some small being out there who's your responsibility?'

'My partner made it very clear. Whatever she chose to do, she didn't want me involved. She was going to take care of it.' But the doctor was right. It hadn't stopped him from wondering. Rarely a day went by when he didn't consider the possibility of a small child out there going through life under the same cloud of uncertainty that he had.

The doctor looked at him. 'I would suggest you look for a resolution, because at the moment your body is telling you loud and clear that it won't risk getting into that kind of trouble again.'

'Is it?'

'Yes. It's saying, "Don't have sex, it leads to unwanted pregnancies..."' Sort things out with your ex and I think you'll find that this is just a passing phase. I'll prescribe you a couple of Viagra though, just in case. That ought to be enough to kick-start you again.' An unfortunate choice of phrase, thought Mariner. 'There might be side effects, of course, including headaches and nausea. But see how you go. You'll need to weigh those against the benefits.' His own line coming back at him.

Taking the prescription, Mariner tucked it into his wallet where it kept ironic company with a pack of three condoms, purchased six months before but still unopened.

CHAPTER 21

DI Mariner was astute, Anna thought as she waited for Jamie to wrestle into his T-shirt. They were getting used to this. For some weird reason, she'd woken up this morning thinking about the detective. She liked him, quite a lot actually. After he'd gone, she'd tried to remember the last time she'd been held by a man, not as a precursor to sex, but just held. She couldn't, not even by her dad. Despite the emotional turmoil going on inside it had felt good. She could still recall that musky smell of a man who's put in an honest day's graft, sweetened by the faintest hint of aftershave.

It came as something of a surprise to her that she could be even remotely attracted to a man like Mariner. She unfailingly went for 'dark and classically handsome,' never for 'pale and interesting,' however blue the eyes. Mariner was thin to the point of skinny too, and older than the men she generally fancied — he must be well into his forties. But there was something about his quiet dependability that she found somehow warm and comforting.

Jamie could have a complete change of clothes today: the new ones she'd bought for him. The rest could go in the wash, including those he'd worn a couple of nights ago. But as Anna turned them inside out something heavy dropped out of the pocket. Jamie pounced on it and she had to wrest it from him. It was a mobile phone. Not hers, but Jonathan's. She had to smile at that. He'd be lost without it, but too proud to contact her to get it back – if he even knew where it was. Just out of curiosity, she had a look at the stored numbers. Hers was the third in the list, probably about what she'd expect. And Melanie? In at number eight and climbing steadily.

In the hall, the letterbox snapped shut. A couple of bills and a package had dropped onto the mat. Anna went to pick them up, turning her attention to the large padded envelope first. Clearly one of the postal service's sorting office disasters, it was battered and crumpled and somewhere along the way one edge had been repaired with adhesive tape. But reading the address made her shiver.

'It's Eddie's writing,' she murmured in disbelief.

'Eddie,' Jamie echoed meaninglessly, continuing to shovel cereal into his mouth, some of the milk not quite making it and running down his chin. Anna had drawn the line at Hula Hoops for breakfast, and after several mornings of scraping various glutinous substances off the walls, had finally found a cereal that he liked.

Anna's hands trembled slightly as she took the thick envelope into the lounge. It was postmarked a week ago last Friday, so it had taken a long time to get here, literally caught up in the system judging by its battered condition. But why was Eddie sending her things through the post, and why now? Had he known then that his time was running out, or was it just an unhappy coincidence? Tearing open the flap, she slid out a blue folder. It contained a series of computer printouts that looked as if they'd been printed off from the internet. With them was an A5 hard-backed notebook. She opened it to see pages and pages of her father's distinctive handwriting, smudged here and there, where the passage of time had caused the ink to bleed into the paper.

It took Anna several moments to work out that the printouts represented information on medication, the kind used to control autistic behaviours and suddenly she got the message. Eddie was helping her out. He'd have known that if anything happened to him, one of the first things she would do was to try and find a residential place for Jamie, and that she would come up against the same insistence on medication as he had. So he was sharing his knowledge with her. Perhaps it was even his way of saying it was all right, he'd had to consider it too.

Not for the first time, Anna wondered what Eddie could possibly have been involved in that would put him in such danger, and felt a stinging guilt that she hadn't been able to help him. All she could do now was accept and make use of what he'd given her. There wasn't time to read it all now, and at first glance she wasn't even sure if she would understand it anyway, so she slid the papers and notebook back into the folder and put it in a drawer for when she could set aside more time.

* * *

The journey to the day centre was becoming routine and Anna no longer had to make a conscious effort to steer the car in the right direction.

'Wow, look at you today,' said Francine to Jamie when she saw him.

'I thought he could do with a new wardrobe,' Anna said. 'We didn't have too bad a night either, he was only up a couple of times.'

'That's great.'

Yes, it was. And in a strange way Anna was beginning to feel like an old hand. She'd planned on going back to the office today, if only to touch base, but the package had brought Eddie back to the forefront of her thoughts. After the funeral, she had requested that his ashes be buried in the garden of remembrance, along with a small commemorative plaque. The crematorium official had told her that it would take at least forty-eight hours to arrange, and now she felt a sudden desire to check that the task had been done. Leaving the day centre, she took a diversion to Lodge Hill.

It had rained during the night and as she crossed the damp grass, a layer of early morning mist hung suspended over the ground. Combined with the noise of several rooks cawing in the trees, it lent the crematorium the quality of a gothic horror, and it was almost a relief to Anna to find that she was not quite alone. As she approached the area where Eddie's plaque should have been planted, she saw another woman, dressed not in the black hooded cloak that would have sustained the illusion, but in jeans and a leather jacket. As Anna came nearer, she realised that the woman was crouching directly in front of Eddie's newly planted memorial, arranging a small bunch of carnations, and unaware of Anna's presence, until she spoke.

'Hello,' said Anna. The effect was immediate. The young woman turned and seeing Anna, scrambled to her feet and began to back away, until with enough distance between them she turned and ran.

But those few brief seconds were enough for Anna to recognise her. 'Wait!' she called, but to no avail. Realising that the woman wasn't going to stop, Anna wasted valuable seconds debating whether to follow on foot, or return to her car. She opted for the chase, running after the woman as she fled from the cemetery out onto the road, and praying that she wouldn't get into a waiting vehicle. An extensive housing estate had grown up around the crematorium, and glancing back occasionally to see Anna in pursuit, the girl kept on running, through the network of almost identical streets, until finally she emerged onto the busy dual carriageway of the main Bristol Road.

She seemed to be heading for the bus stop, which would take her back towards the city centre. If she boarded a bus, Anna didn't have a hope, it would move off long before she could catch up. But for once things were going Anna's way, and there were none to be seen. Anna was gaining ground now and the girl showing signs of panic, until suddenly a black cab appeared from nowhere and with a minimal wave of her hand, the girl flagged it and jumped in. Anna was still too far off to read the cab's license number, but not for the vehicle registration. Rehearsing it over and over to herself, she fumbled in her bag for a pen and scribbled down the number on the palm of her hand. Breathless, but still running on adrenaline, she retraced her steps to the crematorium, where she retrieved her mobile phone from the car. After only minutes she was connected.

'I'd like to speak to Inspector Mariner, please,' she gasped. 'It's urgent.'

* * *

Tony Knox was nearest to the phone in Mariner's office when it rang. He picked it up.

'Anna Barham, boss,' he said watching Mariner's reaction a little too carefully as he handed it over.

'What? Who?' Mariner took the phone, masking, he hoped, the fact that Anna had barely been absent from his thoughts, conscious or unconscious, since last night. She was probably embarrassed now about what had happened, but when she spoke, if anything, she sounded excited.

'I think I've just seen Kerry.'

All thoughts of the previous evening evaporated. 'Where are you?'

'Selly Oak, at the crematorium. She went off in a cab, but I've got the registration.'

It was tenuous, but it was something. 'Okay, go ahead.' But he sensed hesitation.

'On one condition,' she said.

'What?' That we don't talk about what happened last night? Fine. But it was nothing like that.

'I'll give you the number,' Anna said. 'But I want to be there when you talk to her.'

She didn't ask much. 'Alternatively, I could just charge you with obstruction,' he said coolly, but, like that other significant aspect of his life, it was impossible to maintain. 'All right,' he conceded. 'When I talk to her informally you can be there, as long as you stay quiet and don't interfere. But if I have to bring her to the station for formal questioning, you know that will be different, don't you?'

'Of course. Look, I know you're going out on a limb for me. Thanks.'

'Sure.'

She recited the cab's registration number for him to write down.

'It will take time to trace this back,' Mariner warned her. 'And even then we may not be sure. If the taxi has dropped her off somewhere in the city centre, we'll have lost her. Go back to your place and if we do find her, I'll pick you up from there.'

'Thank you.'

More gratitude. He'd save it up for a rainy day.

* * *

A weak sun was trying to push its way through the low, grey cloud as, fifty minutes later, Mariner drove down Millpond Road, one of the shabbier aspects of Edgbaston, with Anna Barham beside him in the passenger seat. They'd been lucky. The taxi driver who picked up Kerry had been able to furnish them with the exact dropping off point and even the number of the house he'd seen her let herself into, perhaps making a note of it for his own personal future reference.

The road comprised mainly Victorian three- and four-storey houses of rusty brick that had long since passed their heyday. Most were now segregated into flats and bedsits, to provide cheap accommodation for asylum seekers, DSS claimants, and anyone else with a high level of desperation. Their residents had little long-term interest in the aesthetic qualities of the properties and consequently gardens were untended, stray rubbish littered the streets and this morning a couple of skinny cats foraged for pickings among the over-spilling bins.

Number seventy-two blended perfectly into the squalor. Torn grey net curtains hung at some of the windows, although those higher up looked new. There was no bell or knocker, so Mariner banged his fist on the door, creating as much noise as he could.

After a faint burst of music and some scuffling, the door was opened by a large African-Caribbean woman of indiscernible age. 'What you want?' she barked, squinting suspiciously at Mariner's proffered warrant card.

'We're looking for Kerry,' he said.

'Kerry?'

'We've got reason to believe she lives here. We just want to talk to her.'

'There's a girl lives on the top floor,' the woman said. 'Don't know what her name is.'

Mariner held out the photograph. 'Is this her?'

The woman peered. 'Yeah, a real sweetie.'

'We need to come in.'

The woman shrugged, turned and shuffled back into her own apartment, slamming the door behind her and leaving them alone in a dark and desolate hallway. Mariner led the way up uncarpeted wooden stairs, through a dim atmosphere, thick with the stench of stale cigarette smoke and rotting food. He cringed on Anna's behalf. It was all in a day's work for him, but for her it must be like a different planet. They passed one landing and continued on up to the next. A door at the top was crudely daubed '1a' in grey paint and had a tarnished knocker in the centre. Mariner rapped on it. Kerry was apparently expecting someone. The door was pulled back almost immediately, wide and welcoming, by a tall slim girl, with glossy shoulder-length chestnut hair and chocolate eyes, which were instantly wary. An inch of her midriff was visible, showing off a small, neat tattoo of a butterfly.

Mariner held out his warrant card again. 'Hello, Kerry.'

Kerry stared at him suspiciously, trying to work out where she'd seen him before, but then she saw Anna, and, recognising her, attempted to slam the door shut again. The door rebounded off the sole of Mariner's shoe. 'We just need to ask you a few questions about Eddie Barham,' he said. 'We can do it here or at the station. It's up to you.' He'd said the magic words and her resistance breached, Kerry led them through a short hallway into a lounge.

The small flat was neat in comparison with the rest of the building. *She doesn't bring her clients back here*, thought Mariner, *it's far too homely and personal.* Even to his undiscriminating eye the decor was tasteful and pleasing, and above all it was spotlessly clean. For Anna's sake he was glad of that. That wasn't the only surprise, either. Kerry, when she spoke, was surprisingly articulate, although her manners didn't extend to offering them a seat. Mariner sat down anyway and Anna followed his lead, leaving Kerry with little choice. Mariner also held back on any introduction of Anna, allowing Kerry to make the assumption that she, too, was a police officer.

'Tell me how you first met Eddie Barham,' he began.

'It was a long time ago, I can't really remember.' She was cool and closed.

'Try.'

Kerry looked over to the window and made a show of trying to recall, though it was more probable that she was weighing up how much to tell him.

'It was a couple of years ago, maybe three. I was living rough. A bunch of us used to go to this café, greasy spoon place near the bus station, when we could afford it. Eddie came in there and we got talking.'

'About what?'

'I don't know, just chit chat, you know. Nothing really, but he was very good at getting stuff out of you. He was just nice, friendly, and he seemed interested.'

'In what?'

'Anything, everything. How we lived. What we did all day. I did think it was a bit weird, until one day he coughed that he was a reporter. He said he was working on some article about what it was like to be living on the streets in Birmingham. He wasn't going to use real names or anything, but just write about how kids ended up there, on the streets, and what happened to them. He said it was a chance to tell our story.'

'And you helped him with it?'

'Yeah. I thought it would be a laugh. Besides he was offering money.'

'Did you know about what was going on at Streetwise?'

Kerry blushed, more in anger than anything. 'Yeah, of course I knew. Everyone did.'

'So you were aware that Frank Crosby was using the drop-in centre as a way of procuring underage kids for prostitution?' Mariner had to be sure of this. From the corner of his eye he saw Anna's eyes widen almost imperceptibly, but he couldn't help that. She'd asked to be here.

'I didn't know about Frank then,' Kerry said. 'I'd seen him around, but I just thought he was a friend of Paul's. Paul was the one who did all the deals.'

'Did you ever do any "work"' for Paul?'

'You know I did.' She held his gaze.

'And you told Eddie about it.'

'I missed one of our meetings. Eddie wanted to know where I'd been, so yes, I told him. I think I wanted to shock him.'

'And did you?'

'Sort of. But Eddie was too much of a pro. He just found it more interesting than the piece he was writing. From then on that was all he wanted to know about.'

'Did you tell him much?'

'Only what had happened to me. I said he'd have to find out the rest himself. I don't grass.' Implicit was her utter contempt for informants. Mariner wondered what she'd have thought if he'd told her that it was how he'd first joined the payroll of the West Midlands Police.

'The next thing I knew, your lot had arrested Paul and Frank Crosby. That was when I first knew who Frank really was. But by then Eddie had paid me enough to put down a deposit on this place, so I didn't have to go to the drop-in anymore.'

'And when did you start working for Frank Crosby yourself, Kerry?' Mariner asked innocently. He hadn't been sure, but her reaction verified it all right.

'I don't work for him,' she said, petulantly. 'I work for myself.'

'And where do you work?' asked Mariner. 'Where do you take your clients?'

'I rent a room.'

'In one of Frank's seedy little hotels?' Mariner could tell from her face that he'd hit the mark. 'And I suppose Frank puts the occasional punter your way, too.'

'It's worth it, they're always generous, Frank's clients. I had to get started somehow.'

As if there was no other option in life. 'I bet Frank doesn't know that you helped Eddie with his story, does he? Does he ever encourage you to offer your clients extra services?'

'Like what?'

'Like a little additional chemical stimulation.'

'No. I don't mess with any of that stuff.' She was rock steady.

Mariner let it go for now. 'And did you see Eddie again after the story broke?'

'Not for a while, no.'

'So when did you see him?'

'A few weeks ago. He'd been in to Maureen's.'

'Heaven's Gate.'

'I know.' Even she could see the irony. 'He'd seen my picture. Maureen gave him one of my cards, so he phoned me.'

'For an appointment?'

Crunch time. But Kerry just laughed. 'Not exactly.'

'So why did he contact you?'

'He wanted a favour.'

'Another story? About what? Frank Crosby?'

'No, it wasn't like that. Eddie's got this brother who's a bit backward, you know?'

The sudden shift in the conversation caught Mariner off guard. 'Jamie?' he said, nonplussed.

'Yeah, that's right. Eddie looked after him. Anyway, he was having trouble with him getting horny. He'd started playing with his dick in public, groping women, that kind of thing. Eddie thought it might help if he actually had sex, you know. He thought it might calm him down. He could hardly ask any of his friends to do it, so he had been trying escort agencies. That's how he finished up at Maureen's. Trouble was, none of the girls would go to his house, and he needed Jamie to learn that sex is something you do in private, in your own place. Then when he saw my picture in Maureen's and she told him what I was doing, he thought I'd be able to help. He knew I looked after myself.'

'And did you agree to do it?' asked Mariner.

'Not straight away. I mean, I felt sorry for the boy. Nearly thirty and had never been laid. Can you imagine that?' Mariner didn't say that actually he was beginning to get an inkling. 'I said I'd want to meet him first,' Kerry went on. 'I didn't know if I could. So one night I met Eddie in the pub and he took me back to his house.'

'When was that?'

'About a month ago, I suppose.'

'And did you do the business?'

Anna visibly flinched, but Kerry remained casual. 'No, but I would have. He was quite sweet and good-looking too. You couldn't really tell that there was anything wrong with him, apart from some of that weird stuff he did. But he wouldn't come near me. It was as if he wanted to, he kept sort of looking, but Eddie said it might take time for him to get used to me.'

'So what did you do?'

'I started just going to see them. I used to stop by at their house on my way back from other appointments. I would have been bloody stupid not to. All I did was sit and watch TV with them, but Eddie still paid me.'

'Did you tell Eddie Barham that you work for Frank—?'

'I told you, I don't.'

'All right then, did Eddie know about your little "arrangement" with Crosby?'

'Not to begin with, no. Why should he? It was none of his business.'

'So who was it who had him beaten up three weeks ago?'

Kerry fell silent, avoiding Mariner's eye. 'Frank must have found out that I'd been seeing Eddie and jumped to the wrong conclusion,' she glared at Mariner. 'Like you did. He wanted me to stop seeing him. Said he knew what crap reporters wrote. I told him it wasn't anything to do with that, but Frank didn't believe me.'

'So he gave Eddie a going over. And then what?'

'Frank told me not to see Eddie again. That if I did, the next time he wouldn't get off so lightly, and me neither. I called round to tell Eddie I couldn't see them anymore. It upset me to do it. I think even Jamie knew something was wrong. He was really sweet, tried to comfort me.' Mariner remembered Jamie's words: Kay no cry. 'Eddie was disappointed of course, but he understood.'

'So when did you see Eddie Barham again?'

'Last Sunday night, he called me. He'd had a bad week. Jamie had walked up to some woman in the swimming baths and grabbed at her breast. Eddie was worried that she might make a complaint. He was desperate. He wanted me to go round, just one last time.'

'And?'

'I told him I couldn't. I had another appointment anyway. Then when I was waiting for the punter to show—'

'Derek.'

Now Kerry realised where she'd seen Mariner before. She looked at him anew. 'Yeah, that's right. While I was waiting for Derek, Eddie turned up. He knew where I met people and he came to talk me into going with him.'

'And you went with him, even though Crosby had warned you not to.'

'Eddie could be persuasive, and like I said, I felt bad. He'd already paid me a lot with nothing to show for it. I wanted to wait to explain to Derek, but Eddie had left Jamie at home on his own so we had to go straight away.'

So that's what the argument was about. 'Did Eddie ask you to bring him a little extra something this time?'

'No. He wasn't into that shit and neither am I.'

'So what happened?' Mariner asked, even though he was already beginning to put it together for himself.

'Eddie took me back to his house in the car. But when we got there, his front door was wide open and there were these two guys inside. Jamie had gone. Eddie went ballistic.'

'What guys? Frank Crosby's men?'

'I'd never seen them before. They were going through Eddie's stuff upstairs, after money I suppose. Eddie tried to take them on, but there were two of them. He didn't stand a chance.'

'And?'

Kerry looked down at her hands. 'What could I do? I was behind Eddie and I didn't think they'd seen me, so I ran to get help. The battery in my mobile was dead and there are no bloody call boxes anywhere any more. I had to go for miles, but in the end I found one and called 999.'

'Very public spirited of you. I thought you said you liked Eddie Barham.'

'I did.' She was defiant.

'So at the first sign of trouble, you just bugger off and leave him.'

'I told you, I went to get help. What else could I do? I was scared. I didn't know what was going to happen, that Eddie would be—'

'Why didn't you go to the neighbours?'

'Oh yeah, like they're going to help me. You should see the way that snotty cow next door looks at me.'

'Are you sure it wasn't more to do with the fact that you knew who those men were? That Frank Crosby told you to disappear? I think you did as you were told, but then your conscience got the better of you, so you waited a while and then called us.'

'That's not true!'

'Crosby had already had Eddie beaten up once, but it hadn't worked, had it? And he was afraid of what Eddie Barham was going to write, wasn't he?'

'It wasn't like that—'

'I think you're lying, Kerry. I think you know very well who killed Eddie Barham. And that's why you ran away that night and why you ran away again today, from Eddie's sister.'

'His sister?' She stared at Anna. Up until then she hadn't realised who she was. She turned back to Mariner. 'I don't know who those men were. I swear it.'

'Who's Sally-Ann?' Mariner asked suddenly.

'Who?'

'Sally-Ann. Is she this friend of yours, or do you sometimes use another name?'

'I've never heard of her.'

'I think you have.'

'All right. I heard the boy mention her once, that's all. But I don't know who she is.'

Mariner stood up. 'Get your coat.'

'What for? You said—'

'You were probably the last person to see Eddie Barham alive, Kerry. We need you to make a formal statement.'

'But I'm expecting—'

'Leave a note on the door. You're the only person who's seen these two men, and even if you didn't know them,' Mariner could barely keep the scepticism from his voice, 'you can give us a description, while I have a little chat with your friend and beneficiary, Frank Crosby.'

Kerry sighed and got her coat. On the way out she turned to Anna. 'I'm sorry, I really am. Eddie was one of the good guys. How's the boy?'

Anna smiled, weakly. 'He's fine.'

'This is where you have to leave it to us,' Mariner told Anna, depositing her outside her flat.

Anna nodded. 'I know. But thanks for letting me hear that. I need to know what happened.'

'I'll stay in touch.'

'Thanks, I appreciate that.'

CHAPTER 22

Mariner left Kerry in the capable hands of a WPC at the Facial Identification Bureau, at Lloyd House, to be shown a selection from the 25,000 or more mugshots they kept on file. The department also operated a sophisticated e-FIT system, which could create a computer image based purely on descriptions Kerry gave them. It was a step or two up from the crude cut-and-paste jobs they were doing when Mariner had started on the force. But if all that state-of-the-art razzmatazz failed, there was always the graphic artist on hand.

Mariner's next stop was DCI Coleman's office. Burly and balding, Jack Coleman was an old generation copper who had risen through the ranks through sheer slog and a powerful conviction that simple but dedicated attention to detail achieved results. It was a doctrine bordering on pedantry that in his previous posting at Severn Road Station had earned him the nickname of 'the Severn Bore.' But Coleman's principles were founded on bitter experience. Only five weeks into the job he'd been one of a handful of officers on foot patrol on the night of 21 November 1974, when a coded warning was received to say that two bombs had been planted in Birmingham city centre.

He'd been present later too, at Steelhouse Lane, when the six Irishmen had been brought in, branded guilty and savagely beaten before they'd even opened their mouths to protest their innocence. He'd seen the fear on their faces and known that it was wrong, but like dozens of others he'd kept silent and had lived with the guilt ever since. These days he made sure that his officers had solid facts before an arrest was sanctioned, and despite the frustration of most of the relief, his squad's high conviction record spoke for itself. Today he was characteristically bedded deep in paperwork when Mariner went in.

'I want to shake Frank Crosby,' Mariner told him, without procrastination.

Coleman put down his pen and sat back in his seat. The glare from his desk lamp bounced off his shining scalp. 'On what grounds?'

Mariner explained what they'd uncovered, including the link with Kerry. Saying it out loud, even to his ears it was beginning to sound flimsy and insubstantial. Unsurprisingly the gaffer apparently felt the same way.

'Eddie Barham's murder doesn't on the face of it look much like Crosby's usual style, does it?' he said. 'He's not known to dress things up, as someone patently did.'

'No, but he does have ready access to drugs and women, so that part at least makes sense. And he has a history with Eddie Barham, too. I just want to talk to him, see his reaction.'

It must have been enough because Coleman didn't argue any further. 'Just go carefully, Tom,' he warned, unnecessarily. 'Frank Crosby bringing a complaint of harassment is something I can honestly live without.'

'Yes, sir.'

'What about Tony Knox?'

'If he's available I'll take him along. The uniform could be an asset.'

'You would seem to be having quite an influence over him,' Coleman remarked.

'He's good at his job,' said Mariner, not having any reason to say otherwise. 'He could be CID material.'

Coleman glanced down at the paperwork on his desk, suddenly avoiding eye contact. 'Yes, I'd heard that he was desperate to get back into plain clothes.'

'Back?'

'Didn't he tell you?'

'We work together. He doesn't confide in me. What happened?'

'Let's just say that during his last spell out of uniform he lacked a certain self-discipline. I'm sure he'll fill in the details for you if he wants to.' So, Tony Knox had been a detective before. No wonder he'd taken to it so well.

* * *

Frank Crosby was taking an afternoon off to get in touch with his human side, playing the role of respectable businessman to improve his swing, putt and very possibly perfect his techniques for employing golf clubs as instruments of torture. Mariner and Knox sat in the car waiting for him to return from the green, watching the clusters of men in gaudy checks and pastels pushing around their golf carts.

'Look at them.' Knox muttered under his breath. 'They're like a bunch of old women with their shopping trolleys.' He shot Mariner a wary sidelong glance. 'You don't play, do you, boss?'

Mariner let him off the hook. 'No, I'm with Twain on this one: *a good walk spoilt*. That's Mark Twain I'm on about, not Shania.'

Knox flashed a sarcastic smile. 'Still,' he added slyly, 'with the state of the football teams down here, there has to be an alternative sport.'

It was too good an opportunity to miss. 'So if you didn't come down here for the football, why did you move to Birmingham?' Mariner asked. 'It wasn't for the clean air.'

'I just fancied a change,' said Knox, without missing a beat. And he escaped further interrogation by the appearance of Frank Crosby, his perambulation apparently over for today.

They watched Crosby and his entourage of two go into the clubhouse, before tracking him down in the members' bar where he was ordering a Campari and soda. Even in their golfing gear, it wasn't hard to pick out Crosby's associates from the general public. It was a question of size, though paradoxically, the exception was Crosby himself.

Less than five feet five of concentrated muscle and teeth, Crosby resembled a pit bull terrier in human form, and enjoyed a reputation for being every bit as vicious. His baby pink polo shirt looked almost grotesque, stretched over his hairy, tattooed arms: like biker's leathers on a new-born infant. Although Kingswood Golf Club was not as exclusive as some, Mariner doubted that many other club members had any idea what Frank Crosby really did for a living. Right now he was enjoying a joke with his cronies.

'Mr Crosby?' Making no effort to lower his voice, Mariner openly displayed his warrant card for the benefit of all those present. 'Detective Inspector Mariner, West Midlands Police. Could I have a word?' With Knox's uniform providing added visual effect, Mariner had succeeded in capturing the attention of everyone in the room: everything so far was going to plan.

Crosby's anger was visible in the flush that spread up through his Donald Trump tan. But this was a man who'd learned over time to control his temper, and by the time he'd picked up his drink and separated from the group there remained only a hint of irritation in his voice. 'Over here,' he said tautly, leading the way to a secluded corner of the room, well away from listening ears. Despite the unnaturally dark hair and gleaming white teeth, Crosby was approaching sixty and running to fat. If you knew where to look, his throat still bore the deep scar sustained in a scuffle in Winson Green, although it was many years since he'd been a guest of Her Majesty. He'd become far too skilled at delegation for that. These days he could afford to be relaxed and play a round or two of golf, give or take the occasional rude interruption from the law. 'What do you want?' he demanded, at a safe distance from his fellow club members. He regarded Mariner like something nasty he'd just stepped in, his annoyance betrayed only by the bulging muscle in his jaw.

'I want you to tell me about Eddie Barham,' Mariner said, with equal directness.

Crosby snorted, almost with relief, making Mariner wonder what he'd thought was on the agenda. 'What about him? He's a reporter. Pain in the arse if you must know,' Crosby said, candidly.

'Really?'

'Yeah. Spends too much time sticking his nose into things that don't concern him.'

'Into your affairs, you mean. He landed you right in it a few years back, didn't he?'

The eyes narrowed. 'I'll remind you I was never charged with anything.'

'Eddie Barham dragged your name through the mud though, didn't he? That must have been bad for business.'

'I got over it.'

'But not the sort of thing you'd want to happen again, if you could help it.' Mariner glanced around him at the opulent surroundings. 'Wouldn't go down well here, would it? Your name splashed all over the papers a second time. It must have made you a bit nervous when Eddie linked up with one of your girls again. I don't suppose you wanted to play the lead in anything else he was about to write. Is that why you had him roughed up?'

Crosby had seen this coming and was far too street-smart to deny it. After all, Eddie Barham hadn't pressed charges so there was nothing to worry about. 'My colleagues offered him a little advice, just in case he was thinking of doing anything stupid.'

'It was hard advice. It left Eddie with enough bruises to fabricate a mugging story.'

'Yeah, well, it's what he's good at, isn't it? Making up stories. I just wanted to make sure that he got the message.'

'But he didn't, did he Frank? So you went back. Was he threatening you with blackmail? Is that why you had to go over his house; to recover any incriminating documentation?'

'What?' Crosby suddenly had the look of a man who had completely lost the plot, though masking his reactions would come naturally by now.

'What were you doing?' interjected Knox, increasing the pressure. 'Following Kerry? Or had you tapped Eddie Barham's phone?'

'Where were you on Sunday, 16 February, Frank?' Mariner demanded. 'The night Eddie Barham was killed.'

Finally his words provoked a reaction, but not the one Mariner had been expecting. 'Killed? What are you on about—?'

'Don't you read the papers, either?'

'Why would I? Full of crap most of the time.' Crosby was on the defensive. Then Mariner remembered someone telling him that Crosby couldn't actually read very well.

Knox pushed again. 'How far were you prepared to go, to keep Eddie Barham quiet, Frank? Or were you doing it for Paul?'

'Paul who?'

'Paul Spink. Forget him already, even though he took the rap for you? Were you repaying the compliment?' Mariner had no idea whether there had been any contact between the two men since Spink's conviction. It was just a simple logical pursuit, but one which, apparently, Crosby was having difficulty keeping up with.

'I don't know what the fuck you're on about,' he said, finally beginning to lose his cool. 'A Sunday night? I'd have been at the dog track all night.'

'And what about your "colleagues?"' Mariner nodded towards the group at the bar, who cast the occasional anxious glance towards them.

'Carl and Terry were with me. We'd have been at the track till two in the morning. Ask anyone.'

'We will,' Mariner assured him. Unexpectedly, Crosby seemed then to relax, again making Mariner wonder what else was bothering him. But seeing the now smug expression, Mariner had a nasty feeling that Crosby was telling the truth — about Eddie Barham at least. There was one more test.

'I'll need you and your monkeys to come in for DNA swabs,' Mariner dropped in, as a last-ditch attempt at unnerving him. 'Just so that we can eliminate you from our enquiries.'

Crosby didn't bat an eyelid. 'Always happy to oblige,' he lied.

* * *

'What do you think, boss?' Knox asked once they were back in the car.

'I think Frank Crosby's an accomplished actor,' said Mariner. 'Let's wait for the swabs.' But even Mariner wasn't holding out much hope. Crosby had taken it all too much in his stride.

'Dinner time?' Knox started the car, ever the pragmatist.

'No thanks,' said Mariner. 'There's something I've got to do.'

'Oh?'

'It's personal,' Mariner said, enigmatically. 'I'm going in search of a resolution, Tony. You should try it sometime.'

But Knox just looked at him as if he was mad.

Mariner tried Greta's office number first. With a small child to clothe and feed, he couldn't imagine that she'd had the luxury of being a stay-at-home mum. He was right.

'Tom! What a surprise.' A mutual one. She sounded not displeased to hear from him. Equally unexpectedly, she agreed to meet him for a quick drink after work in a couple of hours, giving Mariner ample time to make his debut visit to Toys R Us.

* * *

Greta wasn't in the appointed bar when he arrived a few minutes late and it crossed his mind that she might yet stand him up for old times' sake. He'd trailed round every appropriate shop in town to look for a present for the baby, but when it came to it he hadn't a clue what to buy. He didn't know the gender of the child, or what would be suitable for its age. In the end he'd settled on a generic cuddly rabbit.

Greta had chosen as their meeting place a wine bar close to where she worked. Sitting down at a table, Mariner ordered a bottle of obscenely expensive mineral water with two glasses. Greta had never been much of a drinker and he needed to keep a clear head.

When she appeared, short of breath, Mariner was, for several moments, thrown into confusion. 'Greta.' He stood up to kiss her cheek. 'How are you?' But he hadn't really needed to ask. She was clearly blossoming, her belly swollen by about six months of pregnancy.

'I'm great,' she said. 'Really well. Do you want to see?' And with the enthusiasm of any new parent-to-be she sat down, and without waiting for his reply, rifled through her handbag to produce a monochrome snapshot of what resembled, to Mariner, an oversized tadpole. 'The consultant says that she's a perfectly average size, plum in the middle of the fiftieth percentile. If she keeps growing at the same rate, she'll weigh about seven pounds at birth. Sorry, that's probably too much information, but I get told everything. First baby at my age, you can't even fart off the record, especially coming so soon after a miscarriage.' She looked into Mariner's eyes, pausing for the first time. 'I'm afraid ours didn't make it.'

'I'm sorry,' said Mariner, as something stabbed at his chest.

'So am I, but it was probably for the best, wasn't it? Sorry, I should have let you know, but I was— well, let's not go over all that again.'

No, let's not.

'Dominic, an old friend, was very supportive.' She placed her hands on her bump. 'So supportive, in fact, that we ended up with this.'

Finally Mariner recovered his power of speech. 'Congratulations,' he said. 'I'm really happy for you.' It was perfectly true. He remembered the gift. 'I brought you this,' he said, handing over the plastic bag. 'It was for. . . But you can . . .' He tailed off as Greta took out the soft toy.

'Oh, it's sweet, Tom. Thank you.' She leaned across and kissed him. 'Anyway, how about you?'

'Me?'

'Yes. Are you seeing someone?'

Good question. 'Not right now. That's probably for the best, too.'

'Mm. Still working all the hours God sends, I suppose.'

He couldn't really disagree. They talked a little longer about inconsequential things, mutual acquaintances who had really been Greta's friends, and polished off a second bottle of spring water.

'I should be going,' Greta said, at last. 'As it is, I'm going to get all the rush-hour traffic.'

They both went up to the bar to pay. As Mariner took out his wallet, a slim, white sheet of paper fluttered out, landing at Greta's feet. The prescription. Shit! Simultaneously, they stooped to retrieve it, Mariner snatching at it before Greta had the chance.

'Throwing away your love letters now, Tom?' Greta smiled. And Mariner had to stifle a sudden urge to laugh hysterically at the irony of the situation. The bill settled, they hugged and wished each other well for the future, then went their separate ways. Greta back to Dominic, and Mariner into the nearest proper pub, where he ordered a single malt, on duty or not, and knocked it back in a couple of burning mouthfuls.

So now he knew. There was no Mariner junior inhabiting the planet and oddly he wasn't sure whether to be relieved or disappointed. If pressed, he'd have tended towards the former, but either way, he wasn't about to take any more risks with that prescription. On his way back to the car, he took it out from where he'd stuffed it in his pocket, screwed it into a ball and dropped it into the nearest rubbish bin. He felt an unexpected urge to call Anna Barham.

CHAPTER 23

Anna had already left work and was at the day centre collecting Jamie prior to visiting to the residential home recommended by Mark. She'd specifically been asked this time to take Jamie with her.

'The social worker came this morning,' Francine informed her.

'What social worker?'

'I assumed it was to do with your last visit.'

The Beeches. Anna was surprised. She hadn't expected things to move quite so fast, but she wasn't about to complain. 'Did she want to see Jamie?' She recalled the questions about 'challenging behaviour,' hoping that Jamie hadn't done anything that might have put the social worker off.

'It was a he,' Francine said. 'And no, he didn't want to see Jamie. Said it was unnecessary at this stage. He just asked the usual questions, particularly about Jamie's communication skills, level of understanding, that kind of thing.'

It was years since Anna had had any experience of this, and even then it wasn't first hand. Her parents had always arranged everything and she'd given it minimal attention. It seemed odd that no one had contacted her first, but then it was probably the protocol, eliminating the opportunity for any advance preparation.

'I hope it was all right for me to talk to him,' Francine said, suddenly concerned. 'I kept everything very positive.'

'Yes, of course it was. Thanks, Francine. Come on, Jamie, let's go.'

* * *

Unlike The Beeches, Manor Park was out of town, set deep in the Worcestershire countryside, and though based around an old stately home, included modern purpose-built facilities in acres of wooded grounds. According to a commemorative plaque in the lobby, the new facility had been opened just five years before by HRH Princess Anne.

Run by the Autistic Association, it was designed specifically with the needs of autistic adults in mind, subscribing to the principles of the Higashi Institute in Boston, with a focus on physical exercise and a rigidly structured timetable. In addition, a number of different therapies and approaches were favoured, including the use of various functional communication aids. Wherever there were signs in words, there were pictures and symbols too. Colours were muted and displays kept to a minimum, with no strip lighting. Special attention had been given to sound absorption, too, creating a calm and relaxed atmosphere.

Anna didn't detect all this on her own, some of it she read in the glossy prospectus she was given while she and Jamie waited for 'one of the team' to show them around. All the staff, she read with interest, were trained in the use of alternative communication, including PECS, the picture exchange communication system. This was more like it. And above all, there were no funny smells.

'Miss Barham?' Anna was greeted by a man of around thirty-five, blond and tanned, who introduced himself as

Simon Meadows, 'one of the team of care staff.' His accent had an Australian twang to it.

Anna noticed from the picture board on the wall that Simon was actually the senior member of that team, but she liked that he hadn't said that.

'And this is Jamie?' he asked. 'Jamie, hello.'

Jamie responded with a fleeting glance, which Simon answered with a thumbs-up sign. 'That's good looking. Thank you.' He turned to Anna. 'Shall we go?'

Their first stop was 'the gym,' which turned out to be a soft play room for grown-ups, with ball pools and climbing apparatus, its walls and floor padded for protection.

'It's the letting-off-steam area,' Simon explained. 'Essential for the clients and the staff. Jamie probably doesn't want to do the boring tour, so he can stay here.' He called over one of his colleagues and assigned him to watch over Jamie. 'He'll be leaving at quarter past four,' he said. 'You can start counting him down when you're ready.'

Counting him down. Anna had seen Francine doing that with Jamie, preparing him for the end of an activity so that he wasn't upset when it stopped or changed.

They began the tour. Simon was welcoming but pragmatic, and not in the least bit ingratiating. The building was busy with other people, but often Anna was hard pushed to tell the difference between staff and clients. Overall, the age profile was much nearer to Jamie's own and relationships looked friendly and easy. Facilities for men and for women were clearly delineated and there were self-contained facilities for individual independence training. Instead of a heavy question-and-answer session at the end, Simon gently elicited information as they walked around.

'How old is Jamie? Where is he living right now? That must be hard, how is he doing? How is his eating, and his sleeping?' Anna was so impressed with the place, she would have told Meadows anything, and she had no qualms about being completely honest with him.

'His sleeping is awful,' she confessed. 'He's up several times every night, but I don't want to resort to medication.' No harm in making it clear from the start.

'Neither do we,' said Meadows. 'Though I have to say that if we've explored all other options, we do consider it. In isolated cases, the use of medication can be highly successful, but we have to have tried every other strategy first. And, of course, it would only be introduced with your approval.'

Anna was pleased to hear it. 'So when can he start?' she asked, straight away, only half-joking. They'd arrived back in reception.

Meadows smiled. 'Let's just jot down a few details,' he said, as if he hadn't just extracted everything there was to know from Anna. 'We try to operate like a community so we do try to take clients who will benefit from the regime.' He handed her a concise application form. Full name? Easy. Date of birth? Anna even had that off pat now, too. Seventeenth of the third and now she even knew the year. At the end of the document was a small section requesting permission for the staff to administer appropriate medications to regulate sleeping and behaviour.

'As I said, it's when all else fails,' said Meadows, seeing her hesitation. 'Why don't you think that part over, and give us a call.' Finally he handed her a list of charges.

Anna did a double take. 'This is for a year?' she asked.

Meadows made a sympathetic face. 'No, it's quarterly. I know. It's expensive, but the work we do involves very high staff ratios. That's how we can minimise the use of medication. I think you'll find that's not unusual.' So that was the catch.

Meadows glanced up at the clock. It was fourteen minutes past four. 'Now, I guess we'd better not keep Jamie waiting.'

* * *

Late in the afternoon as Mariner walked back into Granville Lane, Tony Knox had bad news. 'Crosby's alibi checks out,' he said. 'We've got a whole pile of witnesses who saw him at the track on that Sunday night, including some of our blokes who were down there keeping an eye on things. He had a successful run apparently and was throwing his money around. Laurel and Hardy were with him, too.'

'Bugger.'

'It's not conclusive though, is it? Even if the swabs turn out to be negative Crosby could easily have hired some temporary help.'

'Maybe, but unless we can identify who that might be, it isn't enough to pull him in either. And if that sum of money in Eddie Barham's bank account wasn't about blackmail, then what was it?'

'For what it's worth, these are the e-fits Kerry came up with.' Knox passed him the crudely assembled photographs. They could have been anyone. In fact, one of them had the look of the pope about him. Mariner wondered what his Excellency was up to last Sunday night. The other had a neat, dark moustache. 'No black mouth,' said Mariner, almost to himself.

'Sorry?' asked Knox.

'No black mouth,' Mariner repeated. It was what Jamie shouted when we took him back to the house. I think he was telling us that one of Eddie's attackers had a moustache – a black mouth.'

'That rules out about nine tenths of the population,' said Knox, helpfully. 'And that's just the women.'

'We're almost there, then,' Mariner replied, matching his sarcasm. The fact of the thing was that it was now almost two weeks since Eddie Barham was murdered, and every hour took them further from the likelihood of finding his killers. Their one tenuous lead had reached a dead end and they were left with virtually nothing. If they had any suspects they could arrange a line up based on

Kerry's descriptions, but Mariner wouldn't know where to start. Who the hell was it who'd wanted Eddie Barham dead?

* * *

Despite the careful preparation, Jamie wasn't too thrilled about leaving Manor Park, and moaned all the way home. Anna had been so impressed with the place that she was tempted to just ring Simon Meadows and tell him that she'd reached her decision, but the cost had taken her breath away. Selling her parents' house would make all the difference, but their will had made it patently clear that in Jamie's lifetime that just wasn't an option. Renting it out might be one creative solution to the problem, but she'd have to be certain of a long-term let and even that could prove to be messy to maintain. Jamie could live to be a very old man, at a time when she herself would be getting older and looking forward to an untroubled retirement.

The enormity of the responsibility felt overwhelming, as it must have been for Mum and Dad and then for Eddie. There was some hard thinking to be done about the medication issue. Even to be considering it made her feel like the family traitor, but DI Mariner was right. Times were changing. Drug therapy was becoming more commonplace because the medicines used were more sophisticated and reliable. And if Manor Park wasn't affordable in the long term it was no good to her, so alternatives would have to be considered. Eddie had clearly been thinking along those lines too because once you started looking at cheaper residential care there seemed little choice. He'd been backed into the same corner.

Retrieving the handouts from Professor Fellowes' talk, Anna spread them out on the kitchen table before seeking out the package that Eddie sent her. She took the blue folder out of the drawer in the lounge. The effect on Jamie was startling. He jumped up from where he was on the floor and hovered a few feet away, staring at the folder with grave suspicion and keening softly. Intrigued, Anna thrust the folder towards him and he immediately backed off, flapping his hands in agitation. Anna laughed. 'What on earth is the matter, Jamie? It's only a folder.' She opened the lid to show him. 'Paper. There's nobody in here.'

But even so, it was some time before he would settle again. Disregarding her father's notebook for the moment, Anna focused on the photocopied sheets and printouts, most of them downloaded from the internet. Cross-referencing them with Professor Fellowes' information there were several common names: Ritalin, Fenfluromine, imipramine. For most, there were chemical formulae, along with descriptions of recent studies that had been carried out relating to their effectiveness. She tried reading one of the articles, but was beaten back by the jargon: *Opioids have long been known to reduce serotonergic transmission by stimulating the presynaptic auto receptors,* she read. *A drug which, unlike serotonin itself would selectively stimulate the post-synaptic receptors, could be of value in controlling aggression and sleep patterns.* Of course it could.

A common factor seemed to be that the drugs apparently acted on the serotonin system, as Professor Fellowes had said, and Anna now wished that she had paid more attention to the talk. She didn't even really know what serotonin was.

Systematically, she worked her way through the internet printouts and every story was the same, doubts raised about the effects of long-term courses of treatment using the drugs mentioned.

The only deviant from this pattern appeared to be something called Pinozalyan, but that was mainly because of the dearth of information on it anyway. All Anna could find was a none-too-clear photocopied paragraph from some kind of medical journal. But interestingly, Eddie had double starred it. Did this mean that it was the one he had settled on at the end of all his research? Anna sifted through the papers and sifted back again. There didn't appear to be any further printouts on it. And there was nothing among the notes from Professor Fellowes. She would have to do her own research. She plugged in her laptop and tapped the unfamiliar names into Google. There was at least some information about the other drugs, again much of it negative, but barely anything on Pinozalyan. Strange.

Yawning, Anna was overcome by a sudden, unexpected wave of fatigue and, glancing up at the clock, saw with a shock that it was twenty past eleven. The flat seemed unnaturally quiet. Jamie! Jamie? He was sprawled on the floor, having fallen asleep where he sat, still clutching a DVD box. The film itself had come to an end, leaving the menu sequence to play in a never-ending loop, as fuddled as Anna's brain felt right now. Her research would have to keep until tomorrow. It might be time to pay Dr Payne another visit, to see if he could enlighten her.

For a moment, Anna considered whether to wake Jamie and put him properly to bed, but decided against it. Instead she tucked a pillow under his head and arranged his duvet around him. He'd be awake soon enough anyway.

CHAPTER 24

She was right, woken at six thirty by Jamie poking a DVD in her face and tugging at her arm. Anna groaned. What wouldn't she give for a lie in? Driving Jamie to the centre, she couldn't shake off the feeling of exhaustion and despondency. Where was all this leading? In the cold light of day, Manor Park seemed an impossible proposition. It was enormously expensive, and despite what Simon Meadows had said, they did employ drug therapy, which her parents would have disapproved of, and on top of that it would mean taking Jamie away from the day centre, at least for some of the time, when the thing he needed most of all was consistency.

As a matter of interest, Anna asked Francine about any other clients at the centre who were taking medication. Francine knew of at least two who were on Ritalin and another who took Impramine, but she hadn't heard of Pinozalyan either. 'Could be something new,' she suggested. 'They're always trying things out.'

Anna tried to contact Professor Fellowes, but was told by his secretary that he was lecturing in London and couldn't be reached. She waited until mid-morning before going to the surgery in the hope that the morning rush would be over. Even so, there were still half a dozen people waiting to see Dr Payne or one of his partners.

The doctor seemed surprised to see Anna again so soon. 'Is everything all right with Jamie?'

'Yes, he's fine,' Anna reassured him. 'Although it is about him that I've called.' Anna explained about her visits to the two homes and the references to medication. 'The one Eddie seemed to have been focused on is called Pinozalyan. Have you come across it?'

Dr Payne frowned and shook his head doubtfully, 'No. I can't say I have.' But there was something else on his mind. 'Are you sure this is the right direction to be taking, Anna?' he asked.

'What?'

'Considering medication for Jamie. Many of these drugs haven't had time for the long-term effects to be known, and may lead to problems with dependency and side effects.' So he felt that way too. 'Your parents and I discussed it at length over several years and I know that neither of them wanted to put Jamie at any kind of risk. Naturally it's your own decision, but—'

But. Always a but. Just when it was looking as if her life was back within grasp, something swung by to knock it out again. She left the surgery dejected and down.

* * *

On top of that, she had to go into the office that day. As she'd expected, there was a mountain of post waiting for her, but seeing Becky provided an immediate distraction. 'Is Mark at work today?'

'I hope so,' said Becky. 'Unless he's swanned off somewhere for some secret passionate affair he hasn't told me about.'

'Do you think I could phone him for some information?'

'He'd love it. He's always had a soft spot for you.'

'He can keep his soft spots to himself. I just want to talk to him.'

Anna smiled, but Becky didn't notice. Absently, she reeled off the number of Mark's surgery. She seemed edgy and Anna soon found out why.

There was a knock on the door. It was Jonathan, looking astonishingly naked. He'd shaved off his goatee. 'Anna, how are you?'

Any cooler and Anna would have shivered. 'I'm fine, thank you,' she responded, frostily. Two could play at that game.

'Well, it's good to see you back again.' His voice lacked a certain sincerity, but he was gone again before Anna could allude to this.

'What happened to the facial hair?' she asked Becky instead.

Her friend had the grace to look embarrassed. 'Melanie doesn't like goatees.'

'Well, that puts me in my place then, doesn't it,' said Anna, cheerfully.

Alone again in her office, Anna ignored her bulging in-tray and keyed in the number Becky had given her. 'Hi Mark, it's Anna.'

'Anna, how are you? Has Becky got you checking up on me?'

'No, you're perfectly safe. I wanted to pick your brains on something.'

'Pick away.'

'I wondered if you'd ever come across of a drug called Pinozalyan? I think it could be something used to help with sleeping, particularly where autism is a factor.'

'Can you spell that for me?' Anna did.

There was a pause at the other end of the line, while Mark considered. 'No, I can't say that I have Anna, but then there are thousands of drugs marketed every year. It's impossible to keep on top of them all. I can look it up on the database for you though, if it's important.'

'It is, Mark. That would be great.'

More helpful than Dr Payne had been, but then, he might not have a surgery full of people waiting. And there was a rider. 'Okay, leave it with me, but I may not get back to you until later in the day, I'm just about to start my rounds.'

No problem. To while away some time, Anna sorted through her pile of urgent phone messages and emails. She responded to a few and wrote some memos, but by the middle of the afternoon she'd had enough. Today she wanted to do the grocery shopping *before* fetching Jamie.

The first thing Anna noticed as she and Jamie entered her flat, in the early evening, was that the bin had moved. She was sure she hadn't left it like that, standing away from the wall. It was a feeling, nothing more, that someone had been in there while she was out. Jamie was oblivious, making a beeline for the now dog-eared Ikea catalogue, squatting on his usual spot on the floor and flicking through the pages. But after stowing the shopping, Anna found that she couldn't relax. She checked her answerphone. No new messages. For a while she paced, undecided, before eventually trying Mariner's number. As she waited for someone at the other end of the line to locate him, she had a tidy up. As usual, this entailed gathering up far too much, and Eddie's package, balanced as it was precariously at the top of the pile, slid off with a crash, scattering the contents.

'Bugger!'

'Everything all right, madam?' asked the voice at the other end of the line.

'Yes, thanks. I just dropped something.'

'I'm sorry, I can't seem to track down Inspector Mariner. Would you like to leave a message?'

Yes, would you tell him that someone has broken into my flat and moved my bin? Suddenly Anna felt foolish. 'No, it's fine,' she said out loud. 'There's no message.' She hung up the phone, regretting the call already. She was being totally paranoid, and about what?

As Anna turned over the empty folder to replace the papers, she caught her finger on something raised just inside the flap. She examined it more closely. Something had been taped to the underside. It was a small, slim envelope. She pulled it off. Inside the envelope was a CD. It wasn't labelled. So what was all this about? Sliding Carol Vorderman into the DVD yet again, to keep Jamie occupied, Anna grabbed her laptop and plugged it in.

She inserted the CD and watched the icon appear. Double click. A dialogue box followed, inviting her to enter the disc's password. Anna attempted to override it, but it wouldn't let her through. She tried to cancel, but the screen returned to Explorer. Damn! This time Eddie had been a mite too clever. She scrutinised the envelope for a second time, hoping to find some cryptic clue written there. But the paper was pristine, naturally. Not much point in having a secret password then advertising it all over the packaging. Okay, she'd have to think of the password. It should be simple. Only fifty thousand words in the English language to choose from, and that was always supposing Eddie hadn't strayed into French, German or Esperanto. She began with the obvious, family names: Eddie/Edward, Jamie/James, Anna, Malcolm, Susan, Mum, Dad. Nothing. Tried them in upper case and lower case, with and without initial capitals. Zilch. The phone rang.

It was Mariner. 'You wanted to speak to me?'

Anna felt foolish. Her feelings of anxiety had evaporated, and she was convinced now that her imagination had just gone into overdrive. 'It was nothing,' she said. 'I thought someone had been in my flat.'

'Has anything been taken?' he was treating it more seriously than was necessary.

'No, I was being ridiculous. Just pure paranoia. I keep forgetting that Jamie's here with me and he moves things.'

'Oh, well, I'm glad you're okay.' He was signing off.

'I've found something else that you might be interested in, though,' Anna said, quickly. 'Eddie sent me a parcel. He must have posted it just before he died, but it got delayed and didn't arrive until yesterday. At first I thought it just contained papers, information about medications and one of Dad's old notebooks. Though it might be helpful, I didn't think it was that important.'

'But?'

'I've just found a CD, too. It was taped to the inside of the envelope, out of sight.'

'What is it?' Mariner audibly perked up.

'I don't know yet. The bad news is that of course it's password protected. I'm trying to get into it right now.'

There was a pause at the other end of the line. 'Kerry helped us to compile some e-fits of the men who were in Eddie's house that night. I'd like you and Jamie to have a look. How about if I bring them by?'

'Okay.'

'Now?'

'Why not?'

Eager to have something to show him when he arrived, Anna took her efforts wider, trawling her brain for any minor detail about Eddie that might hold the key. She knew he had once supported Aston Villa, but did he have a favourite player? What was his favourite food, drink, colour, movie, book? She hadn't a clue. This was the payback for hardly knowing your big brother. She typed in Echo, Greenwood, Countdown . . .

Anna became aware of Jamie hovering at her elbow. 'Want a loops.'

'In a minute,' Anna said, distracted.

'Want Loops, get a loops,' he repeated, tugging at her sleeve.

'In a minute, Jamie,' she shrugged him off impatiently. 'This is hopeless'

Jamie mirrored her exasperation. 'Loops!' he insisted grabbing at her arm.

'Oh! You and your bloody—!' Anna banged on the keys irritably. *Hu-la-Ho-ops*, she typed. And the screen unfurled in front of her.

'Jamie, you're a genius!' Without thinking, she put out her arms to hug him. He backed away in alarm, fearful of the sudden contact, making Anna laugh. 'You can have all the Hula Hoops you like.'

The intercom buzzer sounded, and Anna let in a frowning Mariner. 'Sure you're all right?' he asked.

For a moment, Anna didn't know what he meant. Then she remembered the bin. 'Oh, yes, I'm fine. Going a bit nuts, but fine.'

'Good.' He was examining the door. 'How do you lock this when you go out?'

'On the Yale.'

'Maybe you should consider using the mortise, too.'

'Yes, inspector,' Anna said meekly.

Mariner smiled. 'Okay. Here ends the Mariner lecture for today. Call it compensation for the fact that our enquiries seem to have hit a brick wall. Frank Crosby has got a solid alibi for the night Eddie was killed. So unless there are some other unknown heavies doing his dirty work, it looks as if Kerry was telling the truth and Frank wasn't involved. It leaves us pretty well back at square one.'

'Not quite,' Anna said.

'What?'

'I've found the password to the CD. Jamie's obsession with Hula Hoops finally came in useful.'

CHAPTER 25

'I'm not even going to ask what you mean by that,' Mariner said. 'Have you found anything interesting?'

'Not yet. You're just in time to help me look.' Mariner dragged a chair round to Anna's side of the table so that they could both look at the screen. As he did so, his arm brushed against hers, making her skin tingle. *Focus, Anna, focus,* she told herself sternly. With a curiously wobbly hand, she opened up the drive. It contained a single document. MS Access. Untitled.

'Eddie and his databases,' commented Mariner, shaking his head. 'He had them for everything.'

Anna double clicked the icon and rows of data unfurled on the screen before them.

'It's the same document as we found,' Mariner observed straight away.

'Except that now we've got all the data as well,' said Anna, hopefully, examining around thirty rows and five complete columns containing an assortment of numbers and letters.

'If that makes a difference,' he said, with obvious disappointment. 'There are still no headings to any of the fields, so we don't know what any of the numbers mean.' Without any indication of what the digits represented, the database told them nothing. 'We're no further on.'

But Anna was staring at one of the columns. 'We might be,' she said, slowly. 'I think it's got Jamie on it.'

'Jamie?'

Jamie looked around momentarily from where he lay on the floor in the lounge.

'Look,' she pointed to one of the dates. 'That's Jamie's date of birth. It didn't mean anything when you showed it me before, but since then I've had to memorise it.'

'It's just a date,' Mariner was less sure. 'That could just be a fluke.'

'No, look at the initials.' Anna traced a finger back along the row. 'JB, Jamie Barham, and there in the first column, SB, Susan Barham, that's my mum. That's got to be more than chance, surely?'

Mariner remained sceptical. 'Anyone else you recognise?' he asked, doubtfully.

Anna studied the column of letters, her mind now moving in a new direction. AR, DM, CJ, ET . . . she mulled over each set of initials, searching for a connection. 'It's a long shot, but that could be Liz — Elizabeth Trueman. I hadn't seen her for years, but she came to Eddie's funeral. And that's their son, Michael.' She indicated the MT, further along the row. 'They live in Sutton now but our families were close when we were kids, you know? We used to go and visit them. They had this massive copper beech tree in the garden that Jamie once fell out of.'

'So what we have here are the initials of children and their mothers. That makes sense. The last initial of each pair seems to match up.'

'It's only one child, Eddie and I are not on here.'

'The youngest child?'

'No, Michael's got a younger sister, Carol. But Michael's autistic, like Jamie. It's the autistic child.'

'So this is about autistic children and their parents, and what?'

Anna thought for a moment. 'Medication,' she said, picking up the envelope that came in the post. 'This is what Eddie sent me. The rest of this stuff is about different kinds of medication. Those PSTIs I was telling you about. And when I met Liz Trueman, she was full of how well Michael is doing these days, mainly because of the new medication he's on.'

'But Jamie doesn't take anything, does he?'

'Not yet, but I think Eddie must have been considering it. I didn't want to believe it at first, but given that he was having mega problems with Jamie's behaviour, and all the residential homes seem to want to have that option open to them, he must have been. The ones that don't use medication routinely are incredibly expensive.'

'And Eddie wasn't exactly rolling in it.'

'So he was being more or less forced into it. But Eddie being Eddie, he wouldn't have taken that step without doing some thorough research. I think it's what all this is about.' She indicated the other rows of figures. 'Maybe he wanted to compare Jamie's data, whatever that may be, with others' before making the decision.'

Mariner was unimpressed. 'But if that's the case then this is pretty harmless information. Who else would be even interested in it?'

'I don't know.'

'If this was Eddie's so-called "drug story" Darren was right. It was a wind-up. The drugs Eddie was talking about were these PSTIs. And the project was "personal" because it was for his own use.'

Anna wasn't about to give up so easily. 'But if that's all it was, why would anyone go to the trouble of wiping it off his computer?'

'They could have been after anything,' Mariner pointed out. 'The corrupted database was one of the items that was left. They could have already successfully destroyed what they intended to.'

'So that's it?' Anna was crushed. 'All this stuff is irrelevant after all?'

'Well, it may be helpful to you. But I can't see how it will help us find Eddie's killer.'

'I'm not really sure if it will be much good to me,' Anna said, finally conceding defeat. 'As you said, without titles for any of the fields, there's no way of knowing what the remaining data could be. It's impossible to tell what the units are for these numbers, let alone what they represent. I'm sorry. I seem to have wasted your time, too.'

Mariner smiled. 'Not entirely. It means we've effectively ruled out another lead.'

'Would you like a coffee or something?' Anna said, quickly, partly because she didn't want him to leave yet.

'Okay, thanks.'

Anna got up to put the kettle on. Mariner picked up the envelope. 'This was all Eddie sent you?'

'That's it. Apart from one of dad's old notebooks, which is pretty indecipherable. Oh, and he left a shoebox full of old letters with our solicitor. They went back years, and were addressed to my dad, not Eddie. I left them where they were.'

Mariner was staring thoughtfully at the computer screen. 'If you've got Jamie, it shouldn't be that difficult to work out what the rest of this means,' he said.

Anna came back to the table with the coffee. 'Is there any point?'

'Eddie must have thought so, or why bother?'

Anna shrugged. If he really wanted to, she'd let him get on with it.

'Let's start from what we do know. We've got your mother's initials, Jamie's initials, Jamie's date of birth, then another number: 2.1. How old was Jamie when you found out he had autism?'

'Older than that, much older, in fact, it wasn't really until he went to school, even though Mum had been up at the doctors with him every other week for years. Everything was put down to colic or teething or the terrible twos and she was told he'd grow out of it. It wasn't until he was about five or six that autism was even mentioned.' She looked across the page. 'In fact, this next column is more likely to refer to that.' The fourth column contained a second date that put Jamie at almost six years old. That was more like the time he was diagnosed.'

'Okay, that's good. It would account for the variation across the other kids, too. Presumably they were diagnosed at different ages. So what is this 2.1?' Jamie's rating appeared lower than many of the others, which were anything ranging between four and nine. What could it be measuring if not time? Quantity? But of what? Measurement? Height? No, too small. Suddenly Mariner thought of Greta's tadpole. 'What about Jamie's weight, when he was born?'

'He *was* seriously underweight,' said Anna. 'Tiny, you should see the photographs.'

'So it could be that.'

'I suppose it's possible,' she sounded doubtful, but Mariner pressed on.

'Let's go with that for now. Okay, so we've got some names, dates of birth, birth-weights, dates of diagnosis.'

'So what? It still doesn't tell us why all these people are on the database, except that all these people might be diagnosed autistic on those particular dates.'

'Which still doesn't tell us why it was important enough for Eddie to go to all this trouble.' Mariner picked up the envelope. 'You've been through this information?'

'Yes, it's about various drugs, but the only common factor seems to be that none of them are particularly safe. The only one that doesn't appear to list numerous side effects is this one, Pinozalyan, but that's because there's hardly any information about it.' Anna showed Mariner the short paragraph. 'This is all there is?'

'Yes, I tried the internet, but there was hardly anything. And when I went to ask Dr Payne about it this morning, he'd never heard of it either. Mark, my friend's partner, is a GP. He said he'd look into it for me, but he hasn't come back to me yet.'

'Pinozal-yan,' Mariner read. 'A relaxant. Prescribed for the treatment of insomnia. Acts as a depressant to hormone serotonin, which controls levels of arousal and anxiety. So that would be useful for someone like Jamie, wouldn't it?'

'You bet. Anything to calm him down and help him sleep more would be a miracle-drug.'

'And there's no mention of side effects?'

'That's what makes it unique.'

'But your doctor hadn't heard of it?'

'No, he was pretty dismissive actually. But then he did have quite a few patients waiting to see him. You said it differently. Maybe I didn't pronounce it correctly. What did you call it?

'Pinozal-yan,' Mariner repeated.

'See I thought it was Pino-zalyan.'

'What, like Pinot Noire? Pino-zalyan . . . Pino-zalyan,' Mariner said to himself. 'Actually that does sound more—'

'Sshh!' Anna silenced him. 'Listen!

'Sally-Ann,' murmured Jamie, suddenly, from where he lay on the floor.

'Oh my God,' said Anna.

'God,' repeated Jamie.

Anna tried it again. 'Pino-zalyan,' she said.

'Sally-Ann,' the name bounced back at them. 'No Sally-Ann.'

Mariner shuffled through the papers. 'Impramine,' he said out loud. Nothing. 'Ritalin.' Silence. 'Pinozalyan.'

Jamie shook his head irritably, 'No Sally-Ann.'

Mariner looked at Anna.

'He must have heard Eddie say it,' she shrugged.

'And why would Eddie say it? Because it was of some significance. Maybe Eddie *had* stumbled across a drug that would help Jamie that has no side effects. What exactly did the doctor say when you asked him about it?' Mariner asked, with renewed curiosity.

'Nothing. Just that he hadn't heard of it.'

'Did he ask what it was, or how you'd come across it?'

Anna thought back to her brief meeting with Dr Payne. 'No, he didn't. He just cautioned me against going down that route. He reminded me about my mum and dad's aversion to medication.'

'So without even asking for more information he actively put you off the idea?'

'I suppose he did. Do you think it could be illegal or something?' Suddenly Anna began to share Mariner's gathering interest. 'That might have given Eddie his story.'

But Mariner was less sure. 'If a drug's illegal, normally the first place you'd find it would be on the internet and you've tried that. Unless it's just unavailable.'

'What do you mean?'

'Well, either it's so new that it hasn't yet been clinically approved in this country. Or it could be like Viagra.'

'Viagra?'

Anna began to wonder where this was going.

'Yes, well. When Viagra first came on the market, if you remember, the government tried to withhold it in this country because of the predicted burden the massive demand for it was going to place on the NHS,' he said. 'It was thought to be too expensive and potentially too popular to make it widely available. But in the end, the government had to bow to public pressure, because anyone could get hold of it from the US and a vast internet black market for it was going to develop. Once people knew about Viagra they wanted it. You've been looking at drugs that might be of benefit to Jamie, haven't you? But what puts you off?'

'The side effects.'

'Right, so you don't go for anything. But say one company developed a drug that was both effective *and* free of side effects. What would you do then?'

'I'd grab it with both hands.' Anna was beginning to see what he was getting at.

'As would any other person who's caring for someone with autism. And the NHS would have to foot the bill.'

'Except that there wouldn't be anywhere near as much demand for it as for something like Viagra. There wouldn't be much of a bill.'

'Wouldn't there? I thought autism was on the increase. And don't some treatments for illnesses like multiple sclerosis run into tens of thousands of pounds, just for one person? If Pinozalyan turns out to be considerably more expensive in the first place, then the cost would soon mount up. And what better way to avoid having to pay out for any drug than to suppress it?'

'But that's immoral.'

'Which would make it exactly the kind of story Eddie would have been interested in,' Mariner concluded, with faultless logic. 'This database could be the list Eddie was collating of the people who would potentially benefit from the drug, were it available. Including Jamie. And there's your scandal: all these people being denied an effective drug that doesn't carry the side effects that all the others do.'

'But how would Eddie have found out about it in the first place?'

'He was an investigative journalist. He'd have had ways and means. And he certainly had the motivation. Now, assuming that these other initials also belong to autistic kids, where would Eddie have got the names? Jamie's day centre?'

Anna was doubtful. 'The people there have a whole range of learning disabilities. I'm sure there wouldn't be enough specifically with autism.' Remembering Susannah's parents, she scanned the column of initials. There was no S, but then she remembered the comment from Susannah's father: 'I hope you're not going to start stirring things up . . .' Perhaps Eddie had talked to them, but they didn't want to be involved.

'So maybe it's not just autism we're talking about.'

For a few minutes they both sat staring at the screen, hoping it would yield an answer. It didn't, and eventually Mariner sat back, rubbing his eyes. 'It's like having three random pieces of a 1,000 piece jigsaw and trying to fill in the rest.' Because when it came down to it, all they had was speculation. Without specifics, they had come to another cul-de-sac. Anna knew it, but Mariner wasn't about to admit it. 'There must be a bigger picture, something that would help us to complete it,' he said.

Anna couldn't help but admire his doggedness. It was doubtless what made him good at his job. 'How can you be so sure?'

'Call it a gut thing.' Mariner's stomach chose that moment to announce loudly how empty it was.

Anna looked at him askance. 'You trust a gut that makes that noise?'

'Sorry,' Mariner, mildly embarrassed. 'I'm late for my appointment with Mr Lau.'

'Mr Lau?'

'The proprietor of my local Chinese takeaway.'

'We haven't eaten either,' Anna realised suddenly. 'Jamie will be famished. You can stay and have something with us if you like, though it will only be pizza. I haven't yet found anything else that Jamie will eat. Apart from chocolate ice cream.' She tried to make it sound casual, take-it-or-leave-it, but she hoped he would stay.

'Pizza sounds good, thanks.'

'And how about a proper drink? Or are you on duty?'

'I officially went off-duty hours ago,' said Mariner. 'I could murder a beer.'

'Help yourself. I don't drink the stuff and it doesn't look as if anyone else will be coming back for it.'

'I'm sorry to hear that,' he replied. To Anna's ears, he didn't sound entirely sincere.

* * *

The microwave pinged to indicate that the pizza was ready. Jamie stayed sitting at the kitchen table until he'd eaten two slices.

'That's a record,' Anna observed. 'You must be a good influence.'

'Not on everyone,' Mariner's blue eyes held hers for a moment and something in the air crackled. Then the phone rang.

'Hello, Anna? It's Mark. I'm sorry it took so long, but I've got you the information you asked me for about that drug.'

Fantastic. 'Hold on a minute, Mark.' Anna switched the phone to speaker mode so that Mariner could listen in, too.

'I'm not sure how much use this will be,' Mark went on. 'Are you certain this is what you're looking for?' To double check he spelled it out.

'Yes, I'm sure.'

'Okay, here goes then. But, be warned, we're talking ancient history here. Pinozalyan was on the market thirty years ago or more. It's basically a serotonin-suppressant and was mainly used to treat insomnia. It seems to have been a reasonably successful drug, but was phased out after about ten years.'

So it wasn't brand-new drug at all, it was old. Obsolete in fact. Mariner could barely conceal his disappointment. 'Mark, this is DI Mariner, West Midlands Police,' he said. If Mark was surprised that Anna had a policeman in her flat this late in the evening, he didn't question it. 'If Pinozalyan was successful, why did they stop making it?'

'I expect because it was superseded by something better, more effective. It happens all the time.'

But Mariner wouldn't let it go. 'Would there be any way of getting hold of it again?'

'I doubt it. And if there are better products around, who would want to?' Mark hesitated, apparently confused by the conversation. 'Look, Anna, if you need anything why don't you come in and see me. Are you having trouble sleeping?'

Anna laughed. 'Not me Mark. If Jamie would let me, I'd sleep for a week.'

'What would have replaced Pinozalyan?' Mariner asked. 'Particularly for anyone with autism?'

They could hear Mark tapping keys at the other end of the line. 'There are a number of alternatives around just now,' he said. 'It would depend on the precise nature of the symptoms, but it could be something like Fenfluromine, or Impramine. There's a whole group of them, these days they're commonly referred to as PSTIs.'

'But they have side effects too,' Anna said, practically an expert now.

'Possibly Anna, I don't know too much about them, I'm afraid. I'd have to look them all up individually.'

'Could you email through what you've got on Pinozalyan?' said Mariner.

'Sure, and if you wanted anything more, you could try the Barnes Medical Library at the university.'

'Thanks, Mark.'

Moments later an alert pinged for new mail in Anna's inbox, confirming what Mark had already told them: that once manufactured by pharmaceutical company Bowes Dorrinton, Pinozalyan was no longer on the market, and hadn't been for many years.

'A brilliant theory bites the dust,' said Mariner, ruefully. 'What could possibly have been Eddie's interest in a drug that became obsolete so long ago?'

'You tell me,' said Anna, forcing her mouth back into shape. She was hoping that Mariner hadn't noticed her stifling the yawn, but apparently he had.

'I guess it's one for another day,' he said, getting up to go. She would have liked to ask him to stay, but what was the point? She had a night of fielding Jamie to look forward to.

CHAPTER 26

The house was dark as Mariner let himself in the front door and he noted, with some gratitude, that it was also quiet. On the way home, Anna Barham, together with his wandering imagination, had combined to produce the half-mast erection that he could always rely on when it wasn't needed. Being forced to listen to Knox and Jenny shagging each other senseless tonight would have been more than flesh and blood could stand.

His mind was still buzzing from their discussion, and he didn't feel much like sleep, so cracking open another bottle of home brew, he poured himself a glass. It was a big improvement on the lager Anna Barham had kept in her fridge, but then, he couldn't expect everything.

Jenny, he noticed, was beginning to make her mark on the house. A vase of flowers stood on the mantel shelf, and unless Knox had dramatically updated his musical taste, the pile of CDs by the player had to be her introduction.

The table in the dining room was covered in papers too — Jenny's assignment, an apologetic note to one side explained. Straining to decipher the scrawl, Mariner could see that Jenny already had one major qualification for joining the medical profession. As he stood over the table, his attention was caught by a whole series of striking black-and-white images. At first glance, Mariner thought they looked rather like pictures of cauliflower florets, until he realised that they represented a foetus in different stages of development, right through from embryo to fully formed infant.

Underneath were descriptors explaining which part of the baby developed at which stage; at week six the head, liver, intestines; week ten the nervous system; week fourteen the muscles and sexual organs. Greta's baby was developing like that, he thought, Greta's baby that wasn't his. Mariner still couldn't decide whether he minded that or not. Although at the time the prospect of fatherhood had terrified him, the idea of bumping into a ready-made replica of himself had also been an intriguing one. The way things were going, that chance may never present itself again and a tiny part of him regretted that. Maybe it always would.

The phone rang, shattering the silence. Mariner grabbed at it. At the other end was a small, female voice. 'Hello. I know it's late, and I'm sorry to bother you, but could I speak to Anthony please?'

'I'm sorry,' Mariner began. 'There's no one—' As he recognised that unmistakable Liverpool lilt, a penny fell from a height, spun where it landed and came to rest. 'Ah, you mean Tony. Er, I'm sorry he's not around just now. Can I take a message?'

A pause, then: 'No. There's no message.' Another pause, then the voice even lower. 'Is he still with her?'

'I'm not sure.' Technically it was the truth. Mariner couldn't be certain that at that precise moment they were together, but all the same as he said it he still felt like a shit.

* * *

That night Mariner dreamed he was climbing Tryfan, way up high above the snowline, the spectacular view bearing an uncanny resemblance to the Himalayan range. He was on a steep and narrow winding path, a knife-edge that he had to cling to with both hands, but when he looked down he saw Greta with a whole gaggle of kids, skipping along carelessly like the family Von Trapp from *The Sound of Music*. Sporting brilliant white, beaming smiles, they were waving at him but as he raised his hand to wave back he lost his balance and fell, tumbling down the mountainside until he woke with a jolt to see the first pale traces of dawn creeping over the sky outside.

Almost immediately he became aware of a gentle rhythmic creaking from the bedroom above. He felt a sudden buzz of excitement, but for once it had nothing to do with sex. During the night, in that slow osmotic way that thoughts form and consolidate, Mariner had developed the ghost of an idea about why Eddie Barham had been killed. Details eluded him and thanks to his late-night drinking session, his head felt as though he'd made a recent investment in ear-to-ear cavity wall insulation.

He would need Anna's help in confirming what he thought, so he had to be sure of the logic of what he'd already worked out. He couldn't plough in there at half cock (ho ho!). For one thing, it was bad policing and for another, it would raise her hopes, but most of all — and he even admitted this to himself — Mariner wasn't eager to make a total idiot of himself in front of her. That would come later perhaps. What he needed now was some air and time to think.

Pulling on an old pair of combats and a warm fleece, he drove through the empty streets to the outer limits of the city, where the Lickeys, a huddle of rolling hills that straddled Birmingham and Worcestershire, rose gently out of the urban sprawl. Leaving his car at the Rose and Crown, Mariner put on his boots and strode out on a cushion of brown pine needles up the steep incline through dark conifers, the raw early morning air searing into his lungs and the dank smell of vegetation invading his nostrils. It was a dull and misty morning, and on the climb up he passed no one except a couple of conscientious dog walkers, the impression of isolation dispelled only by the permanent auditory backcloth of the rumbling motorway traffic.

From the mock castle monument on the summit, Mariner looked out over the conurbation spread out at his feet like a bluish grey patchwork, intricate in its detail. It was an unspectacular sunrise, the skies too grey and overcast to be anything more than a sluggish paling of the sky to the east, and at first only the geological features were discernible: to the west the rise of Dudley Castle hill, the north of the city marked by the mound of Barr Beacon. But little by little, landmarks emerged in the developing daylight linking together to form the coherent whole, as the facts of Eddie Barham's death continued to take clearer shape in his head.

Back home, enervated, Mariner showered and ironed himself a clean shirt; a habit he'd clung to since his return to the civilised world all those years ago. When he went downstairs again, Jenny was in the kitchen, wearing what looked like one of Tony Knox's sweaters. It barely covered what it needed to.

'Hi,' said Mariner, keeping his eyes above shoulder level.

She gave him a sleepy smile in return. 'Hi.' Then, noting that he was fully dressed. 'You're keen this morning, aren't you? Want a coffee before you go?'

'No thanks,' Mariner said, raising his half-drunk mug. 'But there is something you can help me with, Jenny. I noticed your project—'

She grimaced. 'Oh, I'm sorry about that. It's just that there's more space here than in halls. I will tidy it up today, promise.'

'No, it's not that. There's something I wanted to ask you. The endocrine system, that's hormones isn't it?'

'A medical student in the making,' Jenny smiled.

'If you took something, some form of medicine that impacted on the system in adults, does it follow that it would also have an effect on the same system in an unborn child?'

'Wow, this is heavy stuff for eight o'clock in the morning. Actually, I couldn't say for sure. Pharmacology isn't until year four, but it would seem logical that it would.'

Knox appeared, looking equally dozy. 'Any chance of a fry up, love?' he asked.

From the expression on Jenny's face, it didn't look much like it and the atmosphere suddenly thickened.

'You haven't got time for that,' Mariner said, partly to relieve the growing tension. 'We've got work to do.'

'Like what?'

'Like when you get into the station, I want you to get hold of whoever dealt with the paperwork on Susan and Malcolm Barham's accident.'

'What for?'

'I'm short of light reading material. See you at the shop.' And swigging back the rest of his coffee, Mariner picked up his keys and headed purposefully out of the house.

From the station, the first thing Mariner did was to phone Anna.

'I'm sorry, she's not in the office yet,' said her secretary. 'Can I take a message?' Mariner asked that she should call him back. His mind on other things, he checked his emails while he waited for Knox to put in an appearance. Eventually there was a knock on the door and Knox entered clutching a manila folder in one hand and a half-eaten canteen bacon sandwich in the other. Add assertiveness to Jenny's many talents.

'Managed to tear yourself away from love's young dream, then?' said Mariner.

Knox only grunted in response, so Mariner turned his attention to the information the constable had come up with. The car accident in which Anna's parents had been killed had occurred over the border in Worcestershire and so had been handled by the West Mercia force, renowned for their paperwork efficiency.

True to form, they had been able to provide the accident report in a relatively short time and Knox had recorded details of one of the officers who had dealt with it. But half an hour later, as Mariner listened to the gentle Worcestershire burr at the other end of the line, his optimism began to fade.

No, there had been nothing suspicious about the accident. Malcolm Barham's car had run off the bridge and into the canal, in treacherously icy conditions. From the pattern of skid marks, the investigators had concluded that he had suddenly lost control of the car, perhaps braked suddenly to avoid hitting something in his path, a badger or a fox, before veering off the road. Yes, the vehicle was checked over and no, there were no overt signs of any tampering or faults to the braking system, although the car was eight years old, so there was the usual wear and tear; some damage to the back of the car suggesting that Malcolm Barham had been in some kind of previous accident.

'Like a shunt?' asked Mariner.

'Could have been, I suppose,' the officer agreed. 'I remember one other thing, too,' he added. 'There was this bloke who kept phoning up for months afterwards, claiming to be a work colleague of Malcolm Barham. Wanted to know if Barham's briefcase had been recovered, and could we let him know as soon as it was.'

'And was it?'

'Never. Which was surprising, given that the canal wasn't especially deep at that point, and there wouldn't have been any current to carry it away. Besides, apart from the cracked windscreen, the car was still completely sealed. That was how they managed to get the kid out alive.'

'Jamie Barham was with them?'

'I don't remember his name, but there was a young lad in the car, yes. He suffered a minor head injury, but otherwise—'

'So what do you think happened to the briefcase?' Mariner broke in.

'Mr Barham obviously didn't have it with him, did he?'

'That's a bit strange, isn't it? I thought he'd been lecturing that night?'

'As Sherlock Holmes used to say,' the sergeant spoke as if the fictional detective had once numbered among his personal friends, 'if you eliminate the impossible, then what remains, however improbable, must be the truth.' Mariner couldn't really argue with that one.

'Do you remember this guy's name, the one who kept phoning?'

'We would have logged it, he was a persistent bugger. Hang on a sec.' A clunk and the line went quiet for several minutes. 'Yes, here we are. Todd. Andrew Todd.' Mariner knew exactly where he'd seen that name before.

'And there were no other witnesses to the accident?' he asked.

'No. But then it's not a particularly well-used road, which is probably why it was so icy. It was a bit of a mystery why Malcolm Barham had taken that route. It's not the most direct way from Droitwich to Birmingham.'

'But it passes close by the radio transmission masts?'

'Yes, it runs right alongside for about two miles.'

Then that was why. The young Jamie Barham was obsessed with masts and pylons. And whoever had shunted into the back of Malcolm Barham's car, causing it to skid off the road, would certainly have known that.

'Thanks for your help,' said Mariner, to the Worcestershire policeman. 'And thanks for getting back so quickly.'

'No problem, the report was to hand anyway. We had another enquiry about it a couple of months back.'

'Oh yes, who was that?'

'The son of the deceased: an Edward Barham.'

Well, well. Thanking the officer again, Mariner went down to the property store where Eddie Barham's personal effects were being held, and took out the wallet. The money was still there, as were the credit cards, along with another old and faded business card. Andrew Todd, Clinical Research Team. And the name of the company he worked for? Bowes Dorrinton Pharmaceuticals. Another brick in the wall.

'So what's all this got to do with anything?' Knox understandably wanted to know.

Mariner told him what he thought.

'You've been overdoing the home brew,' was Knox's verdict. 'It's rotted your brain.'

'Is that why you're like a bear with a sore head today?' slipped in Mariner.

Knox just shot him a venomous look. The phone rang and Knox picked it up. 'Anna Barham,' he said, passing it over. Time to test the water.

'I think I know why Eddie and your parents were killed,' Mariner said, as an opener.

'My parents? What have they got to do with it?'

'Everything. We need to talk to their friend Liz Trueman. Do you remember where she lives?'

'I don't know the address, but I might remember the house. It's up near Sutton Park somewhere. We went there a couple of times when we were kids.'

'Can you take me there?'

'Yes, I think so, but what's this all about?'

'The Brocken Spectre.'

'Oh.' If she thought he'd lost it, there was no clue in her voice.

'I'll pick you up in ten minutes.'

'Want me to come?' asked Knox, sulkily.

Mariner shook his head. 'I think you should take a couple of hours off and go and sort out your personal life.'

'Thank you, sir. If I need any more advice, I'll be sure to come and ask you for it.' And he turned and walked out.

CHAPTER 27

Collecting Anna from her office, Mariner drove them north out of the city, along the six-lane Aston expressway, where fortunately at this time of day most of the traffic was heading in the opposite direction. Over to the left they passed the stately Jacobean towers of Aston Hall nestling incongruously alongside the ultra-modern Villa Park football stadium.

'So what's the Brockle Spectre when it's at home?' Anna asked.

Mariner smiled. 'The *Brocken* Spectre,' he corrected her. 'It's an optical illusion.'

'Oh, *that* Brocken Spectre.'

Mariner pressed on. 'It's called that because it was first seen on Mount Brocken, in Germany. It's a phenomenon that occurs when you're up on a mountain above the clouds. The sun shines down and projects your shadow onto the cloud below, but magnified several times, so you look down on this huge outsized shadow of yourself. It's amazing, very dramatic. But the interesting thing is that however many people are there on the mountain with you, the only shadow you see is your own, you can't see any of the others around it. That's what's happened to us. Me. I've been so focused on Jamie's "shadow" on that database that I couldn't see any of the other people on it, and I completely missed the person it's really all about.'

'Who?'

'I hope that is what we're about to find out.'

'Oh, come on, you have to tell me more than that,' Anna implored.

But Mariner wouldn't. 'I want to hear it from the horse's mouth,' he said. 'Without any hints from us.'

They were coming into Royal Sutton Coldfield, once a small market town in its own right, but now just an outer, if more exclusive annex of the city. Mariner always thought of it as Birmingham's Bel Air, as did many of its residents.

'Okay, where to now?' asked Mariner.

'The house is near Sutton Park itself, close to the south gate. If they still live there, that is.' But approaching the park, Anna began to recognise landmarks. 'It's somewhere along here, I'm sure.' Then she saw it. 'That's it. That's their house,' she said, picking out a solid thirties detached in the shade of a huge spreading copper beech. 'That's the tree Jamie fell out of.' There was a car already parked on the drive. It was a good sign. Mariner pulled in behind it, and Anna rang the doorbell.

After some delay, Liz Trueman appeared, drying her hands and wearing the sort of attire suitable for gardening. Despite the smile, her welcome seemed uncertain. 'Anna, what a surprise. Please, come in. But I'm afraid Michael isn't here.' They followed her into an airy, large and comfortable lounge. Almost immediately Mariner noticed a couple of black-and-white symbols, like those in Eddie's house.

'This is Detective Inspector Mariner,' Anna said, once they were seated and had declined the offer of refreshment.

Mariner proffered his ID. 'This isn't exactly a social call, Mrs Trueman,' he said, sensing that she'd already guessed.

'It's about Eddie, isn't it,' she said, apprehensively.

'Yes, it is. We now know for certain that Eddie's death was not suicide.'

'I knew it,' Liz wrung her hands together anxiously. 'I said that to Richard, my husband. It was all so — unnatural. First Susan and Malcolm, then Eddie.'

'How long had you known Mr and Mrs Barham?' Mariner asked.

'Years. We first met soon after Jamie was diagnosed. Finding out that your child is autistic is a very lonely experience, inspector. Back then it was even worse because there were no ready-made support groups and much less was known about the condition. It was both devastating and isolating. Then one day, completely by accident, I ran into Susan in the doctor's waiting room. That was when we lived in Harborne of course, shortly before we moved out here. The relief of finding someone else who was going through the same emotional turmoil was indescribable. We clung to each other. We grieved together.'

'Grieved?' It seemed an odd choice of word.

'For the sons we didn't have, and never would have,' she said, her voice filled with sadness. 'It never stops, you know. Every time your child fails to reach another milestone you mourn all over again for what might have been. One of the hardest things is when you realise they're not children any more, they're adults and they're never going to change.' Her eyes glistened as momentarily her emotions got the better of her.

Mariner waited for a few seconds while she composed herself. 'Mrs Trueman, have you ever seen this before?' He showed her the database. 'This is Jamie and we think this must be Michael.'

Liz studied the document for a few moments. 'I haven't, but I know what it's about. You're right. It is Michael. Did Eddie put this together?'

'We found it on his computer.'

Liz Trueman sighed. 'Eddie contacted us last summer. He said that he was coming under increasing pressure from Jamie's respite care home to allow them to use some form of medication for Jamie, so he'd begun to research what was available. He'd come across our name and address and said he wanted to renew acquaintance. He was having a difficult time with Jamie, so we were only too willing to offer him some support. He said he was interested in the fact that Michael has been on a programme of medication for several years now, because he was considering it for Jamie too. In retrospect, I think that was just an excuse to come over and talk to me. He and Jamie visited us here a couple of times and spent some time with Michael. Not that Jamie or Michael were in the least bit interested in one another, of course.'

'And is that all you talked about? Michael's medication?'

She shook her head. 'On the second visit Eddie brought one of your father's notebooks with him.'

'Dad's research project?' said Anna.

'What was left of it. Your dad had always been determined to get to the bottom of autism, and so little was known about it back then. I'm sure it was his way of coping with Jamie. Anyway, at the back of this particular notebook was a section about a drug called Pinozalyan, that could treat insomnia, so Eddie thought it might be of benefit to Jamie. He wanted to know if we'd ever heard of it.'

'And had you?' Anna held her breath.

Liz looked suddenly tired, as if she'd been through all this before. 'Oh, yes.'

'But it wasn't for Michael, was it?' said Mariner.

'No.'

'Then what?' Anna was confused.

'Michael didn't take Pinozalyan, I did. Back when I was expecting Michael, I was finding it hard to sleep and my blood pressure had rocketed as a result, so I was prescribed Pinozalyan. It was something else your mother and I found we had in common. When your father realised we had both taken the same drug while we were pregnant, he seized on it.'

'Pinozalyan, which acts on the serotonin system.'

'Yes. Being a chemist, he realised at once that there could be a link between the drug and the fact that our children had both subsequently been diagnosed with autism, displaying the very behaviours that excess serotonin would cause. So, he set about proving it.'

'The Brocken Spectre,' said Mariner, grimly. 'We thought it was all about the treatment, when really it's about the cause.' He turned Liz's attention back to the database. 'So this last row of dates, the ones before Michael was born—'

'Refers to the dates when I was prescribed Pinozalyan. I didn't remember, of course. I had to go back to my GP and ask to see my medical records again.'

'And have you any idea who any of these other people may be?'

Liz frowned. 'No. There were a couple of other local families, but not nearly this number. Although shortly before he was killed, Malcolm did make some kind of breakthrough and got what he considered to be some concrete evidence. I don't know where it came from, but he was very excited about it and published a letter in *Autism Review*. The response he got was overwhelming.'

'The letters,' Anna said, suddenly.

'What letters?'

'The letters at the solicitor's I told you about last night. They were from the parents of autistic children, describing their children's behaviour, the date of diagnosis. They were addressed to Dad, because it was his research in the first place, but Eddie must have been checking back through them.'

'To compile his database.'

'The next thing we heard was that your parents had been in that terrible accident. We just couldn't believe it.'

'But surely you don't think—' Anna began.

But Liz's silent tears made perfectly clear what she was thinking.

* * *

By the return journey however, scepticism had set in. 'I'm sorry,' Anna said. 'It's just too far-fetched, like some second-rate sci-fi film.' They were driving south again, over the tangled roads of spaghetti junction, cars scurrying around its loops and strands like mice in a maze, reflecting the muddled confusion of Anna's thoughts.

'On the contrary,' Mariner argued. 'It all makes perfect sense. Your father discovers the link between a prescribed drug and a debilitating condition, publishes his theory in a magazine. Weeks later he's killed. Then, years after that, Eddie discovers your father's notes and starts following the same line of enquiry, and now he's dead, too. That's quite a coincidence, isn't it? And it explains why Eddie sent you the notebook along with everything else. It wasn't for any sentimental reasons. I'll bet there's further evidence in there of what your father believed. I think that when Eddie went to meet Kerry on the night he died, someone was waiting for him to go out. While he was gone they broke into the house to look for your father's notebooks and any other evidence of what Eddie was up to. They shoved Jamie in the cupboard under the stairs and began to destroy Eddie's computer files. But Eddie and Kerry came back too soon and disturbed them.'

'That's ridiculous,' said Anna. 'It's so melodramatic. Who would kill Eddie just for the sake of some half-baked theory of my father's?'

'Someone who knew he was right. Imagine if your father was really onto something. If he could conclusively prove that Pinozalyan had caused Jamie's autism and that of other kids? It would be the Thalidomide scandal all over again.'

'But that was years ago.'

'It makes no difference. The end result is the same. Once the link between Thalidomide and birth deformities was proven, the company responsible for producing the drug was liable. Think about it.'

Anna did. 'It's mind-blowing,' she said, numbly.

'And all we're left with is the task of proving it.' Even to Mariner's own ears it sounded ridiculously simplistic. 'There was a business card in Eddie's wallet belonging to an Andrew Todd, an employee of Bowes Dorrinton, I'm sure he must be involved somehow.'

Anna looked at him. 'I know that name. A man called Andrew Todd phoned Eddie's house that afternoon, the day you told me he'd been — after you'd gone. When I said what had happened to Eddie, he just hung up. I tried calling him back but the number was unobtainable.'

'He's the connection with the drug company,' Mariner snorted with disgust. 'He was checking that the job had been done.'

'But that's crazy. Surely Eddie wouldn't have been naïve enough to go to the company directly with this.'

'Somebody found out what he was up to,' he said. 'Eddie must have talked to someone apart from Liz Trueman.'

'It wasn't Darren.'

'Darren's only a kid. Who else would Eddie have told? Who would he have trusted?' But as he'd already learned, Eddie was a loner and nobody came to mind.

'So what now?' Anna asked, tentatively.

'It would help if you could get access to your mother's medical records. At least then we'd have confirmation that she took Pinozalyan, too. And we need to get hold of those letters to your father and cross-reference them with the database. Where's your solicitor's office?'

'Harborne High Street.'

'We'll go straight there.'

They'd left the expressway and come almost to a halt in the inevitable queue of traffic. Anna had gone suddenly quiet.

'You all right?' Mariner asked, lightly. From the corner of his eye, he saw that she was staring intently out of the window.

'I was just thinking about what Liz said. I don't think that in all the time I was growing up I ever considered what Mum and Dad might be going through with Jamie. Never once did I acknowledge their courage or their patience. All I ever did was complain about their lack of understanding of me. I never once thanked Eddie for taking on the responsibility of Jamie either. He just did it so that I could get on with my life. Now it's too late to tell any of them.'

'You can't keep beating yourself up over it.' But she was. He could tell. Not knowing what else to say, Mariner laid his upturned hand on the seat beside her. When she put hers in it, he squeezed, gently. It seemed to help. It did wonders for him.

Curiously, a marked patrol car was already stationed outside Jenner, Mason and Partners, and walking into the small office block, Mariner and Anna stepped into a scene of utter devastation. Desk and filing cabinet doors were thrown open, papers strewn everywhere, and the word 'fuck' was spray painted across one wall.

'We've been burgled,' Jenner said, unnecessarily. 'Kids, I suppose. Had too much to drink.' He gestured towards the empty lager cans that littered the floor.

'What about your alarm system?' Mariner asked.

Jenner looked sheepish. 'We've been having some problems with it.'

'Anything missing?' Mariner asked one of the uniformed officers.

'It's difficult to tell yet, sir.' One look at the mess justified the vague reply. Whatever had become of the predicted paper-less office?

'We need to find some letters that had been left here,' Mariner said. 'They're in a bundle, tied with string, all addressed to a Malcolm Barham and were originally in an old shoe box. Let me know if you come across them.'

'We'll keep a look out, sir.' It was the most they could do, but Mariner wasn't hopeful. Someone else had got there first.

'I can't believe it,' said Anna, once they were back in the car. 'I don't understand how anyone else could have known about those letters.'

'Hm, and if they knew about them, why wait until now to get hold of them. Did you tell anyone else about them, where they were?'

'No. To be honest, I'd forgotten myself until last night.'

Last night, when she'd thought her flat had been broken into, that something had moved. Nothing had been taken, but what if something had been left behind?

'Where's that CD now?' Mariner asked.

'At the flat.'

'We need to put it all the material Eddie sent you somewhere more secure.'

'Like where?'

'A safety deposit box would do it.'

Mariner returned to Anna's flat with her to collect it. It took a matter of seconds to transfer the contents of the folder to her handbag, but Mariner insisted on coming with her right into the kitchen while she did it.

'And you're sure this everything?' he asked. 'You've got the CD, the hard-copy documents and the notebook, there's nothing else?'

'Yes.'

'Okay, so we'll put it all in the safety deposit box. Don't leave anything behind.'

'No. Okay.' Anna didn't quite see the need for the running commentary, and thought it strange that he was speaking so loudly. He was being weird.

The bank she used had its main branch in the city centre, within walking distance of her flat, via Victoria Square. Although normally slow, Mariner's warrant card hurried things along and in a matter of half an hour Anna was the proud owner of a credit-card style key to her own safety deposit box. Mariner had insisted on an instant access arrangement, too. He wasn't going to be kept waiting around to get hold of evidence when the need arose.

For Anna the whole process only served to fuel the growing feeling that she was caught up in some low budget spy thriller, and she was a little alarmed at how seriously Mariner seemed to be taking everything. He'd slipped into a different, ultra-professional persona, taking complete control of the situation. With anyone else she would have kicked against it, but somehow Mariner made it feel exciting. His insistence then on accompanying her to collect Jamie from the centre seemed to be taking things a bit far, but it seemed to keep him happy, so Anna went along with it.

Jamie was touchingly pleased to see Anna, but getting him into Mariner's car was a different matter and he pulled back violently. 'No black mouth, no black mouth.' Then Mariner saw what Jamie had seen. The e-fits lay ignored on the back seat and Jamie had recognised them. Scooping them up before Anna noticed, Mariner stalled. 'I'll be back in a minute, wait here.'

* * *

Inside the day centre Mariner showed the pictures to Francine. 'Ever seen these people before?'

'Yes, he's the social worker who came to talk to us about Jamie.'

It confirmed what Mariner had already suspected. Someone was onto Anna, too. But returning to the car, he said nothing. The last thing he wanted to do was to scare her witless.

CHAPTER 28

What Mariner did do, was to go and try to convince Jack
Coleman that some protection for Anna was essential. 'I
believe she could be in danger, sir.'

'From whom?' Nothing, if not grammatically correct,
Coleman.

'I'm not absolutely sure yet.'

On the face of it, this story sounded considerably
more contrived than the Crosby effort, and
understandably, Coleman was reticent. 'Not much in the
way of evidence for all this, other than the circumstantial,
is there, Tom?'

'Not apart from the fact that Miss Barham's parents
and brother have already been killed sir, no.' He could see
Coleman searching his face for sarcasm, but Mariner was a
picture of innocence.

'We don't know for certain that her parents were
murdered though, do we?' Coleman reminded him.

'Their car had damage to the rear, consistent with
being shunted from behind. I think Malcolm Barham was
forced off the road into the canal. It probably wouldn't
have taken much. According to Ann— Miss Barham, her

father was not a confident driver. He'd have been easily unnerved.'

'Even so—'

'And I'm not saying that they intended killing him, just giving him a fright. *We know where you live and where you go*, sort of thing.'

'So you're saying that they were followed? Unless the attacker knew that the Barhams were taking that route. It's not a very popular one.'

'It was with Jamie Barham. He was obsessed with radio transmission masts. He would have made them go that way. Anyone could have known that.' Mariner persevered. 'The pharmaceutical angle ties in with the way Eddie Barham died, too. Who else would have access to pure-grade diamorphine, but a drug company that legally trades in the stuff day in day out? I'm pretty sure that Anna Barham's flat has been bugged, too.'

'*What?*'

'She called me yesterday because she thought her flat had been broken into, something had moved, but nothing taken. She dismissed it as paranoia. Then shortly after we had a discussion about them, some letters were stolen from her solicitor. It's a lot of trouble for someone to go to.'

'Do you want to do a sweep of the flat?' Coleman asked, beginning at last to take notice.

But Mariner shook his head. 'I've thought about that. If we did uncover a listening device, whoever planted it will know that we're onto them. I've kept my suspicions from Anna, too because I don't want her to start behaving differently and give out the same message. I don't think there's anything else to be learned from it, so we may as well let sleeping bugs lie.'

'So what do you want to do?'

'Talk to Andrew Todd. He works for Bowes Dorrinton and has been in recent contact with Eddie Barham. He should be able to clear it up one way or the other. Meanwhile I would feel safer if we posted someone outside An— Miss Barham's flat until I've spoken to him. If Todd can come up with a satisfactory explanation, we'll call them off. All I'm asking is a couple of days, sir.'

Coleman seemed to consider for a moment, although experience told Mariner that he had already made up his mind. 'All right then,' he said at last. 'Just until you've spoken to Todd. Where does he live?'

'Northumberland. That's where the pharmaceutical company Bowes Dorrinton are based. I'll speak to the force up there and try to arrange a meeting with Todd for tomorrow.'

Coleman rolled his eyes. 'So it will mean an overnight?'

'Yes, sir.'

'Well, don't go living it up at the Hilton on police expenses, not if we're providing Anna Barham with a twenty-four-hour watch as well.'

'I'm not sure that there is a Hilton in that exact part of the country, sir.'

Coleman walked him to the door, so Mariner knew there was more. 'You seem to be on easy first name terms with Anna Barham,' he observed. Not much got past him.

'I've had to work closely with her, sir. It's been necessary to the investigation, but the relationship is entirely professional.' *Unless you count what's going on in my head.*

'Just make sure it stays that way, Tom.'

'Yes, sir.'

'At least until the case is closed.'

Coleman's remarks made Mariner think. Perhaps it was time to back off a bit. He phoned Anna. 'We're posting a man outside your block,' he said, trying to make it sound like the most natural thing in the world.

'This is getting scary.'

'Not at all. It's just a precaution, my gaffer's idea,' Mariner lied. 'But it's important that you try to carry on as normal.'

She gave a derisory laugh. 'What's normal?'

'Just try to do the things you would usually do at the weekend.'

'What about you?' she asked.

Mariner had already decided not to tell her about his plans regarding Andrew Todd. If she was under scrutiny, the less she knew the better. 'It's my weekend off,' he said, casually.

'Oh.'

He thought he sensed disappointment, but perhaps he was flattering himself. 'I'll speak to you early next week. And try to relax, okay?' Patronising git, he thought as he put down the phone.

Immediately the connection was severed, Mariner dialled the STD code for Northumberland, followed by the Bowes Dorrinton number, and asked to speak to Andrew Todd. The receptionist had apparently never heard of Todd and asked Mariner to wait one moment. There followed a pause of considerably more than one moment, during which Mariner was treated to the whole of 'Autumn' from Vivaldi's *Four Seasons*. Three months gone, just like that. Eventually a man's voice came on the line. 'I'm sorry, Mr Todd no longer works for this company,' he said, coolly.

'When did he—?' but Mariner was talking to himself. *First sign of madness*, he thought, wryly. So Andrew Todd had left the company. What, Mariner wondered, had precipitated his departure? Whatever had occurred, he was still being protected. If Mariner tried phoning back he would doubtless get profuse apologies that the line had been cut off, but he wasn't going to join in with that farce.

Knox wasn't around so Mariner had to enlist the help of PC Hunter to get hold of Eddie Barham's last phone bill. It was a simple enough task to trace Andrew Todd's home address from the data already collected relating to Eddie Barham's calls.

There was only one Northumberland number on the list. Todd may not be employed by Bowes Dorrinton now, but he still apparently resided in Chapel Dene, the town where the pharmaceutical company was located. This established, Mariner made a courtesy call to a DI Dennis Weightman, a detective on the local force, and briefly outlined his plans, as he was required to do. It would also help for Weightman to be put in the picture in case Mariner needed back up.

'I can contact Mr Todd and set up a meeting for you, if you like, man?' Weightman volunteered straight away in a dense Geordie accent.

But Mariner declined the offer, 'Thanks, but I'd rather not give him time to prepare.' Or to leave town.

* * *

Chapel Dene, little more than a large village tucked away in the remote northern Pennines, seemed an unlikely home to a multi-national pharmaceutical company. To get there meant a potentially tiresome journey up the M6, but for once Mariner relished the prospect of the long uninterrupted drive. Borrowing a pool Mondeo to give him the benefit of a CD player, he threw in some CDs of Bob Marley and The Smiths, along with his boots and a fleece jacket. It was unthinkable to venture up to that part of the world without them.

Childhood holidays with his mother had been simple and economical, motoring round in a succession of dubious vehicles, staying in youth hostels and walking in the countryside, taking in the occasional folk festival along the way. That basic pleasure had stayed with him, though his goals had become ever more ambitious. Over successive summers in his youth he'd tackled the best of Britain's long distance footpaths: the coast-to-coast, Offa's Dyke, the Ridgeway. It was what had helped him to get a grip on his life again. Among the best times of his life had been weekends spent hitchhiking out of the city, walking all day before getting pissed or laid, and on some happy occasions both. One of the most memorable, in his early twenties, had been the year of the Pennine Way, England's last wilderness. Mariner had pounded the wild and rugged, sparsely populated route often alone with only the sheep for company.

Since that time the amount of traffic on the roads had more than doubled and going north on Europe's busiest stretch of motorway on a Friday evening was constant stop-start. By the time Mariner was onto anything resembling open road it was after ten. He checked in, in accordance with Coleman's wishes, at the cheap and cheerless Travelodge off the A66 at Penrith. Thanks to a major agricultural event in the town that weekend, all they could offer him was a double room. It was relatively quiet, but Mariner lay awake anyway, wishing he had someone to share the double bed with, preferably Anna Barham. Coleman was right. He had spent a lot of time with Anna and Jamie, and whether he cared to admit it or not, he was becoming emotionally involved. Greta would have been proud of him.

Before eight the following morning, with a full English breakfast congealing to form a leaden mass in the pit of his stomach, Mariner drove over bleak moorland, following the route described to him over the phone by Dennis Weightman. His memories of the area were of the lush greens of summer, backed by the extravagant trill of the curlew. Now, in February, the countryside was bleak and cold, still in the grip of winter, the ground hard and frozen underfoot and snow across the fells. Skeletal trees stood stark against a milky white sky, rooted in the muted greys and browns of dormant vegetation. Even the sheep were down from the hills for the winter and would not be back up again for weeks. Despite this, there was something uniquely restful about the vast emptiness and that smooth, undulating skyline of the moors.

High Bank turned out to be an inhospitable, ramshackle stonewalled farm, a little way out of the town and set up on the hillside under a cowl of windswept beeches. Progressing slowly towards it along an unfinished track — rough with potholes and clods of grass that scraped at the Mondeo's undercarriage — Mariner wished he hadn't worn a suit. He was going to look like the man from DEFRA.

He parked up outside a rusting five-bar gate and was just unfastening its frayed nylon cord to step into the yard, when, from nowhere, bounded a huge long-haired German shepherd, snarling and barking, and intent on tearing him to shreds. *Shit!* Mariner jumped back, banging the gate shut again as the beast leapt at him. He heard shouting, and from behind a stone byre emerged a small woman of pensionable age, wearing mud-spattered wellingtons and a dark anorak. Mariner half expected to see a twelve-bore nestling in the crook of her arm, but she carried nothing more threatening than a galvanised metal bucket.

The dog had obediently dropped its greeting to a low warning growl, but the woman made no attempt to call off the animal, instead coming right over to the gate where Mariner stood, his palms sweating and heart-beat gradually slowing to normal.

'What canna do for you?' she squinted warily at him.

Mariner took out his warrant card, struggling to keep a steady hand. 'Mrs Todd? I'm Detective Inspector Tom Mariner, West Midlands Police.'

'You're a long way from home,' she observed.

But despite the remark, Mariner got the impression that she wasn't all that surprised to see him. 'I wanted to speak to your husband. Is he here?'

Close up, her face was ruddy from exposure to the elements, and small dark eyes regarded him warily. 'You'd better come in.' Mariner pushed open the gate with more than a little apprehension, but the dog seemed content to grumble at him from a distance. 'Don't mind him,' Mrs Todd ordered, brusquely.

The farm was as cluttered and dilapidated inside as it was out. Removing her boots, she took Mariner through a working kitchen and into a musty smelling lounge, crowded with aging furniture, and randomly piled with books and half-completed knitting projects, its sofa already half taken up by a large complacent-looking tortoiseshell cat. Shooing away the animal, Mrs Todd cleared a space for Mariner to sit down on a garish crocheted Afghan, and grudgingly offered him tea. Mariner accepted, hoping it would have a dual effect on the raging thirst the aberrant cooked breakfast had given him, and his now ragged nerves. Heart and stomach sank in unison when minutes later, along with the tea, came a chunk of solid looking fruit loaf.

'I baked it myself. I hope you've got room for it,' she challenged, and Mariner wondered if this was his penalty for disturbing them. 'My husband will be down,' she added, and left him alone with the disgruntled feline.

Moments later, Andrew Todd entered the room. Once upon a time, his height would have been imposing, but now his shoulders were hunched forward, a weight of anxiety pressing down on them. His eyes swept the room nervously, never resting on anything for more than a few seconds. After introducing himself, he sat on the edge of the seat opposite Mariner, hands on his knees and fingers drumming relentlessly. 'How can I help you, inspector?'

Mariner saw no merit in prevarication. 'Mr Todd, I'm investigating the murder of a journalist named Eddie Barham.'

Todd closed his eyes momentarily. 'So it's true. I hoped that there had been some mistake.'

It wasn't the reaction Mariner had anticipated. 'I'm afraid not,' he said, uncertainly. 'You admit to knowing him, then?'

'I knew *of* him,' Todd corrected. 'We spoke only once on the phone. I knew his father, Malcolm Barham, much better.' Todd's openness caught Mariner off guard, this wasn't going at all the way he'd expected. But maybe this was a calculated strategy. Todd must, after all, have known that Mariner or someone like him would turn up sooner or later.

'What was your relationship with Malcolm Barham?'

'He first contacted me, oh, must be twenty years ago' Todd said. 'He'd come across a paper I'd written and wanted more information.'

'What paper?' Mariner's confusion was growing. He was beginning to lose the plot.

Todd heaved a weary sigh. 'I'm a qualified chemist,' he said. 'And for much of my working life I was employed at Bowes Dorrinton, the pharmaceutical company. They are based not far from here in Chapel Dene. I was on one of their clinical research teams, testing new drugs.' This also astonished Mariner, who hadn't expected Todd to be employed at such a grass-roots level. 'We were responsible for trialling new products, monitoring for any side effects the drugs might cause before they could be approved and put on the open market.'

Mariner remained silent, waging battle with the fruit loaf but allowing Todd to talk, intrigued now about where this was leading.

'In 1961,' Todd went on, 'Thalidomide hit the headlines. You'll know all about that, of course. Hundreds of babies born with limb deformities.' Mariner did indeed. Growing up he was aware of a local man who his mother said had been affected by the drug. In place of arms the man had two flipper-like appendages, about eight inches long. Not that it ever seemed to stop him from doing anything.

'The problem arose with Thalidomide,' Todd continued, 'because its effects on unborn foetuses had never been explored. At the time that was not a procedure required by law, which is why the appalling teratological side effects could never have been predicted. But once it had happened, of course, there were fears that other drugs could have similar effects. In 1968 the Medicines Act was introduced and from that point testing requirements became incrementally stricter. Pinozalyan was subject to the new, more stringent testing regime.' Suddenly Mariner could see how this story would unfold, but he let Todd continue. 'Happily we found that there were no apparent resulting foetal or birth deformities, so the drug was marketed.'

'But?' Mariner prompted through a mouthful of stodgy cake that was resisting descent of his gullet. He took a swig of tea to help it on its way.

'The Thalidomide scandal had alerted us to the possibility of physical anomalies, so that's what we were looking for. I had conducted my tests on Pinozalyan using rats, and as the offspring subsequently born appeared healthy, we retained them for other procedures. Then one day, one of my lab technicians reported that rats in one of the cages were behaving strangely. They were hyperactive, engaging in extreme self-stimulating behaviour, apparently oblivious to the resulting pain. More detailed observation revealed highly disturbed nocturnal patterns and high levels of anxiety too. I carried out some routine checks on them and found that levels of serotonin were abnormally low. It was then that I realised these were the creatures whose mothers had been administered Pinozalyan, which should have stimulated the production of melatonin. It was as if, in response, the second-generation rats had developed a compensatory mechanism to suppress the hormone.'

'Naturally I reported all this straight to the clinical director. We couldn't be certain that it was Pinozalyan that had caused the behaviour, but having eliminated all other environmental factors, I felt that there was a close correlation and therefore an element of risk. Something had caused significant chemical changes within the brains of those rats that were, in turn, influencing the patterns of behaviour. I felt it imperative that we should withdraw Pinozalyan from sale until further tests could be conducted.'

'So why didn't that happen?'

Todd snorted. 'Although the director supported my view, those in the higher echelons of Bowes Dorrinton did not agree. The timing was bad. Pinozalyan was at that time trying to compete with a relatively new, high-profit product that had hit the market; diazepam — Valium to you and me. Withdrawing Pinozalyan then would have been like admitting defeat, so they wanted more concrete evidence before they were prepared to take any action. As you will appreciate this wasn't the kind of data that could be produced overnight. The rats whose behaviour had changed were now several months old. To set up a new experiment would have taken at least a year, and that was too long. In the meantime the most Bowes Dorrinton were prepared to do was issue a drug alert memo individually to GPs, warning of "possible risks."'

'That's *it?*' Mariner was appalled.

'It was the minimum requirement at that time. Such a response was wholly inadequate and I expressed my fears, but no one would listen to me. So I decided to publish my findings in a pretty low-level science journal. At least then I felt I had tried to do something. When the article appeared, I was inevitably asked to leave my post at Bowes Dorrinton for "failing to act in the best interests of the company". As an alternative to direct dismissal I was given the option of taking early retirement on the grounds of mental ill health. Financially it was the sensible thing to do, but it, of course, meant that my research findings could be discredited as the ramblings of a sick man. I was also made to sign a disclaimer, preventing me from passing on any information relating to the work I had done at the company.'

'Is that usual?'

'It's a common enough practice, to guard against commercial espionage, but this one went further. I was also advised, verbally, not to compromise my own or my family's personal safety.'

'An open threat? You didn't report this to the police?'

'What was the point? I couldn't prove anything, and it would have just looked like a pathetic attempt at revenge from a man who had lost his job.' He was right.

'And the company took no further action on Pinozalyan?'

'The memo was the only step taken. And that would have made little difference. Most GPs have a rather unhealthy relationship with the major drugs firms, in my opinion. Pinozalyan continued to be distributed.'

'So why was it finally withdrawn?'

'I don't know for sure, of course. A combination of factors probably. Perhaps, despite the reaction at the time, something of what I said had made an impression. And post-Thalidomide, the idea of reparation and compensation was becoming established, so companies were taking more care. Nowadays the risks and benefits of all medicines have to be regularly reviewed. And also by this time the battle with Valium was lost; it dominated sales worldwide. I suspect it was felt that the commercial potential of Pinozalyan was no longer worth the risk.'

'So your fears were vindicated,' said Mariner.

'If that matters,' snapped the old man, irritably. 'More significantly Pinozalyan remained in circulation for almost ten years, during which time I was entirely impotent.' Mariner tried not to flinch at the word. 'The only positive was that in that time I came across no reports of any negative effects on humans, so I had to conclude that what I had seen was peculiar to rodents. By some miracle Bowes

Dorrinton seemed to have got away with it. But I left the pharmaceutical industry altogether, bought this place and tried to forget. For years I wondered if I had done the right thing or if I had simply overreacted and thrown away my career for nothing.'

'And then Malcolm Barham came along.'

'Malcolm wrote to tell me about his young son, Jamie, who had been diagnosed with autism. In researching possible causes of his son's condition, Malcolm had identified a possible link with Pinozalyan and he'd come across my article, which supported his hypothesis exactly. I tried to put him off. The last thing I wanted was to get involved again, I was afraid of what I might learn, I suppose. But Malcolm was clever. He invited me to go and meet Jamie. It was a surreal experience. The boy exhibited almost exactly the same behaviours as those lab rats: obsessive, repetitive self-stimulation, high anxiety. The disastrous consequences of Pinozalyan were right there, staring me in the face, impossible to ignore. Susan Barham had been prescribed Pinozalyan for three months of her pregnancy.' Andrew Todd stared at a spot on the floor; a nervous tick had taken control of his right eye. Then suddenly he turned to Mariner. 'The worm in the bud,' he said. 'It's devastating corruption invisible until the flower blooms.'

'What did you do?' Mariner asked.

'Malcolm persuaded me to help him, to provide him with the clinical evidence he needed to support his ideas. But one isolated case wasn't enough to verify anything. Although I had the theoretical material, the scientific data, we also needed more in the way of statistics to prove that this wasn't pure chance, and that Jamie didn't have some kind of predisposition. Autism is a complex condition with many and varied causes. For every child whose condition had been caused by the drug there would be many others who had developed it for other reasons. Malcolm and Susan Barham knew other parents of autistic youngsters, so they began to contact them, to find out whether any more of these mothers had taken Pinozalyan during pregnancy. But the cases were few and far between, until Malcolm wrote a letter to some kind of autistic group magazine.'

'And got a huge response,' said Mariner, thinking of the letters in the shoebox and the names on Eddie's database.

'Did he?' Todd said. 'I never knew, because shortly after his letter was published, Malcolm and Susan were killed.'

'The car crash. Did you ever consider that it could be related?'

'I tried to believe that it was just an unhappy coincidence, but afterwards I attempted to establish whether Malcolm's briefcase had been recovered from the scene. I knew he kept a lot of the vital information with him, for security reasons. It never was. It just vanished. I suppose I had a feeling then that there could be more to it.'

'But you never attempted to follow this up yourself?'

'No. I'm ashamed to say that since Malcolm's death I have never pursued it. I didn't have Malcolm's emotional incentive and I was fearful. My family had already been threatened. The implications of this thing are enormous, Inspector. Were this ever to be made public, Bowes Dorrinton would be liable for millions of pounds in compensation. I always suspected that they would do anything in their power to suppress it and as far as I was concerned, Malcolm's death was confirmation of that. But I had no proof.'

'How would Bowes Dorrinton have known what Malcolm Barham was up to?'

'I don't know.'

'Did they know that he'd been in touch with you?'

'I've sometimes wondered about that. Even after leaving the company, I often used to get the feeling that I was being watched, but put it down to my own paranoia. So now I have that on my conscience too. If only I hadn't published that research, if only Malcolm hadn't read it—'

'You couldn't possibly have foreseen the outcome,' Mariner said, feeling unexpected sympathy for the burden this inoffensive man had carried for so long. 'So what happened next?'

'Nothing, for years. I thought that was finally an end to it, until a few weeks ago Eddie tracked me down. He'd discovered his father's original notebooks and begun compiling data from the letters sent to his father. He wanted to meet. I tried to call him back to warn him, but apparently I was too late.'

'That was when you spoke to Anna Barham. His sister.'

'Oh.' He hadn't known who she was. 'Poor girl.'

'Who's behind all this, Mr Todd? Who does Bowes Dorrinton get to do their dirty work?'

'You mean the individuals? They used to have a whole department of people handling complaints. We called them "the bleachers" because they made everything look whiter than white. But this is different, isn't it? I wouldn't know where to start.'

The old man was becoming increasingly agitated, the twitch in his eye more pronounced. 'I've said more than enough. I'd like you to go now.'

'I will have to come back, Mr Todd.'

Mrs Todd walked him to the gate. 'My husband isn't a well man. If anything happens to him, I shall hold you personally responsible,' she said. Her gaze was uncompromising.

CHAPTER 29

Leaving the ramshackle farm, Mariner couldn't help but feel desperately sorry for Andrew Todd. He, Mariner, had got this so spectacularly wrong. Todd was on Malcolm Barham's side and had probably, in his way, suffered just as much: a man with integrity, trying to do the right thing. But where had it got him? He'd exchanged a comfortable indoor job for a run-down farm, and carried the deaths of three people on his conscience. What a thing to wake up to every morning.

Not far up the road began the wild, uninhabited moors. In the distance, Mariner could see a single stone-built chimney standing alone, the sole remnant of the once prevalent smelt mills, built to carry the poisonous filth from populated areas in the valley to be expelled high on the deserted hills, out of harm's way. Unsettled by the interview with Todd, Mariner pulled up on the roadside, discarded his jacket and tie in favour of a fleece, and changed his shoes for boots. He probably looked ridiculous, but there was no one around to see as he walked out over the brown springy heather along the course of the underground flue. The moors were eerily silent, with not even the distant bleat of a sheep.

The higher Mariner walked up the winding single track, the mistier it got, until he was shrouded in a dense freezing fog and a biting wind that whipped at his ears. Visibility was just a few grey yards in each direction. But the route was well marked. Occasionally the sky lightened as the fog drifted, and at the top it suddenly cleared again, exposing a commanding view of the rusty red moorland. It took him twenty minutes to reach the tall, crumbling tower of the chimney and sitting on its plinth, he leaned back against the rough stone, gazing out over the vast exhilarating emptiness, and asking himself, as he always did in such situations, why he didn't leave the city completely. There was nothing keeping him there. Not yet anyway. But if he lived somewhere like this all the time, where would he escape to?

Afterwards Mariner drove into the town to have a look at Bowes Dorrinton Pharmaceuticals. It was totally innocuous: a complex of featureless, factory hangars and a block of offices, set back off the road behind immaculately groomed lawns. The only identifying feature, the company trademark: capitals BDP linked together to form a distinctive logo. The guard at the barrier wasn't overtly armed, but as far as Mariner was concerned, he may as well have been. Somewhere on the other side, within those harmless looking buildings, were individuals who had gone as far as conspiring to murder in order to protect their own interests. The question was, who did they get to pump away their filth?

Not knowing how resistant Todd would be, Mariner had planned to stay in the north-east for another night. But the job was done and it was still only late morning. One of his options was to have a lunchtime drink in a couple of the nearby pubs and chat up a few locals to see if anything interesting turned up. But it was a long shot. He couldn't see anyone around here spilling the beans to a complete stranger, even if there was anything to spill. This was evolving into a different beast, and a far more dangerous one than he had anticipated. These people had the resources and the sophistication, and the conversation with Todd had left Mariner feeling uneasy about Anna Barham, with or without police surveillance.

* * *

Although Mariner had instructed her to do nothing, Anna had found it impossible. Inactivity just was not in her nature. Besides, with the two of them shut in the flat, she and Jamie would drive each other crazy. The climbing club seemed the obvious solution, but when she'd phoned to book, she had been told that Saturday and Sunday mornings were dedicated to under-sixteens. She'd even considered taking Jamie swimming, but couldn't face the complications that getting him changed would cause.

At the surgery Dr Payne was out on call and the officious receptionist was uncertain of the procedure for getting hold of Anna's mother's medical records. She promised to get back to Anna 'as soon as possible.'

The only other useful task Anna could think of was a visit to the library to see if she could locate a copy of her father's letter to *Autism Review*, which surely couldn't do any harm. Mariner had told her to behave normally and normal people went to the library every day. And part of her was intrigued now to know what it was that she'd missed all those years ago. Besides, the city's main central library was only a short walk from her flat.

To be on the safe side Anna decided to employ the tracking device Mariner had given her earlier that week. Activating the handset as Mariner had shown her, as she and Jamie were poised to go out of the door, she surreptitiously dropped the tiny receiver into his shirt pocket. But despite her subtlety Jamie saw immediately and wasn't having that, so he pulled it out again. Diverting his attention, Anna then tried clipping the receiver to the back pocket of his trousers, but he felt it and ripped it off. As a last-ditch distraction tactic, she attached it to a belt loop. This time, it stayed where it was, but only until they got out into the hallway.

'No!' With an emphatic shout Jamie tossed the tiny black button on the floor. Defeated, Anna picked it up and pocketed it, before recognising the stupidity of carrying the now-redundant, bulky transmitter with them. Unlocking the front door again, she dropped the device just inside on the floor. Then, securing the flat once more, she sneaked them out of the back entrance to the apartments, so as to avoid any awkward questions from the young PC who was vigilantly keeping watch outside in his car.

Being a Saturday, the canal basin swarmed with tourists, day trippers queuing for narrow boat excursions along the waterway and shoppers seeking refreshment in the restaurants and coffee houses overlooking the picturesque quayside. Anna and Jamie passed through a bustling Brindley Place without incident, Jamie lagging his customary five feet behind his sister. The library was a quiet haven amid the frenetic activity. Archive copies of *Autism Review*, Anna was told, were not in great demand and were stored on microfiche on the fourth floor. After a brief demonstration from one of the librarians, she stationed herself at one of several machines, leaving Jamie to meander around the aisles. Wary of him straying too far, Anna glanced up to check on him constantly but for once he seemed to be staying out of trouble, content to study and recite the catalogue numbers on the book spines — enough to keep him occupied for hours. Two other people were using the machines, and several students browsed the shelves.

Anna noted that an issue of *Autism Review*, a monthly publication, had been issued three weeks before her parents' deaths. Anna scanned each of its pages, eventually finding what she wanted towards the end of the letters page, from Malcolm Barham, Harborne, Birmingham. *Dear*

Editor, it read. *I am the father of a teenage boy with autism, and am currently looking into possible causes of his condition. I would be interested to hear from the parents of autistic children aged between two and twelve years, particularly where forms of medication were prescribed during pregnancy. Faithfully, Malcolm E. Barham.* It was so true to her father's style, concise and formal, that she could actually hear him reading it. She rubbed at her eyes, cross with herself for being so weepy lately.

Setting up the machine to print off the letters page for her, she went to find Jamie to warn him that they would be going soon and so hopefully avoid a major incident. He'd been brilliant, she'd hardly known he was there. She was definitely going to reward him with lunch at McDonald's, even though twice in one week was rather too much of a good thing for her. She walked over to where she had last sighted his black jacket through the gap in the shelves, but he'd moved on. Gradually Anna worked her away around the rows, scanning each one. 'Jamie? Jamie, where are you?' But Jamie was nowhere to be seen.

Her initial calm began to accelerate into concern, rushing on towards mild panic. Jamie wasn't here. Anna had never considered the possibility that he would ever really wander off without her, but now he'd done it. Why the hell hadn't she insisted on him wearing the tracking device? The transmitter button was burning a hole in her pocket. In case he was simply keeping one step ahead of her, Anna moved more quickly, her eyes sweeping up and down the aisles, desperately seeking out the familiar black coat and cargo pants. At one point she thought she saw his flapping hands, but it was only a middle-aged man scratching his head in concentration.

She'd covered the whole of the fourth floor now, but no Jamie. The lifts were tucked away in one corner. Anna had felt sure he wouldn't have ventured into one alone, but now she had to consider the possibility that he might have done. The problem was, had he gone up or down? It would be impossible to search the whole six-floor library herself. She approached the librarian at the nearest desk, trying to keep the tremor from her voice. 'Excuse me, I need some help. I've lost my brother.'

'Yes, of course.' With a minimal hand signal, the woman summoned a uniformed security guard. 'This lady has lost a little boy, can we do a search?'

'No,' Anna interrupted. 'He's not a child, he's a man, an adult, but he's autistic. He can't communicate and he has no sense of danger. I have to find him.'

The guard was reassuring. 'Don't worry, madam, this kind of thing happens all the time. We'll soon find him.' Taking out a walkie-talkie, he activated a button. 'Put out a call on a missing person, John,' he said and relayed the description Anna provided. Meanwhile, Anna went shakily to the ground-floor atrium where, she was told, the search would be coordinated and Jamie would be brought when he was found.

She waited for an agonising fifteen minutes, at the end of which the original guard came back to her shaking his head. 'I'm sorry, love, we've looked everywhere. He's not in the library. Would you like us to call the police?'

Anna didn't know what to do. She couldn't understand how Jamie could have managed to find his way out of the building on his own. Then, as the automatic doors to the library slid open, she caught sight of something red and shining wafting in the breeze. It was an empty Hula Hoop pack. The ground seemed to shift under her. 'No,' she said. 'No thank you. I'll do that.' Outside the library she took out her phone. 'I need to speak to DI Mariner. It's urgent—'

'I'm sorry, Inspector Mariner isn't in the station today.' Of course, he wasn't. In her distress she had completely forgotten. He'd taken the weekend off and was not expected back until Monday. 'Is there anything I can do to help?' the officer asked.

'I don't know. It's my brother.'

'And what's his—' The line went dead. Anna paced around trying to re-establish a signal, but nothing happened. There was no other option but to terminate the call. She would have to move to somewhere else and try again. But before she could, her phone rang again.

'Thank you for calling back, sergeant,' she began. 'I lost the—'

'Miss Barham?' an unfamiliar male voice cut her off.

'Yes?'

'Let me first reassure you. Your brother is safe and well.'

'What? Who is this?' Anna grappled for understanding. What was going on?

'Don't worry,' the man said. 'I told you: your brother is perfectly safe, but he's going to stay with us for now, because you have something that we want.'

'What do you mean?'

'Why don't you just listen for a moment, and I'll tell you how you can ensure your brother's safe return.' He had an accent. Northern, or was it Welsh? 'It's very simple,' he went on. 'But as soon as we have finished this conversation, I want you to take your phone and drop it into the black rubbish bin, five yards to your right. I have to make sure you won't be tempted to use it again to dial 999.'

Anna looked across to her right. About five yards away was an ornate, cast-iron bin. Whoever she was speaking to had her in his sights. He must be right here in the street with her. She scanned the crowd of people around her in Victoria Square. Everyone seemed to be hurrying purposefully, to the shops, back to the office, in and out of the nearby museum. For once she could see no one speaking into a mobile phone. 'All right,' she said, trying hard to keep her voice steady. 'What do you want me to do?'

'Go to your safety deposit box now and recover all the documentation relating to your father's research. You'll have to hurry up, before the bank closes. Take out everything. The disc, the printouts and the notebook. Don't be tempted to leave anything behind, or to try to make copies of anything. In any case, you won't have time for that.' Anna's head was spinning. How did he know about the safety deposit box? How did he know what was in it?

'When you've got everything, go straight to the International Conference Centre. You'll see there's to be a presentation at two o'clock called "Being an Effective Communicator," which you're to attend. On your way in, you'll pick up a delegate's pack and drop all the information into it. Ten minutes into the presentation, you'll get up and go, leaving the delegate's pack on your seat. Return immediately to your flat and wait for a call. When we're satisfied that we have everything we need, I'll call to let you know where you can find your brother. Don't make any attempt to contact or involve the police, even DI Mariner. If you do that, I'll no longer be able to guarantee your brother's safety. The same will be true if you try to evade us, communicate anything to anyone or otherwise draw attention to yourself. You are being watched. Do you understand?'

'Yes.' Anna's voice was barely a whisper.

'I'm sure you appreciate how serious I am.'

'How do I know that you'll do what you say?'

'I don't think you have a choice, do you?' his conviction was chilling. 'The conference presentation begins at two.'

From where she stood, Anna could see the council house clock. It said 1:15. The bank would close at 1:30pm. 'But that's no time—'

'It's all the time you have.' And the line went dead. Anna had never before felt so alone. Jamie hadn't wandered off at all: he'd been lured away from her. Suddenly she realised: she might never see him again. Except that she must. She just had to do as she'd been told. Sick with fear, she hurried back towards the bank, dodging other pedestrians and forging a way through. On this unseasonably sunny February afternoon there were so many people, men and women in business suits, tourists photographing each other in front of Anthony Gormley's featureless iron man. Someone must be observing her, following her, but she dared not look back. Anna had to resist an urge to grab someone, another woman perhaps, and plead with them, *call the police, I'm in trouble*. Instead she kept an unnatural distance from everyone she encountered.

The bank thronged with people carrying out final transactions before the weekend, and Anna had to wait in a queue that moved agonisingly slowly.

Hurry up! she wanted to scream. *A life is at stake!*

CHAPTER 30

Mariner shifted uncomfortably in his seat. Traffic on the southbound M6 had been going at an uneven, caterpillar crawl since Wolverhampton. He was beginning to get cramp in his right leg and his bladder was uncomfortably full. He'd been considering whether to phone Anna, just to check that everything was all right, and to tell her what he'd learned from Todd . . . but was delaying it while he mentally debated whether his interest was more professional or personal. *Bugger it*, he decided finally and called anyway.

When there was no answer from her flat or her mobile, he phoned the station and spoke to the duty officer. 'It's Tom Mariner. Can you tell me who's doing the surveillance on Anna Barham?'

There was a pause while Sergeant Reilly checked the log. 'Tony Knox is on it now, sir. He took over about a couple of hours ago.'

So he'd reappeared. 'Good,' said Mariner. 'And he hasn't reported anything?'

'He called in at 11:30 and it was all quiet. They haven't been out all day.'

'So why isn't she answering the phone? I've been ringing for the last ten minutes.'

Another interlude while Sergeant Reilly's mind ticked over, 'Oh shit,' he said suddenly, guilt oozing down the phone. 'An Anna Barham called here, about half an hour ago, to speak to you, sir. I didn't make the—'

'What did she want?' Mariner interrupted.

'She said it was her brother.'

'Her brother?' What had Jamie been up to now? 'What about him?'

'I don't know, sir. We didn't get any further because she lost the signal.'

'And she didn't call back?'

'No, sir.'

'What exactly did she say?'

Reilly consulted his notes. 'She asked to speak to you. I told her you weren't here, but asked if there was anything I could help with. She said, "I don't know. It's my brother," then we got cut off.'

'Shit! And she was definitely on a mobile?'

'Must have been, sir,' Reilly was with him now. 'Shall I get Knox to go up and check the flat?'

'Yes.' Mariner tried Anna's mobile number again. It was switched off. His own phone rang. He almost dropped it and, momentarily distracted, veered out into the adjacent lane of traffic, causing the car coming up alongside to slam on his brakes. The driver hooted.

If only you knew, thought Mariner. 'Yes?' he barked into the phone.

'It's Knox. I'm in Anna Barham's flat. There's no one here.'

'I thought they hadn't gone out.'

'How the hell was I meant to know there's a back entrance?' demanded Knox, defensively.

'Bloody brilliant,' said Mariner. 'Wait for me there.' But it was a further twenty minutes before he drew up outside the building where Knox was waiting for him at ground level. He was in civvies, but Mariner didn't ask why. Instead he asked Knox the same question he'd been asking himself. 'Why would she ask to speak to me urgently, and then switch off her phone?'

'Perhaps whatever it was resolved itself and she didn't want you to waste a call,' Knox suggested.

'It was something to do with Jamie.'

'Maybe he ran off again.'

'So why hasn't she phoned us back? And why didn't she alert you? She knew you were here.'

'She found him?' Knox suggested.

'So where are they now?'

'Having their dinner at McDonald's.'

What Knox was saying wasn't unreasonable, so why didn't Mariner buy it? Because he'd talked to Andrew Todd, and because he finally understood what Malcolm, Eddie and now Anna Barham were up against. 'Let's take a look upstairs.'

'I've already done that, sir. There's nothing—'

'So we'll look again. Anyway, I need a pee.'

The disgruntled building supervisor let them into Anna's flat for a second time, but once inside, Mariner was struck by how normal it all looked. In the kitchen, Eddie's folder lay on the table where he'd seen it yesterday, now conspicuously empty. There was no clue whatever about where Anna and Jamie might have gone, but Mariner was convinced that it was an ominous sign.

Then, on his way out of the bathroom, Mariner caught sight of the red light of the discarded Kestrel receiver winking at him, from where it lay discarded on the hall floor. It was still switched on, but the transmitter was nowhere to be seen.

'That looks like one of ours. How did—?' Knox began.

'Not now,' Mariner silenced him. He was studying the LCD display and trying to determine what had happened. 'If Jamie's wearing this then he's not far away.' Crossing to the window, he looked out. 'Somewhere near the conference centre. She must have gone after him.'

'So why didn't she take the tracker?'

'God knows. I'm not even sure that she understood how to use it. But it's all we've got. At least if we can locate the transmitter we should get Jamie.' But something was telling him that there was more to it. They kept moving, but as they walked, Mariner had Knox call through on his mobile to Anna Barham's bank. It was no longer open for business, but the manager was still on site and able to confirm that Anna had accessed her safety deposit box shortly before closing time.

'Why would she do that?' Mariner said. 'The documents were safe there. The only reason she'd go back is if someone forced her to.' Crap. Why hadn't they thought to save copies of that complete database, or at least print off a hard copy. Stupid!

Homing in on the signal, Mariner called for backup, and by the time he and Knox reached the entrance to the International Conference Centre, there were three more officers waiting for them. Crammed into the squad car, Mariner could only brief them with guesswork.

'Anna Barham called in at around 1pm today to speak to me urgently, possibly because Jamie had run off. Since then she has gone silent, though we're getting a signal from the tracking device she had for Jamie,' Mariner said. 'We just need to bear in mind that all may not be as it seems. I have reason to believe that Anna Barham is in some danger, because she holds information that would be highly damaging to a major drugs company. I'm certain that they've killed for it before. I think it's possible that she's been asked to meet someone to hand over that information. She may well have been warned against contacting us, which is why she evaded PC Knox and has switched off her phone. Someone will need to go inside, locate the transmitter and try to establish what's going on. It can't be me, because her observer's likely to know me too.' Scanning the group, his eyes came to rest on Knox, the only other officer not in uniform.

'Looks like I'm the lucky volunteer,' said Knox with a humourless smile.

'Get in there and see if you can see what's happening,' Mariner told him. 'Let me know as soon as you do. The rest of us will take up positions around the building and maintain radio contact at all times.' They watched Knox disappear into the centre, before following him part of the way. Five slow minutes passed before Mariner's phone rang.

'I've got a visual on Anna Barham, sir.' His voice was so low that Mariner could barely hear. 'She seems to be waiting to go into a presentation. She's carrying a delegate's bag and a small handbag, nothing else.'

'What about Jamie?'

'No sign of him. The transmitter must be on her. She looks jumpy.'

It was Saturday. Jamie wouldn't be at his day-care centre, so where the hell was he? 'How big is the bag?' Mariner asked.

'It's just a plastic carrier. It looks bulky though. There's more in it than the one I was given.'

'She must be making a drop.'

'Do you want me to show myself?' Knox was asking.

'Make eye contact, try to let her know you're there, but don't approach her directly. Stick to her like glue, but leave it to her to make the first move. And Knox?'

'Yes, sir?'

'Try to be subtle for once.'

* * *

Anna stood outside the conference hall of the ICC, sipping coffee from a polystyrene cup and trying to control the tremor in her hands. Surreptitiously she glanced around, wondering who was the one watching and waiting.

In front of her a balding man in a black leather jacket dropped his delegate's pack, spilling the contents onto the floor. As he knelt to retrieve the pamphlets, his eyes for a brief second met hers. Recognition turned to relief and then fear. It was Knox, Mariner's colleague. He gave her an almost imperceptible nod, before gathering his papers together and moving off. Anna's heart pounded. Why was he here? Was it because of her? Did they know what was happening? Oh God, if the police intervened it would wreck everything. They had to stay away. She searched the crowded room for Mariner, but saw no more familiar faces. Perhaps Knox's presence here was just a bizarre coincidence and he really was here to learn about being an 'effective communicator.' From his performance when they first met, it wouldn't do him any harm.

At that moment the doors opened and a swell of people began moving into the conference hall itself. Anna took a seat at the back of the vast room, at the end of a row. She hadn't seen Knox again. It seemed an eternity before the audience was settled and the duo of presenters introduced themselves. Anna hoped it wouldn't be one of those events where the delegates were asked to introduce themselves too. *Hello, my name's Anna and I'm being blackmailed.*

On the wall clock ahead of her the passage of time seemed interminable, but finally, as the minute hand hit twelve, Anna got quickly to her feet and, leaving the plastic carrier bag on her seat, walked out of the hall. She half expected someone to hurry after her to point out that she'd forgotten the bag, but they didn't. The door closed behind her and she walked across the now almost deserted lobby, towards the entrance, her footsteps echoing unnaturally loudly on the marble floor. No one followed. Weak with relief, Anna forced her legs to keep moving, telling herself that the ordeal was nearly over. Once they had what they wanted, they'd let Jamie go. She didn't know whether to be pleased or disappointed not to be greeted by a task force of police surrounding the building, but everything outside seemed oddly normal, the world going about its regular business.

The walk back to her flat was one of the longest of her life. She kept her eyes ahead, knowing that she must still be under scrutiny. Back at her flat, her hands shook uncontrollably as she poured herself a strong drink and waited. Then she saw that the tracker box had gone.

* * *

Fifty metres away, from the cover of the carefully concealed squad car, Tom Mariner's heart leapt in his chest when he saw Anna Barham emerge from the conference centre. Against the immense building she looked more vulnerable than ever, and he was astonished by the strength of his urge to run over to her and gather her up safely. Instead, he dispatched PC Karen McLaughlin to tail her at a discreet distance, though he was sure Anna would be returning to her flat. Then he and the other officers left their cars and took up what Mariner hoped were casual-looking positions outside the main entrance of the centre, and waited.

Tony Knox stayed inside the conference hall, having moved to an empty seat just down from the one recently vacated by Anna. He'd been puzzled to see her leave, but catching sight of the carrier bag she'd left behind, he understood what was going on. Knox bided his time. It was just what he wanted, he thought, an hour's presentation on effective communication. The boss should be here. He might pick up a few tips. The rest of the audience seemed enthralled though, and as the lecture drew to an end, it was received with tumultuous applause.

As the clapping died away, people began gathering their things, standing to leave, networking. While appearing to browse his course brochure, Knox kept his eyes riveted to that seat. As it was, he nearly missed the pick-up when it happened. A man shuffling along behind the row, a quick snatch over the back of the seat and it was gone, but Knox had clocked him: medium build, red hair, charcoal suit and white shirt — identical to at least fifty percent of the other people in the room. This one was going to be tricky, particularly as two hundred delegates surged simultaneously towards the exits.

'Excuse me, excuse me,' Knox stumbled his way to the end of the row. Snatcher had moved off at a pace, but Knox caught up and stayed with him, ducking and diving through the mob to keep up. Outside the lecture hall the crowd thinned and his task was easier. Knox had expected Snatcher to make for the main entrance and the pick-up bays, to a waiting car, so was surprised when he seemed to be heading in the opposite direction. He was making for the rear exit of the conference centre, going towards Brindley Place and the canal, away from where Mariner and the other officers were waiting.

As he ran, Knox put a call through to Mariner waiting outside. 'I've got him, sir. IC1 male, about thirty, five-ten, short, stocky, ginger hair, wearing a grey suit and white shirt.'

'Well done, Knox. We'll have him. We've got cars standing by on all exit routes and he'll never get out of the city in this traffic.'

'He doesn't seem to want to. We're going out the back way, towards the canal.'

'Where the hell is he going?'

'Anna Barham's flat?' said someone. It was certainly a possibility. They began moving to the other side of the building. But as Mariner ran, Knox's voice broke in again. 'We're down on the canal-side, sir. Going over Farmer's Bridge towards the Fazeley Canal. Oh, shit! You'd better get round here!'

'What?'

Knox couldn't believe his eyes. Approaching the canal side, Snatcher had suddenly broken into a run, at about the same time as Knox became aware of background revving of a high-powered motor. Moored to the side of the canal was a motor-driven inflatable dinghy. It was over in no time. Snatcher jumped in, and the dinghy roared away, up the canal.

'Stop! Police!' Knox shouted ineffectually after the receding vessel. 'Oh fuck! They've got away!'

'No, they haven't,' said Mariner arriving at his side, gasping for breath. 'The canal doesn't go on forever. I know where they're going.' Knowing the network of canals as well as he did, it didn't take superhuman powers to work out their destination. They needed a map.

'This is where they're heading,' said Mariner and indicated the point at which the canal met one of the largest road intersections in Europe. Spaghetti junction. 'They're going back up the M6 to the north.'

CHAPTER 31

Traffic around the city ring road was gridlocked and in an unmarked car, even with the aid of hazard lights and siren, Knox could only stagger through the reluctantly parting lines of vehicles. 'Move, you pillock!' he yelled at one driver who was particularly slow to respond.

'Let's find out where big bird is,' said Mariner. 'We could use some help.' Based out at Birmingham International Airport, the Air Operations Unit could be anywhere in the West Midlands in under ten minutes, with a flying time of up to two and a half hours before needing to refuel. It was standing by and only minutes later, the McDonnell Douglas MD 902 Explorer came into view. *Alpha Oscar One, to Delta Victor Two-Four, awaiting instructions.* They had airborne support.

Mariner rapidly briefed the crew, and as he and Knox continued to plough their way onto the expressway, got the response he was hoping for.

'Delta Victor Two-Four, we have a red, inflatable dinghy heading north along the Birmingham-Fazeley canal, just coming round the back of the UCE, two occupants.' They were neck and neck.

'Received,' *and relieved*, thought Mariner. 'Do a sweep to see if there's any sign of a pick-up vehicle at, on or around spaghetti junction,' he instructed. 'Suspects are thought to be heading north up the M6. Don't stick too closely to the dinghy. I don't want them to know they're getting any special attention.'

'Understood.'

Moments later the helicopter was back in contact: 'We have a possible, sir. A blue transit parked on Argyll Street, adjacent to Cuckoo Road Bridge, and about fifty yards down from the motorway junction.'

Mariner consulted his map. Cuckoo Road was a side street off the main Lichfield Road and joined the northbound M6 within a quarter of a mile. The canal passed right underneath. It was the ideal spot. 'And the status of the van?' he asked.

'Just parked up, facing out, looks as if the driver's sitting tight.'

Weaving through the heavy traffic, progress was still painfully slow, so Mariner mustered two unmarked units from the nearest NPU to keep a closer watch over the van. Meanwhile, he had time to check in with PC McLaughlin.

'Anna Barham's still in her flat, sir, she hasn't moved.'

'No sign of Jamie Barham?'

'No sir.'

'Because he's in the back of that van,' muttered Mariner to himself, and then, to Karen: 'Give Anna a call, as an old friend, ringing to see how she is. Don't identify yourself or give any clue that we're abreast of the situation. Nothing clever, just a fishing call.' And as an afterthought, 'Give your name as "Karen Brocken."'

McLaughlin called back as the jumbled carriageways of spaghetti junction loomed, HGVs trundling high along the M6 like a procession of lethargic snails. 'Contact made, sir. She caught on straight away, too. Jamie has "gone out" with friends. She doesn't know where they've taken him, but she's waiting for a call to say when and where she can collect him.'

'He *is* in the back of that van.'

Knox killed the lights and siren. 'You think they're planning to keep him?' he said.

'Or dump him at a motorway services somewhere. What could be more natural? They can make it look as if they're dropping off a hitch-hiker, then blend straight back into the traffic.' Leaving Jamie Barham to fend for himself.

The radio crackled again, 'Two-man dinghy passing through Salford Trading estate, approaching Cuckoo Bridge, at about two hundred yards, all units standing by, sir.' It was said just as the blue transit came into view. Knox drove straight past it, round the corner and out of sight, made a three-point turn, doubled back and pulled into a gap between kerb-side vehicles thirty yards away. The driver of the transit may have seen them, but Mariner doubted it. He was too busy watching for someone else.

'Wait for my signal,' said Mariner. 'When all suspects are in the van, we move in.'

Knox glanced across at him. 'Wouldn't it be better to follow them, wait until they make contact with the recipient, sir? If we take them now, all we get are the errand boys.'

Mariner had considered that option, but he could only think of Anna Barham, sick with anxiety for her brother. He was unequivocal. 'They've got Jamie Barham. I want him safely recovered, now.'

But in the end, the task proved impossible. With surprise on their side, the operation was over in minutes. On Mariner's instruction the teams at the scene watched as the dinghy approached Cuckoo Bridge. As predicted the two men abandoned their getaway craft and, scrambling up the steps from the bridge, made a dash for the van. Immediately the rear door opened and it began to pull away. Mariner gave the order — 'Go!' — and the officers moved in, blocking the van and giving chase to the men.

Two were caught immediately, but the driver of the transit escaped back down the steps and onto the canal, running off along the towpath beneath the soaring concrete pillars that shored up thousands of tons of continuously-flowing motorway vehicles.

Mariner gave chase into a dark and dank no man's land of harsh concrete and scrubby wasteland that echoed to the constant and deafening thunder of overhead traffic. The man dodged behind a concrete support and into a tunnel. Mariner trailed him, his lungs already burning, splatting through oily puddles that soaked his socks, pursuing his quarry out and onto one of the walkways that crossed and double-crossed the canal. Cat and mouse in the centre of a vast and deadly theme park ride.

For a while it looked as if Mariner would lose the man in the complex mass of tunnels and bridges, but following under a low, dark flyover, he emerged to be confronted by a sheer forty-foot wall, the only way out via an iron ladder leading up to a slip road high above. Undeterred, the driver was heaving himself upward, already twenty feet from the ground. But this was Mariner's territory and launching himself at the wall, he ascended quickly and began to gain ground. Almost within grasp, he made a lunge for the man's ankle, but simultaneously the driver kicked out viciously, causing Mariner to momentarily lose his footing. For several seconds he flailed in mid-air, struggling to regain a hold, before slithering down again over the jagged concrete, landing hard in the dirt at the bottom.

The driver gave a triumphant leer back over his shoulder, before vaulting over the crash barrier to freedom. Almost instantaneously, there came a prolonged, blood-chilling screech followed by the smallest muffled thud. A cloud of bluish smoke billowed into the air. It was a freedom short-lived. Mariner knelt over in the dirt and vomited.

When the retching subsided, Mariner brushed himself down, buttoning his jacket over the blood that had begun seeping through his shirt, before calling for an ambulance and staggering back to Cuckoo Bridge. His priority now was to make sure that Jamie Barham was well looked after. But he was in for another disappointment. All that had been found in the back of the van were sleeping bags, clothing and empty fast-food cartons. Jamie Barham wasn't there.

'What happened to the package, the documents?' Mariner asked the nearest uniform, hoping to at least salvage something from the fiasco.

The officer looked sheepish. 'It's down there, sir.' He pointed to the grille of a drain in the gutter. 'He did it before we could stop him.'

Mariner walked over to the drain and peered down into the foul black abyss.

'Well, get someone down here to get it out,' said Mariner calmly.

'Yes, sir.'

* * *

The transit driver was declared dead at the scene and Mariner was present when the other two men were booked in at the station. Initially they could be detained for resisting arrest and possession of stolen goods, though Mariner was confident that those charges would be just the start.

'Don't look much like hitmen, do they?' was Knox's observation, seeing the way that Snatcher's conference suit unhappily accommodated his bulky frame. 'But I bet the only time he's ever put on a suit before is for court appearances.'

Mariner hoped that it would be to their advantage. That discomfort might just give them the edge.

The smaller man was dark with rodent-like features and a moustache to match his lank, oily hair. Jamie's 'black mouth.' He had a facial injury identical to Mariner's, the bruising around his beak-like nose faded to greyish yellow blotches. 'I see you're acquainted with Jamie Barham too,' Mariner said, but all he got in return was a blankly defiant look.

'Take a blood sample,' Mariner ordered. 'It will match with the stain that was on Jamie Barham's shirt.' But it wasn't going to help them find the boy.

* * *

The interviews didn't get off to a promising start. Bobby Weller and John 'Snatcher' Holmes were both, as Mariner had guessed, residents of Tyneside. The PNC database produced surprisingly light rap sheets, mainly detailing drugs-related offences. It meant that they were either new to this or smart enough not to have been caught before now. It soon became clear that the second of these was true. Although Weller, from the outset, seemed the brighter of the two, it transpired that they were both experienced at this game. Their first move was a blatant stalling tactic.

'I want to wait for my brief to get here,' Weller said, with some satisfaction.

Fortunately Mariner had already discussed the issue with Jack Coleman, who was inclined to agree with his view. 'Sorry, no can do,' he said pleasantly. 'We believe you know of the whereabouts of Jamie Barham, who may well be in danger, so if you're going to be that choosy you'll have to start without legal representation.'

Weller's other option in the circumstances could have been to exercise his right to silence, but perversely he chose not to take it. Unlike his partner, he seemed happy to talk. It smacked of an agreement between the two that Weller would act as spokesman. So, out of necessity, Mariner concentrated his efforts on him. Weller coughed and spluttered his way through the interview, allowing him convenient opportunities to pause and keep his story on track while surreptitiously sipping at a beaker of water.

'What were you doing in Birmingham today?' Mariner began, when the preliminaries had been gone through.

'We came to collect a parcel,' Weller said.

'What was in this parcel?'

'I don't know.'

'So why did you want it?'

'We were collecting it for a friend.'

'Without knowing what was inside? That's very trusting of you.' Mariner observed.

'It was documents,' said Weller, vaguely.

'This friend must be quite a mate for you to go to all the trouble of coming down here, just to collect some documents. Most people would use email.'

'He doesn't trust technology.'

'So who is he, this friend?'

'Al.'

'You'll have to do better than that.'

'It's all I know.'

'And you call him a friend?'

'Let's say he's more of a business associate.'

'But you don't know his full name.'

'He just contacted me to do a job. He does that sometimes.'

'So this "business acquaintance" calls you up, asks you to do something for him, and you just jump.'

'He pays well.'

'He must do. That was quite a performance today. What I don't understand is, if this was all so straightforward, why not just knock on Anna Barham's door and ask for these documents?' Mariner asked.

A shrug. 'We just did what we were asked to do — collect the package from the conference. It had already been set up.'

'By this friend. That was convenient. And what about Jamie Barham's abduction? Was that pre-arranged, too?'

Weller shook his head uncomprehendingly. 'Sorry, you've lost me there.'

'You needed an incentive to persuade Anna Barham to give up those documents, and her brother was it. That's why you snatched him from the library.'

'I don't know what you're talking about.'

Mariner switched to a different tack. 'You were in quite a hurry to leave once you'd got your package.'

'There were other interested parties. Our friend wanted the documents pronto.'

'So why not just leave the city by car or train like most other people?'

'I like boats.'

'So, tell us a bit more about this friend,' Mariner said. 'How does he contact you?'

'On the moby, how else?'

'So where's your phone?' Mariner had seen the bagged-up possessions when they'd been logged into custody, there was no mobile phone among them.

And for the first time during the interview, Weller looked mildly unsettled. 'I must have dropped it somewhere,' he said.

Mariner was prepared to lay bets on the canal being the most likely resting place. He'd have to find out if anyone had seen Weller ditch it. Alternatively, it could have gone into the drain along with the package. A search team was working on that at this very moment. Perhaps that's what bothered Weller – the realisation that his phone, and all the information on it, might be recovered. It was some small comfort.

'Have you worked for this friend before?'

'A couple of times.'

'Including Sunday, 16 February, the night someone got into Eddie Barham's house, locked his brother in the cupboard and turned over his house before injecting him with a fatal quantity of heroin?'

Weller shook his head doubtfully. 'I'm sure I'd remember something like that.'

'What were you looking for then? More documents?' A blank look. 'Are you denying that you were in Birmingham that weekend?'

'I don't know. I'll have to check with my secretary.'

That was when Mariner would have liked to take a swing at him. Instead, straining to contain his frustration, he suspended the interview. On one level Mariner had to admire the man for being so composed under pressure and sticking rigidly to his story. He was consistent and plausible and from the Crown Prosecution's point of view, had said nothing incriminating. And they had no leverage. Knox was right, all they'd got were the errand boys, and they were having a laugh on him.

Worst of all, he couldn't even balance the books with the recovery of Jamie Barham. He'd just disappeared into thin air. Weller simply denied all knowledge of him. According to him, he'd just been attacked in the street, 'some nutter' had walked up and headbutted him, completely unprovoked, which would neatly explain why a sample of his blood was going to match with the stains on Jamie's shirt.

Among the items that had been bagged up by the custody sergeant was a bill for two nights' accommodation at a cheap motel on Lee Bank, which indicated that they'd checked out earlier in the day. By the time a team of officers was dispatched, the chambermaid had cleared up the detritus and had discovered no bodies dead or alive. They'd check for fingerprints but Mariner doubted that Jamie Barham had made it that far. Mariner felt as if he was trapped in a maze. What had felt, earlier in the day, like a limitless number of possibilities, was gradually narrowing as each, one by one, led them into a blind alley.

The one remaining hope of prising open the case was the man who knew the whole history. But the news that finally came through from Dennis Weightman wasn't good.

'Have you brought him in?' Mariner demanded, his patience beginning to fray at the edges.

'We couldn't,' said Weightman. 'We went up to the farm, but his wife hasn't seen him since this morning. She claims not to know where he's gone.'

It was a growing trend. Mariner pushed a hand through his hair, fighting back a feeling of the world falling down around him.

* * *

Anna Barham was wandering among the ruins of her own life. On returning to her flat, she'd sat for almost an hour over the phone, willing it to ring so hard that it physically hurt. Then, instead, her door buzzer had sounded. Cautiously, leaving on the chain, she opened it and peered out. To her surprise it was a woman, a police officer.

'Anna Barham?'

'Yes?' What the hell was she doing here? What was going on?

'DI Mariner asked me to call round. We need to ask you some questions.'

It had seemed unreal, like days ago, when PC McLaughlin had come to tell her about the chase and the arrests. 'Where's Jamie?' Anna kept asking, but all that came back at her were more questions: 'Who did you speak to?' 'Would you recognise his voice?' Then gradually it began to dawn. They hadn't got Jamie.

'Where is he?' she demanded, finally, angrily.

And at last PC McLaughlin admitted it. 'I'm sorry. We don't know.'

CHAPTER 32

Fury quickly gave way to fear, and as soon as she was left alone, Anna knew she had to take action. Okay, so according to PC McLaughlin, the police had issued a description citywide, and there would be an appeal broadcast on tonight's local news bulletin, but Jamie was hardly likely to turn himself in on the strength of that. Someone had to get out there and look for him, and if the police weren't going to do it then she'd have to do it herself.

As soon as McLaughlin had gone, when it had already begun to get dark outside, Anna had embarked on her own search. Since then she'd been trudging the streets for hours, praying for a glimpse of her younger brother, even though deep down she knew it was a vain hope. England's second largest city, Birmingham's population was a little over one million. It was like trying to find a needle in a whole field of haystacks. But Anna couldn't bear the thought of Jamie out there on the streets, lying in a gutter or worse, while she sat at home and did nothing. She had to do something to assuage the guilt that was gnawing away at her inside.

She'd let everyone down: her parents, Eddie and now Jamie, too. For fourteen years Eddie had successfully looked after Jamie, and now after little more than a week she'd failed spectacularly. Voices in her head berated her: if only she'd stayed at home, if only she'd watched Jamie more closely, if only she'd been more attentive to Eddie and less absorbed in her own pathetic life. It was all her fault. She was responsible.

Unable to come up with anything more logical, she'd begun her search back at the conference centre. Someone had to have been waiting there to collect her package and perhaps, having achieved their aim, they had released Jamie somewhere in the vicinity, too. They had no reason to hold him any longer. He was of no further use to them. Keeping a steady pace, she scoured the inside of the building, before moving out to its surrounding walkways, the warren of underground car parks, searching each face she saw, studying the movements of people as they walked, frantic for a glimpse of Jamie's gangling walk.

She carried a photograph of Jamie with her, and occasionally showed it to passers-by, but all she got in return were blank looks, slow shakes of the head. The population on the streets began to diminish as people went home, and faces began to blur and merge. What she had begun systematically, quickly degenerated into an aimless lurching from one passage to another, her movements driven by fear and desperation, her inner voices getting louder and more insistent.

All the time she walked Anna tried not to think about how Jamie might be holding up. It was bitterly cold and he would be freezing. The rain earlier in the day meant he might be soaked through, too, and beyond his carefully maintained environment he would be petrified. But as the minutes and hours ticked by, the vision that loomed terrifyingly larger was of Jamie lying lifeless and beyond fear in some dirty, backstreet alleyway. As darkness enveloped the city, shadows lurked in the emptiness. The lights were inadequate and Anna realised that she would need a torch if she was to cover everywhere, and she was exhausted. She would go home and eat something, have a short rest, collect a torch and then she would start again.

* * *

Mariner left the office late. He could no longer think straight, which was probably why, ten minutes later, he found himself sitting in his car outside Anna Barham's flat. He didn't know quite why he was here. What was he planning to do? Apologise? Explain? Offer some comfort? Ha! That was a joke. He caught a whiff of something acrid and unpleasant. His clothes reeked of the filth and heat of the interview room, so before going into her building, he walked over to the canal to allow some clean air to wash over him.

Up on Farmer's Bridge he leaned his elbows on the railings and looked along the glistening oily strand dotted with lamplight that disappeared into the darkness. Just up ahead the canal split. To the left began the Farmer's Bridge locks, a series of deep watery vaults that took the canal down underneath the city. Up ahead, five hundred yards along the main route, the bright lights of the Brindley Place restaurants vibrant with activity; friends and couples enjoying a night out. He'd never been part of that. This was exactly where he belonged, on the outside looking in.

If you carried on beyond that past the tourist areas, through the university complex and beyond, eventually you'd come to his home. It made him and Anna Barham practically neighbours, he thought suddenly, on the same continuum but poles apart.

He was procrastinating. Mariner hadn't imagined he could ever be reluctant to see Anna Barham, but facing up to her now was one of the hardest things he'd ever had to do. He had no answers, only more questions. The desire to turn back the clock and make everything right again burned him like a physical pain. He stood a little longer, mustering the courage to go up to her flat, but in the end he didn't have to. As he looked out over the canal a diminutive yet familiar figure emerged from the gloom on the towpath below. Initially he couldn't be sure that it was her. The posture was all wrong. Her shoulders were hunched, and her feet dragging. Christ, he thought, I've done that.

'Anna?' he called out to her. Immediately her face lifted, and her pace quickened as she hurried towards him, injected with sudden optimism. The transformation cut through him.

'You've found him! Have you found him?'

'No.' Mariner shook his head, extinguishing the flame of hope with a single word. 'I'm sorry.'

She crumpled again, devastated. 'What do you want then? Why are you here?' Even in the dim halo cast by the streetlights, she looked pale, and her eyes red-rimmed.

'I just came to see that you're okay,' he said, lamely.

'Okay?' she was incredulous, though her lower lip trembled. 'You've got a nerve.' Anger began to take over. 'This is all down to you. If you hadn't barged in—'

'I thought you were in danger. You *were* in danger. You vanished without telling anyone where you were. What did you expect me to do?'

'Nothing. It was *your weekend off!* Don't you get it? They had Jamie! They told me if I contacted the police they wouldn't guarantee his safety! And you gate crashed the whole thing like a bull in a fucking china shop! What the hell were you playing at?'

'I was trying to help,' said Mariner, feebly

'Well, you didn't, did you? You've ruined everything. You shouldn't have interfered!' And unable to contain her fury any longer, she hit him, a stinging blow across the face that jarred his still fragile nose. Despite the sudden rush of warmth down the inside of his left nostril, Mariner didn't move. Unable to meet his eyes, she looked away, jamming her hands down in her pockets. Tears flowed freely down her cheeks, though she seemed not to notice.

'You're bleeding again,' she said, finally, glancing up at him. Her anger had moved on like a passing storm, leaving her weary and desolate. 'You'd better come up.' Cupping a hand under his dripping nose, Mariner followed her in silence. Standing in the lift he wanted to reach out and put a comforting arm around her, but she kept her distance.

Her flat wasn't the same one he'd been into just a couple of nights previously. There were spent coffee mugs and glasses on nearly every surface. Clothes were draped over furniture and it was untidy and neglected. In the dazzling light he could see that she too was changed. She wore no make-up and her hair was unbrushed, her baggy clothes carelessly thrown on.

Mariner followed her into the living room where, from beneath a pile of clothing, she unearthed a box of tissues.

'Thanks.' Mariner took it from her as his mobile rang. It was Knox. 'Boss? I've just picked up something on the radio. A serious RTA involving a young IC one male, close to the city centre. He was behaving erratically and ran out in front of a vehicle.' A wave of revulsion struck Mariner and he struggled to keep his voice normal. 'Okay, thanks. Give me a minute.'

'I've got to go,' he said to Anna, hoping that his tone didn't betray the emotions raging inside him. 'Please stay here now. We'll find Jamie. I promise you.' Pressing a wad of tissues to his nose, he hoped to God that they hadn't already.

'How can you be so sure?' She was scathing. 'You have no idea. He could be anywhere. He could be . . .' but she couldn't bring herself to complete the sentence. 'You should have stayed away,' Anna told him.

'I'm sorry. I did what I thought was right.' How many times in his life had he said that?

* * *

In his car, Mariner patched back through to Knox. 'Let's have the details.'

'It's at the Bristol Road, the junction with Lee Bank Middleway. It doesn't sound good.'

The nightmare was escalating. With blues and twos to speed him, Mariner was at the scene in minutes. The roadside was chaotic, lit by the strobing lights of the emergency vehicles. The HGV involved had swerved into the crash barrier and was blocking the carriageway. Uniforms were diverting the traffic around it. Mariner parked some distance away and walked towards the melee. As he approached he could hear the remonstrations of the van driver.

'I didn't stand a chance, he just ran out in front of me! I couldn't do anything!' A PC was trying to calm him.

A small group of green-clad paramedics crouched over something at the side of the road. As Mariner headed towards them, one sat back on his haunches. 'What a waste,' he said. There were murmurs of assent around the group.

Getting nearer, Mariner saw the crumpled and twisted body on the ground, its upper half now respectfully covered by a blanket, awaiting a stretcher. He took out his warrant card and waved it at the nearest paramedic.

'I'm DI Mariner. I need to get a look at him. I may know who he is.'

The man appraised him warily, taking in Mariner's dishevelled appearance, the bloodstained clothing. 'Go ahead, mate. You might save us some bother,' was the almost indifferent reply. With incidents like this commonplace, it was pure self-preservation.

As Mariner got nearer, the commotion seemed to fade away into the background, leaving only the sound of his own heart punching at his ribs and pulsing the blood in his ears. He knelt down beside the broken figure and gingerly raised the blanket, then closed his eyes as an express train roared its way around his skull. The boy had bleached hair and a single gold hoop in his ear. It wasn't Jamie.

'Any luck?' asked the paramedic.

Mariner felt weak enough to pass out. 'No, sorry. It's not who I thought.'

Somehow Mariner communicated this to the senior officer at the scene, who also seemed to study him too carefully, before lurching back to his car, nauseous with relief. He called Tony Knox. 'It's not him. Keep looking.'

'Thank God for that,' said Knox. 'Just leaves us with the muggers and perverts then.'

* * *

Mariner caught sight of himself in the rear-view mirror. He wasn't a pretty sight. His face was pale and unshaven, there was a thin crust of dried blood around his nose and looking down he saw that blood had stippled his tie and shirt. He should get cleaned up. Knox would contact him if there were any developments. He also felt an urge to wash away the nasty taste left by Knox's words. His first port of call was the Boatman, where Beryl didn't give him a second look.

In Mariner's estimation the biggest threat to Jamie out there wasn't from perverts, but that wasn't to say that it didn't exist. Back when he was living in the squat, there were several occasions when Mariner had woken up to find unwelcome hands pawing at him. He'd been strong enough and aware enough to fend them off. Jamie Barham wouldn't have that advantage.

Suddenly he realised he hadn't eaten much today and the two pints and whisky chaser were starting to make his head spin. He staggered home while he still could. The house was dark, but for the comforting glow of the wood-burner. He didn't bother with the lights.

'Bad day?' said a voice as he crossed the room.

Christ! He hadn't noticed Jenny sitting there, curled up in the armchair. 'Hideous,' he said recovering from the shock. 'Couldn't get much worse, but I won't bore you with the details. Couldn't even if I wanted to.'

'Anything I can do to help?'

Jesus, what an offer. 'No, I'm fine,' Mariner slumped onto the sofa. 'Anyway, what are you doing up and about at this hour?' he asked, eventually.

'I couldn't sleep. Tony's gone. Back to his wife.'

'Ah.' That explained a lot.

'I don't mind,' she said. 'It was only a fling. We both knew that.' She said it with the worldliness of a forty-year-old. 'Thing is,' she went on. 'I was wondering if you'd let me stay on. I really like it here. I'd pay rent and everything, and Tony said you were looking for a lodger.'

A young, pretty, female lodger; never in his wildest dreams had Mariner imagined— 'Sure,' he said. 'Why not?'

'Great,' she said. 'You won't regret it.'

That settled, Mariner, closed his eyes. After a while, out of the darkness, Mariner heard Jenny get up and pad over to him and felt the warmth from her body as she plopped down beside him, very close. 'Are you sure there's nothing I can do?' A hand snaked over him, finding its way inside his coat, opening up his jacket, and moving down to massage his crotch. 'I'll do anything you like,' she whispered, close to his ear, her hand moving faster, pressing harder. Mariner groaned in response. 'How about something special?' But as she enunciated the last word, Mariner exploded, his orgasm rushing uncontrollably through him.

'Oh God, I'm sor—' but when his eyes snapped open, the sky was lightening to a pale grey, and he was completely alone, Jenny an illusion manufactured by his overactive brain. The fire had died, leaving the room icy cold as rain lashed against the windows; the same rain that would be beating down on Jamie Barham, wherever he was.

Mariner didn't dare think about where the boy might be now, or in what condition. A statistic flashed unbidden into his mind; 200,000 people go missing in Britain every year. Three thousand of them are never found.

And, reasonably enough, Anna Barham blamed him. It was the most monumental fuck-up of his career.

Heaving himself out of the chair he hung up his coat and dragged himself upstairs where he stood under the shower for twenty minutes trying to get warm. Afterwards he lay on the bed, waiting for dawn to break.

CHAPTER 33

When it did, nothing had changed. Mariner slipped out of the house early before Jenny surfaced. Even though it was only a dream, he couldn't face her after that imagined moonlight encounter.

As Mariner turned the car ignition, the radio came on too, tuned to local station BRMB. He caught the end of the news bulletin: '. . . growing concerns for the safety of twenty-nine-year-old James Barham, who went missing in the city yesterday. Mr Barham, who has autism and severe learning difficulties, is described as being of medium build with short brown hair and green eyes. He was last seen in the vicinity of Birmingham Central Library. Police are appealing to anyone who may have witnessed anything unusual in or around the library at around midday.'

Mariner was certain Anna hadn't slept much last night either.

At Granville Lane a shake of the duty sergeant's head told him all he needed to know. Mariner went straight to his office, but it wasn't long before Tony Knox pursued him there. 'I thought I should let you know boss,' he said, sheepishly. 'I've—'

'Moved back home. I know, thanks.'

'You'll be able to rent the room out,' Knox said, helpfully.

'I already have,' said Mariner. 'Jenny's staying on.'

Knox's face was a picture: almost enough to make Mariner crack a smile. 'That's great, boss,' he said, recovering. Inevitably, a sly grin crept over his face.

'You two should get to know each other, boss. She goes like the—'

'Have you made any progress with that bank account?' asked Mariner, hoping to wipe the smirk off Knox's face.

But the look just turned to smug. 'As a matter of fact, that's what I came to tell you. It belongs to an organisation called the Queensbridge Trust.'

'Which is what, exactly?'

'I don't know, yet. It's not listed in any of the UK business directories I've looked at so far. But it sounds to me like a charity,' said Knox.

Mariner wasn't so easily fooled. 'Just because it sounds like it, doesn't mean it is.'

Knox was hesitant, as if aware that he was on sensitive ground. 'If it was though, it might mean that those payments into Eddie Barham's bank account were legit, and not relevant to his murder.'

But after all that they'd been through, it wasn't a possibility Mariner was prepared to entertain. 'They are,' he said, firmly, fixing his gaze on Knox. 'Keep looking.'

* * *

Weller's brief had arrived in the city from Newcastle and turned up at Granville Lane mid-morning. Mariner didn't hold out much hope of it changing anything and he returned to the interview room with a heavy heart. His fears were borne out, and before long they were going round in the same old circles, so Sergeant Reilly's interruption, soon after the interview commenced, came as a welcome relief. 'There's a Colin Lloyd on the line, sir,' Reilly said, once they were out in the corridor. 'From Hanover's, the law firm. Wants to know if he should still come in to see you.'

Mariner had completely forgotten about Lloyd. He shook his head. 'No, just tell him that things have—' he stopped mid-sentence. What he was about to say was right, things had moved on. The Powell family had been cancelled out of the equation long ago. But on the other hand, Colin Lloyd was a lawyer specialising in compensation claims. It was just possible that he might have something to contribute regardless of that. Mariner reversed his decision. 'Tell him I'll be out to see him in about half an hour.'

'Right you are, sir.'

The offices of Charles Hanover were located close to the old Birmingham law courts and constructed from the same brownstone imported from the Welsh borders nearly two hundred years ago. The leaded, stained glass windows gave the place an ecclesiastical feel and inside, the polished wood floors and oak panelling smelled of old money. Colin Lloyd wasn't your average ambulance chaser. Ancient portraits gazed down on Mariner from the walls as he followed the short-skirted secretary to Lloyd's office.

'Good morning, inspector,' Lloyd stood up from behind his desk and extended a hand in greeting. It was a firm, no-frills handshake and accompanied by a genuine smile. Tall and athletic, Lloyd had the healthy glow of a man who'd just spent a relaxing fortnight in the Seychelles.

'Our first child was conceived there,' he explained, sitting down again opposite Mariner. 'We try and go back when we can. Sentimental reasons, I suppose.'

On his salary, Mariner thought, wryly, it would be no more of a commitment than a weekend jaunt to France.

'I was stunned to hear about Eddie Barham,' Lloyd was saying. 'He seemed like a good man.'

That surprised Mariner. 'You knew him?'

'Mainly it was by reputation, I must admit. A colleague on the criminal side of the business, the one who referred him to me, spoke highly of him. That view was substantiated by the one meeting we had.'

'Regarding Mr and Mrs Powell.'

Lloyd's face creased to a mystified frown, but presumably he couldn't be expected to remember a case that had never materialised.

'Mr and Mrs Stephen Powell versus the Birmingham health authority,' Mariner elaborated, to help him out. 'Expecting a baby post-sterilisation.' But already a creeping realisation was making his spine tingle.

'No, inspector,' Lloyd corrected him calmly. 'Eddie came to talk to me about some research his father had done into a drug called Pinozalyan.'

Now that Lloyd had said it, it was so glaringly obvious. So why the hell hadn't Mariner made that leap before? It was he who had made the assumption that Lloyd and the Powell family were connected, and in his head that connection had lingered. 'Shit!' he said out loud, at his own stupidity.

'You know about all that?' Lloyd asked.

Mariner gave a sardonic laugh. 'Yes. I know all about it. It just hadn't occurred to me that you would, too. I thought Eddie had come to talk to you about something altogether different.'

'So you'll know that Eddie felt that his father had uncovered some pretty conclusive proof that Pinozalyan was responsible for Jamie's autism. Eddie came to me for advice on whether what he'd got would stand up legally, and on how he should proceed.'

'And what did you tell him?'

'Unfortunately, I think, not what he wanted to hear. On the plus side, I felt that with his father's notebooks, the testimony from all those other parents, he probably had a strong case against the drug company. On top of that, of course, he had the backing of one of the clinical researchers, Andrew Todd. Todd had actually published a paper on the harmful effects of the drug. He'd also tried to warn the company management, yet they had failed to act.'

'They circulated a memo to GPs,' Mariner reminded him.

'A drug alert, yes. But post-Thalidomide there would be a powerful argument that it wasn't enough. Not when there were such clear indicators that Pinozalyan was unsafe.'

'But surely all this was exactly what Eddie did want to hear?'

'Oh yes, that part was. The problem was that Eddie was in a hurry. Of course he wanted justice, but I gather he was also under some financial pressure and, as you know, these things can't be resolved overnight. At best, the legal process moves at a snail's pace, and that's without all the obstacles that a company as large as Bowes Dorrinton can throw in the way. And running alongside that are the costs of bringing a case like this. It could amount to hundreds of thousands of pounds. Sure, there might be a big payout at the end, but you have to have the resources to finance it to begin with. Regretfully I think by the time Eddie left here I'd successfully discouraged him from taking any action at all.'

Mariner shook his head. 'Not at all, Mr Lloyd. I think what you did was divert him from the legitimate legal path. Eddie Barham took a shortcut. I think he attempted to blackmail Bowes Dorrinton.'

'Good God,' Lloyd took a moment to absorb the information. 'And you mean his death is tied in with this?'

'Shortly before he died Eddie received two large payments from an offshore bank account, a month apart. We've traced them to an outfit called the Queensbridge Trust. You don't know it, do you?'

'No. Can't say that I do.'

'We haven't yet identified what exactly the organisation is or does, but I'm certain there will be a link with Bowes Dorrinton. I think the company played along with Eddie to begin with, humoured him. But Eddie was a journalist. They could never be sure that he wouldn't expose the truth about Pinozalyan regardless.'

'Or that he wouldn't increase his demands. On principle, major organisations don't give in to blackmail. They either ignore it, if they didn't consider it enough of a threat, or—'

'If they did take the threat seriously?'

'The simplest thing would be to eradicate the source.' Lloyd's words had a chilling formality.

'And you really think they would go that far?'

'What do you think? Pharmaceutical companies have a turnover of millions of pounds annually, inspector,' Lloyd said in reply. 'It's a cut-throat, competitive field. Almost all firms have their own versions of the same drug, so they're completely dependent on advertising and promoting positive image. It's not dissimilar to the rivalry between Coca Cola and Pepsi, though in this case, millions of pounds are spent cosying up to GPs. And on top of that, many of them still like to see themselves as benign entities, the saviours of the modern world, ridding us of disease. If the case were proven, it would cost financially, but far worse, their reputation and public confidence in them would be severely damaged, possibly beyond repair. In my experience drug companies will do whatever they have to do to prevent adverse publicity.' Lloyd's confidence was reassuring. He was the only person who hadn't questioned Mariner's logic.

'Even murder,' said Mariner.

Lloyd didn't contradict him. 'There are plenty of cases where clients have been intimidated by large corporations into withdrawing actions against them, through hate mail, fire bombs — remember Samantha Drummond?'

Mariner did. The five-year-old had been abducted from a playground in north London, prompting a nationwide search.

'Her father was bringing an action against Pierspont for failing to disclose the sugar content of their paediatric products. Samantha was released after three days unharmed, but the message was clear enough. "Watch your back, because this is what we're capable of." Naturally, Drummond withdrew his claim.' Lloyd smiled. 'Samantha's abductors were never traced. The people who specialise in this kind of damage limitation have massive resources at their disposal, they're clever and they're careful. They tidy up after themselves.'

'On the night Eddie was killed his computer was practically wiped. Since then, the letters from other parents who took Pinozalyan have been stolen and as of yesterday, Andrew Todd has disappeared.'

Lloyd remained sanguine. 'Someone's done a highly efficient job, then,' he said.

'You could say that.'

'But if you could track down Andrew Todd—'

'We're working on it, believe me.' Mariner thought for a moment. 'If Eddie did decide to make a direct approach to Bowes Dorrinton, who would he have made it to?'

'That depends on how brave or foolhardy he was. He might have gone for someone right at the top, the chairman or the chief executive.'

'And what would the likely response be?'

'They'd turn to their legal department who would handle any complaints or grievances against the company or its products. Someone would be nominated to look at how much of a threat was being posed and then deal with it accordingly.'

The Bleachers, Andrew Todd had called them. 'So that's where we need to look? At the company's legal department?'

'That's what I would suggest, though I wouldn't expect too much. Those guys will be squeaky clean. I can start you off, if you like.' Opening up a desk drawer, Lloyd took out a plastic wallet, which he passed to Mariner.

'After Eddie Barham came to see me I did a little research of my own into Bowes Dorrinton. I didn't get very far, but you're welcome to it. And if there's anything else I can do to help, I'd be glad to. Gratis.'

Mariner tried to conceal his surprise, but apparently without success.

Lloyd smiled, sardonically. 'That child I told you about, our oldest, Daniel, is on the autistic spectrum. That's partly why Eddie was referred to me. Danny was born long after Pinozalyan had come and gone, of course, and he's a terrific kid. But his life is not going to be easy, so if there's anyone out there who's responsible for inflicting autism on any child, I'd bloody well want to see them hang.'

'Well, whatever happens at the sharp end of all this, there are still all those families out there who have suffered as a result of Pinozalyan,' said Mariner, Anna Barham uppermost in his mind. 'If we could identify them all again— But I don't have the time or the manpower to do it.'

'It should be a simple enough task,' said Lloyd. 'The quickest route would be through the Autistic Association. We could arrange to have a circular sent out, perhaps in the guise of a more general survey. If we log the details of anyone who took the drug all over again, we may be able to instigate a public enquiry into the drug. It will be slow, but at least it would be something. Even better would be some press coverage. That would open up the whole case.'

Mariner thought about Ken Moloney. 'I'm sure that could be arranged,' he said.

* * *

Back in his car, Mariner scanned the information Lloyd had given him. On the list of company personnel, one name on the board of directors had been highlighted. Alan Crowther. Or was that just Al? If it was, Al had got careless. He wondered if it was worth having a chat with

320

Crowther. It was unlikely to turn up much, but it was all they'd got. Mariner deliberated about giving Dennis Weightman another call, but in the event that decision was taken out of his hands. Arriving back at Granville Lane there was a message for him to call Weightman.

The detective got straight to the point. 'We've got Andrew Todd. Some ramblers found him up on the moors in his car, a length of hosepipe leading in from the exhaust. He's alive, but only just and we don't know what state he'll be in if he ever regains consciousness. I'm sorry.'

'Shit.' How many more blows could they take?

'He left a lengthy suicide note detailing what happened over Pinozalyan,' Weightman went on. 'But I doubt that it will be of much use. It reads like a history lesson.'

'Can you email it through, anyway?' asked Mariner, dejected.

'Sure.'

'Oh, and have you ever heard of something called the Queensbridge Trust?'

Weightman considered. 'Yeah,' he said, at last. 'It sounds familiar. I'll see what I can find out.'

'Cheers.'

But still there was nothing on Jamie Barham.

When it came through, Mariner pored over the scan of Todd's letter. The handwriting was shaky and barely legible in places. In it he detailed his research paper on Pinozalyan. His letter concluded with the hope that someone would have the courage that he did not. A separate sheet provided details of meetings and there was a copy of a letter congratulating him on his retirement.

Mariner compared it with the more up to date information given to him by Lloyd, but none of the names matched. Like Weightman had said, it was all in the past. No one named by Todd could be held to account.

* * *

Mid-afternoon, Mariner got a summons to DCI Coleman's office. On Coleman's invitation, he slumped down in the chair facing the gaffer.

'What are you doing about Holmes and Weller?' Coleman asked.

'We've held them for nearly twenty-four hours. Their brief is putting pressure on. And he wasn't particularly impressed that you cleared off after only half an hour and haven't been back since. What are you playing at, Tom? Very soon we'll have to charge them or let them go.'

Mariner gave Coleman a summary of his discussion with Colin Lloyd. 'Ironic isn't it?' he said. 'If we can contact the other parents we can link Pinozalyan to autism all over again. And I'm sure that we'll be able to find a connection between Bowes Dorrinton and the payments made into Eddie Barham's account, but we still have nothing more than circumstantial evidence linking anyone to Eddie's Barham's murder. The guy in the legal department at Bowes Dorrinton who set up the whole thing will be as clean as a whistle, won't he?'

Coleman was inclined to agree. 'I doubt that when their records are seized and scrutinised they'll come up with any invoices for "Hitmen, two," if that's what you mean.'

'To be honest, the interviews with Holmes and Weller are going nowhere.'

'Would Jamie Barham be able to pick them out of a line up?'

'Even if we knew where he was? I doubt it. All we'd find out was if whether he recognised them or not. And that seems a bit immaterial right now, sir.' Mariner got to his feet.

'It's not looking good, is it?' Coleman observed.

'Not especially, no.'

'It could have gone either way, Tom. Self-flagellation isn't going to help.'

'No one else made it happen,' said Mariner and walked out of Coleman's office.

A little later, Dennis Weightman called back. 'I've tracked down the Queensbridge Trust. I thought the name rang bells. It's a local charitable organisation. They were pretty high-profile a few years back, doing "good works" with local deprived kids, that kind of thing. But since then they seem to have slipped into oblivion. They're still registered though, and guess what? Alan Crowther, one of the trustees, is also—'

'On the board of Bowes Dorrinton.'

'You've got it. It's flimsy, but it's better than nothing.'

'Better than nothing will do fine,' said Mariner, wryly. 'Can you go and talk to him, see if he's willing to help with our enquiries, say first thing in the morning? I'd like to know more about the Queensbridge Trust, wouldn't you?'

'Consider it done,' said Weightman. 'I'll keep you posted.'

* * *

By eight o'clock, most of the team had left for the night, but Mariner remained in his office going back over the details of the case again and again, trying to find something, anything, that would link Weller and Holmes to Eddie Barham one way, or to Bowes Dorrinton the other. Knox appeared in the doorway.

'Bugger off,' said Mariner.

Knox ignored him. 'You might want to hear this, boss,' he said. 'St Barnabas, the men's hostel, just phoned. They've had a bloke show up there, bit of a weirdo. They don't think he's on booze or drugs, but the description fits Jamie Barham. They're bringing him in.'

CHAPTER 34

Mariner was waiting at the desk when the manager of St Barnabas arrived with a loudly protesting Jamie. The lad was filthy and his clothes stank, but Mariner wanted to hug him.

'Shall I?' Sergeant Reilly picked up the phone.

'No,' said Mariner. 'I'll do it.' While Reilly took some details from the hostel manager, Mariner put through the call. 'Anna?'

'Yes.' Her voice was stretched taut with anxiety.

'We've found Jamie. He's fine. A bit grubby, but I'm sure he'll clean up.'

'Oh, thank God,' her voice choked with emotion. 'Where is he?'

'We've got him here at the station.'

She must have broken every speed limit to get there, and burst into the station only minutes later. 'Where is he?'

'Through there.'

Immediately he saw his sister, Jamie walked over to her and put a weary head on her shoulder, while his right hand grabbed at her coat, clutching on for dear life.

Her lower lip wobbled. 'Hi, Jamie.'

'If you can wait a few minutes, we can get the surgeon to give him the once over,' Mariner offered.

'No thanks,' she said curtly, with a look that said 'you've done enough damage.' 'His own doctor will do that.'

It hurt, but it was no more than he deserved.

'Come on, Jamie, let's go home.'

Mariner watched them go out of the building. The hostel manager had finished and was leaving too.

'Thanks for contacting us so promptly,' Mariner said. The relief of finding Jamie alive had sapped what remained of his dwindling energy.

'No problem.' But moments later, the manager was back, holding something out to Mariner. 'I forgot to give you this. It was in his pocket. We had to take it off him. Something like this can cause a riot in the hostel. It's partly how we knew he wasn't one of our usual crew.' He handed over a mobile phone, and something inside Mariner crowed.

'Cheers, mate,' he said, with remarkable calm. 'Appreciate it.'

* * *

Jamie had fallen asleep in the car on the short journey home, and Anna had to wake him to get him into the flat. He was so groggy he didn't even protest when Anna put him under the shower, and afterwards he munched his way listlessly through almost a whole pizza while Anna put a call through to Dr Payne's surgery. Inevitably, all she got was the after-hours answering service, but moments later the doctor himself called her back. With some difficulty, Anna explained what had happened during the last forty-eight hours. Dr Payne was typically unfazed. 'How are you?' he asked.

'I'm okay. But I am worried about Jamie. He's too quiet.'

'I'll come straight away and check him over.'

'I'd really appreciate that, thank you.' While she waited, Anna thought about DI Mariner. She'd been pretty unpleasant to him. God, had she actually hit him? Wasn't that an offence? In truth, she'd been annoyed with him for deserting her at the weekend and her anxiety about Jamie had compounded the anger, but all the same, he hadn't really deserved that. He was only doing his job. She must call him to apologise. She'd do it later when Jamie was settled. No she wouldn't, she'd do it now. But, of course, when she tried, Mariner was unavailable. When her door buzzer sounded, just a few minutes later, Anna half hoped that it might be him, but it wasn't, it was Dr Payne with a wonderfully reassuring smile. 'So, how's the patient?'

'Strangely subdued,' Anna said. 'Look who's here, Jamie.'

But Jamie had seen who it was and was suddenly animated again. In fact, rarely had Anna witnessed such a look of sheer abject terror on his face. 'No! No black mouth! No black mouth!' he shouted, backing hastily towards the bedroom.

Anna was horrified. He was more traumatised than she'd realised. 'Jamie! It's all right. It's Dr Payne, Jamie's friend,' she tried to reassure him, casting the doctor an apologetic smile. 'I told you. He's all over the place.' After a few minutes, she managed to calm Jamie by fetching him a drink and putting on a DVD.

Dr Payne dismissed Jamie's reaction with his customary understanding. 'He's been through a lot. It's not at all surprising that he should be reminded of the last ordeal. It might help if I prescribe you something to help him sleep, just for a few nights, until he's back into a normal routine again.' Sitting down at Anna's kitchen table, he took out his prescription pad and pen and scribbled down something. 'Now, let's go and have a look at him.'

This time Jamie remained passive while Anna took off his shirt, and he allowed Dr Payne to listen to his chest. The phone rang.

'I'll take it in the kitchen,' Anna said, as Jamie seemed okay.

It was Mariner. 'Hello, I got your message. How's it going?'

'All right, thanks.' Now that he was on the line, Anna didn't know quite what to say to him. 'Look, I wanted to—' but as she spoke something caught Anna's eye. Something embossed in gold on the leather case of Dr Payne's prescription pad: BDP, the capital letters all interlinked. That was interesting; he knew the company too. Perhaps he'd have some idea—

Snippets of a past conversation crept unbidden into her head. *Who would Eddie have told about this? Who would he have trusted?* Anna's mind raced as she grappled to achieve some kind of coherency to the invading thoughts. Jamie, shouting *No black mouth!*

'Hello? Are you all right, Anna?' Mariner asked, at the other end of the line.

'Yes,' Anna said, immediately distracted by further remembrance . . . *how did they get in so easily?* The voices echoed: *Eddie went out leaving Jamie . . . maybe he always left the door on the latch. Or somebody else had a key to Eddie's house.*

Who would Eddie have trusted? Who had she trusted? The person who knew her family intimately and would have known her mother's medical history, who knew about Jamie's obsessions with Hula Hoops and radio transmission masts, and knew about the spare key to Eddie's house.

Anna shivered as understanding took shape. 'Look, I've got to go,' she said suddenly. 'The doctor is here examining Jamie.'

'Okay,' said Mariner, uncertainly.

'We'll keep in touch.'

'Sure.'

Terminating the call so abruptly, Anna could sense Mariner's confusion at the other end of the line but she had to give herself time to think this through. She must be wrong about this. There would be a reasonable, rational explanation for everything. All she had to do was ask.

'Dr Payne . . .' Anna walked back into the lounge, but unexpectedly the doctor and Jamie weren't there. She went through to the bathroom, and as a last resort, Jamie's bedroom, but the flat was empty. They had gone.

* * *

As weird phone calls went, that one was off the scale, thought Mariner. She hadn't even told him what her original call was about. With Jamie safely recovered, he'd anticipated an opportunity to patch things up, but he'd got it wrong, again. It was becoming a habit. But the last few days had been a hell of a strain on her. She must be exhausted. And so was he. He couldn't do this anymore. He'd have a quiet drink at the Boatman, pick up a takeaway and head for home. Then Knox appeared in the doorway, like a familiar picture in its frame.

* * *

'Doctor Payne?' Anna called out, bewildered. What the hell was going on? Then she noticed that the front door was slightly ajar. Struggling to quell a rising panic, Anna rushed out into the hallway, her fears beginning to crystallise. This late at night, everything was deathly quiet, there was no one around. She ran towards the lifts, but saw that they were both at ground-floor level. Surely there hadn't been time— Then, deafening in the silence, the door at the other end of the hallway, the one leading up to the roof garden, banged shut on its spring.

'No.' Anna gasped out loud.

'Jamie!' Anna raced up the stairwell, taking the stairs two at a time. She burst onto the roof, to see Jamie and Dr

Payne standing beside the waist-height railings, like a couple of old friends admiring the view.

Dr Payne turned towards her. 'Anna,' he said, mildly. 'Come and join us.'

Anna walked slowly towards them. 'What's going on? What are you doing up here?' she asked, her voice barely audible, even to her own ears.

'You must have already worked that out, Anna,' smiled the doctor. 'I'm protecting myself. I have to make sure that no one will ever know.'

Anna was chilled to the marrow; she'd been right. 'I can help you,' she said, quickly, hating herself for sounding so wheedling. 'I can keep it to myself. I won't tell a soul. I promise.'

The doctor shook his head. 'It's too much to expect. I need to be absolutely certain that I will never be implicated in what has happened to your family.' In the white glow cast by the floodlights, his face was grotesque.

'What can you hope to do?' Anna said, finding sudden strength. 'That was Inspector Mariner on the phone. He knows you're here. If anything happens to us—'

'But I'm here to help, Anna. I'm your family doctor, an old friend, and when I tell Mariner what happened, he'll think the same thing as everyone else.' He smiled. 'That it was a tragic accident. He'll have no reason to think otherwise. It's the kind of thing that could have occurred at any time, especially now, when Jamie is so traumatised.'

'What accident? What are you talking about?' But even as she spoke, Anna knew.

'You've come a long way in the last few weeks, Anna,' he said. 'Eddie would be proud of you. But how far would you go? How far would you really go for Jamie?'

And he took a step nearer to the edge.

CHAPTER 35

'I can't believe I didn't see it before. It's been there all the time, staring us right in the face!' Mariner talked as he ran, long strides towards the area car, Knox running to keep up. Within seconds they were on the road and speeding towards Brindley Place. The streets were steady with traffic even at this time in the evening, but with enough slack to clear the way ahead. Mariner dreaded to think what they were going to find. 'Please God, let us not be too late,' he murmured under his breath. As they drove he asked CAD to run a vehicle check. Moments later the radio crackled with the information that the car registered to Dr Owen Payne was a green metallic Lexus. The officer recited the registration.

'And there it is,' said Mariner, as they squealed into the parking bay below Anna's flat, to see it looming alongside Anna's bright red Mazda. There was even a 'Doctor on Call' sign resting audaciously on the dashboard. Knox skidded to a halt. 'Have we got back up, boss?' he asked, but Mariner didn't hear. He was already out of the car and running towards the building where he hammered on the doors loudly until the doorman appeared.

'All right, keep your hair on,' he grumbled, as Mariner and Knox thrust identification in his face.

'Has anyone left the building during the last fifteen minutes?' Knox asked him.

'No.'

'You sure?'

'Positive. What is—?'

'What about the back entrance?'

'I locked that up hours ago.'

So they must still be here.

'Don't let anyone out of this building until we say you can,' ordered Knox, running after Mariner who was already racing up the stairs.

'I can't—' But his protests went unheard.

The third floor was surprisingly undisturbed. Emerging from the stairwell Mariner and Knox moved slowly along the landing towards Anna's flat. Seeing the door slightly ajar, Mariner pushed it, gently. 'Anna? Is everything all right?' There was no reply. The flat was empty. They checked each of the rooms in turn. 'So where the fuck are they?' said Mariner.

He walked through Anna's flat and into the kitchen, trying to figure it out. Looking out of the window onto the car park, everything was quiet and normal. What he'd expected to be a siege was beginning now to look like another abduction. 'But if Payne's car is still there . . .' he said, thinking aloud. 'Where have they gone?' His gaze swept over the canal, its towpath dark and empty at this time of night. 'Go and talk to the doorman again,' he said, to Knox. 'Make sure there isn't any other way of getting out.'

'Right, boss.' Knox disappeared down the hallway.

Then, turning away from the window, Mariner happened to glance down at the table. 'Knox!' he yelled. 'Get back here!'

* * *

Anna had always considered the roof garden beautiful. An effort had been made to create a soothing green oasis away from the stress of city living. But in the light of the horror unfolding before her it had become monstrous and ugly. She was exhausted and part of her just wanted this to be over. She wanted to close her eyes and for this to end. But she had to keep Dr Payne talking. If he let go of Jamie now, it would be disastrous. But she needn't have worried. The last couple of days had reaped one advantage at least, and Jamie was clinging to the doctor like a leech.

'So you were the one Eddie trusted,' Anna said, advancing slowly, straining to form the words.

The doctor smiled ruefully. 'Eddie and your parents, yes. I do regret that Anna. I hope you can believe me. I'm truly sorry for the way things have worked out.'

He was sickening. Anna couldn't imagine now how she'd ever even liked the man. 'So why didn't you put a stop to it?' she said, coldly. 'You could have done. You could have warned my parents and Eddie that they were in danger.'

'No, Anna. I couldn't afford to allow your father or Eddie to make that information public, any more than the drug company could. When it was first suspected that there might be a problem with Pinozalyan, Bowes Dorrinton sent out a memo, warning of the dangers, long before I prescribed it for your mother. Oh, other GPs probably ignored the warning too, but if your father's little campaign had succeeded, I would have been the one singled out and accused of negligence. Bowes Dorrinton would have made sure of that. They'd have needed a scapegoat. Not to mention the details about Pinozalyan I later removed from your mother's medical records. I could have been struck off.' He was becoming agitated, his breathing fast and uneven. 'Bowes Dorrinton knew it, so they used me to keep an eye on your father and provide them with any additional inside information they needed to get things under control.'

'Like where Dad was giving his lectures. And Jamie's obsession with transmission masts,' Anna said, bitterly.

'You have to understand my position Anna. I was a young GP, just starting out. I had my own family to think of, debts to pay off. Alongside that warning were the financial rewards for prescribing drugs. What was I to do? I was offered good incentives for my co-operation, too; holidays abroad, the odd bonus payment to supplement my pension fund. I'd have been a fool not to go along with it. And up until your parents' accident, I really had no idea of how far they would go. That came as quite a shock, believe me, but by then it was too late. When Eddie started pursuing the same line of enquiry, I was in too deep. I had to stop him.' Beads of sweat had broken out on the doctor's upper lip. Anna was close enough now to see them glistening in the light.

'Did you kill Eddie?' Anna asked, her voice a whisper.

'No Anna, I didn't kill Eddie. I merely provided access to the house and a sterile syringe. It wouldn't even have been needed if Eddie hadn't come back so soon. All they wanted were your father's notebooks.' Jamie moaned and struggled at his side. 'Jamie's getting bored,' he said. 'We should get this over with.'

'And the people at Bowes Dorrinton?' Anna persisted. 'Is this their idea, too?'

'Oh no, this is what you might call simple self-preservation. I've no other option. But the final decision is yours Anna. Who is it going to be? Jamie, or you?'

'How do I know that you won't let Jamie fall anyway? After all that you've done, why should I trust anything you say?'

'That's your choice, of course. But you're his only chance, Anna.' Payne relinquished his grasp slightly and Jamie struggled to wrench himself free.

'Wait!' Anna blurted, desperately. 'I'll do it. You don't have to hurt him. He won't give you away. Look, I'll do it.' Feeling suddenly weightless with fear, her legs shaking almost uncontrollably, Anna stepped up onto the first and then second rung of the railings. Payne watched, urging her on with his eyes. She glanced below to where the city streets swayed and blurred. So this was how her life would end, in ultimate, futile sacrifice.

'Anna, stop!' Another voice rang out over the roof and, with a jolt, Anna recognised it as Mariner's. 'You don't have to,' he said. 'It's over. Walk away from the edge, Owen. And bring Jamie with you.' Everything on the rooftop froze. 'It's the only sensible thing, doctor,' Mariner continued, persuasively. 'You can't win this. We know what you've done. We have records of your calls. We've just listened to your confession. You have nothing to gain by this now. There's nowhere else to go.'

For what seemed an eternity nothing happened as Payne hesitated, weighing up his situation. Anna halted, poised on the precipice. Seconds ticked by, everything deathly silent, but for the background hum of an ignorant city, amplified by the light rain that had begun to fall. Then miraculously Dr Payne began, inch by inch, to move back across the roof towards the policemen. For a moment it looked as if he would comply, until suddenly, as Anna's foot touched back down on the roof, he shoved Jamie to one side, turned and lunged for the railings.

Mariner and Knox exploded from the doorway as Jamie, panicked by the sudden activity, started running towards the outer edge of the roof.

'No!' Anna screamed. Mariner took a flying leap at Jamie, bringing them both crashing heavily onto the concrete, but for Owen Payne it was too late. Blocked by furniture and plant pots, Knox couldn't get to him fast enough to prevent him from hurling himself over the brink to certain death.

The sirens of the summoned backup team grew louder. Retaining a tight hold on Jamie's shirt, Mariner got to his feet and walked over to where Anna stood, dazed and shaking. He put a protective arm around her. 'Come on,' he said. 'Let's get off here.'

Behind them Knox turned to his radio. 'Echo Charlie Two-Nine; ambulance required at Brindley Place.'

* * *

In Anna's flat, officers came and went and statements were taken. Mariner went down to watch the mutilated body of Dr Owen Payne being secured into its body bag and loaded into the coroner's van. When he got back, most of the others had gone, leaving Knox alone with Anna. Jamie wasn't around.

'Asleep,' Knox told him, gesturing towards the bedroom. Exhausted by two days wandering the streets, for once he was peaceful. And as if that wasn't surprise enough for one day, Knox was offering to make tea. But Mariner declined, so there was nothing more for him to do. 'I'll get going then, boss,' he said.

Mariner saw him out. 'Thanks, Tony. You've done a good job,' he said.

Knox smiled sardonically. 'First time for everything. Put in a word for me with the gaffer, eh?'

'I'll see what I can do.'

'I'll even promise to stay away from his missus.'

'Is that's why you moved—?'

Knox grinned. 'I was more ambitious then: Assistant Chief Constable's wife. Not for nothing did they call me "Opportunity Knox."'

'Someone found out?'

'Caught us at it, actually.'

'You bloody idiot.'

'Oh, I don't know. Look where I ended up. See you, boss.'

Mariner knew that he should go too, but as Anna hadn't suggested it yet, neither would he. He walked through to where she was in the kitchen.

'What made you come back here tonight?' she asked him. 'Was it my phone call?'

'It certainly got me wondering. But when Jamie was picked up, he had a mobile phone in his pocket that he must have lifted from Weller — one of his abductors. The manager at St Barnabas gave it to me after you'd gone. We traced the calls on it. Just after I spoke to you, Knox came to tell me that one of the names that featured on the account regularly in the last few days was a Dr Owen Payne. We got here and I saw those.' Jamie's pictures were scattered across the table, among them the snowflake and the garden.

'Not bad for a beginner. Thanks for showing up.'

'It's what I'm paid to do.'

'And I'm sorry, I've been a bitch.'

'Well, the last couple of days haven't been much fun, have they?' *But if you want to make it up to me—*

'I probably shouldn't have hit you, though.'

Mariner shrugged it off.

'That shirt's a mistake by the way,' she said, to bridge the awkward silence. 'I'm not sure that the bloodstain effect really works.'

Mariner glanced down at where blood had seeped through again. 'No? Well, that's police work for you. No respect for fashion.'

'Let me see.' Before he could argue, she was unbuttoning his shirt and pulling it loose from his trousers. At one point her fingertips touched his bare flesh making Mariner draw breath. A series of raw abrasions an inch wide spread from his stomach down over his abdomen, angry red against his pale skin.

'You should get those seen to.'

'I'll be all right.'

'Well, at least let me put something on them.' She returned from the bathroom, moments later, with antiseptic cream, which she started to lightly massage into his skin with her fingertips, working her way down until the abrasions disappeared beneath his waistband. She looked up at him, a mischievous gleam in her eyes, before Mariner felt a tug on his belt and heard the rasp of his zip. Oh God. Why, oh why, had he ditched that prescription?

'Look,' he began. 'I've got this—'

But suddenly, uttering an expletive, she jumped back from him, and Mariner turned to see Jamie shuffling sleepily into the room.

'Want a drink,' he said, walking over to Anna and tugging her arm.

She gave Mariner an anguished glance. 'Sorry,' she mouthed.

Jesus, so am I. 'I'd better go.' With a silent howl of frustration, Mariner turned away from them and zipped up.

Jamie provided for, Anna walked Mariner to the door. 'Thanks for everything,' she said.

'Don't you mean, thanks for screwing everything up?'

'You were there when we needed you.'

'Now that we have evidence of Payne's involvement, we can press charges for Eddie's murder,' Mariner said, still trying to wrench his mind away from the disappointment. 'We've got a lawyer working on the case now, too. And if Andrew Todd pulls through, the case against Bowes Dorrinton will be blown wide open.' He'd make the phone call himself to Ken Moloney first thing in the morning. 'You and all the other families can look forward to the justice and the compensation you deserve. You'll be able to get your life back.'

'If I want it.' Suddenly she seemed less certain. 'The last few days have brought a few things into sharp focus. Look I'm sorry about—' she gestured back towards the kitchen. 'Some other time perhaps?'

'Sure.' Perhaps.

* * *

Outside, the rain had turned into a steady downpour, and Knox, of course, had taken the car. Turning up his collar ineffectually against the torrent, Mariner started towards Broad Street to flag a taxi.

THE END

Afterword

Since this book was first written autism has featured in a number of popular fiction pieces, from novels to films to TV productions. This is perhaps not surprising given the increased prevalence; more than 1 in 100 people in the UK are diagnosed with the condition, with the ratio of males to females approximately 4:1. Predominantly fictional characters have high-functioning autism or Asperger's syndrome. Jamie Barham, on the other hand, has severe autism coupled with learning disabilities, which is rather more common. While growing recognition has led to a corresponding increase in research into autism that identifies some clear genetic factors, there remains no single known cause of the condition.

Thank you for reading this book. If you enjoyed it please leave feedback on Amazon, and if there is anything we missed or you have a question about then please get in touch. The author and publishing team appreciate your feedback and time reading this book.

Our email is office@joffebooks.com

www.joffebooks.com

DI TOM MARINER SERIES

Made in the USA
Coppell, TX
12 October 2021